A DAISY FOR THE SINGLE DAD

O'SULLIVAN SISTERS BOOK 5

SOPHIA QUINN

FLP

———————

ISBN: 978-1-99-103410-6 (Paperback)
ISBN: 978-1-99-103409-0 (Kindle)

Forever Love Publishing Ltd
www.foreverlovepublishing.com
2022 - USA

CHAPTER 1

L evi loved his daughter to the moon and back.

He tried to remind himself of this as her shrill voice filled his car, and he dipped his chin with a defeated sigh.

"But it's not fair!" she said.

For what had to be the tenth time.

Nothing was ever fair in Mikayla's life. He lifted his head, fixing his gaze on the stretch of Main Street where he was parked. As sheriff, it was second nature to assess the pedestrians and storefronts, searching for any signs of trouble...even while dealing with his permanently cranky thirteen-year-old.

"Shelley gets to go," Mikayla whined.

"Shelley doesn't have two little brothers to babysit this afternoon."

"Why can't Aunt Helen do it?"

"Because your aunt Helen has other plans." They'd been over this three times already. "And besides, you're too young to be going out on the town by yourself."

"Out on the town? Seriously, Dad, how old are you? I

just want to hang out with some of my friends. Everyone else my age is allowed to walk around town without adult supervision!"

Levi shut his eyes for a second. "I don't care what everyone else your age does. You're my daughter, which means you're my concern—"

"Oh, so you don't trust me to hang out alone with my friends, but you trust me to look after the boys?"

Oh for the love of... "It's not that I don't trust you, Mikayla!"

He squeezed his eyes shut and counted to ten. How many times had he said that already? He'd lost track. And he'd also lost his patience.

Again.

He pinched the bridge of his nose and tried to focus on his breathing.

He hadn't always been a small-town sheriff. He'd been a cop in the bigger town of Bozeman and before that in Denver. He'd seen enough to know all the horrors out there in the world, and it took everything in him not to spell it out for her now.

But her innocence, her naivete...he didn't want to take that from her. He just wanted to protect her. Was that asking too much?

"You're such a jerk, Dad."

Apparently it was.

He pulled the phone away from his ear to stare at it in dismay. Had she just called him...?

"Mikayla May Baker," he started, his already gruff voice turning hard. His cop-voice, the boys called it. "You don't talk to your father—"

A click sounded.

"Did she just—"

Yes she had.

She'd hung up on him.

He let out a growl, resisting the urge to shout like a maniac.

"Now what?" he said aloud, his heart pounding with anger and frustration. It felt like this was his constant lately, especially with Mikayla.

There was no answer, of course. There never was. He wasn't even sure who he'd been asking.

Maybe Beth? A smile curled his lips at the memory of his wife even as that familiar ache filled his chest. "You'd know what to do." He found a little comfort thinking that maybe she could hear him. "She'd listen to you."

He shook his head, his gaze catching on his reflection in the rearview mirror. What would Beth think if she could see him now? He ran a hand over his short, trimmed beard. He hadn't had it three years ago when she was still alive.

He hadn't had the permanent air of exhaustion either.

"In all that planning we did about what me and the kids would do after you were gone, we never thought to talk about the teen years," he muttered.

The answering silence felt deafening.

He stared down at his phone. He ought to call Mikayla back and read her the riot act.

Again.

Good grief, it was exhausting parenting a teenage girl. His finger hovered over the Call button for a minute before he swiped the screen away with a sigh. He didn't have it in him for another round with the surly teenager who'd taken possession of his sweet little girl.

When had this happened?

She used to be daddy's little girl, all smiles and

3

sunshine, and then…poof. She grew up and caught a feral case of bad attitude.

He scrolled through his contacts. His good friends Ethan and Dex were always offering to help out. But Dex was on call at the clinic, and besides, Levi was almost certain he was helping his new wife, Rose, move in today.

He found Ethan's number and called.

"Hey, man, what's up?" Ethan sounded like he was out of breath.

"You at work?"

"Yeah, I'm on at the fire station today," he said. "It's been a slow shift, so I'm just doing some lifting. What do you need?"

Levi winced even as gratitude swelled in his chest. He hadn't been born and raised in this town the way Beth had —he'd only moved here when she'd wanted to be closer to her family when she was pregnant with Mikayla. But he wasn't sure how he'd ever have survived these past few years without the help of this town and his friends.

"Helen's out of town," he started. "And Mikayla wants to go out with her friends to—"

"Say no more, man." Ethan chuckled. "You know I love hanging with Dawson and Ronnie."

Levi sank back in his seat, letting out a long sigh of relief. "Thanks, buddy. You may have saved me from World War III when I get off duty tonight."

Ethan chuckled. "That bad, huh?"

"I'm not fair, I'm stricter than the other parents, I'm mean…" He rattled off the more persistent of Mikayla's complaints. "Oh, and I just found out that I'm also a jerk."

Ethan whistled. "She's not happy with you today."

"She's not happy with me any day, and that's what worries me." He scrubbed at his eyes, weariness settling over him like a lead weight. "She's bound for trouble at this rate."

"She's just being a teenager," Ethan murmured.

Levi nodded. He heard it all the time from Ethan, Dex...even his sister-in-law, Helen, and her husband, Bob. He supposed they ought to know. Their kids were grown and off to college. But still, he'd seen too many teens head down a destructive path, and he couldn't just sit back and watch Mikayla do the same.

"She's acting too rebelliously," he muttered. "She has no respect for me anymore."

"Again, she's a teenager. Far as I know, that's all par for the course."

"I wasn't like that," Levi said. "Were you?"

Ethan laughed. "First of all, man, it's not fair to compare her teen years to yours. You didn't lose your mother, and you weren't a girl. Not to mention, not all of us grew up loving the rules like you do."

Levi rolled his eyes. He was used to the teasing. Even Beth used to laugh at how by-the-book he was. He believed in rules and respect, timeliness and duty...

All things his daughter seemed to think were forms of cruel and unusual punishment.

"Maybe you're right." He sighed, finally breaking the silence.

He knew Ethan and Dex thought he was too strict with the kids. But they didn't know what it was like being the only person who stood between three innocent, vulnerable little ones and a world filled with all sorts of danger.

Being a single parent was no joke. He was responsible for everything—their health, their safety, their happiness. And the older they got, the harder it was to protect them.

"I should be off duty in about an hour," Ethan said. "You want me to go relieve Mikayla?"

Levi's gut twisted with tension. *No. Go to the house and tell her to go to her room and stay there.*

That was what he wished he could say. He wished he could threaten her with a time-out and get a pouty lip in turn. But those days were gone, and he knew enough to know he had to pick his battles.

And an afternoon hanging out with her friends was not one of them.

"Yeah." He sighed. "Tell Mikayla she can go, but only if she tells you who she's going with and when she'll be back."

"Yes, sir," Ethan joked.

Levi felt his lips twitching upward. "Sorry."

Sometimes his work and his role as dad leaked into his personal life. He eyed a skateboarder who nearly hit an old lady on the sidewalk.

It wasn't easy to turn off the law enforcement or the strict-dad routine, and some days he wasn't sure he knew how any more.

Beth used to know how to make him relax. She was a joyful woman, and she loved to laugh. After a long day on the streets, no matter what he'd seen or heard, she could always make him smile.

But she wasn't here anymore, and no amount of wishing would change things. She wasn't here to be the parent Mikayla needed, but he was.

"Tell her…" He started and stopped. "Tell her to have fun, but that she and I are going to have a talk when we get home."

"You got it."

"And Ethan…thanks."

"Anytime, man. You know that. You're not in this alone."

He nodded but couldn't quite bring himself to agree. "I'll be home as soon as my shift's over."

Ethan hung up, and Levi turned back to the street. He was lucky to have his friends, and his family, and Beth's family, and the wonderful people of this town...

But none of that made up for Beth's absence. She'd been joyful, yes, but she'd also known how to be a great mom, and how to set a good example. She'd been kind, and thoughtful, reliable and steadfast, and—

The sight of a pale blue Beetle flying past him cut through his reverie. He straightened, irritation flaring hot and his duty as sheriff shifting into place like a coat of armor.

It wasn't just his kids who depended on him to keep them safe.

The whole town did.

His eyes narrowed on the VW Beetle. It looked to be straight out of the 60s with a rattling exhaust pipe and a dent in the back bumper. A broken taillight too. The thing was a speeding traffic hazard.

He flipped on his lights and pulled out behind the car.

He might not have a clue how to handle Mikayla. But a speeding, reckless driver?

This was his forte.

CHAPTER 2

W *hoop!*
A single siren blast sounded over the blaring music and gave Daisy a jolt as she came to a stop at the cute little town's stoplight. She winced when she glanced in the mirror, then flicked off the radio.

Crap. A sheriff's car was right behind her. Had she been speeding?

She blew a long blonde lock out of her face as she wrinkled her nose.

Probably.

She tapped her fingers on the steering wheel as she tried to push the gathering storm clouds away. The last thing she could afford right now was a ticket.

The light turned green, and for half a second, she considered driving away. But if she couldn't afford a ticket, she definitely couldn't afford bail when she eventually got caught evading the law.

So with a sigh, she pulled forward and to the right, parking at the curb in front of an adorable, old-fashioned little diner. She grinned as she craned her neck for a better view of Main Street.

Aspire really was a cute ol' town. Rose's descriptions were not an exaggeration. No wonder her little sister loved this place so much.

Daisy's smile spread as she took in a quaint coffee shop across the road, and a bookstore, and two hot cowboys striding down the sidewalk in her direction.

Yes, sir, this town was perfect. For a little while, at least. Just long enough to spend some time with her sisters, shake Benny's money-hungry goons, and then be on her way.

Her smile was brilliant as she turned off the car.

The drive from Los Angeles might have taken an eternity, but it was definitely the right call. Her gaze caught on the wing mirror as the man in uniform got out of the squad car behind her and started striding toward her door.

All she had to do was sweet-talk her way out of a ticket and she'd be home free. No biggie. She checked her smile in the rearview mirror and widened it even farther.

She'd been pulled over too many times to count, but she'd never once gotten a ticket, and today was no different.

Rolling down her window, she pulled in a breath as he drew closer and peeked her head out for a better look.

Well, hello, handsome.

Oooh. This was going to be fun.

A uniform had a way of making any man look sexier than he was, but this guy was a hottie to begin with. Older —but that was the way she liked 'em. His face had a weathered, workingman appeal. She liked his thick brown hair and broad shoulders, and it was impossible not to notice the curve of his biceps and imagine what would no doubt be a sculpted body beneath that beige shirt of his.

And check out that beard. Wonder what that'd feel like brushing over my skin.

Desire flared through her, and she bit her bottom lip, wishing he'd walk a little slower so she could really admire the view.

But the closer he got, the more she liked what she saw. Beneath the beard he had classically handsome features. Sorta like a scruffier Ryan Gosling.

Oh yes, baby. This is definitely going to be fun.

And the fact that her very first interaction in this town was with a Ryan Gosling lookalike?

This was totally a sign. Coming to Aspire had been her best idea yet.

"Hi there, Officer," she sang in her sweetest voice.

His lips didn't so much as twitch.

But that was fine. Sometimes they took a little while to warm up.

"Driver's license and registration, please."

She got a little shiver at the low, gruff tone. She didn't even have to feign breathlessness when she batted her eyelashes. "Is there something wrong?"

He wasn't wearing opaque sunglasses, but he might as well have been for all his eyes gave away. "Driver's license and registration."

Her brows hitched up slightly. *Well, okay, then.* She reached into the glove compartment and rummaged around past the makeup case and toiletries she'd stashed there until she found what he wanted. She beamed up at him as she handed it over. "Sure hope I didn't cause any trouble, Officer."

"It's Sheriff." His tone was so curt she didn't even take in what he said.

"What was that?"

He took a deep breath and let it out in a sharp exhale, exasperation clear in his tone as he kept his gaze on her paperwork. "I'm the sheriff. And in these parts we have deputies, not officers."

"Oh, I..." She laughed. She couldn't help it. "Sorry, *Sheriff*. I'm new to these here parts."

She'd hoped to make him grin with her low-voiced imitation that made her feel like she was in the deep South, even though they were practically all the way to Canada.

He didn't smile. He didn't even blink.

Jeepers. Tough crowd.

She bulged her eyes and lightly tapped the steering wheel, trying to carry on with her upbeat tone and bright smile. "Anyway, I'm sure you see all sorts coming through this town with a job like yours."

When in doubt, kill 'em with friendliness.

No one had actually taught Daisy this lesson as a child. Not that she could remember, at least. But she'd learned it, nonetheless.

"Do you get many tourists?" she asked.

No answer.

"I'm here to visit family myself. What about you?" She tilted her head slightly, hoping to catch his gaze. "Do you have family here?"

A wife, perhaps?

No?

Oh, well then...lucky me.

She made herself giggle as she played out the ridiculous scene in her head.

12

He stopped scribbling to stare down at her. "Is something amusing, ma'am?"

She clamped her lips shut, but the urge to laugh only grew. "Ma'am?" She giggled, earning herself a narrow-eyed glare.

Huh. How about that? She'd gone and found the first uncharmable man in existence, and on the one week when she really, truly needed all the help she could get.

The thought made a flicker of fear spark in her chest before she doused it.

She was fine. Everything was fine.

All she had to do was lie low for a while and this would all blow over.

And just like that her smile was back in full force. "I am sorry, Sheriff. I didn't mean any offense. I just like to laugh, that's all."

He peered at her. "Have you been drinking, ma'am?"

Her chin jerked back. *Okay, wait…what?* It was one thing to not smile at her good-natured small talk. But was he accusing her of being…drunk?

Fear spiked again before she could brush it off. She wasn't drunk. Obviously. But what if he didn't have a Breathalyzer? What if she couldn't walk a straight line? Was she supposed to know how to say the alphabet backward?

That's it. She rested her elbows on the open window. He might be a grumpy man, but he was still a man, and all men caved eventually. "I swear on my life, Your Honor," she said with comically wide eyes. "I have not been drinking at…" She made a point of glancing at her phone. "Eleven in the morning."

His face was unreadable as he turned back to her license. "Says you're from New York."

"The Big Apple," she chirped by way of confirmation. "Have you ever been?"

"Your license is about to expire."

"Oh." Her smile faded ever so slightly.

Look at me. Take your eyes off my license and look at me.

She tried to will his gaze on her, because goshdarnit, she still had her secret weapon.

No one could still be a grump when she gave them *the smile.*

He looked up, but her ultra-watt, dimpled grin—the one that had gotten her free drinks for years—froze into a grimace when she heard her twin sister's voice.

"Hey, Levi. Everything okay over here?"

"Fine, thanks, Dahlia. Just a routine stop to chat about a broken taillight."

Broken taillight? Was that what this was about?

Daisy frowned. How long had she been driving with a broken taillight?

But as her thoughts spun, she...sank.

She couldn't help it. Dahlia's voice was growing louder, and this was so not how she'd planned on making the big appearance back into her sisters' lives. It was supposed to be a surprise. A happy one.

Not one she'd be hearing a lecture about for the rest of the week.

Maybe Dahlia hadn't recognized her. Or her blue Beetle.

She winced right as Dahlia's dark hair fell into view and then her paternal twin's face appeared. "Hey, Daisy."

It was time to fake it with an extra burst of sunshine.

Daisy's smile bloomed as she threw herself toward the door. "Dee!"

Dahlia chuckled when Daisy bounded out of the car, nearly knocking the sheriff over in the process.

She ignored his "Oof!" and threw her arms around her sister. Then Daisy spotted Rose waddling toward them across the street and Daisy dropped her arms, her mouth popping open. "Oh my…"

Dahlia was laughing behind her as she leapt on Rose, hugging her smiling sister and then twirling her around. "My little Rosie, look at you! You're so fat!" She laughed along with her teasing, then swept it all away with a teary-eyed smile. "I love it. You are so beautiful."

"Thanks." Rose beamed as she stroked circles over her rounded belly.

Daisy touched the bump, too, true awe filling her voice. "I can't believe it. I mean, I know I've known for ages, but it's different actually seeing it, and…"

"And you're here," Dahlia murmured.

To Daisy's surprise, Dahlia wrapped her in another embrace, and there was a shocking lack of sarcastic resentment in her voice when she whispered, "It's so good to see you, Dais."

Rose smiled at Daisy over Dahlia's shoulder as if to say, "See? Told you she's lightened up."

Daisy reached out and tugged Rose into the hug as well, and soon all three of them were laughing and dancing in a circle. Daisy nearly knocked them off-balance with her exuberance.

Her happiness wasn't feigned anymore. There was no need to fake this. As soon as she pulled her sisters into her arms, it all felt right. Pure joy.

Not even a meanie sheriff staring from the sidelines could smother her happiness.

She hadn't realized just how much she'd missed her sisters until she saw them again, and the swell of emotions caught her off guard.

She was safe now. With her sisters.

And off the grid.

CHAPTER 3

The sound of the sisters' laughter and shrieks of delight was deafening, and for the second time that day, Levi found himself wincing on behalf of his poor eardrums.

But, considering the pretty blonde's joy was a total one-eighty from Mikayla's bratty tantrum, it was hard to be too annoyed.

He cleared his throat to get their attention. Mainly *her* attention. He still had her license in his hand, but she seemed to have forgotten about him and her impending ticket as she greeted her sisters.

Levi leaned back against the hood of her car and crossed his arms. His lips twitched with the urge to smile at the sight before him. It was nice to see Rose so happy. He'd grown more and more fond of his best friend's wife these past few months, but it was still rare to see the shy, sweet woman laughing so loudly, oblivious to the scene they were causing.

Even stranger was seeing Dahlia so carefree. Oh, sure, she'd been loosening up some since she first came to town, but JJ's girlfriend wasn't exactly known for dancing in the street, and that was precisely what she and Daisy were doing right now. It was a sort of hugging dance that had him cocking his head and smothering a smile.

No, sir, this little scene was all Daisy's doing. She was like a bright ball of sunshine, and it was almost hard to look directly at her without squinting.

Their hugging dance turned them so Daisy was facing him, and for a second, Levi felt like he'd taken a sucker punch to the gut. The air was knocked right out of him.

She was beautiful, there was no doubt about it. That smile could light the entire town. But it wasn't her pretty smile or her twinkling eyes that had first caught his attention.

Oddly enough, it had been her scent. He'd been hit with a wave of peaches and vanilla and something flowery. Heck, he didn't know what the name of her scent was, but it had wrapped around him and charmed him before she'd even opened her mouth.

He dipped his head to hide a smile. Once she'd opened her mouth...forget it. The girl was adorable. Her attempts at flirting were harmless and cute. There was nothing coy about it, just simple and straightforward. A woman who knew what she wanted and precisely how to get it.

The effort it took to keep a straight face and ask for her license and registration without his voice breaking was commendable. He couldn't let some pretty woman weaken his defenses. He was here to uphold the law and keep his town safe.

"You did not!" Daisy shrieked, her eyes comically wide as her mouth dropped open.

Levi missed what Dahlia had just said, but she tipped her head back with a laugh. Keeping up with their conversation was basically impossible. They were talking over each in high speed, their sentences punctuated by laughter rather than pauses for breath.

This could take all day.

He straightened, rubbing a hand over his beard and smoothing out the smile while he was at it. He couldn't go giving away how cute he thought this all was. He'd totally lose his authority, and there was no way Aspire could run as safely as it did if people thought he was a softy.

"Excuse me, ladies."

They all ignored him.

Or maybe they just didn't hear him.

He found himself standing there gawking on the sidelines like a pimple-faced kid enamored by the cheer squad.

He huffed. This was ridiculous. The woman might be cute and bubbly, but she was still a reckless driver and irresponsible with her vehicle's upkeep.

The thought had him scowling. It was a glare that had most delinquent teens and wayward criminals quaking in their boots.

Daisy didn't seem to notice.

She was too busy taking Rose's hands and lifting them, stepping back to admire her sister's big belly. "You really are so fat." Her tone was filled with reverence and adoration.

Rose giggled. "I'm still trying to decide if I should be taking that as a compliment."

"You should! You absolutely should!" Daisy laughed. "Seriously, sweetie. I never thought I'd see your skinny self look so round…and beautiful. Pregnancy looks good on you."

"I know, right?" Rose twisted from one side to another

19

to show off the bump. "Dex says it makes me hotter than ever."

"Of course he does." Dahlia rolled her eyes, but she was wearing an indulgent smile as she added, "That man has hearts in his eyes when he looks at you."

"Oh, like it's any different with you and JJ," Rose shot back. She turned to Daisy to stage-whisper, "You should see the way they moon over each other."

"No." Daisy shook her head, and her long, loose, light blonde locks went flying. "I can't believe it. I won't believe it until I see it with my own eyes."

Levi cleared his throat. He'd had quite enough of eavesdropping on this particular conversation.

Once again he went ignored as Daisy launched into a story of her drive here, and for some reason, it seemed to require large hand gestures as she made the other two giggle.

He planted his hands on his hips. "Excuse me, ma'am!"

She stilled in the middle of speaking. Only for a second, but long enough for him to know Daisy was ignoring him on purpose.

Did she honestly think her ticket troubles would just go away if she laughed and smiled long enough?

He moved closer until that dang smell of hers was impossible to ignore.

Was it shampoo? Some sort of soap? It was spring in Montana, yet she smelled more like spring than the breeze did.

He crossed his arms again and found himself watching her gestures and her movements. It was entirely too easy to get caught up in her storytelling, so he focused on assessing her instead. It was partly habit to clock people and partly a way of maintaining his skills. Body language said a lot about a person.

As did their clothes.

And everything about Daisy's flared, tattered jeans, her flip-flops, and her long, flowy white shirt said carefree. Her waves of loose hair were a reckless match to her ensemble. She didn't seem to have any makeup on, but her skin glowed, and her cheeks and lips were a pretty shade of pink, and…

He shook his head. What was wrong with him? He was supposed to be gauging her body language, not taking note of the exact shade of her lips.

Dang it.

He moved closer, until he was near enough to touch her. "Excuse me, ladies!"

He'd spoken loudly. Rose gave a start and then flashed him a sheepish smile. Dahlia arched her brows and gave him a pointed look that said "I know you did not just shout at me." And Daisy…

Daisy turned slowly, like she had all the time in the world, and gave him a smile that nearly cut him down at the knees. It was…radiant. There was no other word for it. She had a glow about her anyway, but this smile directed that glow like a ray of sunshine, and he got the full force of it. Dimples flashed as her white teeth glinted.

The girl was a walking toothpaste commercial.

She tilted her head to the side, her long hair flowing over her shoulder. "I'm sorry, Sheriff. Did you want something?"

For a moment his mind went blank.

Did he want something? It was like the question only had one answer, and she knew it.

He wanted her.

He blinked. Then he gave his head a shake and took a long, deep breath. When he finally tore his gaze away from hers, he saw Rose and Dahlia giving him odd little smiles.

Knowing smiles. Rose's even seemed a little sympathetic.

Dahlia's was wry, like she knew exactly what was happening to him and found it amusing.

He straightened and shifted his focus to the ticket book he pulled out of his pocket.

"Oh now, Sheriff…" Daisy placed a hand on his arm, and it felt like hot iron searing his skin. "Surely you don't need to go to all this trouble for little ol' me."

He lifted his gaze to meet hers, and she blinked.

No…she batted her lashes.

He felt a smile tugging at his lips again, along with a laugh bubbling up in his chest. But that was precisely what she wanted. She wasn't trying to seduce him, just charm him. She was being cute and lovable and not even trying to hide her agenda.

It was almost impossible not to go along with it.

But then he heard Dahlia's little snort of amusement. They all knew what she was doing, and no doubt it was how this lady always got herself out of trouble.

A flicker of irritation shot through him at his own weakness. It was his job to uphold the laws and dole out punishments fairly. It wasn't his place to go easy on anyone or rewrite the laws. So he dipped his head, finished scrawling on the ticket, and tore it off.

"There's a car repair shop at the far end of Main Street," he said. "They'll be happy to help you with that taillight."

"But…" She sputtered, staring indignantly at the piece of paper flapping in the breeze between them. "But…"

"It's the law, ma'am." He handed her the ticket.

She reluctantly took it, and for a second, his chest tightened painfully at the flicker of genuine emotion that passed through her eyes. For one brief moment, that brightness and laughter were replaced by...fear.

Ah heck. He shifted toward her, some primal instinct making him want to reassure her.

But she sensed his movement and took a step back. Her bright smile returned in a flash, although she wasn't fast enough to hide the hint of desperation in her laugh. "But surely a warning would suffice."

As much as he wanted to snatch that ticket back and crumple it in his fist, he stood firm. It would take all of two seconds for word to spread that Sheriff Baker took it easy on the pretty blonde, and he'd have complaints about fairness coming in one ear and everybody else trying to sweet-talk him out of their misdemeanors.

No, he had a job to do.

"Get it taken care of straight away please, ma'am." He gave her a curt nod and headed for his car. "I won't be so lenient if I catch you a second time."

"Lenient? You gave me a ticket!" she shouted at his back.

He turned, one hand on his car door as he took in her wide eyes and gaping mouth. She looked more adorable than ever with her flushed cheeks and angry glare. The urge to smile was nearly impossible to deny.

But he managed.

CHAPTER 4

D aisy scowled at the ticket in her hand. "I can't believe he went through with it."

"Sorry, Daisy," Rose said with genuine sympathy in her voice. "But don't take it personally. Levi's pretty by-the-book like that."

Dahlia wrapped an arm around her shoulders as she snickered. "Is that the first time your superpower has failed you?"

Rose giggled. Daisy rolled her eyes. But the answer was yes.

"Come on." Dahlia chuckled as she nudged Daisy forward. "Rose and I were at the coffee shop when we saw you get pulled over. I'll buy you a cup of tea."

"Thanks." She wrapped an arm around Dahlia's waist and rested her head on her sister's shoulder.

Rose was right. Dahlia was definitely not her normal uptight self these days. She'd gotten hints of it on the phone, but seeing it was something else entirely.

They stepped inside, and Daisy grinned at the

charming little bistro decor and the homey smell of coffees and pastries.

"Be right back with a chamomile," Dahlia murmured, already heading to the counter.

Daisy grinned. "Thanks, Dee."

"Rosie," a man called from a table in the corner. "Who's your friend?"

Rose smiled and tugged on Daisy's arm. "Come on, I want you to meet the guys."

Her little sister tugged her toward a round table full of old men.

Daisy loved them instantly. They reminded her of the seven dwarves. There was Happy and Grumpy and Doc and Bashful.

She grinned as the man's cheeks turned pink when Rose introduced her.

Dr. Bob, the local veterinarian, Norman, Chicken Joe, and a few others all gave her friendly grins.

"You another one of them sisters, eh?" Norman pointed at her. "Soon you O'Sullivan girls will be taking over the town."

Daisy leaned forward with a wink. "You don't know the half of it."

The older men chuckled, and Daisy chatted them up, asking questions and making them laugh.

Rose watched her with an indulgent smile.

"So why do they call you Chicken Joe?" she asked.

The man shrugged, a smile in his eyes. "Soon as I moved here, I ordered five hundred chickens."

"Five hundred!" She gaped.

"And he didn't know a darn thing about taking care of 'em," Dr. Bob added.

A few more customers came in while she was laughing

at their stories, and Daisy heard the whispers, felt the stares. So when Dahlia came over with the cup of tea, Daisy turned and faced the room with a smile. "Hello, everybody. I'm Daisy O'Sullivan of the notorious O'Sullivan gang."

There were some titters of laughter from the far table.

"And you heard right," she said. "Frank's daughters are planning on taking over this fine town."

Norman laughed. "I knew it!"

She was still laughing with the men when Dahlia dragged her over to their table. "Must you always be on?"

Daisy shrugged. "Can't help it. I like to make people smile."

Dahlia sighed, but there was a small grin curving her lips rather than a scowl of disapproval. "You're unbelievable."

"I'm unbelievably what? Cute? Charming?"

"Incorrigible."

Daisy laughed. "Why, thank you."

Dahlia gave in to a little snicker before Rose killed the mood with an innocent question she had no idea would rattle Daisy so badly.

"So, why are you here?" She leaned forward, elbows on the table. "Why didn't you tell us you were coming?"

Daisy forced her frantic brain to calm down, keeping her smile in place and trying to act like these questions were no big deal.

Turn it back on them.

She cradled the cup of tea in her hand and shrugged. "What do you mean? You asked me to come, silly." She wagged a finger between them. "Both of you have been nagging me to come here and check out this ranch or whatever..." She waved a dismissive hand. "Although why I need to see it when we're just gonna sell it is beyond me."

She didn't miss the look her sisters exchanged, but neither said anything about the ranch. Dahlia arched a brow. "We asked you to come for Rose's wedding."

Daisy winced, guilt niggling as she turned to Rose. "I'm sorry I missed it, Rosie."

"It's fine. It was just the courthouse ceremony anyway," she said. "But I do hope you'll be back for the real wedding. We don't have an exact date yet, but I'm hoping it'll be this year."

Daisy smiled. "I wouldn't miss it."

The silence that followed made her uneasy. She waited for Dahlia to point out all the times she'd promised something and flaked. She braced for it.

But Dahlia just said, "It would mean the world to Rose if you can make it back here for that."

Daisy's smile felt brittle. "I said I would, didn't I?" She turned to Rose. "I really did want to be here for the ceremony, sis. The album just took way longer than I thought, and it was one thing after another, and…"

"It's fine." Rose patted her hand. "I understand, really."

Daisy bobbed her head and took a sip of tea, managing to burn her tongue in the process.

"Is it done now?" Dahlia passed her a glass of cold water. "The album."

Daisy's insides froze, and she bought some time by gulping down the entire glass. Again her frantic brain started to panic, but she hid it all behind a bright smile. "Yes," she lied. "It's all done, so there's nothing in the world that could keep me from your wedding, Rosie."

Rose smiled.

Daisy did her best to ignore the churning in her gut as her sisters watched her carefully.

"How long do you plan on staying?" Dahlia finally asked, her smile back as she reached for her coffee.

"Oh, I don't know..." Daisy shrugged. *Just long enough to get a loan shark off my back. Just long enough to figure out where I should go next.*

A tense anxiety seized her stomach, making the chamomile tea feel like acid. She swallowed hard, shoving thoughts of LA aside. "You know me. I'll stay until the wind takes me."

Rose giggled while Dahlia rolled her eyes.

But Dahlia was smiling. Again.

That had to be some sort of record.

Daisy turned to Rose. "So, tell me everything I missed at the courthouse ceremony."

Rose lit up instantly. "Well, Emma and Lizzy were there." She squeezed Daisy's hand. "They are going to be so excited to meet you in person!"

Daisy grinned. "I can't wait to meet them too."

"And of course they brought Nash and Kit. Dahlia and JJ were there, obviously—"

"Dahlia and JJ." Daisy giggled as she winked at Dahlia. "I love hearing you be part of a pair like that. Why do I get the feeling more wedding bells are in our future?"

Daisy's jaw dropped when Dahlia...blushed.

She *blushed*.

Her hard-as-nails sister blushed.

Rose didn't seem to find it odd because she kept talking. "And then we had to invite Dex's grandfather, and Ethan and Levi, of course. The sheriff is Dex's best friend."

Daisy nodded but stilled as the name registered. "Wait, the sheriff. As in..." She gestured to the street out front, her earlier irritation flaring hot and sudden before she shook it off with a rueful laugh.

"Yes," Rose confirmed. "Levi was the one who gave you a ticket."

"And he's Dex's best friend?"

"Yep."

She'd heard nothing but good things about Dr. Dex, but she was seriously going to have to reconsider his taste in friends.

As if she could read her mind, Rose's eyes widened. "Don't be too mad at Levi. He's a really good guy. He just takes his role as sheriff very seriously."

"Uh-huh." She didn't try to hide her disbelief.

Rose looked so earnest and worried that Daisy grinned again and changed the topic. "Okay, so now let's get to the good part." She wiggled her eyebrows and adopted a stage whisper. "The wedding *night*. Did you guys play doctor? I bet you did." She shared a teasing look with Dahlia, who started laughing while Rose turned beet red.

"Daisy!"

"I'm just guessing he was really good at it." Daisy joined Dahlia's laughter, and soon even a red-cheeked Rose was joining in on the giggles.

CHAPTER 5

L evi smoothed a hand over his beard and took a deep breath.

He immediately wished he hadn't when he got a lungful of barnyard smells.

"Mr. Cooper, I'm not saying you're not in the right," Levi started.

But yet again, the old rancher leapt in before he could finish. "That's my side of the property, Sheriff." He jabbed a finger at the cow that was minding its own business...on the wrong side of the fence.

"I understand that." Levi tried his best to keep the exasperation out of his tone. "But Billy said—"

"I already said I'd fix the fence!" the younger, louder, and no less irritating rancher shouted.

Levi winced. His head was starting to pound from all the yelling.

And he still had to call Mikayla back, so the shouting was far from over.

"Gentlemen!" Levi raised his hands when the bickering

started up all over again. "I really don't see how this is a matter for law enforcement."

"Because he said—" Billy started.

"This young hooligan started it—" Mr. Cooper shouted over top of him.

"Unless you want me to take you both down to the station for disturbing the peace, I suggest you work this out among yourselves." Levi was using his cop voice, and both men fell silent. Finally.

"Now." Levi exhaled loudly, trying to ignore the insistent pounding in his skull. "Billy already offered to fix the fence—"

"He's said that before."

"And I will be by in two days' time to make sure it's done," he finished as if the older man hadn't interrupted.

Both ranchers were scowling at him now. But that was fine. Levi was used to being the bad guy.

Inexplicably, the thought called up an image of a gorgeous blonde with a megawatt smile. His lips twitched despite the pounding headache as he remembered her dumbfounded stare just before he'd walked away.

Good grief, she was adorable.

He gave his head a shake.

And trouble.

The fact that she was pretty and sweet had nothing to do with the matter. He already had more trouble in his life than he could handle.

"Take care, gentlemen." Levi ignored their bickering as he headed to his car.

He took out his phone and eyed Mikayla's number. His gut churned with unease. Was she all right? Was she still angry?

Would calling her to check in just make her want to rebel more?

He pinched the bridge of his nose. The last thing he wanted was to drive her even further away than she already was.

One more push and he was afraid he'd lose her for good.

That was just fear talking, though, right? He sat there listening to the silence in his car. No answers were coming. He just had to keep trying to do his best to protect her and hope like heck that they made it through this phase without a permanent rift in their relationship.

With a sigh, he swiped away Mikayla's name and called Ethan instead.

"Hey, Levi—" Ethan was cut short by the sound of screaming.

Levi straightened. "What's going on? Do you need backup?"

Ethan's laugh put him at ease. "Calm down, man. The boys are just having fun."

Another scream. This time he could make out Ronnie's voice, and it was filled with laughter.

Levi sank back into his seat and let his heart rate return to normal. "Mikayla's out, I take it."

"Yup. She bolted as soon as I got here. She told me she was meeting up with friends at Mama's Kitchen and would be home by dinner."

Levi nodded, that ever-present worry making his gut feel like a pit of acid. Beth used to say he was going to give himself an ulcer.

Maybe she had a point. Maybe he ought to find ways to destress and relax and…

And then, just like that, she was back in his mind's eye.

Daisy O'Sullivan, with her tinkling laughter and her bright, warm smile, and the air of a person who didn't have a care in the world.

Except for that one little glimpse he'd seen. He frowned at the road as he ended the call with Ethan and pulled out onto the highway that would take him back into town.

He hadn't been imagining it. The flicker of fear in her eyes had been like a summer storm, thoroughly blocking out the sunshine—there and gone in a heartbeat. But it had been there, and the thought of it had his brows furrowing in concern.

Great. Just what he needed. Another person to worry about.

He shook his head, calling in to the station to make sure there were no other fires he had to put out before heading home. He'd just reached the intersection that would either take him home or to Main Street when he couldn't abide the nagging doubts a second longer.

Mama's Kitchen with her friends. That was what she'd told Ethan.

And Levi wished like heck he could believe her. But he'd caught Mikayla in one too many lies lately. Small white lies and a few missed curfews.

His fingers clenched the wheel.

But this was how it started, wasn't it? A little experimenting here, testing the boundaries there…

A muscle in his jaw ticked, and on instinct he turned onto a street that would take him past Mama's Kitchen. He didn't want to drive her away with his overprotectiveness, but he couldn't bear the thought of losing her either.

And there were so many ways he could lose her. His mind was all but spinning with a slideshow of worst-case scenarios by the time he drove past the beloved diner. He slowed his car to a crawl, and relief flooded him when he spotted Mikayla right there in the window, looking like a carefree little girl again as she laughed and drank a milk-shake alongside her friends.

He let out a shaky exhale through pursed lips as he kept going.

His little girl was safe.

For now, at least.

CHAPTER 6

"We'll have it ready for you by the morning."

The grease-covered overalls read Fred.

Daisy leaned over the counter at the auto repair shop. "Thank you so much, Fred."

He turned a little pink as he wiped his hands on a rag. "That's what we do, ma'am."

"Oh no, please. Call me Daisy." She stuck her hand out, and when he hesitated, looking down at the grease on his hands, she laughed. "A little grease never hurt anyone."

He matched her grin as he took her hand. "All right then, Miss Daisy."

She wrinkled her nose. "Miss Daisy makes me feel like I'm an old lady being driven around in a town car."

He chuckled.

She kept going, ticking them off on her finger. "And ma'am makes me feel a hundred years old. And Miss O'Sullivan?" She arched a brow meaningfully. "Half the town would come running."

He was all-out laughing now.

She gave him a dimpled smile. "So you'll have to call me Daisy."

"Well, all right then...Daisy."

Daisy heard Dahlia sigh with impatience behind her. But was it really so awful to make a boring chore a little more enjoyable for everyone involved?

And he gave her a discount in return, so all the better.

She was trying hard not to think about the cost of a tail-light. It couldn't be that much, right?

"If you don't mind, Daisy..." His eyes got all wide and earnest. "I'd sure like to check under your hood."

Daisy blinked. Dahlia made a choking noise behind her.

"Um..." Maybe Daisy had gone a little too far with the flirting.

"You've been on the road for a long time," Fred continued. "And that car is no spring chicken. It must be right out of the 70s, I'd say."

"Oh." She turned to look at her beloved blue Beetle. "Yes. Uh...a '74, I think."

"They sure built 'em to last." He grinned. "But she's getting on in years, and I think it's worth giving this blue bug a tune-up."

"That would be great."

He bent down to scribble something on a notepad, and Daisy felt a flicker of fear. Wait...how much would it cost to 'look under the hood'?

Was that included?

"I'll let you look under my hood under one condition, Fred." She put on her flirty smile and kept her voice smooth as honey.

He blinked up at her. "What's that?"

"You promise not to work too hard." She grinned. "It's

the weekend. And I bet a guy like you has a pretty wife or girlfriend just waiting to be taken out. Am I right?"

"Well, actually…" He looked at his feet, the blush deepening.

"I knew it. Guys like you are always taken." She winked when he waved her off with an aw-shucks chuckle.

Dahlia gripped her arm and tugged. "Thanks for everything, Fred."

"My pleasure, ma'am."

"Bye-bye," Daisy sang over her shoulder as Dahlia led her back out into the sunshine.

"Was that necessary?" Dahlia asked as she climbed into the driver's seat of an enormous truck. It was JJ's apparently, and Daisy was more than a little impressed by how at home Dahlia looked behind the wheel. Like she'd grown up driving monster trucks in the country, not navigating public transit in New York City.

"Fred is a very nice man," her sister continued.

Daisy blinked. "And?"

"And you shouldn't get his hopes up like that." Dahlia frowned.

Daisy's insides instantly tensed. Here she was, the bossy sister she'd been waiting to see. Pinching her lips tight, she looked out the window. They'd dropped Rose off at her new home earlier, and Daisy suddenly wished they hadn't. Rose had always been better at dealing with Dahlia.

But then Dahlia sighed. "I'm sorry."

Daisy whipped her head around to face her. "What?"

Dahlia shrugged, like it was no big deal that she was apologizing. Meanwhile Daisy's jaw was hanging somewhere near her feet.

"I know it's just in your nature," Dahlia said. "You've been flirting with people since you were a baby." She shot her a sidelong look. "At least, that's what Mom used to say."

Daisy smiled at her sister's peace offering, but she so did not feel like dwelling on the things "Mom used to say."

Daisy didn't remember much about her life before their father, Frank, left when Rose was born, but she vividly remembered the time after he left. Their grandmother told them that their mother had always battled mental health issues, and between postpartum depression after Rose was born and losing the husband who she'd built her world around…

Well, she was pretty much useless to them after that. Their grandmother stepped in for a while, and after she passed, Dahlia became the de facto mom, even though she was the same age as Daisy and not that much older than Rose.

"So…" Dahlia shifted in the large seat, her gaze back on the road. "I'm sorry. I shouldn't have lectured you like that. Old habits die hard."

Daisy frowned at her, shaking her head and muttering, "Okay, who are you, and what have you done with my sister?"

Dahlia smirked. "I'm still me, Dais. But I've been learning to…let go a little."

"Because of JJ?" she guessed.

Dahlia didn't answer, but her blush gave her away.

"All this time you just needed a good man, huh?" Daisy teased.

"No!" Dahlia made a tsking sound that was very familiar. "Of course not. It's just that JJ… He helped me figure some things out, you know?"

Daisy stared at her sister's profile. No, she didn't know. But she was afraid to ask. With their mom and their upbringing…there were a lot of topics Daisy didn't like to go near. And she had a hunch that whatever great epiphany JJ had awakened had something to do with their past.

"And it's not just JJ." Dahlia smiled. "I mean, he helped me see where I was getting in my own way, not letting myself be happy, but it's also…this place." She made a sweeping gesture toward the sprawling ranches that lined the road to her right. "I guess Rose told you that I've been working at our ranch, right?"

Our ranch. Daisy tried not to wince. Rose had mentioned it…but Daisy hadn't thought it was such a big deal. "You're just pitching in to get the books straight or whatever, right?"

"Nash handed over a lot of the managerial tasks. And I really like it. I mean, I've always been good at admin work, but it's more meaningful putting those skills to use in a business I actually care about."

"That you care about." Daisy couldn't hide her disbelief. "I thought you were dead set on selling this place."

"Yeah, well…that was before." Dahlia shrugged.

Fear curled like a snake in her belly. "But all the sisters have to be in agreement, right? That was the deal?"

Suddenly she wished she'd paid more attention to Rose's chatter during their phone calls. Or answered Dahlia's calls. But nine times out of ten, Rose caught her when she and the band were touring or in the studio, and Dahlia…

Well, she hadn't been in a place to deal with Dahlia's lectures.

But now she was scrambling to remember what the deal was, exactly, because she'd sort of been banking on the fact that there was some kind of financial boon coming her way.

Dahlia gave her an odd look, and Daisy forced her posture to relax and her lips to curve up in a smile. "Doesn't everyone get a vote?"

"Yeah, definitely. But Emma's still trying to track down Sierra, and April, the youngest, is refusing to have anything to do with her. Or us."

"Okay." Daisy tapped her foot restlessly. Sierra and April, the infamous missing sisters, as she was starting to think of them. Their father had been a crappy dad to Daisy, Dahlia, and Rose, but he'd straight-up abandoned four other girls. No one knew why he'd decided to leave his ranch to all seven of them, or to add in this annoying clause about having to come to a unanimous decision about buying or selling, but Daisy was not exactly feeling the love for her dearly departed dad right now.

She fidgeted with the frayed strap of her messenger bag that was in her lap. "So now you, Rose, Emma, and Lizzy all want to keep the place? But, like, couldn't you buy out the sisters who don't want it?"

"Maybe, but we're not sure it'll come to that." Dahlia glanced over at her. "I think what Emma's hoping—what we're all hoping—is that all the sisters will agree to keep it and be content with dividing the profits rather than selling and getting a lump sum. A large chunk of cash is nice, but we ran the numbers, and it'll actually be more profitable for all of us in the long run if we keep it. Nash has a bunch of plans for how we can increase—"

"But can we get our cut now?"

Dahlia looked over in surprise, and Daisy had to force another smile and a shrug. "Just curious."

"Not this year." Dahlia shook her head. "We're reinvesting every spare penny to make the changes Nash suggested, but if all goes according to plan, there should be enough profit to go around next summer."

Next summer.

Dread pooled in her belly and made her fidgety.

"But hey, at least you have a free place to stay whenever you come to visit." Dahlia flashed her a smile, her brows arched high with eagerness. Like she actually wanted Daisy to come visit often.

Next summer. That felt like an eternity.

"You okay, Dais?"

It was the gentleness in Dahlia's voice that startled her. A snippy, harsh, judgmental Dahlia she knew how to handle. But this new Dahlia was a whole other beast.

"Yes, of course." She laughed and mussed Dahlia's perfectly blown-out hair. Some things hadn't changed, it seemed. "You worry too much."

Dahlia's lips curved in a rueful smile as she straightened her dark locks. "So I hear." She checked her reflection in the rearview mirror, then focused back on the road. "So, the album is finished? That's exciting."

"Mmm." Daisy turned to look out the window.

"And Tanya and Brian? They're still good?"

At the mention of her bandmates, her stomach turned, but she managed an airy "Yeah, they're good. Great. Hey, is that the ranch up there?"

"No, that's Nash's family's property, right next to ours." Dahlia pointed out the big house in the distance, then started telling Daisy about the huge gatherings that often took place there.

Daisy welcomed the subject change and peppered her with more questions even though she couldn't care less about the answers. It kept Dahlia talking, and most importantly, it kept her from asking any more questions.

CHAPTER 7

D ahlia cut herself off in the middle of a long tirade about beef prices. "I hope you're ready for this."

Daisy glanced over in surprise at the warning tone as Dahlia turned onto a winding dirt road that led up the hill-side. But before she could ask what Dahlia meant, her sister flashed her a wry smile. "Wait, never mind, you're good with hugging."

Daisy arched her brows. "Hugging?"

Dahlia looked like she was trying not to laugh. "Pre-pare yourself for hugging, Daisy. Lots and lots of it."

A minute later they crested the top of the hill, and Daisy knew what her sister meant. Two blonde women were flying out the front door of the sprawling ranch house. And for a second, it was all too much to take in.

This house...this had been her dad's house.

A weird knot formed in her throat before she could remind herself that she'd barely known the man. Even the memory of his face was kind of fuzzy now.

But even as she thought it, her mind was trying to register the next shock. The smiling sweetheart and the chic, taller blonde right beside her…these were her half sisters. She swallowed hard.

She'd known she had sisters, of course. Unlike Emma and Lizzy, she and her sisters had been aware that their father had been a busy man, procreating daughters like it was his job. And ever since Rose had arrived here months ago, she'd heard all about them.

But still…

"It's weird, right?" Dahlia murmured beside her, and not without a surprising amount of sympathy.

"Yeah." But Daisy started to laugh as she reached for the door. She didn't do heavy emotions, and new sisters were something to celebrate. She leapt out of the truck and straight into Emma's and Lizzy's arms. They took turns hugging her and exclaiming how excited they were that she'd decided to come.

If a flicker of wariness sparked in her belly at the knowledge that they were excited she was here so they could make a decision about the ranch, she ignored it.

How often did one get to meet new sisters, right?

"How long can you stay?" Lizzy was asking.

"I've already started making up the guest bedroom," Emma said.

But Daisy was too distracted to comment because a scruffy, bearded man with a trucker hat had come from the side of the ranch house, headed straight to Dahlia. He lifted her off her feet like she weighed nothing.

Crazier than that…Dahlia just giggled.

Giggled!

Daisy's jaw dropped as she watched her uptight, straightlaced twin kiss the scruffy cowboy like this was some farewell scene in a movie.

"So cute, right?" Emma nudged her.

46

Daisy left her mouth gaping as she turned back to Emma and Lizzy. They both laughed at her expression.

"You get used to it," Lizzy assured her. And then she added, "Eventually."

Emma snagged her hand. "Come on inside. One of the guys will bring your bags in later."

"Yes, you have to meet everyone." Lizzy fell into step on the other side.

Daisy was flanked, and she kind of didn't mind.

Everyone, it turned out, was Emma's husband, Nash, who Daisy had already heard a lot about from Dahlia since they were working together to run this place, and Kit, Lizzy's husband.

Daisy blinked dazedly a few times in the face of the handsome cowboy, but she knew better than to flirt with a happily married man.

Unless she was trying to get out of a ticket. Her mind instantly called up the hottie sheriff. Was he married?

He hadn't been wearing a ring, but some guys didn't. She should have asked Rose.

"Daisy." Kit grinned as he pulled her in for a hug as if it was totally natural. She had a feeling she was going to like these people. "We've heard so much about you."

And then two little voices were joining the mix.

"Aunt Daisy!"

"Wait. Are you our aunt too?"

Daisy laughed as two adorable little ones surrounded her. "Well, who do we have here?"

"I'm Corbin." The little boy stuck his chest out with pride.

"And I'm Chloe."

"We're twins, just like you and Aunt Dahlia," Corbin added.

47

"Then welcome to the club." Daisy grinned as she stuck out her hand to shake the little boy's.

"Do we get a special ring or something?" Chloe's brows were knitted together, so very earnest about the twin club and what it entailed that Daisy had to press her lips together to stifle a laugh.

"Actually, I think all twins have to wear homemade hats," Lizzy said. She reached a hand down for Chloe's. "Come on, let's see what you and I can whip up with your art supplies."

She shot Daisy a wink before leading the little girl into another room.

"Sorry your first day here is so chaotic." Emma grimaced. "We do a lot of family dinners around here on the weekends, and this family, well…"

Dahlia chuckled. "It just keeps getting bigger and bigger."

Emma laughed. "Exactly."

Daisy beamed. "Well, I love meeting new people, so bring on the whole crazy family."

She got what she asked for. A couple hours later, the house was full to overflowing with everyone and their mother.

Literally. Nash's mother showed up, along with his father and his sister Casey, whose husband was out of town. Then Kit's younger brother Cody showed up and promptly became a climbing post for the twins—the little ones, not Daisy and Dahlia—and the last to arrive was Rose and her new husband, Dex.

Daisy liked Dex instantly. He was so very sweet and kind and doted on her baby sister…and handsome. So very handsome.

"You've done well, Rosebud," Daisy teased as she nudged her little sister.

Rose giggled and grinned, a blush seeping into her cheeks. "I'm so glad you two finally met. It didn't feel right, you two being strangers and all."

A pang of guilt caught Daisy unexpectedly. She really had meant to come to the courthouse wedding, but life kept getting in the way.

"Well, I'm here now, so your cutie doctor and I will just have to spend lots of quality time together before I go."

"And when will that be?" Emma looked worried as she joined in the conversation. "I hope you won't have to leave too soon…"

"Oh no," Daisy said quickly. "I'm in no hurry to go anywhere."

And I can't afford to even if I wanted to.

She brushed the thought aside. She was safe now. There'd be plenty of time to sort out her troubles, or, better yet, let them just disappear while she spent some time with her new family.

And what a family it was. She grinned as she looked around the busy kitchen and took in all the easy chatter and the laughter and the good-natured bickering over who was going to set the table.

For a moment, she took a step back to take it all in. She saw Dahlia cuddled up to JJ, who was whispering something in her ear that made her laugh, and Rose snuggling with Dex on the couch in the other room, her hand resting on her belly as she grinned at Corbin's and Chloe's playful antics.

It was perfect. Daisy had definitely made the right decision to come.

"I hope we're not overwhelming you." Emma joined

Daisy in the archway. "We haven't even given you a proper tour of the house yet, and you've had to meet everyone all at once."

"I love it." Daisy linked her arm through her newfound sister's. "And there is no place I'd rather be."

Emma got a little teary at that, but then Lizzy came up to them. "Come on, you two, grab a seat. Kit and I are putting the food on the table."

Dinner itself was a raucous affair, with too many people at the table, and so many people talking at once it was hard to keep up. Daisy had her end of the table laughing over dessert with her tales from the tour.

Rose and Dex had to cut out early, but when everyone else got up to help clear the plates and do the dishes, Daisy offered to get her guitar and play some music for everyone.

She played some songs the kids knew so they could sing along, and when Kit caught Lizzy from behind while she was drying dishes and pulled her into a dance, cleanup turned into a hoedown. JJ got Dahlia to dance, and the twins were little whirling dervishes in the midst of it all.

Cody joined Daisy on the couch, and she discovered he had a great voice, so the two of them sang some favorite country duets, including some Johnny Cash and June Carter numbers that had everyone clapping and singing along. You couldn't go past the classics.

Eventually she took a break, and Cody brought her some water. They chatted easily as she watched the happy couples break off to snuggle and chat among themselves.

"Sure am glad you showed up," Cody said, nodding toward his brother and Lizzy with a grin as they canoodled on another couch. "It gets old being the odd man out."

She laughed and smacked his arm. "Something tells me you could have any girl you wanted in this town."

He shrugged, his smile sheepish. But he didn't deny it.

Even though he wasn't much younger, he had a boyish air about him. Something sweet and open that made him easy to laugh with, but Daisy had no desire to flirt. It would be like taking candy from a baby.

But they did settle into a fun conversation about music, and she treated him like the little brother-in-law he kinda was.

What she liked was a challenge, she supposed. And just like that he was back—the unreadable, unflappable, painfully serious sheriff.

Now there was a man she'd like to tease and flirt with until he grinned and let out a belly laugh. She took a sip of her drink and sank back into the couch.

When was the last time that man had any fun?

She'd bet the last of her money that it'd been an age…if ever.

She bit her lip, a laugh bubbling up at the memory of his scowl.

Someone really ought to do something about that.

CHAPTER 8

L evi winced as he put a hand on the doorknob. He meant to be home over an hour ago but got a last-minute call just after passing Mama's Kitchen.

Thankfully it was easily resolved, and Mrs. Nefler was found less than half a mile into the forest behind her son's house. The poor woman had dementia and had wandered out of the house unnoticed, which sent her son into a panic.

Walking the confused old woman back to the house took some coaxing, but they managed in the end, and he scored himself a grateful hug from the daughter-in-law and the grandson.

As good as it was to be appreciated, he was now thoroughly done for the day. He should be relieved to be getting home after the long shift, but instead he found himself bracing for battle.

Thankfully, when he opened the door to his two-level house just north of Main Street, it was relatively quiet. He heard Ethan in the kitchen, and when he passed through the living room, he got a couple waves and a mumbled "Hi, Dad" from Ronnie and Dawson. They were so engrossed in a video game, he wasn't sure they'd actually clocked his arrival.

But since no one was shouting or in pain, he called it a win.

"Thanks again, Ethan," he said when he walked into the kitchen.

Ethan was making grilled cheese for the boys. "No problem. You know that's what we're here for."

Levi nodded, resting against the doorframe. "Where's Mikayla?"

"Still out." Ethan shot him a wary look. "She said she'd be home by dinnertime, but…" He glanced at his watch and winced. "It's still on the early side, right?"

Levi clenched his jaw, his gut twisting as he stared at the time on the stove. "We usually would have eaten by now."

"Don't stress. Just give her a little leeway. I'm sure she'll be home any second."

His gaze kept snagging on his phone, and he was on alert for any sound of the front door opening as he cleaned up and changed out of his uniform.

When Mikayla still wasn't home by the time he came back out, that worried knot kept growing. "Who was she with at the diner?"

Ethan's brow furrowed. "Gina was the only one I recognized. I don't know the names of the other girls."

Levi nodded and pulled out his phone.

"She's not that late," Ethan started.

Levi just barely bit back a sigh. Ethan and Dex were always trying to get him to lighten up with his kids. But they had no idea what it felt like to have kids, let alone to be the only parent.

54

What would Beth do?

He had no idea. Mikayla had been a sweetheart of a ten-year-old when her mom passed. Beth wouldn't recognize their daughter if she saw her today.

He stood there with his phone in hand debating his options. Finally, he called Mikayla. If she wanted to be treated like a responsible teenager, then she could explain what was taking her so long.

But Mikayla didn't answer.

And Gina's mom's phone went right to voice mail.

"You okay, Dad?" Ronnie asked.

Levi stopped short. He hadn't realized he'd been pacing until Ronnie stopped him. He looked over to see his sons studying him like they were trying to read his mind.

Guilt flared hot and sharp. He knew it was taking a toll on them too, this constant battle between him and their older sister. But he had no idea how to shield them from the tension any more than he knew how to fix it.

"I'm fine, son." He tried for a smile.

Dawson handed him a controller. "Want to play?"

No. But sitting there staring at his phone wasn't helping anything, and it was much too early to go into full-blown panic mode.

Wasn't it?

He scrubbed the back of his head, all too aware of Ethan's concerned gaze, ready to step in and smooth things over for his sons.

Levi cleared his throat and took the controller with a smile. "Sure. Why not?"

One game and then, if she still wasn't home, he'd put out an APB. That was reasonable enough, right?

There was a knock on the door, and Levi dropped the controller halfway through his turn.

Ronnie was the first one up, and he ran to the door eagerly. Levi tensed. Mikayla wouldn't knock.

But Dex would, and that was who appeared in the doorway. Levi approached and saw Rose at Dex's side, with Mikayla hovering behind them, her head hung low and a nasty scowl distorting her pretty features.

"What's going on?" He stood behind Ronnie, who was bouncing on his toes.

"Hey, Rose. Hey, Dex! Wanna come in?"

"Ronnie, stop," he barked, then noticed the way everyone gave a little jerk of surprise at his harsh tone.

He swallowed and tried for a smile. "That's really good manners, but, uh…can you give us a sec?"

"Okay," Ronnie mumbled, shuffling away with a frown.

Levi gritted his teeth and tried to ignore the twinge of guilt. Focusing back on Dex, he gave his friend an expectant look.

"Uh…" Dex gripped the back of his neck.

Not a good sign.

"Well…" he started, but before he could say anything else, Mikayla huffed and rushed past him, rudely jostling Dex and Rose aside as she stormed into the house.

"Mikayla! Come back here!"

She ignored Levi's shouts as she raced to her room, her feet pounding on the wooden stairs.

Levi was left to stare at Dex and Rose. "What happened?"

Rose winced. "We were driving back home from the ranch, and Dex needed to stop at the clinic…" She looked to her husband.

Dex's brows were set in a stern line. "I'm afraid I caught Mikayla and her friends vaping behind my office."

Levi sucked in a deep breath. The news felt like a punch to the gut. His baby girl. Vaping. An ugly image of smoke steaming out Mikayla's mouth made him grimace.

He ran a hand over his face, only half listening as Dex and Rose took turns explaining how they'd confronted her and called her friends' parents. How Dex had given her a lecture on the dangers of vaping while he drove her home.

"She knows," Levi murmured. The words tasted like ash.

Beth might not have had lung cancer, but Mikayla knew all about the horrible disease, and he'd given her countless speeches on how smoking and vaping could lead to it.

"She knows," he said again, trying to keep his voice even.

She knew, and she did it anyway.

Rose put a hand on his arm. "She's clearly going through a tough time, Levi."

He nodded, but his throat was choked. She was. He knew it. And he had no idea what to do about it. Or how to help her.

His gaze dropped to Rose's belly. He hoped she never knew what it felt like to see her child suffer and not be able to stop it. But her kind gaze and Dex's sympathetic expression had him listening to reason.

"Maybe give her a minute to calm down." Dex winced.

Ethan came to join them, and Rose filled him in.

"Her pride's probably smarting after being caught," he agreed. "She's not going anywhere tonight. Why not give her some space so both of you can cool off?"

He nodded and then moved back so Rose and Dex

could enter. "You care to join us for some dinner? We've got grilled cheese sandwiches and some leftovers."

"We ate already," Dex said.

"But we'd love to keep you company," Rose added.

Her smile was so sweet and sympathetic, he couldn't even bring himself to turn down the offer. "Well, all right then."

So he and Ethan ate while Dex and Rose filled them in on who was up at the O'Sullivan ranch and how Daisy had entertained everyone with tales of her wild adventures. Apparently she'd been pulling out her guitar, about to perform a concert just as Rose and Dex were leaving.

He shook his head with a rueful chuckle. Of course she was.

His smile faltered. It was hard to laugh and listen to stories of carefree Daisy O'Sullivan when his daughter was currently sulking in her room.

He'd have to talk to her at some point, but he dreaded the conversation.

What he wouldn't give to know the magic words that would make everything right.

CHAPTER 9

After Ethan, Dex, and Rose went home, there was no putting it off any longer.

He checked in on the boys, who were watching a movie, and then headed up to Mikayla's room. He knocked, and when she didn't answer, he let himself in, a tray of grilled cheese in his free hand.

She sat on her bed hunched over her phone.

"Hey," he said.

She didn't look up.

"I brought you some dinner."

Her eyes darted to the tray, then back down to her phone. "Not hungry," she mumbled.

He stood there for a long moment, trying to figure out what a good parent would say or do. Part of him wanted to dump the tray on the end of her bed and shout, "You're eating it anyway!"

And another part of him wanted to turn and walk out the door because he didn't know the best way to handle this.

And yet another part wanted to drop to his knees and

ask where his sweet little girl had disappeared to. Beg her to come back and be her happy, giggling self again.

What would Beth say?

She used to instinctively know the best way to manage the children. It was so wrong that she was the one to pass away. The kids would have been so much better off if it'd been him.

She wouldn't give up. She'd make Mikayla talk no matter how awkward it got.

He cleared his throat, but when his daughter continued to ignore him, he set the grilled cheese down on her desk. "Mikayla."

He might as well have been a ghost for all the attention she paid him.

"You can't just ignore me."

She sniffed, her lips pursing as she continued to stare at her phone screen.

With a heavy sigh, he rested his hands on his hips and gave her a final warning. "Don't make me take your phone away."

That did it. With a loud huff she slapped her phone on the bed and glared at him. Her sneer made her look like a stranger. "What?"

"Really?" He gave her a deadpan stare, crossing his arms and struggling for the right words. "Come on, you're smarter than that. You know exactly why I'm up here."

She rolled her eyes. "It wasn't a big deal."

"Uh...yes, it was. Do you have any idea how bad vaping is for your health? You do realize—"

"D-ad!" She stomped her foot on the bed. "I've heard this all from Dex already. Do I really have to suffer a repeat? I'm not an idiot."

"Then why were you acting like one?"

She clamped her mouth shut, her eyebrows dipping into a sharp frown.

"Was it your friends? Did they…" He inwardly winced as he navigated what had become a new minefield—her friends. He never knew who she was fighting with or who was a bad influence. "Did they pressure you?"

She made a tsking sound as she rolled her eyes so hard it looked painful. "No, Dad. Gah! You don't know anything."

"Then explain it to me."

She shook her head, dismissing him as she went back to her phone. "You wouldn't understand. You don't understand anything."

His insides were at war. Anger and hurt, regret and guilt.

Beth, help me! What do I say to this stubborn little—

He stared at the top of his daughter's head, and between all his raging emotions, pain won out. He was sad beyond belief on her behalf. That she didn't have a mother to turn to, and that she was stuck with him…

But pitying her wouldn't keep her from making bad decisions. And he couldn't bear the thought of her getting sick. Or worse, what if vaping was the gateway? What if the next step was drugs and skipping school and—

"The way you behaved is not good enough. You're smarter than this, and you can't just ignore me."

Her head snapped up at his tone. The derision on her face said she was unimpressed by the "cop" voice.

"Or what?" Her voice was a mocking, lazy drawl.

A muscle in his jaw ticked. He ordered about grown men, and not one soul in this town would dare speak to him like this.

Except her. His own daughter.

"Show a little respect," he clipped.

"Whatever." She shrugged and looked back down at her phone.

He took three deep breaths to keep cool. It didn't work.

Snatching the phone out of her hand, he shoved it in his back pocket.

"Hey! Give that back!"

"I will soon enough. For now, we have to talk about the consequences of your actions."

"Ugh! You are such a jerk!"

"I'm well aware of that!" he snapped. "But I can't just let you get away with this stuff. It's for your own good."

"That phone is mine! Give it back."

"I paid for it, and I keep your plan going, so technically it's mine. You just have borrowing rights."

She bulged her eyes and looked ready to scream.

"Now." He folded his arms, fighting for calm as he laid down the law. "You are grounded for the rest of this week, including the weekend. I will be collecting you from the bus each day after school."

"What?" Her cheeks flushed red.

"And you will get your phone back as soon as you've written me an essay."

She blinked at him as if he'd just told her she had to wear a chicken suit to school on Monday. Oddly enough he felt a flicker of triumph at the surprise in her eyes.

He arched his brows. "Two pages, single spaced on the dangers of vaping. And I want scientific research and references."

Her lips parted.

He could all but see her disbelief. "If you don't have that to me by the end of day on Monday, you can say goodbye to your phone for the rest of the month."

She gasped as if he was threatening to cut off her hand. "But...Dad..." Her tone turned whiny, and suddenly he saw a glimpse of the kid she was trying so hard not to be. "That's not fair."

"What's not fair is being disrespected by my daughter who I feed and clothe and—" He was about to say "love," but her sigh was so loud it cut him off.

She rolled her eyes again and...

And he'd lost her. The kid was gone, and the little hellraiser was back.

He took a step toward her desk, lightly tapping it with his finger. "I'd get on it if I were you."

"Whatever you say, warden," she muttered.

He flinched at the word and had to resist the urge to bawl her out for that as well.

Warden?

She felt like home was a prison?

She had no idea. He was tempted to take her down to the station and let her spend the night in a cell.

And she thought *he* didn't know anything.

With a sigh, he shook his head and left the room before temptation got the better of him. The second he was out in the hallway he slumped against the wall with a sigh. The sound of the boys' movie greeted him along with their bickering. He found himself heading toward the sound of fighting out of habit.

He couldn't handle an all-out war between those two tonight.

"Hey!" He grabbed their attention, and they both whipped around to look at him. Their expressions were ones of fear, and it made his gut twist uncomfortably. He softened his voice. "No fighting."

They nodded, turning back to the screen in silence.

Scrubbing a hand over his face, Levi walked toward the kitchen, calling Helen on the way.

He had to swallow down a surge of resentment as he lifted the phone to his ear. He hated that he relied so much on Beth's sister.

Hated that she always knew what to say and do with his kids when he was permanently messing up.

"Good evening, Sheriff Baker. How can I help you?" Her voice was strong and chipper, as per usual.

"Hey, Helen," he rasped. "Sorry to bother you."

In a few short sentences, he filled her in, and like he'd expected, her tone was unconcerned. "Teenagers experiment. It's what they do."

But it's not what my daughter does.

He pinched the bridge of his nose. What did he know? Sometimes he wasn't sure he knew his daughter at all anymore.

"She'll be fine," Helen said. "Look, I'll talk to her next time I see her, all right?"

"That would be great, thanks. She could use a woman to talk to, I think."

"Mmm, she definitely could use a mother." Helen sighed as she always did when the topic came anywhere near Beth and her absence.

More than once, Helen had made a comment about how Beth would want him to move on. How she'd want him to find a good woman who'd make a fine stepmother and…

Ugh. It made his insides flat just thinking about it.

He'd already had love, and while he didn't regret a second of his marriage, he also knew now the flip side of that sort of happiness.

He knew very well how bleak it could be when it came

to an end. And to put himself through that again? Or his kids?

He couldn't even think about it.

"Will we see you guys at church tomorrow?" Helen asked.

"Yes, ma'am." He hoped. If he could wrangle all three of them into their good clothes and out the door in time.

They were late more often than not, and he hated being late.

"Well, all right then. You try to relax and have a good night, Levi."

"Thanks." No sooner had he hung up when he heard the sound of shouting coming from the living room.

He stalked toward his boys with a bark. "All right, you two. That's enough."

CHAPTER 10

Daisy rose to the smell of coffee and the sound of birds chirping. From where she lay in bed, she had a gorgeous view of a sunny spring day on the ranch. Green grass sprawled ahead and met with a brilliant blue sky dotted with puffy white clouds.

She stretched her arms with a smile and leapt out of bed. Unlike yesterday morning, when everyone had been crowding the kitchen before and after church, the downstairs was eerily empty.

She padded around, exploring her father's house in a way she hadn't been able to over the weekend, but it didn't take long for her to grow bored.

Emma wouldn't be home from teaching for ages, and she had no idea when Dahlia, Nash, and the other cowboys swung by for lunch. The silence in the house grew suffocating, so she hurried her way through a shower and let her long hair dry naturally as she donned her favorite flowy blouse and a pair of comfy jeans.

The sunshine was calling to her, so she made her way out back, coffee mug in hand. She settled in on the porch, marveling at the view before her. Amazed to think that she was part owner of all this. Well, until they sold the place… if they did sell the place.

Her stomach clenched.

When her phone rang and it was a local number, she frowned in confusion, but she recognized Fred's voice before he even said his name.

"Is my car ready to be picked up?"

"I'm afraid not, Miss…er, Daisy," he said.

Her stomach fell, a tight knot whistling down to her knees. There was something in his voice that made her wary, and her coffee sloshed, spilling over the edge and spraying droplets over her jeans. She brushed them off and tried for a teasing tone. "Give it to me straight, Doc. How bad is it?"

Fred sighed. "You need a new transmission."

Her mouth went dry as she stared unseeing at the scene before her. "How much is that?"

She didn't want to know. Then he named the price, and she really, *really* didn't want to know.

"I've already called around to see who can get one in for you," Fred was saying.

"Oh no, that's not necessary." She tried to argue, but Fred was insistent.

"You won't be able to get far without one."

That was the argument that finally got through to her, and she shut her eyes with a sigh. She needed that car to leave town…eventually. It wasn't like she could stay here forever. And once she lined up work in New York, she'd have to drive all the way across the country and—

"Daisy? You still there?"

She swallowed hard. "Yeah, I'm here. Go ahead and get that transmission. Thanks, Fred."

68

She hung up and let her head droop with a groan. She couldn't afford any of this. And no amount of flirting would pay for a transmission. She rubbed her eyes. There was nothing she could do about it now, though, right?

She ought to relax and focus on the positives. She lifted her head to the bright blue sky. She was here, after all. She was safe and with her family. She wasn't going to ruin this precious time by worrying. That was all there was to it.

Her phone dinged, and she reached for it eagerly. Maybe it was Rose wanting to meet up or—

She froze, the phone in midair as she caught sight of the LA number. It didn't have a name attached, but it didn't need one because the message made it obvious.

You can't run away from this. You owe me, and I will find you.

She swallowed hard and then shut off her phone before any more messages could come through. Jumping to her feet, she left her coffee on the seat and paced the porch, a sudden flood of adrenaline making her antsy and nauseous all at once.

When she reached the stairs, she rushed down them and started to walk, even though she didn't know where she was heading.

How was she going to pay him back? What was she going to do?

She gave her head a shake and fixed her gaze on the cute pigs in their sty straight ahead. She didn't need to think about it now. And besides, she was safe here, and it wasn't like she'd never have money. She'd find a way to repay him…

69

Eventually.

And for now…

She forced a smile as she reached the pigs, setting her chin on her arms as she watched them. "For now, I'm here, right? There's no point in worrying over the future."

She got a snort in response, and that made her smile more genuine. "Exactly. And besides, it's not like I have no skills. I know how to make money."

Was it her imagination or was the pig looking at her in disbelief.

"It's true!" she argued, then grinned at her own silliness.

She was squabbling with a pig, there was no denying that.

"I'll have you know I have an excellent singing voice."

Snort.

"And I've got some great guitar skills too. But really I'm a lead singer by nature. That's where I shine."

The pigs moved closer, and she took that to be a good sign. The universe was in agreement. She was on the right path. These recent hiccups were just detours, that was all. What she needed to do was keep moving forward.

"I'm going to be messaging my contacts in New York, seeing if I can set up some solo gigs. I've never really done solo before, but I can do it. I'm sure I can." She nodded, trying to ignore the jitters racing through her. "You know what?" She lightly slapped the top of the fence post. "I should find a way to make money singing now."

Snort.

"That's right. Here in Aspire."

A chuckle gave her a start, and she turned to see Kit grinning at her. "You know, Emma likes to talk to the pigs too."

She laughed. "Maybe an affinity for swine runs in the family."

He arched his brows, dubious. "If so, it skipped my Lizzy."

"Not a fan?"

"Of barnyard smells?" He shook his head with a laugh. "Definitely not."

She wrinkled her nose. "Now that you mention it..." She gave the pigs side-eye. "Y'all could use some deodorant."

Kit chuckled. "You getting lonely in that big house?"

She cast another meaningful glance toward the pigs. "Is it that obvious?"

"Well, if you want to check out Aspire, Cody and JJ will be taking a trip into town soon. You could hitch a ride in and come back with Emma or get a ride back with Rose or Dex."

She perked up at the thought. For years back in her teens she'd made do with the cash she earned busking on the streets of New York City. Why not try and do the same here? After all, it was a gorgeous day, and she had nothing better to do.

"That's a great idea. I'll just grab my guitar, and then I'll be ready!"

"Your...guitar?" Kit sounded a little confused. "O-kay."

A little while later, she found herself tucked between JJ and Cody in JJ's truck as they headed to town, her guitar safely in the back.

"Thanks for the ride." She smiled at Cody, who gave her a shy grin before she turned to look at JJ, who was driving.

The scruffy cowboy gave her an easy smile in return.

71

She couldn't imagine anyone less like Dahlia, but she supposed sometimes opposites really did attract.

"I was hoping to have a word with you, actually," JJ murmured.

Cody nudged her arm and gave her a little wink.

"You were?"

JJ's hands fidgeted on the wheel, the only sign that maybe he wasn't so at ease as he seemed. "I, uh...I was hoping to get your permission to ask Dahlia to marry me."

Her gasp sounded absurdly loud in the truck's cab, and Cody burst out laughing beside her. She shot him a quick look. So that was what the nudge had been about. He'd known this was coming.

JJ, meanwhile, still wore a smile, but he wasn't laughing. He was serious.

"JJ, you don't need my permission. Dahlia is a grown woman, and besides, she's actually a few minutes older than me."

His smile widened. "I know I don't need it, but it feels right. It seems...proper."

"Right and proper, huh?" she teased. "I guess maybe Dahlia's rubbed off on you as much as you've influenced her."

His grin widened once more, and his eyes sparkled with laughter as he murmured, "I sure hope so."

Aww. She felt a surge of joy on her sister's behalf. They might not have gotten along, but Dahlia was still her sister, and to see her so perfectly matched made her happy to her core. Not envious, though. Daisy couldn't imagine ever liking any guy enough to get hitched.

The very thought of being tied down like that gave her the heebie-jeebies. But for Dahlia?

"You two are perfect together," she said, leaning over

to nudge his shoulder. "Of course I give you my blessing. I'd be honored to have you as a brother-in-law."

She was rewarded with a side hug and a gruff "Thanks, Daisy."

Shortly after that they arrived on Main Street, and Daisy took in the light crowd with a grin. What a gorgeous day to make some music...

And some money.

Hopefully.

"Could you let me off here?"

JJ pulled over, and she jumped out and bid her farewells, then set off down Main Street in search of the perfect spot to make camp for the day.

CHAPTER 11

Levi was making his rounds, the way he did most Monday afternoons. Being able to get to know the business owners and residents in his town was a luxury he hadn't had before moving to Aspire, and he didn't take it for granted.

So, after a lunch at Mama's Kitchen, he headed toward the end of Main Street. As he drew close to the library, he heard it.

Music.

He stopped in his tracks for a moment as the sound wrapped around him. A hauntingly beautiful female voice. The soft strum of a guitar.

Confusion had him pausing—who on earth would be singing on the streets of Aspire?

But it was another emotion entirely that captured his heart and held him captive.

There was something soulful about the voice. He couldn't make out the words, but he could feel the emotions behind it.

Beth used to sing in the choir at church, and she'd always brought the joy of music home with her, teaching the kids how to harmonize and sing along.

"You trying to turn us into that family from *The Sound of Music*?" he'd tease.

She'd laugh every time, and then she'd go right back to teaching the little ones the importance of music.

Slowly he started walking again. The voice he heard, it wasn't Beth's…obviously. And it didn't belong here.

He was frowning by the time he reached the small clearing along Main Street that held a gazebo and a small garden, and there she was.

Daisy. He should have known.

He stopped short again, this time held captive by the sight of her. Her fair hair seemed to glow in the sunshine, and her eyes were half closed, her expression one of bliss as her voice rose high and clear on the chorus.

He felt it in his lungs. In his chest. Maybe even in his heart. Like her voice had some sort of magic that made a man feel.

But then she caught him staring. Her eyes widened, and those pretty pink lips curved up, and…

"What are you doing?" he snapped.

It came out harsher than intended, but something about the way she'd stirred memories of Beth irritated him more than he could admit.

But she just laughed. "What does it look like?"

"That was real pretty, hon," Chicken Joe murmured as he moved toward Daisy and dropped a dollar bill in her open guitar case. "Take it easy, Sheriff. This angel's just brightening up our afternoon."

Levi's eyes widened. He hadn't even taken note of the

small crowd that had paused before her. He, who prided himself on being observant in every situation, hadn't noticed a dang crowd.

That was...unsettling. The woman had some sort of witchcraft about her.

He blinked a few times as he watched her laughing and chatting with an older married couple who bent down to give her cash.

"You are too kind." Her voice floated in the air like cotton candy.

Once the crowd had dispersed, he moved forward, hands on his holster. "Do you have a permit, Miss O'Sullivan?"

She laughed harder at that. As if he'd made a joke. "A permit?"

She exchanged a smile with a young man who approached her shyly with a dollar in hand.

"I'm serious, Miss O'Sullivan."

"Please don't call me that." She wrinkled her nose, her lips still curved in a smile like that was their default state.

"It's your name."

"No, my name is Daisy." She said it slowly like he was a child. "Just like your name, I now know...is Levi."

She looked entirely too pleased with herself, but good grief if it wasn't difficult not to return that grin.

"No matter your name, you need a permit to perform in public in this town."

Her smile faltered a bit. "You're serious?"

He nodded.

"But..." She pointedly looked around them at the few pedestrians walking by on this fine spring Monday. "Why?"

"What do you mean, 'why?' It's the rules."

She cocked her head to the side like a puppy. Dang it, she was too cute. "But I don't get it."

He sighed and crossed his arms, willing himself not to smile. If he let the rules slide for one woman just because she was cute and pretty, then that would make him a hypocrite when summer came and the tourists arrived, and buskers along with them.

Anywhere tourists went, buskers and outdoor vendors followed.

Food trucks too.

His mouth flattened with a scowl. Dang food trucks. Few of them ever followed the rules.

"You got another tune coming?" It was that young man again, still loitering around with a goofy look on his face. He looked like he was college aged. Too young for Daisy.

Although…

Levi frowned. How old was she?

Too young for you.

She couldn't be older than thirty, and probably a few years younger than that. He found himself doing more math than was good for him. She had to be at least a decade younger than him, so…too young.

Not that it mattered. He wasn't in the market to date anyone anyway.

And yet…

He found himself glaring when the young man approached her again, hands in his pockets.

Daisy might be too young for him, but she shouldn't be flirting with college guys either.

"I sure would love to hear another," the guy was saying.

Daisy leaned forward with a beaming grin that would

have knocked Levi straight off his feet if she'd aimed that thing at him. She gave the kid her undivided attention as she asked his favorite song.

The guy was getting cockier with her every smile, and as Levi drew closer, he heard the man bragging about how he was getting his MBA.

"Wow, that's impressive," she said, all wide-eyed.

Was he the only one who spotted the lie? The woman was good, he'd give her that. But not good enough to fool a trained lawman.

But the MBA student was preening like a peacock as he told her that he was here on vacation and blah blah blah.

"That's fascinating," she said.

Levi scoffed. He couldn't help it. If she was fascinated, he was a mermaid. But she shot him a teacherly pout that said "Now, now, don't be rude."

And Levi had officially had enough.

"Young man, I suggest you move along now." He gave the guy a stern look. "Miss...Daisy," he amended, "is about to stop playing because she does not have a permit."

Daisy snickered and shook her head while the college kid eyed him up, his chest nearly puffing out until his eyes darted to the emblems on Levi's shirt. With a little sigh, he waved goodbye to Daisy and shuffled off.

Levi stepped in a little closer and put on his cop voice. "I'm going to have to ask you to get yourself a permit. It's the only way I can allow you to keep busking."

"But—"

"It's twenty dollars, and you can purchase it from the sheriff's station." He pointed over his shoulder, vaguely indicating where it was. He had a mind to walk her down there himself, but he wasn't sure how much more of her sunshine he could withstand. A man only had so much

79

self-control, and his was dwindling with each passing moment. Even standing this close he could detect *Essence of Daisy*—the sweet scent enough to send his insides reeling with unbidden desire. Walking next to her all the way to the station? Definitely not a good idea.

"You cannot be serious." She snapped him out of his fleeting "walking in the sun" daydream.

She truly sounded like she didn't believe him. Not for the first time he wondered if anyone had ever said no to this woman before. She didn't seem to be comfortable with it. "It's the rules around here, Daisy, and if you plan to stay—"

"I don't." She followed the brisk comment with a bright smile.

Holding her chin high, she gave him a little sniff before packing up her guitar and shoving the loose cash and change into a bag that was slung across her body. "You don't have to watch me like I'm some criminal," she managed to say through a smile that was becoming increasingly more tight-lipped.

He rocked back on his heels, his arms crossed. He didn't stop watching until she had her guitar case in hand and was turning away from him with a loud huff.

She strode off, her flared jeans frayed at the edges and her hair flying behind her like a kite. It wasn't until she reached the end of the block that he let his lips twitch upward. A soft chuckle escaped as he turned away.

He had an odd desire to follow her. To see what she'd do next. He had a feeling that the woman was incapable of staying away from trouble for long. But he had a job to get back to. And besides, he planned on picking the boys up and then meeting Mikayla at her bus stop so she couldn't get "lost" on the way home.

But he dipped his head as he walked away, his mind still on the beautiful blonde with the angelic voice and sunshine smile.

That woman was trouble, all right.

But she was awfully cute.

CHAPTER 12

T*he nerve of that man.*
    Daisy took a deep breath as she walked away.
And then another. Then one more. But no amount of
deep breathing seemed to calm her racing heart.

What a day. She closed her eyes briefly and focused on
inhaling, but that only had her stumbling when she
brushed against a lamppost.

Was it her imagination or were the sheriff's eyes still on
her? She wasn't typically paranoid, but she felt like she
had a laser between her shoulder blades. Seriously, did he
really have to watch her like a hawk while she packed up?

Acting like she was some criminal just because she was
singing and making people smile.

Geez.

She waited until she reached the end of the block
before turning to see if he was still staring, but he was
walking in the opposite direction, so...fine.

Good.

She watched him for another minute, her gaze trailing
down his body and her lips quirking into a smile as she

lingered over his butt for just a moment too long. Okay, so those uniform pants fit him perfectly. He turned the corner and disappeared from sight. Such a shame, really. The man was so handsome. He'd be a total ten if he ever smiled. Or cracked a joke. Or...showed any sort of emotion, really.

She shook her head and turned back the way she'd been heading. She was certainly not about to go get a permit. The whole point was to make money, not spend it.

She was out here playing for tips. Did it look like she had twenty bucks to spare? She kept walking until she got to the end of the main strip. It wasn't as busy on this side of Main Street, but she found a lovely spot in the sun right in front of a flower shop that smelled divine.

She cast a few glances up and down the street, but there was no sign of that irritating stick-in-the-mud sheriff, so she planted herself atop a picnic table with her guitar case open on the bench below her feet. Then she gave the guitar a quick tune and started to strum.

The few pedestrians walking by stopped to listen.

She grinned, her earlier annoyance forgotten as she lost herself in a song, and then another. It was the sort of folk pop she'd always listened to as a kid—the music that made her home life bearable. And it was the same kind of music she and her band created...

Or the kind they *had* created.

She swallowed hard and shook off the thought of her LA nightmare, then threw herself back into the music.

You couldn't dwell in the negative when you were singing about love. It was a proven fact.

The pedestrians came and went. Never any great crowds—Times Square this was not—but between songs she leaned over to see a nicely growing pile of coins and cash.

She wasn't about to make enough money for a trans-mission in one afternoon, but it was a start. It was better than nothing. And besides, she'd missed singing with abandon.

Sitting here playing music in the sunshine had her feeling like herself again.

After a while, a school bus pulled up, and Daisy beamed as high school students got off. Most of them gathered around, enthralled, no doubt, by the rare sight of a musician on their streets.

What with the *Footloose* sheriff running this town, maybe this was the first music they'd ever heard. The thought made her laugh, and the crowd of teens bright-ened her spirits. Some of the gangly boys were trying to catch her eye, and that made her grin even more.

But there was one girl with sandy shoulder-length hair who caught her attention. She had a forlorn air about her, and her gaze wasn't on Daisy's outdated bell bottoms or her hair, but on her fingers.

On the guitar.

Curious, she set the guitar down after the crowd of teens dispersed. A few girls asked if she was coming, but the girl shook her head, mumbling something like "I can't, remember?"

They all frowned together, and the girls walked off, muttering darkly under their breath. She watched her friends leave with a sad pout.

"You okay?" Daisy asked and beckoned for the girl to approach.

The girl rolled her shoulders, looking hesitant. Glancing down the road, she scanned the street, then shuf-fled forward.

"How's it going?" Daisy grinned.

The girl gave her a cautious smile and shrugged.

"Friend troubles?"

"Not really." She shook her head, her eyebrows dipping together until she started eyeing up the guitar again.

"So, you like Buddy, huh?"

The girl gave her a confused grin. "Buddy?"

"My guitar. I call him Bud for short."

She let out a little laugh and nodded. "He's really cool."

Daisy held it up for her to see. "He's old and has seen some good times. Maybe a few bad as well," she said with a grin. "But he was my first guitar and will always be my favorite."

The girl's smile grew a little wider as ran her fingers lightly down the strings.

The guitar let out a noise of approval, a sweet little trill that made Daisy laugh. "Do you play?"

She started to shake her head, then shrugged. "Not really."

Daisy nodded, her heart going out to this young teen. She wasn't so old that she couldn't remember what it was like to be that age. When insecurity was ever present and everyone around you was judge and jury.

Daisy got through that phase like she'd gotten through everything else in her life—with music and a smile. "Come on up." She shifted to make room for the girl on the table.

The girl looked around, uncertain once more. Daisy had no idea who she was checking for. Maybe an overly strict parent or some bullies she was afraid of.

"It's okay. I've got your back." Daisy grinned, and the girl gave her a shy smile before dumping her bag on the

86

ground and sitting up beside her. "I'm Daisy, by the way. You want to sing with me?"

The girl shook her head, but the movement was too quick, and Daisy caught the actual emotion on her face. She wanted to. She was just embarrassed.

"Tell you what," she said. "How 'bout if I start, and you join in if you feel like it."

The girl nodded, peeking over with a shy smile. "You have a real pretty singing voice."

"Aw, thanks."

"You…you kinda sound like my mom when you sing."

Daisy's heart clenched at the sadness that was written all over the girl's face. Where was her mom now?

It wasn't her place to ask.

She tipped her head down and focused on plucking the strings. "I sound like my mom too."

The girl laughed. "Really?"

Daisy nodded, her smile growing strained as memories threatened. "My mom had this way of singing…" She swallowed hard. "When she sang it would light up a room."

The girl nodded eagerly. "Yeah, my mom too."

They shared a smile, and Daisy forced her mind to stay focused on those memories, those rare, fleeting times when her mom was happy. When the world was bright and filled with hope and…

Well, those times didn't last long, so Daisy learned that you had to enjoy the heck out of them when they came. Focus on the happy times, forget about the bad.

"Come on," she said, nudging the girl gently with an elbow as she grinned and strummed a few chords. "Let's make our moms proud, what do you say?"

The girl laughed softly and nodded.

Daisy started, a simple folk tune that had an easy melody to follow and simple lyrics. The girl nodded along, her expression lost in thought as she listened. Then when the chorus came around again, she joined in, softly at first and then with more conviction.

Daisy's eyes widened, and she beamed at the girl as she broke out in a harmony that gave Daisy goose bumps.

The girl's answering smile was shy but pleased. She was proud of herself, and Daisy's heart gave a hard slam against her rib cage.

When the song came to an end, they both started laughing as the pedestrians who'd stopped to listen burst out in applause.

The girl ducked her head, but Daisy wrapped an arm around her shoulders and squeezed. "You're a natural, hon."

"Thanks."

"What's your name?"

The girl lifted her head to meet her gaze. "Mikayla."

CHAPTER 13

Levi paused for the tenth time on the short walk to Mikayla's bus stop. He was already running late to collect her, and it was making him antsy. She'd respect him even less if he didn't keep his word. And not being there gave her way too many opportunities to sneak off with her friends. He wanted to be standing there when the bus pulled up.

Why did he let Dawson talk him into stopping at Mama's Kitchen on the way? He thought they'd have time, but then—

"Boys!" he barked.

Usually one word said that way was enough to get Ronnie and Dawson to stop bickering. But today they both ignored him completely.

Great. Now even his boys were learning how to tune him out. He walked back to where they'd stopped.

"It was your fault," Ronnie accused, his little face red with anger.

"Oh, like I made you spill your milkshake," Dawson taunted.

"You didn't have to laugh!"

"Why not? It was hilarious." Dawson started laughing all over again as Ronnie's hands curled into fists.

Levi sighed. Though at eight years old, Ronnie was younger than his ten-year-old brother, he was typically the more mature of the two. Dawson had always been more of a class clown—loud, aggressive, though he had a good heart. He just had more energy than he knew what to do with—that was what Beth used to say.

In contrast, Ronnie had always been on the quiet side. He was small for his age and preferred to go to the library than play sports. And overall, he didn't have much of a temper. But Dawson knew exactly how to rile him and never missed a chance.

"We're already late to pick up your sister," he said, hoping one of them would stop their staring contest to at least glance at him.

"We wouldn't be late at all if Ronnie hadn't been a klutz and spilled his milkshake."

"You bumped me!"

"Did not."

"Did too."

Levi stepped between them, a hand on each shoulder, studiously ignoring the amused glances from passersby. "Neither of you will have another milkshake for the rest of your life if you don't end this squabble right now."

They both clamped their mouths shut, but the glaring continued even after he turned around. He heard Ronnie whisper to Dawson, "How would he keep us from getting a milkshake when we're grown-ups?"

Dawson snickered.

Levi felt a little smile tugging at his lips. He didn't mind being the butt of the joke so long as they were getting along. They were actually laughing together by the time they reached the corner near the bus stop, and for the second time that day, music drifted toward him.

Daisy.

She must've gotten that permit after all. And truthfully, he found he was glad she had. Her voice was soft and sweet, and once again it seemed to reach inside him and wreak havoc with his chest.

It was a voice that ought to be shared and appreciated.

"...right, Dad?" Ronnie said.

Levi cleared his throat and glanced down. "Uh, sorry, what?"

Ronnie asked again if they were having chicken tenders for dinner—his favorite meal.

Levi gave him a distracted nod and walked forward. Dawson started talking about his day at school, and this time Levi tried to pay attention, but his feet were picking up the pace, and he felt like the music was drawing him forward by an invisible cord.

As they turned the corner, he heard a second voice join in and...magic.

It sounded like magic and joy and...

Beth.

It sounded like his Beth was right there with them.

"Look, Dad, it's Mikayla," Dawson said.

Levi blinked. He'd been expecting the sight of Daisy in all her pretty sunshine-y glory. But to see Mikayla sitting beside her...to see her singing...

His heart caught in his throat. She sounded just like her mother.

How had he not known she'd gotten her mother's singing voice?

Pain clenched his chest, but it was bittersweet. It was

memories of Beth mixed with gratitude for the children she'd given him, alongside a deep and abiding love for this little girl who was smiling.

Smiling.

His throat tightened as he stared at Mikayla's face. How long had it been since he'd seen that smile?

Not one filled with sarcasm, and not a sneer of disdain. But a genuine smile filled with joy as she closed her eyes and tipped her head back, holding a long note like it was the best she'd done all year.

"They're good." Ronnie crossed his arms and assessed them like he was a music producer scouting for new talent.

It was the understatement of the century. Daisy's voice was just as soulful and pure as he remembered. And Mikayla…

Her voice was perfect.

All too soon the song was over, and he watched Mikayla smile and laugh with Daisy in a way he hadn't seen in what felt like forever.

"Who is she?" Dawson's question pulled him back to reality just as Daisy caught him staring.

Levi swallowed, taking Ronnie's hand and gripping Dawson's shoulder as he led them forward. Mikayla caught sight of them, too, and…

He nearly tripped over his own feet at the smile she gave them. Almost like she forgot that she was permanently angry with him and annoyed by her brothers.

"You sounded great, Mikayla." Ronnie ran up to stand beside her.

She ruffled his hair and laughed. "Thanks."

"Daisy." Levi tipped his hat.

Her smile widened, her eyes sparkling like he'd just said something funny. "Sheriff."

"Dad, you know Daisy?" Mikayla's voice was high, like this was truly shocking.

"Dad?" Daisy repeated, her eyes widening.

"We met," he said. He tried not to laugh as Daisy wrinkled her nose, no doubt at the memory. To Daisy, he added, "I see you've met my daughter, Mikayla." He gestured to his sons. "This is Dawson and Ronnie."

"Well, now I see the resemblance." She pursed her lips as she eyed the boys and then Levi. "Yup. Three so very handsome men. It's clear you're family. But you..." She nudged Mikayla. "Where'd you get that gorgeous smile? Definitely not from your dad."

All three of his kids laughed as Daisy narrowed her eyes and curved her lips down in what he assumed was an imitation of him.

Mikayla laughed hardest of all. And once again, Levi felt his own lips starting to curve up in a grin. Yup. He'd happily be the butt of the joke if it meant hearing his kids laugh and have fun together.

But Daisy caught them all off guard when she added, "You must've gotten your smile from your mother, just like your singing voice."

Levi felt the air in his lungs evaporate at the easy mention of Beth. Somehow Beth's name, her very existence —it had become a sort of sacred topic. People in town either never mentioned her or, when it was unavoidable, they spoke of her in sad, low tones, like even three years later they were still hovering over her deathbed.

To hear her spoken of like...well, like that...

Worry had him looking to his children, gauging their reactions.

Mikayla's smile brightened. "I guess so!"

Ronnie and Dawson were nodding eagerly.

"You do have her smile," Dawson said.

"What about mine?" Ronnie's smile was more of a cheesy grimace that had everyone cracking up.

And then Daisy was challenging the boys to see who could make a funnier face, and then his surly thirteen-year-old was laughing so hard she actually snorted, which set the two boys off all over again.

Levi watched the scene in amazement. Daisy was chatting with all three of them so easily. Just like she talked so easily to everyone, it seemed. And she made each of them light up like that smile of hers was contagious. Or maybe it was the undivided attention she gave to whichever of his kids was talking.

She spared none of that attention for him, and that was just fine. He didn't need her trying to flirt with him again. It wasn't like she'd been seriously interested in him, anyway; she'd only been looking to get out of trouble.

His gaze drifted to the open guitar case beside her. She did get that permit, right?

Mikayla let out a loud laugh at whatever Daisy said.

He'd ask her next time he saw her. For now…

"Come on, kids. We've got to get home and get homework out of the way before dinner."

Mikayla groaned, but it was a mock, exaggerated one that made Daisy grin.

"Bye, Daisy!" Ronnie shouted, turning to wave enthusiastically.

Dawson and Mikayla were shouting back to her as well as they walked away. And even after they'd turned the corner toward their street, the playful, light banter continued between his children.

It felt like some kind of miracle.

"What are we having for dinner, Dad?" Mikayla asked, turning back to look at him with wide eyes, untainted with all that insecurity and sadness that seemed to be plaguing her lately.

"Chicken tenders is on the menu. Does that sound good to you?"

"As long as you make that special dipping sauce to go with them."

He hadn't planned to, but that just changed. "Of course."

She smiled at him again, and Levi's heart swelled with gratitude when he wrapped an arm around her shoulders and she didn't pull away.

CHAPTER 14

S *o the sheriff has a family.*
         His poor wife.

Daisy watched them walk away with a snicker. But her laughter faded as she remembered Mikayla's odd tone when she'd spoken of her mother. Was she still in the picture? Were they divorced?

She shook her head. None of her business. She should just be grateful he hadn't asked to see the permit. She played a few more songs, but the pedestrians became few and far between, so she packed up her things and took a walk to stretch her legs.

Along the way, she texted two of her contacts in New York. She hadn't spoken to them in months, so she was doubtful of a quick reply...or any reply at all, but she wanted to have some things in motion so that once she had enough money for that transmission, she could get going.

She then texted her sisters and quickly found out that Rose was hard at work trying to finish all her editing projects before the baby came, and Dahlia was swamped trying to set up a new accounting program for the ranch. But Emma had offered to give her a ride back after she wrapped up at school, and Lizzy had told her to swing by the clothing boutique where she worked part-time.

Daisy headed that way, and this time she took her time strolling, taking in the old-timey architecture along Main Street and the parks and community gardens just beyond.

It was an adorable little town. Like something off a postcard, or the backdrop for some Hallmark movie.

She grinned at the thought. It was no wonder Rose had decided to stay here. It fit her sweet, romantic nature to a T.

Dahlia, on the other hand...

Well, Daisy would not have predicted that her city-loving sis would find her perfect home in the mountains of Montana, but no one could deny that she was thriving here. With JJ, being close to Rose and the others... It was good for her. Maybe it was the sort of happy home she needed after their own toxic upbringing.

Daisy shook off the thought. She didn't like to go there. What mattered was that her sisters had found a place to call home. And men who made them happy.

She smiled as she turned onto the street Lizzy had told her to.

Good for them. She couldn't imagine loving any one place or person enough to be tied down. She wrinkled her nose at the mere thought. Getting hitched, buying a house. It sounded like prison.

But to each their own, right?

The bells above the door tinkled lightly when she stepped inside. And after standing still for a second to let her eyes adjust to the light, Daisy gasped.

"What do you think?" Lizzy stepped toward her from

behind a back counter, gesturing broadly to the displays and mannequins.

"It's gorgeous in here," Daisy gushed.

Lizzy beamed. "We try."

Daisy's eyes were wide, and she was only exaggerating a little as she oohed and aahed over the fancy scarves and the high-end purses. "It's like a legit boutique!"

"I know, right? You'd never guess there was something like this in Aspire." Lizzy laughed. "When I first got here, I thought the stores didn't sell anything but flannel."

When Daisy touched a silk blouse, Lizzy asked, "Want to try something on?"

"Oh no," Daisy said quickly. "It's not really my style."

And she couldn't afford a single thing in this place. But what she'd said was true too. "I'm more of a secondhand-store girl myself."

"Fair enough." Lizzy went back behind the counter and rested her elbows on it. "But you didn't bring much luggage, and the seasons change quickly here, so if you ever need some new items in your wardrobe, let me know." She winked. "I'll give you a good deal on something new, or you can always borrow stuff." She eyed Daisy with a professional eye. "I'd say we're about the same size."

Daisy grinned. "Thanks for the offer, but I don't think I'll be here that long."

"Oh." Lizzy's expression fell, but she brightened quickly. "Bet you've got a lot of exciting stuff to get back to in Los Angeles, huh?"

"Mmm." Daisy kept her gaze on the scarves draped over the end table.

"Rose was telling us about your tour. That must have been exciting."

Daisy nodded, but her insides were starting to twist uncomfortably. The tour was supposed to have been everything their band had worked so hard for, and instead…

She took a deep breath, trying not to think about the bickering and the fights. Daisy had been so sure it was just a side effect of being on the road together for so long. But then they'd gotten to LA, and things had gotten even worse when they were all crammed together in the studio.

"I bet you can't wait to get back to your music and the limelight…" Lizzy gave a funny little sigh as if she was jealous, but Daisy wasn't fooled. She'd seen how happy Lizzy was with Kit and the twins.

Daisy bet she couldn't pay Lizzy to leave Aspire, and certainly not for a nomadic life in LA.

But Daisy nodded, her smile real when she said, "I do miss the music."

Her heart gave an uncomfortable squeeze as Lizzy's gaze turned sympathetic. "Well, I hope you don't rush off too soon. We'll be sad to see you go."

Daisy felt another jolt, but this one sent her heading toward the door. She didn't want people giving her a guilt trip for leaving, or getting ideas that she might be willing to stay. Like always, this sort of talk made her muscles tense and her skin itchy.

"Always running from responsibility." Her mother's voice was loud in her ears. *"Just like your father."*

Daisy flinched. Where had that come from?

She lifted a hand to say goodbye. "I'd better head over to Emma's school so I don't hold her up."

"'Kay. See you soon!"

Daisy took a deep breath when she got outside, and the sunshine and fresh air did wonders to help her regain her earlier peaceful mood. Lizzy hadn't meant anything by that. It was just being around all this family, that was all.

She wasn't used to it. She'd forgotten that with family came expectations and obligations.

She smiled determinedly as she waved at the old men she'd met the other day. They were camped out around a table in front of the coffee shop and called out a greeting.

She'd just enjoy this town and her family while she was here.

Because soon enough she'd be on her way.

CHAPTER 15

L evi turned to face Mikayla in the passenger seat.
"Did you remember your homework?"

She sighed. "I already told you yes. Why do you have
to nag me first thing in the morning?"

"That's just one of the joys that come with parenthood,
I guess."

She rolled her eyes as they inched forward behind
another car in the drop-off line.

"Don't forget you're watching the boys until—"

"I know, Dad. Geez." She huffed as she looked out the
window.

"Look, I'm not trying to annoy you—" He cut himself
off when she made a scoffing sound. "If you hadn't missed
your bus this morning, you could have avoided all the
nagging."

"And now a guilt trip," she muttered. "Nice."

His jaw worked as his hands tightened on the steering
wheel. "Where is the sweet little girl who was singing like
an angel the other day?"

He hadn't really meant to say it aloud, but it tumbled

out. He'd been wondering it all morning. The girl was so hot and cold, all over the board with her emotions. Maybe that was normal to some extent—Helen assured him it was.

But somehow, seeing her all light and happy with Daisy two days before made her newfound bad attitude that much worse.

"I wasn't a sweet little angel," she said, so low and soft he almost didn't hear her. "I just liked singing, that's all."

He stared at her profile in disbelief. That was the most she'd said without an insult or a sigh attached in twenty-four hours. He wanted to ask her more, but he had to choose his questions wisely or she might turn back into a snapping turtle again.

He cleared his throat. "I know you and your mom used to like playing music together. Do you, uh...do you miss it?"

She lifted a shoulder.

He took that to be a yes.

"Maybe..." He inched the car forward again. "Maybe you could join the church choir—"

"With all the old ladies?"

She sounded so horrified he quickly moved on. "Or the school's band or—"

"No, Dad." She made "Dad" sound like an insult, and he still wasn't sure how. "My friends would think I'm a dork."

He opened his mouth, then closed it again, holding back a few choice words he had to say about her friends. He knew better than to suggest that maybe she shouldn't listen to those girls.

"Well, maybe we could—"

"I gotta go." She hopped out before he could finish his thought.

"Don't forget to watch your brothers—"

The car door slammed.

"After school," he finished. "Aunt Helen will pop in to check on things," he murmured, pretending she was still in the car, listening with all her attention the way she used to.

He drove forward as Mikayla ran off without a backward glance. He was on duty, so he headed straight to the station and checked in with his staff.

Mikayla missing her bus had made him late. It was not the way he liked to start any morning. Thankfully, his neighbor agreed to walk the boys to school so he would only miss the start of the morning briefing.

Mikayla was on his mind as he met with his deputies, wrapping up the end of the meeting before they went on patrol, and then with a concerned citizen from an outlying community that had been seeing more than its fair share of vandalism.

At midmorning, he took a break and headed across the wide-open grassy lawn that lay between the station and the coffee shop on Main Street.

This time he saw her first. How could he not?

Daisy's hair seemed to be a halo in the sunlight, and her white, off-the-shoulder blouse and long swingy skirt amid the sea of denim and leather made her look like the out-of-towner she was.

Her laughter was clear as day, and her head fell back with it, revealing a long, slim neck. The guitar was in her hands, but she was chatting with the small crowd as some dropped money in before walking away.

She spotted him just as the last of the crowd walked

away, and her smile was adorably knowing. "If you've come over here to read me the riot act for performing without a permit, you're too late." She grinned as she slid the strap of her guitar case over her shoulder. "I was just leaving."

He winced slightly, because...well, he had been about to ask her about the permit, and while he normally prided himself on being a rule enforcer, for one second he found himself wishing he wasn't so very predictable.

Wouldn't it be nice if she saw him coming and smiled rather than sighed with irritation like Mikayla always did?

Oh, Daisy hid her annoyance better than his daughter, but he caught a whiff of it when she turned away, her chin held high.

He didn't want to see her go. And then he realized why. This woman...the way she'd made Mikayla so happy, even if for a short time...

He found himself hurrying after her. "Daisy, wait."

She shook her head, which made her long hair fly in the breeze. "So you can slap me with a fine or give me another ticket or whatever?" She flapped a hand like he was a bug to be shooed away. "I don't think so."

"No, that's not why I want to talk to you." He picked up his pace. She was surprisingly quick for a woman wearing flip-flops and carrying an instrument.

She cast him a narrow-eyed look over her shoulder. "So you didn't come over to me in that sexy uniform of yours to give me another lecture about performing without a permit?"

"No." He reached her side, and one side of his mouth tugged up against his will as her words registered. "You think the uniform is sexy?"

"You know it is." She did another shooing wave again.

"But since you didn't actually catch me playing, you can't do anything about my lack of a permit."

He crossed his arms, the lawman side of him at war with the side that was still preening just a little at the "sexy uniform" comment. "You're making too big a deal out of that," he said. "It's just a formality. And it's only twenty bucks."

"Yeah, well, twenty dollars is a lot for some people."

He slowed down to look at her, but she glossed over it quickly, going on a little tirade about how music should be free for everyone. But she was just trying to distract him. And suddenly he was remembering that flicker of fear in her eyes the first day they'd met when he handed her the ticket.

She'd glossed over that too. But he knew what he saw. And what he'd heard in her voice just now. Fear. Worry.

And that did not sit right by him. In fact, it made him feel like he'd swallowed glass. "Daisy—"

She turned around so quickly, he nearly bumped into her. "What?" Her smile was fading, and she looked...frazzled. Or maybe a little tired, like sleep wasn't coming so easy.

He knew that feeling all too well.

"I, uh…" He licked his lips. "I wanted to thank you." Ah heck, his voice was too stiff.

She cocked a brow. "For what?"

"For singing with my daughter. That was…"

She started to laugh, and the sound rivaled her melodic tones. "That was my pleasure. She's got a killer voice."

"Yeah, well…" *She got it from her mother.*

He couldn't bring himself to mention Beth right then, so he switched topics to the idea that had been brewing since the moment he'd spotted her this morning. "What do you think about giving Mikayla music lessons?"

Her brows drew in tight. "What kind?"

"Well, she used to play a little guitar and piano…"

He could see the "no" on her lips in the sad little smile she was giving him. "I'd like to, but…"

"I'll pay you," he added quickly. "Of course."

Her lips parted, but she hesitated.

"Say twenty bucks a lesson?"

She tilted her head from side to side, and he saw the inner debate. The woman clearly needed money.

"Look, she seems like a good kid, and I'd like to help you out, but I'm not planning on sticking around long, so you'd probably do best to find someone else."

She gave him another apologetic little grimace before turning to head toward Main Street again.

Find someone else. Some other miracle worker who could make his daughter come alive? Who could make her smile and talk and…and sing?

He chased after Daisy. "Please. It's important. It has to be you."

She slowed to a stop, and her gaze searched his, no doubt looking for a trick or some kind of play.

But there was none. He was serious.

Whatever she saw, she gave a resigned little sigh along with a nod. "Tell you what. You buy me a tea and tell me just why it's so vitally important that I be the one to give your daughter lessons"—she spun on her heel and hitched up the guitar—"and then I'll decide."

For a second, he watched her lead the way, her skirt swishing around her ankles and her long hair wild in the wind. And then he followed in her wake…

A grin spreading across his face.

CHAPTER 16

The morning rush had faded since Daisy had stopped into Cal's for a glass of water and a trip to the restroom an hour before. Now it was just down to the old men in the corner, who waved and shouted her name like she was Norm from *Cheers*, and a few tables of patrons chatting quietly over their drinks.

"What would you like?" Levi asked as he joined her at the counter.

He was standing right behind her, and his voice was low and rumbly in her ear. Butterflies burst into flight in her belly before she could stop them. She gave her head a rueful shake.

So he was attractive. Didn't mean she had to go and get all giddy about it.

He's a married man, she reminded those butterflies. Not to mention a father of three. So basically, he was the exact opposite of what she looked for in a relationship.

Not that she really did relationships, but he wasn't the guy for her.

She liked men who were just as uncomplicated as she

was. No strings. No attachments. She took a deep breath and smiled at the girl behind the counter, who was waiting patiently for her order. "A chamomile tea, please."

"The usual for me. Thanks, Gracie." Levi nodded at the girl, and she gave him a friendly smile before walking off to get their drinks.

The usual.

It made Daisy smile. She couldn't imagine ever living in a place long enough for someone to know her *usual.*

They stood there in silence, Daisy twisting the mood ring on her pointer finger until Levi asked, "Do you want some food as well?"

She blinked up at him in surprise. Mainly because the offer had come out grudgingly. It almost sounded like it was against his will.

She grinned. She wasn't about to look a gift horse in the mouth. She leaned over the counter. "I'd like one of those croissants, please. Oh, and a muffin." She peeked over her shoulder and saw a hint of amusement in the stern sheriff's eyes as she used a stage whisper to add, "And a cupcake."

The girl had returned in time to hear it all, and she giggled, fetching the food as if it were her absolute pleasure.

"You're really gonna eat all that?" Levi pointed at the plates piling up on the counter.

"Of course not." She winked at him.

He arched a brow, and she couldn't have looked away from his amused gaze if she'd tried. "Well, I hope you didn't order for me. I don't eat sweets."

She laughed. "Of course you don't." She patted his arm. "I'll save the cupcake for lunch."

His lips twitched, and she caught the faintest hint of a smile before he squelched it.

Dang. She had a feeling his smile would be something to see.

When their drinks were ready, Levi helped her carry everything over to a small table by the window. He sipped his black coffee—of course he drank it black—as he watched her devour her croissant. "You were hungry."

She shrugged. She didn't like the hint of concern in his eyes. She'd seen it earlier when she'd stupidly made a comment about not having any money. She hurriedly changed the topic. "All right, now you have to spill, Sheriff."

He tensed, his gaze growing wary.

Her own belly clenched as well, so she grinned and added, "Why don't you eat sweets? Is it a health thing, or you just don't like to be happy?"

The wariness faded, replaced by exasperated amusement. "Sugar is bad for you, in case you hadn't heard."

"Oh, I've heard. But I've also heard you only live once." She tore off a piece of the muffin and popped it in her mouth. "Life is short and all that." She talked around her mouthful of food.

The amusement in his eyes faded again, and he looked far too serious for a man surrounded by muffins and cupcakes.

She swallowed her mouthful and wiped the edge of her lips while he let out a soft sigh.

"Yeah, well, I'd like to live long enough to meet my grandchildren, so I take my health seriously."

"You take everything seriously," she shot back, softening the taunt with a grin.

"Maybe."

She straightened and picked up her tea. "I bet you work out, too, don'tcha?"

His lips twitched. "What makes you say that?"

"Uh…aside from those killer biceps and the way you fill out your shirt?"

He dipped his head down and made a choking sound. He was embarrassed, and that was…kind of adorable.

He's married. It was Dahlia's voice in her head.

Was he, though? The way Mikayla spoke about her mom, Daisy suspected she was out of the picture. Probably divorced. Too messy for her, either way, but she couldn't resist adding, "Bet you've got killer abs too," before taking a sip of her tea.

He scrubbed a hand over his face and then smoothed down his beard. "You finished?"

She lifted her shoulders with a look of pure innocence that had his lips twitching again.

Goodness, what would it take to make this guy smile?

"Do you do Pilates?"

He rolled his eyes. "I jog every morning before the kids wake and hit the gym at least twice a week. Satisfied?"

She batted her eyelashes as she made a show of checking him out. "Very."

A chuckle slipped out of him, low and rumbly. "You're incorrigible."

"And you just sounded so much like my sister Dahlia that I think maybe you're her twin and not me." She got another lip twitch with that one. But his eyes were back to being all light with amusement, so she leaned forward and tilted her head to the side. "Wanna tell me why you're so keen on getting your daughter music lessons?"

His flinch was slight but noticeable as he rubbed the back of his neck. "She's a teenager…"

112

"I noticed."

"And she's...well, she seems to be going through a phase or something. Or, at least, I hope it's a phase." His brows drew together, and Daisy had the most ridiculous urge to lean forward and smooth a hand over his forehead so she could rub away those frown lines. He looked like a walking, talking headache.

"She's gotten so distant, and moody, and...and she's talking back."

She tried hard not to smile. Not because his issues were funny but because the way he talked was so earnest and...sweet.

What would it have been like to have a dad who cared so much? Her heart ached a bit with the thought.

But at the same time, she leaned back in her seat, already preparing to say no again. She felt for him. She did. But she couldn't go getting involved with another family's problems. She couldn't have people depending on her.

"I'm sorry she's struggling," Daisy said when he stopped talking. "But I don't think I'm the one to help. I don't know the first thing about kids—"

"You were great with her the other day," he argued.

She continued as if he hadn't interrupted. "And I'm not gonna be here for long. So I really can't commit—"

"I'll take whatever you can give," he interrupted again. There was a desperation in his voice that had her hesitating when she meant to go on with her rejection. "Even if it's just for a few days or a week. I don't need a commitment."

The words soothed her a bit, and she settled back in her seat to turn over all he'd said.

"You were so good with her, and she really lit up with

the singing…" He leaned forward, his gaze fixed on her. "I think she needs this."

"What about her mother?"

He stared at her, and for a second, she wasn't sure, but it seemed like he'd gone pale behind that neat beard of his.

Her stomach turned with apprehension, but the silence was unbearable. They'd been talking so easily for a little while there, and that made his sudden tension feel like a heavy weight. "Levi?" she said tentatively. "She said her mother sang, and played the guitar, and… Why can't her mother teach her?"

He dipped his head, and those straight shoulders sagged until he looked like a man carrying the weight of the world. She started to reach out to him but stopped herself.

It wasn't her place.

She didn't need Dahlia's voice to point that out. This was a man with a complicated family…and that was so not her thing.

She swallowed hard. "You know what? Forget it. It's none of my business, and—"

"No." He lifted his head, and the sadness in his eyes made her heart ache. "You should know…"

CHAPTER 17

D espite his declaration, Levi almost stopped right there.

What was he doing? He glanced around at the clusters of patrons. Most of whom he knew, all of whom nodded or said hello when he'd entered.

And the weight that always bore down on him when he so much as thought of Beth was crushing. There was no way he could talk about this here and now.

But then Daisy placed a hand on his, her eyes soft and searching. "You don't have to talk to me, Levi. I understand if you don't want to."

"No." He cleared his throat, his tone too gruff. But he'd seen the way she was about to walk away from him...from Mikayla. And she might be his one chance to get through to his little girl. She was the first person to make her smile in months, and he had to fight for this chance.

She deserved more of an explanation, especially if she ended up saying yes.

So he forced out one word after another. "Beth got cancer."

Daisy's eyes widened, and the sympathy he saw there was nearly his undoing.

"It was aggressive, and we were too late by the time we found out..." The words were coming out clunky and abrasive, as if he were choking on them. He didn't dare glance around to see if anyone noticed.

He was the sheriff. People looked up to him; they expected him to protect them. He couldn't lose it in front of this crowd.

But Daisy's gaze held his steady, and he focused on that. On her. On the way her eyes crinkled at the edges even when she wasn't smiling, like she was ready to at any moment.

But she wasn't smiling now, and the sadness in her expression gave him the sense that he wasn't alone. Like she was shouldering some of the weight of this crushing grief. Enough, at least, that he managed to get out the rest. "She made it ten months." He tried for a smile and failed. "They only gave her six, but she was determined to be there for Ronnie's fifth birthday."

Daisy smiled for him. "I bet she was so happy she made it."

He nodded. "She died three days after the party."

Her eyes welled with tears as she squeezed his hand. "I'm sorry."

"The worst part was the funeral." Good grief, why was he still talking? But she nodded in empathy, and he couldn't seem to stop. Her soft eyes and sweet expression seemed to be pulling the words out of him. "I'd tried to prepare the kids. But you can't. Not really. There was nothing I could do to protect them from that."

"No," she agreed softly. "There was nothing either of

you could have said or done to shield them from the pain of losing a parent."

Levi stilled, and for a second, he wasn't sure if he could draw another breath because the words hit so hard. Something about the simplicity in her tone, the way she wasn't trying to make him feel better. She said it like a fact.

Whether it made sense or not, her words and the way she said them...

He had this feeling of absolution.

There was nothing more he could have done.

He pinched the bridge of his nose, painfully aware of all the people in this coffee shop who could see him as he cleared his throat. "Thank you for saying that."

She didn't respond, and finally he lifted his head to meet her gaze. He was a little startled by the sheen of emotions that she didn't try to hide.

It was strange to see this ray of sunshine not grinning. Even when she was annoyed with him or teasing him, she had a joyful energy about her.

But right now she was quiet and still as she stared deep into his eyes.

He had an odd notion to ask her what she saw.

Whatever it was, it had her sitting back in her seat with a resigned sigh. He felt the loss of her heat when she pulled her hand back from his and crossed her arms. "All right. I'll do it."

He blinked in surprise, and for half a second, he had no idea what she was talking about. It came back to him with a jolt.

Mikayla. Music lessons.

How had he forgotten that was what this whole conversation was about? He leaned back, trying to regain his senses. "I didn't, uh..." He cleared his throat. "I didn't mean to guilt you into saying yes."

She laughed. And the sound made him feel like dark storm clouds were parting and warmth was flooding in.

"I know that," she said with a wave of her hand.

"I mean it." Pride had him straightening. "I wanted you to know why I'm worried about Mikayla, but I'd never use my wife's passing to make you feel like—"

She groaned comically loud. Loud enough that the neighboring tables were looking their way. Then she flopped forward like she was too weary to sit upright. "Doesn't it ever get exhausting being so good all the time?"

His lips parted but no sound came out.

"Of course you weren't trying to guilt-trip me." She brushed her hand through the air again. "I'd bet you don't have a manipulative bone in your body."

He couldn't refute that. He prided himself on being straightforward.

Her smile turned impish. "You know, if I were you, I'd be getting all the perks I could get from the situation."

"Pardon me?"

"Oh you bet." She nodded enthusiastically. "If I had a dead husband, I'd be using people's pity to get all sorts of things."

For a moment, he didn't know whether to be horrified or amused.

But when he caught the glint of laughter in her eyes, saw the teasing that lay underneath, he realized she was doing it on purpose. Shocking him out of his maudlin state.

"Why, I bet you could have gotten your coffee for free." She pointed a thumb toward the counter, eyes wide with feigned innocence. She gasped and leaned forward to whisper, "You might've even gotten a biscotti if you really worked it."

Laughter caught him by surprise, and he made an odd choking sound.

She sat back with a satisfied smile. "So no, Sheriff," she teased. "I didn't think for one second you were trying to guilt-trip me."

His lips twitched. "You could have just said so."

"I made my point." She lifted a shoulder.

And she'd made him laugh. He shook his head in awe. "Mikayla could use you."

Her smile widened. "That's why I changed my mind."

"So..." He toyed with the handle of his mug. "Not because you feel sorry for me?"

Her scoff was over the top. "Of course not."

They shared a little smile at her obvious lie. But then she grew serious, and her voice turned painfully gentle. "I do feel sympathy for you, Levi. But that's not why I'm saying yes. I can't promise to stick around for long, but while I'm here, I'd love to hang out with her."

"Yeah?" His chest felt tight again, but for a very different reason.

She nodded. "I saw the way she lit up when she was singing. And that's the magic of music, you know?"

"Is it?"

"Of course." She reached for the cupcake, apparently forgetting that she was supposed to save that for later as she unwrapped it and took a bite. "Music makes everything better."

He felt a twitch in his lips, but for the first time in a long time, he couldn't squelch it. Or maybe he just didn't want to. And so he smiled, and she grinned right back.

Levi was in a good mood when he left the coffee shop, and those good spirits carried him throughout the day. He felt lighter.

Maybe it was the extra coffee Daisy had convinced him to order so he could continue to keep her company while she ate the last of her sugary feast.

He shook his head with a rueful smile as he let himself into the house at the end of the day. How often did she eat like that? She ought to have a proper meal now and again—

"Thank goodness you're home!" Helen's exasperated greeting when he walked in brought him back to the moment.

"Hi, Helen. Is everything okay?"

She puffed out her cheeks and blew out a slow breath with a roll of her eyes that he assumed was supposed to be comical. But he and Helen did not share a similar sense of humor.

He tensed. "Is everyone okay?"

"They are *now*," she said, following him as he set down a bag of groceries in the kitchen. "But I'll tell you what, those kids make me glad my own are off at college."

She let out a guffaw, and he gave her a grimace in return. "That bad?"

She laughed her way into a monologue about how Ronnie convinced Dawson that he was old enough to start shaving, but then Dawson nicked his chin, and the bathroom became a crime scene of bloody shaving cream, screams, yells, and murder threats.

All of this was, of course, going on while Helen was dealing with Mikayla, who'd decided that turning three pairs of her jeans into shorts so tiny you could see her underwear was a brilliant idea.

He stared at her with a sinking sensation.

Had he been in a good mood before?

It was hard to remember why right about now.

"Thanks, Helen," he said when he realized she was finally done talking. "I owe you—"

"Oh no, no," she interrupted. "This is what family's for."

He nodded. She and her husband said that a lot—it had become a sort of catchphrase for them, Beth's parents, and his own family ever since his lovely wife had passed. But he was starting to wonder if maybe he was taking advantage.

Helen had already raised two kids of her own. And her presence, while appreciated, didn't seem to be helping matters.

More than once he'd caught her tsking sadly when she looked at Mikayla and made a comment about how much she looked like her mother.

Not a bad thing to say, of course—Beth was beautiful—but the way she said it, all maudlin and wistful, it always made Mikayla deflate.

Unlike Daisy's comment about Mikayla's smile.

He frowned as he turned that over.

"You okay if I leave?" Helen was already reaching for her purse.

"Yeah. We're fine."

Fine. That was a bit of an understatement.

He followed her to the door and wished her a good night, then turned back and hesitated at the bottom of the stairs. Part of him wanted to just go to the kitchen and make supper in peace. But he really ought to check in with them…

And make sure Mikayla knew she wasn't allowed to leave this house wearing shorty-short-shorts!

His footsteps were heavy as he climbed the stairs, and a quick glance showed the boys were doing their homework.

"Hey, Dad!" Dawson called out.

Levi nodded, his gaze catching on the Band-Aid covering his chin. He didn't have the heart to give the boy a lecture, especially since he'd likely already learned his lesson, so he moved on to Mikayla's room.

She was on her bed. Hopefully studying. Definitely listening to music. He gestured for her to take out her earbuds, which she did with an irritated sigh. "What?"

A muscle in his jaw ticked. Should he talk to her about the shorts?

Her gaze seemed to be challenging him already.

Helen said she'd handled it, so he swallowed down the words crowding out his mouth and cleared his throat instead. "I have some news…"

This was met with a blank stare.

"I got you music lessons."

Her nose started to wrinkle, her brows coming down. "Dad." She turned the word into three syllables with her whine. "I told you, none of my friends—"

"It's not through school." He took a step inside the room. "I asked that woman you met the other day. Daisy. Remember her?"

Her impertinent expression remained, but she stopped arguing.

"She's gonna be in town for a little while, and she thinks you have real talent."

Her shoulders lowered a little, her gaze wary but not hostile. "Really?"

"Yeah. And she plays guitar and piano...and she sings, obviously. So, I thought..." He cleared his throat, reminding himself that if he tried to make her do this, she'd probably say no. How did he convince her this was an awesome idea?

Scratching his whiskers, he played it cool, throwing in a shrug for good measure. "I mean, it's up to you, of course."

Her brows hitched.

What would he do if she said no? The thought had him opening his mouth to contradict himself. *You'll take the lessons, and you'll like it.*

But then she said, "Okay."

He blinked. "Okay?"

She shrugged. "Daisy seems cool."

"Yeah." He felt a surge of triumph that he tried to hide. "She does seem pretty cool, doesn't she?"

CHAPTER 18

D aisy could practically feel Dahlia's mind working from where she sat in the passenger seat on Monday afternoon.

"It's just..." Dahlia took a deep breath, and Daisy had to bite the inside of her lip to stop a laugh.

Dahlia had made great strides in the "chilling out" department, but she was still Dahlia.

And she couldn't stand not having a plan. Which would be fine, except that she also couldn't seem to handle her sisters not having a plan.

"I mean, do you have any sort of time frame on how long you're going to be staying?" Dahlia asked.

It was the fifth time she'd asked that question in some way or another over the last few days.

"Why?" Daisy sipped the thermos full of tea she'd brought with her. "Have I overstayed my welcome?"

Dahlia huffed and shot her a sidelong glare. "Of course not. Don't be silly. You know it's your home too. You're welcome for as long as you'd like."

Daisy smirked. Sometimes the best defense was

offense, right? And Dahlia fell for it every time. She shifted in her seat and reached for the radio dial, assuming the conversation was over…for now, at least.

But Dahlia piped up again. "It's just that the summer is almost here, and the bunkhouse will be filling up with seasonal workers, and the house is already full—"

"Aren't you and JJ going to move in together?" *When you get engaged?* She clamped her mouth shut. She might be desperate to change the conversation, but she wasn't about to ruin whatever surprise JJ had in store.

"Eventually, yes," she said.

This time it was Dahlia who was shifting in her seat, and that was when it clicked. She was fretting over Daisy's plans because she was uncertain of her own future.

"I mean, I think so." Dahlia frowned. "Last time I brought up us moving in, JJ got all weird."

Daisy had to bite her tongue this time to hold in a giggle. "You don't say."

"I mean, we've agreed to take things slow, but logistically it makes sense for us to start talking about that sort of thing, you know?"

"Mmm."

Dahlia shot her a sharp look, and Daisy looked out the window. Poor JJ. He'd better propose soon or her sister might just do it for him.

"Anyway," Dahlia continued, "I just figured you'd have something coming up. More studio time or another tour or something."

Daisy tensed, buying time by taking a few extra sips of tea. Her heart started to pound, and her stomach writhed.

This was exactly the conversation she was hoping to avoid.

Preferably forever.

Dahlia stopped at an intersection and turned to face her. Daisy pretended to be engrossed by the scenery.

"Don't you have to do something for the album's release?" Dahlia sounded tentative. Daisy's twin was a smarty-pants, but when it came to the world of music, she was clueless.

A fact which Daisy had no problem exploiting. "No, the manager is handling all that."

Guilt stabbed at her. Their manager *would* be handling all that...if he hadn't ghosted them.

Daisy tried to focus on the scenery, counting the cows that dotted the hillside and then focusing on the puffy white clouds. But Dahlia's silence felt stifling, and the emotions she'd been trying to outrun were catching up with her.

"So, where are Tanya and Brian?"

Daisy nibbled on her lip. "Hmm?"

"Tanya? Brian?" Dahlia's voice held a hint of amusement. "You know, the two people you've been playing music with since you were fifteen?"

Daisy swallowed hard at the reminder. More than a decade together and they'd left her. They'd just...left.

She swallowed convulsively as her insides tried to turn knot tying into an artform.

That's what people did, right? She should have known better than to think a band was any different than any other relationship.

But she had. She'd thought their shared love of music was a bond that was stronger than most. She never expected boyfriends to stick around, or her mother, obviously, and her father had been the first one to teach her that love didn't last.

But music?

She gripped the thermos hard, all too aware of Dahlia's searching gaze. "We're all just taking a little breather from each other, you know? The album recording was...a lot of hard work, and it was suggested we take a break. You know, rest is good for your health and all that." Dahlia didn't say anything, and Daisy kept her stinging eyes on the horizon. "Tim...our manager...he's working on lining up more gigs for us."

Liar. You are such a liar.

Guilt had her steering closer to the truth. "And Tanya and Brian, well...I think they need to work on their relationship for a while, you know? Being on the road like we all were, it was intense."

"I bet," Dahlia murmured.

The hint of concern in her voice had Daisy shifting in her seat. "We're just in a little vaycay phase, that's all. The album's being edited and readied for sale. You know...uh, technical stuff that I don't really understand, and while that's happening, we all just decided to take a little break."

"Oh."

Oh. That was it. But somehow the one little syllable made Daisy feel like dirt. Did Dahlia know she was lying?

"I was thinking I'll head back to New York next."

"Really?" Dahlia sounded confused.

But why? That was where they were from. It was where Daisy had contacts. She could find something. Someone would give her a gig...if they ever texted her back.

"Yeah, sounds fun to go back to my roots, you know? Maybe play some of the clubs where we first started."

Her stomach twisted and dove. *Yeah, real fun. Going backward. Starting over. Fun, fun, fun.* "Just for a little while," she added when Dahlia didn't speak. "While we're taking a break."

"If you guys need a break, then maybe you should take one. A real one. I mean, you've been working so hard. Maybe you shouldn't be looking for stuff in New York when you could be relaxing here. A vacation is supposed to be just that—relaxing." Her eyebrows rose, and Daisy turned away from her twin's pointed look. "How long will the album take to get edited?"

She shrugged, the tea in her belly sloshing dangerously. "They're gonna let me know."

Daisy didn't mind little white lies or a slight bend in the truth. But straight-up lying to her sister made her queasy.

"But I like the idea of doing a few solo gigs in New York. It'll be fun."

"Really?" Dahlia seemed surprised. "You always made it sound like the band was everything to you. Do you think they'll mind if you branch out?"

Daisy's heart clenched painfully.

They left her. She still couldn't quite believe it.

"They're cool with it. You know we always support each other. That's what friends do, right?"

The words tasted like ash, and her throat was painfully tight when she turned to flash Dahlia a smile.

"Yeah. Right." Dahlia nodded. "Well, just so long as you're happy."

Daisy's smile started to tremble, her lungs froze, and she felt dangerously close to a hiccupy sob. For the first time ever, she had this urge to turn to Dahlia and pour out all her troubles.

She forced herself to look out the window again.

Spilling it all would just end in a series of lectures and "I told you so's" that would only make her feel worse.

Nope. She just had to keep her lips sealed on this whole thing.

They'd reached downtown Aspire, and the end of this ride was in sight. Thank goodness.

Talk about needing a break.

Daisy was desperate for an end to this trip.

But just as Dahlia slowed for traffic, Daisy's phone dinged with a text.

She scrambled to pull it out of her pocket, hoping a New York contact was finally replying. But the words on the screen turned her insides to ash.

You can't keep ignoring me. We had a deal.

"Who's that?" Dahlia asked.

Daisy's blood ran ice-cold as she eyed the text. Then she quickly swiped it away. And, still not satisfied, she deleted it.

As if that'll make him go away.

"Everything okay?" Dahlia was studying her, no doubt trying to read her mind.

Not happening, sis!

Daisy snapped her head up and shoved her phone in her bag. "Yup. Fine. Just one of those promo texts offering me discounts if I upgrade my phone plan. Ugh. So not happening." She forced a bright smile while her mind scrambled for a solution.

Maybe she could change her number. Or just ditch her phone altogether.

Instantly she thought of Dahlia's response if she couldn't get a hold of her. The National Guard would be alerted. Hounds would be sent off with her scent.

Not to mention Levi.

A ghost of a smile curved her lips as amusement flared to life and helped her to shove all thoughts of her phone and that text aside.

He'd texted twice and called three times over the weekend, just to make sure she'd be at his house at the appointed time.

She snickered into her tea. Such a worrywart.

"This is it." Dahlia pulled over to the curb in front of a modest ranch home with a tidy yard and potted flowers out front.

The perfect middle-American suburban house. Exactly what she'd expect from the do-gooder family man.

"Thanks for the ride, Dee," she called as she jumped out.

The fresh air and the birds chirping as she strode toward the door with her guitar put her in a much better mood. By the time Mikayla answered the knock on the door, all thoughts of her bandmates and her debts were nicely tucked away once more, and her smile was back in full form. She lifted her guitar. "Who's ready to rock 'n' roll?"

Mikayla giggled at her over-the-top comment. "Uh, I guess I am?"

"Good answer." She followed the girl inside. "Do you want to start with the guitar or piano?"

"Um, I'm not sure."

She came to a stop behind the girl in the living room, and she couldn't help but grin. Yup. Just as she'd imagined. Everything in its place, and perfectly tidy and neat.

There were framed pictures on the mantel, but other than that, the room had a sort of sterile feel. Not cold but not warm either. There were no splashes of color or childlike mess. The only sound was the ticking clock on the wall, and for some reason, that small beat seemed almost oppressive.

It felt like a waiting room.

A limbo of living rooms, she decided.

With a little huff of laughter, she headed toward the piano. She knew how to fix the stifling silence, at least. Without any warning, she started in with a few chords, feeling out the keyboard. It was a little out of tune but not terrible.

She grinned over at Mikayla. "Yup. We can work with this."

CHAPTER 19

L evi paused with one hand on the knob of his front door.

The sound of their piano drifted out—a pretty little melody that made him smile. But it was followed by an even prettier sound.

Mikayla's giggle.

He chuckled when Daisy's louder, more confident laughter joined in with his daughter's.

It was working. Daisy's music lessons were working.

"Dad, can you open the door?" Ronnie whined. "I have to pee, and you said I can't go on the lawn anymore and—"

"Yeah. Yeah, of course." He pushed the door open. "Boys, don't disturb Mikayla's les—"

"Hey, Micky!" Ronnie shouted as he raced toward the bathroom.

Levi sighed. "Dawson, don't—"

Dawson ran straight into the living room. "Hey, Mik, you sound good."

Levi followed Dawson in with a sigh. "Don't disturb

her lesson," he finished. But apparently he was only speaking to himself, because Dawson was standing right next to Mikayla, already chatting with Daisy. She was asking him about his day.

"Did you just come from baseball practice?"

He grinned and looked down at his uniform. "I'm playing first base."

"Ooh, like Lou Gehrig. Nice." She nodded appreciatively.

Dawson's eyes widened. "You know who Lou Gehrig is?"

Daisy rolled her eyes. "I grew up in New York. It's kinda mandatory to know all the legendary Yankees."

"That's cool," Dawson breathed.

Levi scrubbed a hand over his mouth to hide a grin before smoothing down his beard as Daisy glanced his way. "Hey, Sheriff."

"Daisy."

She winked, her eyes sparkling with laughter. "You didn't tell me Mikayla was already such a pro on the piano."

Mikayla grinned, her cheeks turning pink as she, too, spun on the piano stool to smile at him.

"Yeah, well, she had a good teacher." The words just… came out. And for a second, Levi held his breath, worried he'd ruined the mood with the mention of Beth.

But Mikayla's smile widened. "I did." She turned to Daisy. "My mom made all of us learn how to pick out middle C before we even knew how to walk." She dipped her head with a shrug. "At least, that's what Aunt Helen said."

"I don't remember that." Dawson looked confused.

"Of course not, stupid. You weren't even old enough to walk."

Dawson started to argue, and Levi went to intervene, but Daisy's laughter cut through the bickering more thoroughly than his barking commands ever had. "You two crack me up."

They stopped to look at her. Levi did too.

"My sisters and I used to argue just like you three do," she continued, turning her attention back to the keys and playing a tune while she spoke, oblivious to the fact that she held all three of them in her thrall just by talking. She tilted her head to the side, lost in thought. "Well...one of my sisters and I fought all the time. My sister Rose was always too sweet for any of that."

"I know Rose," Mikayla said. "She's really nice."

"She's the best. And Dahlia's pretty cool, too," she added, almost as if it was an afterthought.

"So what happened? Do you guys still fight?" Dawson asked.

Levi tucked his hands in his pockets, uncertain whether he should intervene. Mikayla had been doing so well, and now he and Dawson were intruding.

But Daisy smiled at Dawson. "Sometimes. Me and Dahlia are so different that we can't seem to help butting heads. But, you know, when times are tough, they're the only two people I have to turn to."

Dawson and Mikayla stared at her, and Levi wondered if they had as many questions as he did.

He wondered if they also saw the flicker of fear and sadness that passed over her face, there and gone in an instant before she turned back to the kids with a grin. "So fight all you want now, but just know..." She leaned toward them and lowered her voice to a menacing growl. "You're stuck with each other for life."

They both burst out laughing, and Dawson turned to leave. "Hear that, Miks? You're stuck with us."

She poked her tongue out at him as he ran away, but she was smiling. And the moment was oddly…sweet.

Levi rocked back on his heels as he considered this blonde bombshell before him. He wasn't a man who believed in magic, but if it existed, she had it. That was the only explanation he could come up with for how she managed to turn their latest round of fighting into a nice moment.

"You ready to try again?" Daisy flipped a page of sheet music.

Mikayla glanced over at him, not with a sneer or a roll of her eyes, but he saw her wariness. He widened his eyes, held his hands up, and backed away toward the kitchen. "Don't mind me."

Daisy laughed as she watched him back up like Mikayla was holding a weapon on him. A second later, just as Levi was about to slip out the door, he heard Mikayla giggle too.

He stopped in the hallway and leaned against the door-frame, out of sight but well within hearing range. He really should be getting dinner ready, but hearing Mikayla's laughter, and the sound of music that hadn't filled these hallways since Beth passed…

It was sweet.

And it was torture.

He swallowed hard and let his head fall back against the wall with a thud. It was bittersweet, he supposed. But as the familiar song wrapped around him, his gaze caught on a framed family photo that hung on the hallway wall.

Beth smiled back at him from behind the three kids, all so much younger than they were right now.

It was a silly notion, perhaps, but for a second, he let himself believe that her smile in that photo was meant for him. Right now. Right here.

He let himself believe that maybe Beth was with them, in the music, and with their daughter.

Fanciful notion or not, it made him smile when he finally pushed away from the wall and headed to the kitchen to make his family dinner.

CHAPTER 20

Daisy almost felt guilty taking the twenty-dollar bill when Levi handed it to her.

"Thanks, Daisy." His voice was low and serious.

"My pleasure," she said. And she meant it. She always loved playing music, but teaching someone who was equally smitten...

It had been a trip.

"Well, I, uh..." He looked down at his feet and took a deep breath like he was about to say something heavy. "I appreciate it."

She laughed. How did he manage to sound so very serious?

Maybe that was the way he always sounded. But today she found herself wondering if he'd always been so solemn or if that was grief's work.

She still took the money, of course, and she waved away Levi's offer to drive her back to the ranch while Mikayla watched the boys.

"You stay and enjoy your kids," she said. "I'll find a

way back. This town is overflowing with siblings and their significant others. Someone will give me a lift."

His lips twitched a bit.

"If not, I'll hitch a ride."

His eyes flared wide with alarm. "Don't you dare—"

"Kidding, kidding." She waved as she skipped down his front steps and onto the sidewalk.

She hummed as she walked through quaint suburbia and popped out onto Main Street.

It was bustling on this nice spring evening, and the setting sun gave everything a warm, romantic glow. She called her sisters while she walked and came up with a plan to get a ride back to the ranch with Rose and Dex, since they were coming over for dinner anyway. But she had some time to kill, and she always loved chitchatting with Lizzy, so she swung by the boutique again.

"Perfect timing," Lizzy called out when she came in. "We don't close for another twenty minutes, and I was hoping for some company."

Daisy cast her arms out wide. "That's what I'm here for."

"Emma told me you were teaching Levi's daughter music lessons. How'd it go?" Lizzy was a little ball of energy, and Daisy loved leaning back against the counter and watching her flit about as she straightened stacks of clothes and rearranged mannequins' scarves.

"It went great. Mikayla is a sweetheart."

"Really?" Lizzy grinned over at her. "All I hear is the trouble she gets into."

Daisy shrugged. "She's thirteen. Who doesn't get into trouble when they're that age?"

Lizzy's eyes widened. "Um, Emma?"

"And Rose," Daisy added with a laugh.

140

Lizzy shook her head, crossing her arms. "I can't imagine Dahlia was a troublemaker."

"Miss Responsible? Of course not." Daisy rolled her eyes, but she was grinning.

Lizzy giggled. "So maybe not everyone gets into trouble."

Daisy arched her brows. "So…just us?"

Lizzy pursed her lips, pretending to give it thought. "Maybe Sierra and April are rebels."

"We can only hope. Otherwise…" Daisy adopted a stage whisper. "We might be the bad sisters."

Lizzy burst out laughing before sniffing and holding her head up high. "Maybe we were, but I, for one, am now a mature young lady."

"Uh-huh," Daisy teased.

"Seriously, though. Becoming a stepmom to the twins has made me grow up."

Daisy wrinkled her nose. "That's sad."

"No it's not." Lizzy laughed. "It's good. It's natural. It's…the way it should be, I guess."

"I guess." Daisy didn't try to hide her disbelief.

"In some ways, I have more fun now that I've 'settled down.'"

The comment made Daisy snort.

"I'm serious! The kids are so much fun. And being a part of a family, feeling like I'm needed and knowing they can rely on me…" She sighed. "I don't know how to explain it, but it's nice. It feels like I'm exactly where I belong."

"Then I'm happy for you."

Lizzy arched a brow. "I take it you never intend to settle down."

"No, ma'am." She gave an exaggerated shake of her

head. "No offense to this town or anything, but I could never settle down here."

Lizzy started to laugh.

"What?"

"Nothing, it's just...you sound like me before I met Kit. I was so sure I knew where my future lay, and then..." She shrugged. "I don't know. I guess love has a way of turning everything upside down."

Daisy's laughter faded along with her smile. Lizzy's words hit a little too close to the mark. Her mind instantly went back to her bandmates who'd abandoned her. It was their breakup that led to the band falling apart.

And then there was her mom, whose entire life fell apart when their dad left.

She shook her head, but she couldn't shake off the icky feelings that were taking root in her belly.

Love might turn some people's lives upside down. But for her?

All it did was lead to ruin.

Her phone dinged, and Daisy jumped, fear making her heart leap into her throat before she could stop it.

"You okay?" Lizzy asked.

"Yeah. Fine. Just..." She dreaded pulling out her phone, terrified of what text she might see.

But it was just Rose saying they were pulling up to the boutique now.

"My ride's here." She leaned forward to kiss Lizzy's cheek. "Tell Kit and the kids I say hi."

"Oh, you can tell them yourself. We're coming to dinner too." She grinned. "I'm picking the kids up from their grandparents' place in thirty minutes.

"Perfect. I'll see you guys soon, then."

Daisy smiled as she walked out, and she grinned even

more as she greeted Dex and Rose in the car. But the thought of a family dinner weighed on her, and Lizzy's words were still ringing in her ears.

Love had gotten her into this mess. If her bandmates had just stayed together, and if their manager hadn't gotten greedy and bailed, and if they could have all just worked out their issues so they could finish the album…

Tears stung the backs of her eyes, but she blinked them away.

Her dreams were in tatters, and the last thing she wanted to do was sit around a table and answer questions about the future. Or tell lies about the past. Or watch all the happy couples be all sickeningly in love when she was on her own.

Again.

Like always.

She swallowed hard, occasionally murmuring a response to Dex and Rose's chatter in the front seat. But her mind was elsewhere. She found herself wondering what Levi and his kids were doing tonight. If Mikayla was practicing and if the boys were fighting…

A smile started to tug at her lips, and she caught sight of it in the window's reflection. She almost wished she was heading back there instead. It was impossible to think about the album, her band, or anything too serious when there were kids rushing about in need of attention…and a sheriff who was desperately in need of some cheering up.

When dinner ended, Daisy found herself with some rare sisters-only time as Kit recruited Dex, JJ, and Nash to play a game of soccer with the kids. They even called Cody and

Boone to join in, and the competitive shouts from outside floated through the windows.

Emma kept gazing toward the window, a look of longing sweeping over her face before her eyes skimmed Rose's belly.

Someone had baby fever.

Daisy wondered if she was already pregnant, but that wistful look told her Emma was in the *dreaming about being a mom* phase.

The thought made her simultaneously giddy with delight for Emma and wary of what that would mean.

It was one thing to be living here at this ranch while her husband worked here and she was still trying to track down all the sisters to come to some sort of agreement on the will, but to start a family here? Make it a real home?

As if reading her mind, Dahlia brought up the topic as she and Daisy did the dishes. "Any progress on the great O'Sullivan sister hunt, Emma?"

"Nothing new." Lizzy was the one who answered. She'd been helping Emma with the seemingly fruitless task of trying to get in touch with the last two daughters.

"I can't believe they're not at least a little curious." Rose's comment trailed off with a yawn. She kept trying to help with the cleanup, and the other sisters kept taking turns ushering her back to her seat because it was clear the poor girl was exhausted just sitting there.

"I swear Sierra doesn't actually exist," Lizzy added as she hopped up on the counter beside Daisy. "Who doesn't have any social media presence these days? I mean, really."

"Yeah, that is odd," Daisy agreed.

"It's kinda admirable." Dahlia rinsed off a plate and

144

passed it to Daisy for drying. "Must be nice to be off the grid like that."

"Says the woman who's fallen for a mountain man," Rose said with a laugh. "The two of you can go off the grid together for your own happily ever after."

Dahlia laughed. "What can I say? JJ's shown me the beauty of peace and quiet."

"This from a city girl?" Daisy tsked.

Dahlia shrugged.

Emma laughed. "Every one of us was a city girl before we came here. What have these men done to us?"

"It is kind of crazy, isn't it?" Lizzy mused. "All four of us moved to this town, not expecting to stay long, and then...boom. We've fallen in love and settled down here."

Rose giggled. "It's contagious."

"More like it's a plague," Daisy muttered.

"You're next, Dais. Just you wait. Your time is coming." Rose put on an ominous voice while Daisy laughed and tossed a dry dish towel at her head.

Dahlia nudged Daisy with her hip. "She's right, you know."

"Oh no she's not." Daisy shook her head. "I don't date men who expect me to settle down.

Dahlia laughed. "Has it ever occurred to you that maybe these men *do* want you to settle down? You just run before they can catch you."

Daisy stilled as the others all hooted and giggled.

"It's true, Daisy," Rose added. "You've never stayed in any one place for long."

She looked down at her hands. They were teasing, she knew that. But she still felt a flicker of...what? Regret, maybe? She'd been thinking more and more about how Dahlia had stepped up when they were kids. How she'd looked after Rose—and even Daisy—when their mother was going through one of her bad spells. Sometimes weeks would go by when their mom didn't even get out of bed.

These days she was getting the help she needed, and she didn't even pretend to be a part of her life anymore. But back then, she'd been in the same house but not there at all. And Daisy...well, she'd barely been there at all too.

She'd been off with her bandmates, skipping school, hitching rides to other towns for gigs or to watch shows...

Dahlia had been there, though.

"Maybe that's how we can lure Sierra here," Lizzy said, laughing as she kicked her feet against the counter. "Come home to Aspire, where every city girl finds her man."

Emma laughed. "I don't think that'll work for April. She grew up here. She probably went to school with every guy her age."

"Yeah, well, maybe that'll work to our advantage. She has to come back eventually, right? It's her childhood home." Rose rubbed her belly, looking pensive.

Dahlia made a little scoffing noise, and Daisy was pretty sure she was the only one who heard Dahlia's murmur. "That wasn't exactly a selling point for us. We never went back there."

Daisy smiled, hating that prickle of emotion that always got stirred up when talk turned to their childhood. But she pushed that aside and nudged Dahlia's arm. "But we're all together now, aren't we?"

Dahlia nodded, and when she glanced over, her eyes were suspiciously wet. "And I'm grateful for that. I really am glad you're here, Daisy."

Daisy ducked her head. "You know I can't stay forever though—"

"Oh, I know." Dahlia's voice returned to normal. "No one expects you to."

Daisy smiled and nodded. That was a good thing. Right? No expectations meant no demands. No obligations. For some odd reason, her mind conjured up an image of the much-too-serious sheriff.

Now *there* was a man who was drowning in obligations. Poor guy.

Emma's voice brought her back to the moment with a jolt. "Still, I think if we can get April to come back here to talk to us, we can convince her to keep this place in the family."

"She's got history here," Rose agreed. "That'll count for something."

"It's Sierra who's the real wild card," Lizzy said. "Who knows what she'll want? She may be in need of quick cash and insist on selling."

Daisy bit her lip, keeping her head down as the others talked. It wasn't that she didn't like this place. And she was beyond happy that her sisters had found such happiness here. But a little part of her selfishly hoped that Sierra and April insisted on selling so she could get her hands on some cash.

Her phone felt heavy in her back pocket as she reached for another dirty dish and rinsed it. The texts and calls were coming more often lately. And the tone was getting more and more intense.

I'll find you.

She swallowed hard.

"Daisy?" Dahlia said.

Daisy lifted her head with a start. "Sorry…what?"

The others laughed.

"We were just talking about how JJ's taking Dahlia away on a romantic trip to California," Rose said.

"Oh, right. That'll be fun."

Dahlia's grin was adorable, and her sister's giddiness helped Daisy forget her troubles. She'd send some more texts and make actual calls to her contacts in the New York music world tomorrow. Her car would be fixed up any day now, and although she didn't have enough money to pay for it yet, she was hoping she could sweet-talk Fred into some kind of payment plan.

Some paying gigs were bound to turn up soon. And in the meantime…

"We were hoping you could give us some recommendations on fun things to do," Dahlia said.

"Are you kidding?" Daisy tossed her hair back over her shoulder. "Fun is my middle name."

CHAPTER 21

L evi was not a man who fidgeted. But that Thursday afternoon he couldn't seem to stop himself from pacing his house as he waited for Daisy to arrive for Mikayla's guitar lesson.

"Dad, she'll be here," Mikayla said when he came through the living room to peek out the front window.

"She's late."

Mikayla didn't look up from her phone. "It literally just turned four right this second. She's not late yet."

"Well, she will be," he muttered. He hated tardiness. Always had. Maybe it was the fact that his father had been a military man, or that his mother believed arriving on time was a sign of respect, but he hated being late himself and disliked it in others.

Most of all, he hated when his kids made him late.

But right now he found himself getting more and more tense as the time of Mikayla's lesson got closer and then passed.

He looked out the window again, and Mikayla sighed

from the couch where she was still on her phone. Doing what?

Who knew?

But at least if she was on her phone in here, she wasn't out there getting into trouble. That was what Helen said, at least. He winced as he watched her so thoroughly absorbed by that little screen.

He had a hunch she could get into just as much trouble on that dang device as she could anywhere else.

A sound of pounding footsteps had him turning toward the stairs where Dawson and Ronnie were racing each other, shouting about something he couldn't make out.

This time he was the one to sigh with exasperation.

But the distraction didn't last long, and soon he was looking out the window again.

A minute later, she appeared. Or rather Nash's truck pulled up, and she hopped out.

Levi let out a shaky breath, his belly doing something strange again, like it had been all afternoon as he'd waited for her arrival. He wasn't nervous, necessarily, just…on edge. And he couldn't explain why.

But as she turned back and gave Nash a wave and a bright, beaming smile, he felt his whole body respond like she'd just flipped a switch with that carefree wave and that effervescent smile.

"She's here." Mikayla shot him a pointed look. Though how she knew, he wasn't sure, because up until that moment, her gaze had never left her phone.

He started toward the front door, but Ronnie beat him to it, shouting, "She's here!" as he threw open the door.

Daisy was already laughing as she looked around and then behind her. "Who's here?" she teased.

"*You* are," Ronnie shot back with a grin so big it had Levi blinking in surprise.

Daisy's gasp made Ronnie giggle. "I am?"

He was still giggling as Dawson appeared, seemingly out of breath from running to get to the front door. "Hi, Daisy!"

And then to Levi's great surprise, Mikayla nudged him aside so she, too, could join in on the welcome at the front door.

"All right," Levi said, placing a hand on each boy's shoulder. "Let the lady through. Mikayla's got a lesson to get to."

Neither of his sons moved quickly. They were too busy pestering Daisy with questions about how famous she was and if she ever played in front of a stadium full of people. At least, that was what he thought they were talking about. The boys were talking over each other as Mikayla added snide little jabs in between telling them to shut up and let Daisy in.

Levi lifted his head to apologize on their behalf and got struck with the full force of her smile. For a second it stunned him into silence.

"Let me in, fellas." Her voice was good-natured and filled with sunshine...if such a thing was possible. "I'm already a few minutes late, and we all know your dad's gonna start turning red and exhaling smoke out his nostrils if I don't get Mikayla's lesson going right away."

All his children burst out laughing, but they made way for her and followed her into the living room like Daisy's own personal entourage.

"You should have seen my dad pacing." Mikayla rolled her eyes.

He scowled at her. "I'm surprised you saw me doing anything with your eyes glued to your phone."

"Can eyes be glued to a phone?" Ronnie asked.

"He wasn't being literal, moron," Dawson said as he smacked Ronnie upside the head.

"I know that! But it's still a valid question."

"No it's not." Dawson frowned.

A fight was about to break out, but Daisy cut it off with a grin as she laid her guitar case on the ground. "Which big, strong boy can open this up and get my guitar out for me?"

Ronnie and Dawson dove for the case so quickly, Levi had to cover his mouth to hide a smile. Then she had Mikayla sorting through sheet music and sent the boys to find a makeshift music stand, and...

Suddenly his house was bustling with three active, eager, happy-to-help kids. He and Daisy watched it all for a moment, and then he leaned over and murmured, "I'm starting to think maybe you were Mary Poppins in another life."

Her head fell back with a laugh so sweet and lovely it made his chest go warm and soft.

"You know Mary Poppins wasn't real, right?" Her eyes sparkled with amusement, and her lips were curved in a gorgeous grin.

He felt a smile of his own trying to break free. "You know what I mean. You're good with kids."

"Nah." She waved off the compliment.

He arched a brow as he shot a meaningful look toward his sons, who were starting to argue over who would fetch Daisy a glass of water.

She laughed and shook her head. "I wouldn't say I'm good with kids. I have zero experience watching little ones. Except maybe Rose, but it's been a minute since she needed a babysitter."

He folded his arms, more curious than he cared to admit about her upbringing. He knew Rose well enough and was getting to know Dahlia. And one thing was clear —Daisy was nothing like either of them. So how had she gotten into music? Why was she so certain she wouldn't stick around for long?

But it wasn't his place to ask, so he settled for "If you're not good with kids, what do you call this?"

She laughed again as they watched his kids racing around to make her happy.

"I'm not good with kids, in particular, but I am good with people." She lowered her voice to a whisper and pretended like she was telling him a secret. "And I hate to break this to you, but...kids are people."

A chuckle caught him unaware, and it had all three of his kids stopping to stare at him. He cleared his throat. "Yes, I think I read that somewhere."

She laughed, her eyes lighting up as he went along with the joke. "So you're in on the secret, then, huh? Good. Grown-ups tend to forget."

She was still teasing, he knew that. But her words caught him off guard all the same.

"I'm ready," Mikayla chirped.

He and Daisy turned to see her standing in the middle of the living room with a guitar in hand.

Her mother's guitar.

Levi felt a blow to the gut at the sight of it. He should have realized...

Heck, he should have thought of it himself. But he'd just assumed they'd both use Daisy's guitar, and now...

now here he was. Staring at a reminder of Beth he'd almost forgotten about.

Guilt and grief hit him hard.

"She's a beauty," Daisy breathed as she gently took the instrument from Mikayla's hands. "Your mom's?"

Mikayla nodded, and Levi saw the pride that filled her glassy eyes as Daisy gushed over it. "Where'd she get it?"

Mikayla frowned. "Oh. Um...I don't know..."

"From her father," Levi rasped. His voice sounded too gruff, but Daisy gave him a sweet little smile that seemed to draw more words out of him. "His father gave it to her. They didn't have a lot of money, so it was his treasure, and he gave it to Beth...to your mother when she turned sixteen."

Mikayla's lips were parted as she drank in the story. "Wow. That's so cool."

Daisy nodded. "There's a lot of love in this guitar. And I bet you anything your mother can hear its music wherever she is."

Levi and Mikayla both gaped at her, but she didn't seem to notice. Mikayla glanced at him, and he saw Dawson and Ronnie staring at him, too, from the doorway, waiting to see....what?

If he believed that too?

He swallowed hard. They all went to church every Sunday, and he believed in heaven. But they never spoke about it like this.

"That's right," he said to Mikayla. "I'm sure your mother can hear you playing the music she loved." He glanced over at his boys. "Just like I know she's watching out for all three of you every second of every day."

A long silence fell, and the moment felt...heavy. But sweet. So unbearably sweet. And for a second, he was

154

certain he could feel Beth there with them. He had a feeling like if he concentrated hard enough, he'd hear her voice and smell her scent. Not a ghost but her spirit. In their hearts and in the music that was now filling the air as Daisy strummed some chords and tuned the old guitar.

"All right, boys," he said, moving to herd them out of the room. "Let's not disturb Mikayla's lesson."

"If you do, you have to pick an instrument and join in!" Daisy's voice rang with laughter, and he shook his head.

How did she do that? How did she make them all feel so much? His head was spinning with the emotions she'd conjured in the short time she'd been there.

It was a gift, he decided. Or maybe it was just a form of bravery that had her facing emotions most people ran from.

They'd only just reached the hallway when his phone rang. The office was calling. "Sheriff Baker here."

He listened to the dispatcher on duty, but he didn't have to hear much before knowing what this was about. Old Man Cooper and his neighbor were at it again. "Isn't Deputy Lewis on duty?"

She explained that everyone else was busy, and while these confrontations rarely came to blows, he couldn't just ignore the call.

With a sigh, he slipped his phone away and walked out to the living room. The second Daisy spotted him, she stopped playing and asked, "Everything okay?"

"Yeah, I just…" He winced. "I have to run out for a bit, and…" He looked to Mikayla, about to tell her she needed to keep an eye on the boys, but it would be dinnertime soon, and he hated leaving them on their own.

"I'll keep an eye on these guys." Daisy smiled. "Go. Do your thing. We'll be fine until you get back."

He widened his eyes in surprise. "You sure?"

She waved him off. "Of course. Go on. We'll be just great."

None of the kids argued. If anything, they looked excited about this turn of events. And he had to admit, it was nice not to have to call in Helen or give Mikayla a lecture on all the do's and don'ts while he was away.

He found himself relaxing just a little as he reached his car.

Yup, it was pretty nice to have another adult around who could make sure everything was under control.

CHAPTER 22

Daisy wasn't exactly sure when the chaos broke out, but it wasn't long after Levi stepped foot out the front door.

It started with the boys continuously interrupting the music lesson, which Daisy didn't really mind, but Mikayla clearly did. So she'd yell at them, and then they'd blame each other, and Daisy stopped counting how many times she had to physically step in the middle to break up a burgeoning fight.

When the hour-long lesson finally ended, there was no sign of the sheriff—which was fine. She could totally handle this.

"What do you guys normally do for dinner?" she asked.

"Pizza!" Ronnie's shout was a little too quick, and his siblings exchanged a not-so-subtle look behind his back.

"Dad always lets us order pizza when he's not home," Dawson added, his eyes much too wide for genuine innocence.

"Is that so?" Daisy tapped a finger to her chin. "Maybe

I should just text your dad and make sure he's okay with—"

"No!" All three of them shouted it at once.

Mikayla sank back against the counter. "If Aunt Helen were here, she'd make us a casserole or something."

Daisy tried and failed to squash a laugh at the sight of their identical pouts. "Okay, and your dad…"

"He'd make something way too healthy for any of us to actually eat," Dawson said.

She snickered. Yeah, she could definitely see that from Mr. 'I jog every morning before dawn.'

"Well, I have no interest in making you kids food you won't eat," she said. "So what do you say we work together and come up with a happy medium somewhere between pizza and casseroles?"

"Like what?" Ronnie asked.

"Well…" She opened the fridge and started pulling out eggs. "My personal favorite is breakfast-for-dinner."

"Like…pancakes?" Ronnie asked.

She shrugged. "Sure. Pancakes sound good to me. Give 'em to me smothered in butter and maple syrup, and I am one happy girl."

The kids exchanged looks of surprise and glee.

She smiled as she turned to get the rest of the ingredients. But, of course, that was the last time they all agreed on anything for the next half hour. She was starting to get a minor headache by the time they sat down to eat.

"Serious question," she said as she reached for the syrup. "How do you all manage to find something to fight about all the time? It seems like it would be exhausting."

Dawson looked thoughtful. "I guess we just have a talent."

Mikayla laughed first, then Ronnie, and finally Daisy

joined them with a shake of her head. "No wonder your dad is so tense all the time."

"Nah, that's because our mom is dead." Dawson took a bite after he said this like it was no big deal.

Daisy froze with a fork right in front of her mouth.

"It's true," Mikayla murmured. "He used to smile. He used to be...happy. But now..."

"Now he doesn't like it when we have fun," Ronnie finished.

Daisy gave a snort. "I'm sure that's not true."

They looked at her like she was a sweet, sweet child... who knew nothing.

She waved her fork in the air as she reached for her water. "Give him a break. It's gotta be hard being a single dad. And raising three little stinkers like you?"

She arched her brows, and they all cracked up.

"He's just sad," Dawson said. "Because of Mom."

"We all are," Mikayla muttered so softly that Daisy was pretty sure no one else was supposed to hear.

"Well, here's the awesome thing about humans." She waited until all eyes were on her. "We can feel more than one emotion at a time."

"We can?" Ronnie looked dubious.

"Of course. And what's even cooler than that is you can choose what you focus on." She leaned over and tapped Dawson's skull. "That's a cool trick right there."

"So when Dawson makes me angry, I don't have to get mad," Ronnie said.

"Well, you can, and you probably will. But you might also see something funny about the situation, and so then you can decide: Do you want to yell or laugh?" She shrugged. "It's up to you."

All three of them stared at her like she was speaking a

159

foreign language. And maybe she was. This was just something she'd figured out as a kid—a way to not get swallowed up by her mother's emotional meltdowns. She chewed on her pancakes as the kids stewed that over.

After dinner, the fighting started again over who got to pick what they watched on TV. Daisy ended it by declaring no TV for the night. This went over...not so well. But then she declared they were having a cookie baking contest instead, and the mood lightened considerably.

"A contest?" Ronnie asked.

"Think *Iron Chef* but with candy and chocolate chips," she called out over the music she had playing from her phone.

"Iron what?" Dawson asked.

"We all make the same base recipe and then get to add in our own extras, and we'll see which contestant's cookies taste the best," Mikayla explained while she and Daisy scavenged the pantry for baking ingredients and every candy, nut, sprinkle, and topping they could find.

"Ladies and gentlemen, are you ready to make the most delicious cookies ever known to man?" Daisy hollered as they gathered around the small island. "This recipe has been passed down to me via the Internet."

Mikayla snorted and shook her head.

Daisy continued with her dramatic announcement. "And tonight, we shall see who can make the most mouthwatering cookie imaginable."

Mikayla giggled as Dawson reached into the bag of chocolate chips and grabbed a handful.

"Not yet!" Ronnie was dragging a stool over to the fridge. "Dad thinks we don't know where he keeps the Halloween and Easter candy."

Daisy laughed as he dragged it down and set it among the rest.

"*Now* we're ready," he said.

"Where do we start?" Dawson asked.

"Uh, duh," Mikayla said as she stuck her hand into the bag of flour and grabbed a handful of powder. "With this."

She flung the handful at her brother, who shouted and laughed before declaring retaliation.

Daisy laughed and turned up the music. "He who throws the next ingredient has to make up a dance move!"

And so a new game began. One filled with flying food, impromptu dance contests, and singalongs whenever a song they liked came on.

Was it still chaos?

Yes. Definitely.

But Daisy's belly hurt from laughing so hard as the two boys came up with a dance move that involved Ronnie trying to lift his bigger brother off his feet as he flapped his arms like wings.

This was the kind of chaos Daisy lived for.

CHAPTER 23

Levi was exhausted by the time he pulled up to his house after dark. But he felt a smile forming at the sight of a warm glow coming from the windows.

Daisy was in there. Maybe even playing music with his daughter or teaching the boys a few chords.

He couldn't remember the last time he'd felt so good while leaving the kids behind. Even with Helen there he fretted and worried that they'd drive her away once and for all. But tonight, despite his frustrations with cranky old Cooper and belligerent Billy, it was thoughts of home that cheered him, and as he'd sat in the office typing up his report, he'd been antsy to get back to see just how nicely they were all still behaving.

Heck, maybe Ronnie was in bed already. He reached for the doorknob. And maybe Mikayla didn't spend the entire night on her phone. And—

He stopped short in the front entryway, his heart slamming against his ribs at the cacophony of sound that hit him.

Music blared, and pots and pans clattered, but it was

the ear-piercing shriek that sent him flying toward the kitchen. He expected to find blood, maybe a broken limb or two, but what he found…was worse.

It was a madhouse. No, it was the monkey house at the zoo but with terrifying creatures throwing food instead of feces. And in the middle of it all was Daisy, looking beautiful, and covered in flour and—

"What is going on here?" His roar cut through the music, and Ronnie froze in the middle of dancing on top of the table. Dawson's arm stayed in midair, and for a second, the candied cherry that landed on Mikayla's hair looked like it was flying in slow motion as his kids turned to him with wide eyes.

"Oh, hey, Sheriff." Daisy's voice was light and calm in the midst of the chaotic storm.

Mikayla reached over and clicked a button, shutting off the music.

His kids remained quiet as they watched him with wariness and shame.

But Daisy…

He gaped in disbelief as she brushed her hands off— apparently not noticing that the cocoa powder on her hands was the least of her problems—and strode toward him with a beatific smile. "How was your night?"

"How was my…what the…who…" He stopped, hating the fact that with his every rage-filled outburst her lips trembled more and more as she held her breath in a clear attempt to stop herself from laughing at him.

She lost the battle, falling forward with a loud snort. "Oh my gosh, look at your face." She pointed at his nose. "It's hilarious."

"How do you expect me to look?" His gaze scanned the room again, realizing it was even worse than he'd first

164

thought. Broken eggs dripped off the counter, and while something smelled amazing in the oven, there was not a single inch of floor not covered in this mess. "What did you do to my kitchen?"

"We were baking." Daisy grinned.

The "duh" was unspoken, but he heard it. Her tone said he was acting irrational and that the question was a silly one. As if he were the crazy person here.

"This...this is not baking..." He met his kids' stares and saw that they were still frozen, fear in their little eyes.

He backed up a step, gesturing to all of them. "You... This mess..."

Daisy let out another snort of amusement as she clapped a hand over her mouth. But this time his kids seemed to realize that she was laughing, and he watched as their fear and horror turned to amusement of their own.

A snicker escaped Dawson, and then Mikayla was smothering a laugh, and Ronnie turned beet red as he clamped his lips shut and shook with silent laughter.

Great. Just great.

Now his kids were laughing at him.

He jabbed a finger at Daisy. "Fix it!"

She gave him a salute as he turned away, his pulse still too fast as anger coursed through him. This was his house. His kids. He was doing all he could to raise them to have good manners and clean up after themselves and be... well, good, dang it.

And then Daisy comes along and leads them into complete and utter chaos?

He stomped up the steps to change out of his uniform. Maybe he'd take a shower while he was at it to cool down.

That would give them more time to make things right before he faced them again and...

Well, what could he do? Could he honestly punish Mikayla and the boys when Daisy was their ringleader?

He shook his head.

What had she been thinking?

No, better question. What had *he* been thinking to trust her with his kids?

He turned on the shower and let the steam fill the bathroom.

One thing was clear—asking Daisy to watch his kids was the biggest mistake he'd ever made.

CHAPTER 24

Daisy clapped a hand over her mouth, but of course it was too late. She'd lost the battle with laughter a long time ago.

Even now, with guilt niggling at her gut, she couldn't shake the memory of the look on Levi's face. She turned to Mikayla, who was laughing so hard her shoulders were shaking as she sat in a mess of spilled flour. "That was… that was…"

Daisy made a snorting sound behind her hand, and that set the boys off all over again.

"Oh my goodness," Daisy wheezed when she could finally breathe. "His face…"

Mikayla wiped at her eyes. "That was hilarious. A little bit scary," she admitted, "but also super funny."

As she calmed down, guilt rose in her chest. "Ugh, he was really mad."

Mikayla waved away her words. "Don't worry about that. He's always mad."

"Like the Hulk," Dawson put on a gravelly monster voice.

"Aunt Helen says he's ultraprotective," Ronnie said matter-of-factly. "And I think that makes him grumpy."

Daisy and Mikayla exchanged a glance, and Mikayla choked on another giggle.

"Do you mean *over*protective?" Daisy suggested.

Ronnie nodded. "That's what I said."

It took an effort, but Daisy kept a straight face. "You're right, you did."

Dawson started to argue the point, but Daisy cut him off. "All right, kiddos, you heard the man. Time to clean this place up."

Dawson groaned. "I don't wanna."

"Yeah, I have to do my homework." Ronnie edged toward the door.

"Me too." Mikayla jumped up and made a beeline after him.

"Nuh-uh!" Daisy leapt forward and blocked the way before any of them could escape. "You are not abandoning me in my time of need. We all fought this food war, and we all must clean it up. Together!" She put on a voice, trying to erase their whiny groans.

Ronnie gave a little snicker, and so she went the extra mile, acting like a slapstick, idiotic general in the army and ordering them around until Ronnie's laughter became genuine and Dawson jumped in on the act too.

It was her crazy way of getting compliance and the exact opposite of what Dahlia used to do.

But even so, bossing these kids around was sort of like seeing her own past through a different person's eyes. She remembered the way Dahlia used to order her and Rose around and make them clean up their messes when she was no older than Mikayla.

Younger, actually.

She'd been giving them orders since they were old enough to talk, and Daisy had always hated it, but right now...

Right now she could only feel sorry for that little girl who'd had to take charge and keep the house clean and her sisters fed and—

No wonder she hardly ever laughed or got silly.

All that responsibility.

All the time.

"Daisy? You got any more orders for us?" Dawson grabbed her attention, obviously disappointed she'd stopped playing the game.

She blinked, snapping back into her role of General Silly Pants.

"Hop to it, lads!" She put on her best attempt at a British accent. "Cleaning is fun."

"Fun?" Mikayla's voice was doubtful.

"Uh, duh." Daisy tossed her hair back over her shoulder, jumping into a Barbie Beach Girl character for a moment. "Did you think this would be, like... boring?"

"Yes," Mikayla retorted. "Because no amount of lame British accents or stupid acting can change the fact that cleaning *sucks*." Her expression was turning petulant, her feisty gaze hungry for a fight.

Well, she was fresh out of luck.

With a pleasant smile, Daisy turned the music back on, becoming herself once more as she clapped her hands together.

"Okay. New game," she called out over the booming bass. "Whoever comes up with the best lyrics about how much cleaning *sucks* wins."

"What do we win?" Ronnie asked.

"Um…" She looked around, but just then the timer dinged. "Whoever wins gets the first cookie!"

She snagged an oven mitt and pulled out the fresh-baked cookies with a moan. "They smell so good."

"I can't wait to try mine one." Dawson pointed at the large lump in the center that he'd declared a cookie mountain.

"Looks good," she murmured, though she wasn't entirely sure his attempt at baking was going to win any prizes.

"Mmm." Mikayla inhaled a big sniff, then dropped a quick rap. "They smell delicious, and I can't wait to have myself a little taste. But first we have to clean this place because it is a big disgrace. Cleaning su-cks. Cleaning su-cks. Clean su-su-su-su-sucks!"

Daisy laughed, impressed by Mikayla's quick thinking as she set the baking sheet down and tore off the oven mitt, then pointed at the disaster that surrounded them.

"If you want to taste deliciousness, then get to work."

"Aww," Ronnie started to whine.

"You make up some lyrics, Ronnie," Daisy shouted. She reached for the garbage bin and started to toss away the broken eggshells.

Ronnie had them all laughing as he did a terrible rap over top of the original song. Dawson found the handheld vacuum while Mikayla got to work loading the dishwasher. Cleaning wasn't exactly fun, but they got through it with a whole lot of laughs and tons of singing.

By the time they were almost back to the super squeaky-clean way Levi had left it, they were also exhausted. Daisy included.

"I think that's good enough for now," she declared, wiping her hands off on her jeans. "What do you think?"

She eyed the tray of cookies. "Who takes first place in the lyrics competition?"

All four of them exchanged mischievous looks before Daisy shouted, "Four-way tie!"

They all lunged for the tray, each grabbing a cookie as they laughed.

A little while later, they were all happily munching away on their cookies as they sat cross-legged on the kitchen floor.

And that was how Levi found them when he came back into the kitchen looking more serious than she'd ever seen him.

She stopped chewing as his dark gaze met hers. Yep, that shower had done nothing to cool him off. He placed his hands on his hips, eyeing the kitchen critically. If he spotted one thing wrong, she was sure he'd jump all over it. The top of his head would start to rattle, and then steam would shoot right out of his ears. The image made her belly tremble with laughter, and a soft snort escaped before she could stop it.

She was all too aware that the three kids had gone silent, their hands stilled in eating as they watched and waited.

Daisy hated their tension. Actually, she hated Levi's tension even more. It was ruining what had been a perfectly lovely time eating cookies on the floor.

She dropped her cookie onto the plate with a loud sigh. "You need to lighten up, Sheriff."

His brows hitched slightly.

She suspected criminals started shaking right about now.

But she was no criminal. And his kids…

She winced inwardly as she remembered how they'd

all told her to ignore his anger because he was so mad all the time. Her heart suddenly hurt on his behalf.

He was a good dad. He loved his kids. But all they saw was...

Mr. Ultraprotective.

She wrinkled her nose as she took in his fierce glory. His hair was still wet from the shower, his beard perfectly trimmed, and his jaw was hard as stone as he glared down at them.

The urge to see him smile, to see him laugh with his kids, hit her like a ton of bricks, and it made her want to do something—*anything*—just so long as it broke through that hard shell of his.

And so, without really thinking it through, she picked an M&M out of the large, misshapen oatmeal cookie she'd been munching on, and she threw it.

At his face.

She and the kids looked on with bated breath as it hit him right smack in the middle of his cheek.

Surprise flared in his eyes, and his lips parted as he aimed that fierce glare directly at her.

Uh-oh.

Daisy pressed her lips together to hide a smile.

She was in for it now.

CHAPTER 25

L evi froze. For a second, time seemed to stand still as everyone in the kitchen held their breath, waiting for his reaction.

And for a split second, he had no idea how to respond.

He could safely say that in his thirty-nine years of living, no one had ever thrown an M&M at his face. Or any food, for that matter.

Daisy's eyes were impossibly wide as they met his, and then...she burst out laughing. And the sound made his heart leap, her melodic giggle holding him like a leash. His gaze moved to his kids, and his heart leapt again, but this time with a mix of emotions he couldn't begin to name.

They looked so happy. So ready to laugh. But they were watching him with...fear.

But one of them—Dawson, he suspected—had the nerve to throw a jelly bean at him.

Levi saw it coming this time and caught it.

There was a collective gasp, and he was sure they were all waiting to see what he would do.

He caught Mikayla's eyes. Saw her wariness battling

with the urge to laugh like Daisy had. So he tossed the jelly bean into his mouth and grunted like a big bear.

Daisy's head fell back with a shriek of laughter, and after a second of shocked silence, the kids joined in with giggles that made his heart swell and dance.

And then suddenly he was being pelted with chocolate chips and jelly beans and who knew what else.

"That's it," he roared. But this time his roar was filled with feigned anger, and everyone knew it. He puffed his chest and unleashed another battle cry, which had Ronnie falling over with laughter, holding his belly like he was in pain.

When was the last time he'd laughed that hard?

Levi swallowed against a wave of emotion. Too long. It'd been too long since he'd seen any of his kids have this much fun.

And so when Daisy nailed him with another piece of candy, hitting his chest before bouncing off, he leapt into action, scooping up the candy that had fallen to the floor and pelting it back at her as she screamed in mock horror.

Mikayla was staring at him with wide eyes. Disbelief was written all over her face. So he threw the next jelly bean at her. She gasped and pretended outrage. "Oh no you didn't!" Her voice came out breathy as she started to giggle.

He threw his hands out wide. "It's on!"

"Bring it, old man!" Dawson shouted.

He choked on a laugh, but then his gaze caught on the open jar of old Easter candy.

"Uh-oh," Daisy shrieked. "Kids, man your stations! Prepare for battle!"

He dove for the jar, baring his teeth as he growled at them. Jelly beans were bouncing off him, and the kitchen

174

was rapidly devolving back to the chaotic mess they'd just cleaned up, but…

He didn't care.

For once, he honestly didn't care.

Not only that. He liked it. No, he loved it. Their laughter and their squeals, the way they were smiling at him with such unabashed joy.

He ducked behind the counter with his candy jar and let his heart catch up with this tidal wave of emotions.

"You're next, Ronnie," he shouted. "I've got a jelly bean here with your name on it."

"Oh no!" Ronnie cried in mock horror.

"I've got you, bro," Dawson said. "He'll have to get through me first!"

Levi ducked his head as a quiet chuckle slipped out.

"Me too!" Mikayla shouted. "You'll never take us alive!"

He peeked around the corner and saw Daisy was curled up on the floor, laughing too hard to shout anything at all. His kids were huddled around her, clearly adoring her unbridled show of joy.

"Daisy, you're not helping." Mikayla giggled, nudging Daisy's shoulder.

"Sorry, sorry!" Daisy sat up, and her eyes locked on his. He felt her gaze like she'd just reached inside his chest and squeezed. Her eyes sparkled like diamonds, and her smile held a world of joy with maybe just a hint of heat.

An electric shock of desire raced through him, his heart swelling as if it might expand right out of his chest.

Sitting there on the floor, surrounded by his grinning children and an epic mess, Daisy had never looked more beautiful. She glowed with life and laughter, and this time the wave of emotions nearly drowned him. It was a swell of gratitude and a tidal wave of affection so fierce it brought with it a surge of fear.

He pulled back behind the counter and let the sound of his kids' taunts and laughter surround him. The noise was sweeter than all the jelly beans in the world.

Mikayla's giggles made his chest feel so soft and warm he had to shut his eyes and drink it in.

"You too scared to show your face, Sheriff?" Daisy proceeded to make chicken sounds that made Mikayla scream with laughter. Ronnie and Dawson were quick to join in, and Levi grinned as a chorus of chicken sounds filled the kitchen.

Levi shot to his feet with another loud roar and started pelting his kids with candy.

"Take cover!" Mikayla shouted.

Daisy reached for a pot lid and held it in front of her like a shield. "Ronnie, behind me!"

As his son used Daisy as a human shield, he and Daisy shared another smile. Something knowing and sweet that made him feel like she knew exactly how much this moment meant to him.

Maybe she'd known all along that this was what he'd needed. What his family needed.

And that she was the one to give it to them.

CHAPTER 26

Nash was having lunch in the kitchen when Daisy grabbed the keys to her Beetle.

"Hey there, bro-in-law," she called.

"Hey, Daisy." His lips curled up into that soft grin he always gave her when they bumped into each other. Yep, he was a cutie. Tall, rugged, handsome...and kinda shy. It was a sweet combination, and she understood why Emma adored her husband so much.

Daisy didn't actually see him that often since he was an early bird and she was a night owl, so it was a pleasant surprise to find him eating at the kitchen table.

"You heading in to give music lessons already?" He glanced at the clock. "Isn't it a little early?"

She shrugged. "I figured I'd swing by and see Rose, maybe visit with Lizzy..."

And stop by the auto body shop to give Fred another payment.

He'd been nice enough to let her pay in installments. But even with the discount he got her and the installment plan, she had to find a way to make more money.

Not that she was in a hurry to give up music lessons. It had been two weeks since the food fight, and she found herself counting the seconds until each visit. Mikayla was a natural, and it was sheer joy watching her come into her own as a musician. The boys were a hoot, and the sheriff...

Well, he was growing on her. A silly little grin toyed with her lips as she reached for an apple on the table.

Okay, maybe she had a little crush. She was an adult; she could admit she was attracted. But of course, it would never go further than that. No matter how cute he was when he gave her one of those rare smiles, or how much she enjoyed teasing him, or how hot he was in that uniform, he was still a single father with more roots in this town than an oak tree.

And she was just lying low for a while, that was all.

Sometimes she could almost forget that fact. Some days, she found herself getting a little too comfortable. But like clockwork a text would come in or a call from an unknown number, and she was reminded all over again why she was here...and why she couldn't stay.

Music lessons were nice and all, but the real money lay in the big cities where a few good gigs could actually make a dent in the debt she owed.

"Emma's making a roast tonight if you're back in time for dinner," Nash called after her. "You think you'll be joining us?"

She flashed him a smile and a wave as she headed for the door. "Maybe. But don't wait up."

It was what she always said, and Nash gave her an indulgent grin.

It wasn't that she didn't enjoy dinners here on the ranch, but being surrounded by happy couples all the time got a little tiresome. Talk always turned to the future and family plans, all of which made Daisy feel like she was sitting in the hot seat.

At least she'd gotten a reprieve from Dahlia's questions about her plans for the future. She and JJ were on vacation, and Daisy would bet all the money she didn't have that when Dahlia came home, she'd be sporting a ring on her finger.

Which was awesome. Daisy adored JJ and couldn't wait until he was officially family. He was so good for her sister. Just like Dex was perfect for shy, sweet Rose.

Her Beetle was working better than ever, and her first stop in town was to give Fred another meager payment.

He gave her a nod and a wink as he took the cash she offered. He'd been a sweetheart to keep the details of their arrangement under wraps. She could only imagine the questions she'd have to face from her sisters if they found out she was too broke to pay for her car repairs.

Next she headed toward Rose's house. She worked from home, and Daisy loved to swing by and see her when she was in town. Their little house and its adorable nursery were always a treat. But as she was driving, she spotted a familiar face.

She narrowed her eyes and...yup. That was Mikayla, all right. She was hunched in on herself as she walked quickly along the sidewalk.

And away from the high school.

Daisy chuckled as she pulled her car up to the curb and called out the window. "Hey, don't I know you?"

Mikayla's eyes flared wide with alarm.

Daisy laughed as she leaned over to talk through the open passenger-side window. "Aren't you supposed to be at school?"

Mikayla's mouth opened and closed.

"That is one mighty fine fish impersonation." Daisy giggled.

Mikayla's mouth clamped shut, a red hue climbing up her neck.

Daisy took pity on the girl and opened the passenger door. "Come on, get in before your dad or one of his deputies drives by and sees you."

Mikayla's look of terror at the mere mention of her father had Daisy swallowing another laugh. Poor Levi. The more she got to know him and his kids, the clearer it was that he adored them. But he was such a stick in the mud that all they saw was his stern side. The one exception was the candy fight, which had to be cleaned up, and it was during those post-giggle complaints that Levi's strict side came back into play. The kitchen ended up spotless, but three quiet kids trudged up to bed.

Mikayla slid into the seat and hurriedly slammed the door shut behind her.

Daisy stepped on the gas as Mikayla buckled up.

"Where are we going?" The girl's voice was wary as she glanced over her shoulder like she was making sure they weren't being followed. "Are you taking me to my dad? He's not at the station."

Daisy rolled her eyes. "Relax, Micky May, I'm not turning you over to the sheriff."

Mikayla sighed as she sank back in her seat. "You're not?"

"No." She gave her a sidelong look. "But if you're playing hooky, you're taking me with you."

Mikayla's lips twitched up, and she looked so much like her father as she tried not to smile that it made Daisy's heart give a little squeeze.

"Where are we going?" Mikayla asked again as they

left Aspire, but this time she didn't sound fearful, just curious.

"Somewhere your dad will never find us," Daisy teased. She kept driving until they hit Wellsprings—the next town over.

"This place is cute," Daisy said as she and Mikayla strolled along the town's main street, enjoying the sunshine and checking out the little stores and restaurants.

"My mom used to take us here a lot." Mikayla pointed to an ice cream shop at the end of the block. "Rocky road was her favorite."

"Mmm, a woman after my own heart." Daisy nudged the girl's elbow. "Come on. My treat."

They raced toward the ice cream shop and were laughing when they stepped inside to order. They found a little table out front and settled in. "So," Daisy said slowly, "when are you gonna tell me why you were skipping school?"

Mikayla winced. "Are you going to give me a lecture too?"

"No. I'm definitely not in a position to give a lecture on this particular topic."

Mikayla's brows arched. "Why not?"

Daisy leaned forward and whispered, "I used to skip all the time."

Mikayla grinned. "You did?"

"I did." Daisy licked her ice cream.

"Where did you go?"

"Well, when it was cold out, I'd usually just hide in one of the music rooms." She shrugged. "I wasn't much good at any other subject, so what was the point, you know? I already knew I wanted to be a musician, so, like...why

181

suffer through calculus? Honestly, I figured I was doing my calculus teacher a favor."

Mikayla giggled.

"On nice days, I'd go to Central Park or Washington Square Park and set up shop." She grinned. "I used to make mad money just playing music all afternoon long."

"Wow. That's so cool." Mikayla's gaze was filled with such adoration that Daisy felt a little thrill.

"My best friends and I had formed this band, and some days we'd all skip and make loads of cash performing on street corners."

Mikayla's eyes were so wide with wonder, Daisy had to stifle a laugh.

This was good, right? They were bonding. Heaven knew Daisy would have killed for an older sister figure when she was Mikayla's age. Someone who understood…

"I hated school," she said. "And I hated home even more."

"Really?" Mikayla's voice pitched in surprise, and honestly Daisy was a little shocked herself. She rarely talked about her home life growing up, and she hadn't really meant to go there now. But Daisy just knew deep down that the only way Mikayla would trust her was if she opened up first.

"My dad left us when we were little, and my mom…"

Mikayla froze with her ice cream cone in front of her face as Daisy tried to think of the words to finish that statement.

"My mom was there, but she wasn't." She grimaced. "It's hard to explain. She had…issues. And it made our house kind of a nightmare."

"I know what you mean," Mikayla muttered. "My dad

makes our house feel like a nightmare...or a prison anyway."

Daisy gave a little snort of amusement. "Uh, no. I know your dad is strict and all, but trust me...you've got a good father. Your house is no prison." She shook her head, licking the end of her spoon and smiling. "He's only looking out for you."

"Uh-huh. Right." Mikayla's eyes rolled, and then her gaze dropped.

Daisy could feel her pulling away.

Okay, so maybe sticking up for Levi wasn't the best course here.

"Anyway, I got really good at playing the system at school." Daisy changed the direction back to school and music. It seemed like a safer topic. "The money from busking was so good that eventually I took off with my bandmates and never looked back."

"Did you graduate?"

"Nope." Daisy shrugged. "What was the point, right? You don't need a degree to play music."

"Wow," Mikayla breathed.

Daisy smiled and leaned forward. "Now it's your turn. What's so bad at school that you're risking the sheriff's wrath?" She put on a voice to make it funny.

Mikayla half grinned and shrugged.

"Oh, come on." Daisy pointed her spoon across the table. "It's not like you were leaving to do something super fun in Aspire. There's nothing going on there."

Mikayla giggled. "That's true."

"So clearly you're not happy at school..." Daisy arched her brows and then settled back in her seat to wait her out.

Mikayla caved with a sigh. "It's my friends." She rolled

her eyes and used air quotes. "Or should I say my 'friends.'"

"Ahhh."

"Yeah." Mikayla shrugged. "I don't know. Sometimes I think we're cool, but then it's like they gang up on me, and suddenly I'm just the sheriff's daughter and not good enough for their stupid circle anymore." She started blinking, her voice catching on the words.

For the next few minutes, Mikayla filled her in on the intense and complicated dynamics between her and her friends. "…and then Jessie told Margo that I'm a narc." She stopped to draw in a deep breath. "And it's all because of my dad. No one invites me to parties anymore because he always finds out, and he ruins everything."

"Ugh, that is tough," Daisy murmured.

"So you get it, right?" Mikayla's eyes were brimming with tears, and there was a hopefulness in her expression that tugged at Daisy's heart.

She wanted to be understood. She needed that.

Daisy sighed. "Yeah, I get it."

Mikayla slumped over with a sigh. "I'm glad somebody does."

"And I always will. I know this is easier said than done, but try not to stress too much over those girls. True friends don't run hot and cold. They stick like glue, no matter what. You just haven't found your people yet." She licked a blob of ice cream off her spoon. "And there's nothing wrong with being a free spirit either. There's a certain safety in flying solo."

Mikayla studied her with a doubtful frown, but then the words seemed to sink in, and she began to nod. "I like that. Free like a bird."

"You can fly anywhere you like."

She gave Daisy a little grin. "You know, you're pretty cool for a grown-up."

Daisy laughed. "Yeah, well…I try."

"What did you do when you left high school?" Mikayla asked.

For the next hour, as they finished ice cream and drove back to Aspire, Daisy regaled the younger girl with tales from her time on the road. But when they pulled up in front of Mikayla's house, they both fell silent.

"Levi," Daisy whispered.

At the same time, Mikayla groaned. "Dad."

He was waiting for them with arms crossed as they slowly climbed out of the car.

"Howdy, Sheriff!" Daisy tried to lighten the mood.

It didn't work. His gaze never left his daughter. "The school called. And your phone mustn't be working because you've ignored my texts and—"

"I turned it off." Mikayla flushed, reaching into her bag to find her phone.

"That isn't good enough. You know better than to skip school."

Daisy could see Mikayla wilting beside her. Gone was the smiling, happy girl she'd spent the afternoon with. The sullen frown that washed over Mikayla's expression made her heart sink.

Daisy hated to see it happening, especially when she'd watched the way Levi lit up when his daughter was happy.

"It's my fault!" The words came tumbling out before she really thought it through.

Levi's eyes widened as his gaze met hers.

Her belly did a silly little flip when their eyes locked.

"It is?" he asked.

She didn't look over at Mikayla, but she could feel the girl's stare.

"Um…" Daisy smiled. "Yes. I, uh…" She glanced over at Mikayla, who was no help at all. "I was driving by the school at lunchtime, and all the kids were out for…recess."

Mikayla's eye bulged, and she mouthed, "Recess?"

"Or…whatever," Daisy added. A laugh was starting to bubble up in her chest because there was no way Levi believed her. But when she glanced back at him, she caught a flicker of dry amusement in his eyes.

"I spotted Mikayla, and I asked her to come hang out with me so we could…"

"Rehearse!" Mikayla finished the sentence far too loudly.

Levi rolled his lips inward, his nostrils flaring. But it was clear to Daisy that he was trying not to smile over their pathetic lie. "I see. And what exactly did you have to rehearse during school hours?"

Daisy looked to Mikayla, and they were both battling to hold back laughter.

"A new song we've been working on?" Daisy offered.

Mikayla gave a little snort before clamping her mouth shut to stop the giggle.

"I see." Levi rocked back on his heels, arms crossed, while Daisy and Mikayla waited. Eventually, he dropped his arms with a sigh. "The school's going to be giving you detention tomorrow."

Mikayla swallowed. "Okay. And you?"

He worked his jaw to the side but then nodded. "I'm gonna leave it at that." He narrowed his eyes, his forehead wrinkling with a frown. "This time. And *only* this time."

CHAPTER 27

L evi could hear Mikayla's lesson from where he worked in the kitchen, and he found himself wearing a smile the entire time. When it wasn't music coming from the living room, it was Mikayla's and Daisy's laughter. And Levi wasn't sure which was more beautiful.

He knew he should be mad over Mikayla's decision to skip school, but watching her and Daisy fudge their way through that ridiculous lie was plain adorable. Not to mention the comfort it gave him knowing his daughter had been looked after, and no doubt entertained, by a ball of pure sunshine and joy.

By the time the music lesson came to an end, he barely even noticed Ronnie's and Dawson's whining as they set the table behind him. All his attention was captured by the beautiful blonde in the other room.

His heart had leapt at the sight of her when they pulled up to the house. He'd just been getting ready to drive around town and start hunting for Mikayla. But then Daisy's Beetle had appeared, and the sense of relief coursing through him was matched only by the sizzling desire at seeing Daisy in her short denim skirt and flowing white blouse. It fell off her shoulder while she was weaving her tale, and he couldn't keep his eyes off her smooth skin or the way her wild hair curled down past her collarbone.

And her legs.

He couldn't resist stealing a glance at those shapely calf muscles when Daisy turned to Mikayla. She was gorgeous from the tips of her painted toenails to the top of her head.

He'd never been a good liar. Not to others, and definitely not to himself. So when he finally heard their voices come into the hallway, he could admit that he wanted to see her again before she left.

He set his knife down and rinsed his hands. It was attraction, that was all. He was a grown man, and she was a woman, and…it didn't mean anything more than that.

And yet his pace quickened so he could catch up with her before she reached the door. "Daisy!"

She stopped short and turned to face him with that smile that seemed to have more of a physical effect on him each time he saw it.

Today it knocked the wind out of him as surely as a sucker punch.

She tilted her head to the side in question, and Mikayla arched her brows expectantly. "Uh…"

He'd already paid her for the lesson, so he had no reason to delay her. He needed to stop paying her in advance so he could have an excuse to be alone with her for a few minutes before she left for the night.

"Yes, Sheriff?" Her eyes sparkled with amusement, and her smile was teasing, as if she knew full well that he'd just wanted to see her.

He cleared his throat. "I just wanted to say thank you…

again. For your help earlier with Mikayla." He glanced at Mikayla, who was looking up at the ceiling with feigned innocence.

"It was my pleasure."

She turned to go, but Mikayla suddenly straightened. "Hey, Dad, can Daisy stay for dinner?"

He and Daisy both turned to her in surprise, but Daisy recovered first. "That sounds fun, but...do you have enough food to go around?"

A smile spread across his face before he could stop it. "Of course."

Her beaming grin made his heart do a backflip. He swallowed hard. He shouldn't have said yes so quickly. Spending more time with her wasn't going to help this attraction any. But he couldn't bring himself to regret the invite when her presence in the kitchen was met with smiles and laughter from his boys.

"You're staying?" Dawson said. "Cool!"

"Can she sit next to me, Dad?" Ronnie asked.

"I don't see why not." He turned to Daisy with his hands tucked in his pockets, telling himself it was absolutely ridiculous to be nervous in his own home.

And it wasn't really *nervous*, necessarily, just...

Off-balance.

She looked so comfortable there in the kitchen as she helped the boys finish setting the table, asking them questions about their day at school, and making the atmosphere in the room a million times lighter with her easy chatter.

When she asked Dawson, "How'd the math test go?" Levi blinked in surprise.

Math test. Had he known about a math test?

He turned to question Dawson, but he was already shrugging. "Easy A."

Daisy tousled his hair. "I knew it. You're a smarty-pants just like your dad, huh?"

Levi chuckled. "You're giving me too much credit. I did all right in school, but Beth was the one who got all As."

"Yeah, Mom was validation," Ronnie said, his chest puffing out with pride.

Mikayla smacked the back of his head as she passed behind him. "It's valedictorian, doofus."

"That's what he said!" Daisy called out cheerfully at the same time Ronnie said, "That's what I said!"

Everyone burst out laughing, and any brewing friction vanished before it could start.

Levi leaned back against the counter as he watched them. Watched *her*.

She made it look so easy. And then she was asking questions about Beth—what else was she good at? What was her favorite song to sing?

Mikayla said it was "Amazing Grace." "She sang it all the time."

Levi felt a smile tugging at his lips even as emotions made his throat tighten. She was wrong. Beth did love "Amazing Grace," and it was one she sang often, both in the church choir and at home. But her favorite song to sing was "You Are My Sunshine"—that was the one she reserved for her kids alone. She sang it to each of them when they were babies, but he supposed they were too young to remember that.

Maybe it was up to him to remind them.

His heart tried to expand and contract at the same time as he watched his children light up with joy as they talked about their mother. And Daisy's laughter at their

190

responses, her enthusiasm about the topic, it was awe-inspiring.

How did she do it? It was like she was bringing Beth's memory to life right before his eyes. And the fact that his children weren't crying at the mention of their mother, but rather lighting up with happiness, made his lungs hitch with emotion.

He turned to the oven and took a deep breath. The timer dinged, and he was grateful to have something to keep his hands busy as he listened to the conversation behind him. He pulled out the lasagna and set it aside to cool as he tossed together a simple salad.

"Can I help?" Daisy's voice was close, and he looked over to see her standing right beside him, so close he could smell that sweet, heady scent of hers and see the little dimple at the corner of her mouth when she smiled. "I think I can handle a salad," she teased.

"I'm sure you can, but I'm already finished." He handed her the bowl. "You can take it to the table if you want to help."

She headed over and slid into the seat beside Ronnie while Luke took his seat at the head of the table. It felt far more crowded with another person there, but somehow that also made it seem cozier.

Or maybe that was just Daisy. Like always, she had the kids talking and laughing, which was such a change from their normal sullen silences and squabbling, he was content to sit back and enjoy it all as he ate his meal.

At one point, Daisy sank back in her seat with a moan. "Sheriff, you are one amazing cook."

Pleasure bloomed before he could stop it. She was just being nice. But he had been working hard to learn how to cook for his family, and he realized right now that Daisy was the first person to remark on it.

"It's just a simple lasagna," he muttered.

"It's not a 'simple' anything." She leaned forward, resting her elbows on the table. "Does he always cook like this?"

Ronnie nodded eagerly. "Yeah, he's a really good cook."

Levi's fork hung in midair, surprise making him pause.

"Yeah, he cooks almost every night," Dawson said.

Mikayla was nodding. "He's pretty good."

Levi's jaw dropped. Daisy caught his shock and burst out laughing. "Hear that, Sheriff? Even Mikayla thinks you're *pretty good*."

He smiled. It was hard not to when she was grinning at him like this…like they were in on a joke together.

The rest of the dinner flew by all too quickly, and Levi found himself wishing it would last longer. He couldn't remember the last time a family dinner had been so easy, or so fun. But they'd lingered over the meal, and then during dessert—a special treat since they had a guest— and by the time everyone was standing up and clearing plates, he realized it was later than usual.

"It's my night to do dishes," Dawson said glumly.

But Levi shook his head. "It's getting late, and you still have homework to do. I'll do dish duty tonight. You kids go wash up and crack open those books."

"I'll help," Daisy said as the kids cleared out.

"You don't have to," he started.

"Oh please." She rolled her eyes. "I might be useless as a cook, but I can handle doing the dishes."

"You don't cook, huh?" He turned on the sink as she

cleared the last of the plates. "I guess that makes sense with all the traveling you do."

"Mmm."

"Did your mom cook?"

She kept busy beside him, but he didn't miss the way she was fidgeting with unease. "Um, no. Dahlia was the one who made sure we were fed, and she wasn't much of a cook."

She went still beside him, and her silence felt tense. "But then again, she was only a kid, so…" Her laugh sounded brittle. "Maybe boxed mac 'n' cheese was the best she could do, huh?"

He didn't know what to say to that, so he turned to face her, to ask her what she meant…but by the time he met her gaze, she was already brightening, her smile wide as she changed the subject. "But where did you learn to cook like that?"

He hesitated. Curiosity about her childhood, her life on the road, it made him want to steer the topic back to her. But it was clear she didn't want to talk about herself, so he shrugged with a rueful smile. "It's called the school of necessity."

"Oh yeah? I've never heard of this culinary school. It must be exclusive."

He handed her a wet plate, and she took it to dry.

"Yup, it's based on the principle that three hungry kids ought to be fed."

"Imagine that."

He found himself smiling. "I still have a ways to go before I graduate. I only know how to make a handful of meals."

"Still more than I know, Sheriff. Your kids are lucky to have you."

The words were said so lightly, so sweetly. Did she have any idea how much they meant to him? His voice was too gruff as he dipped his head with a shrug. "I don't know if they'd agree, but thank you." He glanced over and caught a hint of that gorgeous smile. She seemed to always be on the verge of grinning. "And it's Levi," he added. "You don't have to call me Sheriff."

"Oh, I know," she shot back. "But I don't want to forget who I'm talking to."

He rested a hip against the counter. "Why? Do you have a warrant out for your arrest or something?"

A flicker of unease crossed her face, and he tipped his head with an apologetic smile.

"I'm only kidding."

"I know." She gave him a teasing wink.

He chuckled as she nudged him out of the way, handing him the dish towel. "Here. You did all the cooking. Let me do the scrubbing. You can dry and put away."

"Yes, ma'am," he murmured, making her giggle.

They worked in companionable silence for a few minutes, and a thought kept nagging at him. He didn't really want to talk about what had happened earlier that day, but the responsible parent in him knew he had to address it. "Hey, Daisy…"

She looked up, her big eyes so beautiful he lost his train of thought for a moment.

"I, uh…" He set down the dish towel and had to focus on the countertop for a moment. She was too distracting, and he needed to get this out. "I know you had good intentions earlier…with Mikayla, I mean."

She leaned against the counter. His eyes darted to her hip and the way it so beautifully curved up into her narrow waist. He wondered what it'd feel like to run his

194

hands along the outline of her body. His skin tingled just thinking about it.

Curling his fingers into a light fist, he forced his gaze to the dish towel he was holding.

"Are you talking about me taking the blame this afternoon?"

He let out a huff of laughter at her easy admission. "Yeah. That...and the fact that you didn't take her back to school."

He glanced up in time to see her nose crinkle. She looked so freakin' adorable he had this urge to pull her into his arms.

"I'm sorry," she murmured. "I guess I can relate a little too much with what she's going through."

"And I appreciate that. I do. I'm glad she's found an adult she can relate to, but..."

"But it can't happen again," she finished for him.

He nodded. "Exactly."

"You have my word, Sheriff." She gave a mock salute.

He sighed, but a smile was already forming. "I told you, it's Levi."

She shifted, stepping so close he could feel the heat from her body. Her heavenly scent wrapped around him as she whispered, "I'll tell you what..."

His gaze zoned in on those gorgeous blue eyes, on the lush, pink lips that were so quick to smile. He found himself leaning down just like she was leaning up toward him. His head was fuzzy, unable to form real thoughts, yet all his senses were on overdrive.

Smell, sight, sound...touch.

He wanted to touch her. Taste those sweet lips.

His world came down to one thing—Daisy.

Her lips curled into a delectable smile as she softly

teased him. "I promise to call you Levi—" She leaned in so close he could feel her warm breath on his neck. "—if you promise to *lighten up.*"

On the last words, she scooped up a handful of bubbles from the sink and blew them at him.

It jolted him out of his trance, and he shook his head, shocked laughter bursting out of him as he wiped the suds from his beard.

"You did not just do that," he growled.

Her answering laughter was high and sweet, and he couldn't stop himself from reaching for her. She shrieked with a girly giggle as his hands found her sides and started tickling.

And then he was wrapping his arms around her as she squirmed, trying her best to reach for another handful of suds.

"I don't think so," he said through his laughter.

The next time she wriggled, she nearly fell out of his arms, so he caught her before she could hit the floor. But the move had him tipping sideways. He swiveled to catch her so she wouldn't get hurt, but he couldn't stop the tumble. They rolled once, and she was pinned beneath him, her wild hair splayed across the wooden floor. Her sparkling laughter softly died away, and he caught the look in her eyes. Her gaze darted to his lips, her pupils dilating as her breath became just a little ragged.

So she felt it, too, this spark he couldn't deny. It passed between them now—crackling and electric. As he lay on top of her, he could sense it catching fire. It burned right through him, and that heat of attraction mixed with this all-consuming affection made him powerless.

He held her gaze as he leaned down, pausing just above her lips in case she wanted to turn away. He half expected a joke or a giggle. A funny quip to break the spell. But the moment her lips parted and her soft breath hit him, he closed the space between them.

Their lips met, and for a moment, the shock of heat was so overwhelming that all he could do was absorb the mind-numbing sensation and revel in the feel of her mouth pressed against his. But then her lips were parting slightly, and his body responded in kind. She tasted just as sweet as she smelled, and the way she responded and moved with him, the way she appeared to sink into him, her arms twining around his neck—they seemed to fit together in a way that felt destined somehow.

Like finding some missing part of himself, she molded to him like a puzzle piece, her sighs so sweet and perfect, it was better than any sound he could imagine. His hands couldn't seem to get enough of her warmth, or the softness of her skin, or the shape she made from her hip to her waist. He followed the outline of her body, all the way to her neck, before letting his fingers dive into her long, untamed hair.

He was so thoroughly lost in kissing Daisy, he wasn't sure when he would have stopped...if they hadn't been interrupted.

CHAPTER 28

Daisy was drowning in a sea of pleasure. Her mind had gone blank the moment Levi's lips touched hers, and now he was everything. His body, which she was happy to confirm had the sculpted muscles she predicted, his weight on top of her, and the way his hands traveled from her hip to her hair.

And his kiss…it consumed her.

For a little while, she forgot all the reasons this was wrong, and all the fears that had been harder and harder to ignore.

Because all that existed were the safety of Levi's arms, the strength of his embrace, and the warm, sweet bliss of his kiss.

Until…

"Dad, why are you giving Daisy mouth-to-mouth?"

Ronnie's voice cut through the moment like a cold splash of water. In a heartbeat, Levi was off her and gaping at his son. Daisy sat upright with a start, trying to catch her breath.

"Uh…" Levi managed.

Ronnie shook his head with a grimace. "We learned CPR in health class, and you are definitely doing it wrong."

He reached for the glass of water he'd left on the counter and turned to leave.

Levi and Daisy stared after him, Daisy blinking stupidly until she turned to Levi, who was sitting on the floor beside her. His wide-eyed stare must have matched hers, and all at once, the reality of what just happened hit her.

She clapped a hand over her mouth, but there was no point trying to stop the burst of laughter that came bubbling out of her. Half a second later, Levi's shocked expression vanished and he was laughing too.

"We're doing CPR wrong." He chuckled the words rather than spoke them.

This set Daisy off all over again, and she watched his beautiful face light with laughter as he joined her.

The sound was even better than she'd expected. It was loud and rumbly, and when he leaned over and pulled her into his arms, they shook together as the laughs kept coming. When he buried his face in her neck and his beard brushed her sensitive skin, she felt a thrill race through her, but she couldn't stop clinging to him as they laughed like children on the floor.

They'd just pulled apart and Daisy was swiping tears out of her eyes when Mikayla arrived in the doorway. She gave them a look of disgust that had Daisy stifling laughter all over again. "What are you guys laughing about?"

Levi took a deep breath beside her, but Daisy quickly

said, "I slipped on some dish soap and fell, and then your dad fell too, and..." She exhaled loudly and waved a dismissive hand. "It was just really funny."

Mikayla arched a brow and then shrugged as if to say, "If you say so." But it was Levi's reaction to her lie that caught her off guard. He looked surprised and maybe...disappointed.

Her belly sank in response.

She turned to Levi when Mikayla walked out. "I figured you wouldn't want Mikayla to know we were making out on the kitchen floor."

"No, yeah, I..." He ran a hand over his beard and gave his head a little shake. "You're right. I just... I try not to lie to my kids."

Her insides took another dive. He wasn't chiding her. He wasn't angry in the slightest, but her own conscience nagged.

When had lying become so easy?

When had it become her default?

These past few weeks, the lies in response to her sisters' questions had gotten more and more elaborate.

She'd been ignoring the underlying guilt, but that flicker of disappointment in Levi's eyes had it all crashing in at once.

"You're right, I shouldn't have lied," she murmured.

He got to his feet and reached a hand down to help her up. "Honestly, I had no response handy, so..." He shrugged. "Maybe lying was for the best. I don't know how to explain...this." He was still holding her hand, and he gave a little tug to pull her closer.

This.

What was...this?

The thought made her belly flip and her heart race. She fidgeted, pulling her hand from his.

She didn't know what this was, and she didn't want to know what he thought. Not right now, at least. Her lips were still tingling from that kiss, and her insides turned to molten lava when he wrapped an arm around her waist to keep her close.

It was just a kiss. And there was no reason to worry about the future—not when she had a hot sheriff holding her close and looking at her like she hung the moon.

She swallowed hard in the face of his adoration. There was nothing guarded about it. No pretenses and no facades. Just a genuine, serious, good-hearted man gazing down at her with affection so warm, sweet, and pure that she felt it flood through her veins like honey.

Goodness.

She let out a shaky breath.

A girl could get used to this look.

The thought had her pulling back until his arm fell away. "It's getting late."

He nodded, but his gaze was still heavy-lidded and filled with longing. "It is."

She swallowed hard, then licked her lips, torn between giddy excitement and wariness. She wanted to stay…and she didn't.

If she stayed, they'd have to talk. She'd have to think this through.

She took another step back. Tonight had been so perfect; she wasn't about to ruin it by overthinking matters.

"I should go." She headed toward the door, but he was close behind her. She poked her head into the living room, and her heart gave another weird little kick at the sight of the three Baker kids, strewn over the furniture with their noses buried in schoolwork.

"Bye, Daisy!" they all called out to her, and she was still grinning when they reached the front door.

"Do you need a ride home?" Levi asked. "I can leave the kids for a little while—"

"No." She'd said it too quickly, but as much as she wanted to be alone with him, she needed space more. "I've got my little bug."

"Of course you do." He looked so disappointed by this simple fact that she gave him a quick kiss on the cheek.

"I wish you could stick around longer," he murmured, wrapping his arm around her waist and keeping her close. "But I get it. It's getting late."

Her heart clenched at the sad flicker in his eyes, and she heard Dahlia's voice loud as day in her ears. *You run before they can catch you.*

Daisy gently stepped back, and his arms dropped away. She shuffled a little farther and ended up tripping over the doorway. Levi caught her by her elbow and steadied her. His smile was small, and sweet, and…oh goodness, it made him look more handsome than ever.

"You okay?" His voice was low and gruff, and concern darkened his gaze even further.

She forced a bright smile. "Of course I am."

His gaze met hers and held, and…there it was again. A draw as real as gravity, making her breathing too shallow and her skin too raw. His gaze dipped to her lips, and she swallowed hard, butterflies bursting into flight in her belly.

She'd never felt like this, not even as a teenager with her very first kiss.

He leaned in close, and the rest of the world seemed to

fade away. "Thanks for staying for dinner. Thanks for…everything."

She smiled, and before she could stop herself, she was giving in to temptation and touching the scruff of his beard. His answering smile as he caught her hand and held it to his jaw made her insides melt.

What was he saying? Oh right. The fact that she'd stayed. That she'd had a family dinner with him and his kids.

"It was fun," she whispered.

That's all this is, right? Just fun.

Yes. That's all it can ever be.

Oblivious to her turmoil, Levi pulled her close again, his gaze raking over her face like he was trying to drink her in. The look in his eyes made her feel beautiful. "It was definitely fun," he murmured, and then his lips were touching hers once more.

The kiss was slow and sweet.

She sank into on a sigh, but didn't try to deepen it.

The kids were just in the other room.

Cutting it short, she took a deep breath as she reluctantly backed away. "I better get going."

"Text me when you get home. Or call." His grin was so hopeful and sweet. "I just want to make sure you get home safe."

How adorable was he?

She gave him a mock salute. "Yes, Sheriff."

He grinned, and the sight nearly knocked her over. "Good night, Daisy."

She spun on the doorstep and practically skipped to her car. In spite of all her silent warnings and doubts, she couldn't deny the bubbles bursting inside her. Kissing Levi was the best!

With a smile so wide it made her cheeks ache, she pumped up the volume on her car stereo and sang her way home. She wasn't sure she'd ever felt this giddy.

CHAPTER 29

I t was a beautiful spring Sunday, and it seemed as though half the congregation lingered outside to soak in the sunshine and make small talk before the service began.

Ronnie stopped in front of the church and turned back to Levi. "Dad, are you coming?"

Levi blinked. "Right behind you."

He'd been caught scanning the crowd…again. He couldn't seem to help himself from seeking out a certain blonde with wild, loose waves and a brilliant smile. But he didn't see her, just like he hadn't caught sight of her in town since she'd left his house Thursday night.

He could have called her, of course.

And said what?

That was what had stopped him every time he'd pulled his phone out with the intention to call.

She'd texted him to say she was home safe, just like he'd asked her to, and he'd sent back a thumbs-up and then a sleeping emoji.

Since then, they'd had no communication, and he couldn't stop obsessing over it.

The only reason he'd used an emoji was because her text had been peppered with them. But did she think it was stupid that he'd used them too?

Maybe she'd been wanting more than a thumbs-up. A love heart, maybe.

But that felt too soon.

Every time he went to pick up his phone to start a conversation, his brain dried up like the Salt Flats, and he didn't know what to say.

I want to see you again.

That was the truth, but it felt like he'd be saying too much with that simple statement.

Did he want to see her again?

Yes. Desperately, if he were being honest.

He hadn't been able to stop thinking of her, or that kiss, for days.

But what was he really looking for?

More make-out sessions that had his mind turning to mush? Or something more?

It wasn't like he was looking for a new relationship. And he was a father of three, so he was in no position to have some casual fling. He'd never done casual in his life, even before he'd had kids. But she wasn't even planning on staying in town.

Was she? He hadn't heard her talk about leaving again recently...

An unbidden flicker of hope sparked as he searched for her among the crowd within the church. But instead his gaze caught on Helen and her husband, who waved from the far side.

The sight of Beth's sister made guilt rise up hard and swift as he waved back.

What was he doing even thinking about another woman, let alone wondering what sort of future they might have?

Helen beckoned them over, but at the same time, Dawson pointed to the middle pews. "Hey, look, there's Dr. Dex and Rose."

He saw his friends smiling and waving, and he steered the boys in their direction with Mikayla trailing behind them. Ethan sat on the far side of Dex and gave Levi and the family a wave as Levi slid into the pew beside Rose, his kids filling in after him.

"How're you feeling?" He kissed her cheek and noted the way her hand rested on her basketball belly.

Her smile was sweet, and it was similar enough to Daisy's that it sent him thinking about her all over again.

"I'm fine." She wriggled on the pew, trying to get comfortable. Because she was so petite, her belly seemed to take up most of her body as she squirmed. "I can't believe I still have another five weeks to go."

Dex leaned forward and grinned. "I made the ob-gyn double-check it wasn't twins."

Rose giggled as she smacked his arm. "Not funny and you know it."

He kissed the side of her head as he wrapped an arm around her shoulders, easing her weight against his. "Better?"

She snuggled up to him with an adoring smile. "Much."

Levi watched the happy couple, his chest giving a little tug of yearning. It had been years since he'd had that sort of intimacy in his life. He'd changed so much these past few years that sometimes it felt like another lifetime when he was that contented family man with no cares except for maybe which family they'd spend the holidays with.

He found himself thinking about those days with a sense of nostalgia. What would Beth think about him kissing another woman?

It was a thought he'd been grappling with for days now, and it never got any easier. Logically he knew he wasn't cheating on his wife. When he thought it over, he could even admit that Beth would want him to move on and find love again.

But it was one thing to think it and another to relinquish these deep-seated feelings of doubt and guilt. He couldn't shake the sense that it would be a betrayal to be happy again. To find love again.

He swallowed hard as he scanned the crowd. That wasn't what this was...was it?

He couldn't be falling in love with the fly-by-night hippie who had no plans for the future...could he?

He ran a hand over his beard and shushed the boys when they got too loud. Mikayla was on her phone—a fact he'd have to remedy. But until the service started, he didn't see the harm.

Ethan leaned forward to talk to him over Dex and Rose. "We haven't seen much of you lately, man. Where've you been hiding?"

He smiled. "Oh, you know, busy at work and with the kids."

Dex shook his head. "You need to get out more."

"Says the man who's always on call." Rose rolled her eyes.

All three men chuckled at that. Levi supposed one of the reasons they were all such good friends was that they were all dedicated to their jobs, and all of their jobs involved helping others. But Rose had a point. Dex was just as committed to his patients as Levi was to this community.

Yet another reminder of why he shouldn't be letting himself lose his head over a woman who would most likely be gone soon. He wasn't about to leave this town, so if he was going to move on, it ought to be with someone who wanted to be here.

And yet, even as he thought it, his gaze was seeking Daisy out again, and his heart was yearning for that smile.

He shook his head. Maybe he did need a night out with his friends. Maybe they could help him make sense of these confusing emotions and the battle currently going on between his head and his heart.

What he needed was guidance. His gaze moved to the front of the church where the minister was preparing. Clasping his hands in his lap, he found himself pouring out all his confusion and his troubles. He silently prayed to God, and then he was talking to Beth. It was a hard habit to break. He'd never stopped talking to her, even after she'd died, and whenever he felt lost or lonely, she seemed his first port of call.

Right now, he wasn't sure what to think or feel, and he had no idea how to act.

His kids came first, that much he knew. Would they be hurt if they got close to Daisy only to have her leave? Would Beth be angry or happy to know that he'd started to have feelings for another woman? He had so many questions, and nowhere else to turn.

Beth, if you're able to hear me, if you're watching over us the way I think you are…please give me a sign. Let me know if I'm right to follow my heart or if—

"Dad," Ronnie hissed.

Levi's eyes flew open.

"Dawson won't share his gum," he complained.

Levi sighed. So much for signs and answered prayers. He had three kids to look after, and that was all that mattered.

The service started just as Dawson reluctantly passed a piece of gum to his little brother, and for a while, Levi's attention was absorbed on the sermon...and keeping his kids quiet throughout the service.

When it came to an end and the congregation started to file out, Levi finally spotted her.

"Dad, there's Daisy!" Ronnie shouted.

"I see that, buddy."

Levi couldn't bring himself to look away. She was a vision in a pale pink sundress, her hair loose and curling around her shoulders. Her lips matched her dress as she smiled and chatted with Emma and Nash, who were walking beside her.

"I'm gonna say hi." Ronnie bolted off to greet her.

As he watched, Daisy lit up at the sight of his youngest son and dropped down to her knees without a second thought to open her arms wide and catch the little boy who hurtled toward her.

She squeezed her eyes shut, a huge smile on her face as she hugged him.

And that was it. Levi's heart skipped and thudded so hard and loud he was sure the whole church must be able to hear it. And that was when he knew.

Whether it was right or not, whether it made sense or not...

He was falling hard and fast for Daisy O'Sullivan.

CHAPTER 30

Daisy looked out the kitchen window to see another car pulling up the drive. She turned to Emma, who was taking leftovers out of the fridge. Or rather, Emma was trying to, but Nash had his arms around her and was whispering in her ear, making her giggle.

"Okay, you two." Daisy feigned exasperation. "You've had your honeymoon, and the rest can wait. Apparently we're feeding half the town lunch."

Nash chuckled as he let Emma go. "Pretty sure Emma invited the entire congregation."

Lizzy walked in with Kit and the twins, who raced past them to get outside where the other kids were already playing.

"An impromptu party." Lizzy grinned. "I love it."

Kit came over to stand beside Daisy. "Any word from Dahlia yet?"

Daisy glanced at her phone. She'd had it on silent for church and never turned the sound back on. Some days it was just easier to avoid her phone than to deal with the ever-increasing number of texts and missed calls from the Los Angeles number.

There was one from Dahlia, but in true Dahlia fashion, it was just the facts. "She said their flight is on time, and they'll be back—" She glanced at the clock. "—any minute now."

Lizzy lifted her left hand and wiggled her ring finger. "And hopefully sporting a new accessory!"

Daisy's mouth gaped as she looked from Emma to Lizzy and back again. They were sharing a mischievous little grin, and Daisy burst out laughing. "Wait a second, is that what today's party is all about? Is this an engagement party?"

"Shhh." Rose shushed her from the doorway as she walked in—or rather, waddled in, with Dex at her side. "We're not calling it that."

Dex chuckled. "There's still a chance Dahlia said no."

Lizzy snorted. "No way. Dahlia's a smitten kitten. I've never seen anyone more in love."

Kit cleared his throat, and Lizzy laughed, going up on tiptoe to kiss his cheek. "Except for me. Obviously."

He grinned down at her. "Obviously."

Dex had a supportive hand on Rose's lower back as he helped her ease down into one of the kitchen table chairs. "I don't think there's much doubt what her answer was, but it would be pretty awkward if they showed up today and we all shouted 'congratulations!' only to find that there's nothing to celebrate."

Daisy laughed at the image. "Okay, so everyone you invited…"

"Thinks we're just hosting an impromptu after-church brunch." Emma's grin was so impish Daisy had to laugh again.

"A devious Emma." She wiggled her eyebrows. "I like it."

Nash nodded, narrowing his eyes at Emma as if giving it serious thought. "Devious looks good on you."

"Right?" Lizzy pointed at her sister. "I've been telling people for years she's not as angelic as she appears." She arched her brows. "And now you all see what I'm talking about."

Rose went along with Lizzy's teasing, tsking as she shook her head. "Really, Emma. I never thought you could be so sneaky."

Emma laughed. "Okay, cut it out, you guys. Dahlia and JJ will be back here any minute, and we've got a ton of people to feed in the meantime."

"Yes, ma'am." Kit gave her a little salute. "What can I do to help?"

Soon Emma was doling out chores, and all the sisters and their husbands were scattering to do as they were told. Daisy included. Although, she was still kicking herself for not finding a way to ask Emma if she'd invited Levi and his family.

If she had, maybe she wouldn't be lingering over setting up lawn chairs as she scoped out the crowd gathering around the grill. Why hadn't she just asked? For the first time ever, she'd felt...shy. Which was weird, and not at all like her.

Her gaze scanned Nash's family and Kit's parents, and then over to Cody, who was chasing the twins around the yard.

When she spotted Levi coming around the side of the house, his three kids trailing him, her heart did the cha-cha in her chest, and butterflies swarmed in her belly.

She let out a breathless laugh when his gaze met hers and he smiled.

Goodness, that smile.

Giddiness swept over her, and for a second, she forgot entirely about the lawn chairs she was supposed to be setting up while she stood there and grinned like a dope as he walked toward her.

"Need a hand?" he murmured.

She blinked, and then she realized he was looking at the chairs she still held in her hand. "Oh. Yes. Thank you."

She let him take over as each of the Baker kids said hello and gave her a hug. Her heart felt soft and squishy at seeing them here.

"Where's the couple of the hour?" Levi asked.

She laughed. "So you figured out what this party is really about?"

He shrugged, amusement softening his features and making him look younger. "JJ and I are friends. Let's just say he had some questions about how to figure out a lady's ring size."

"Ahhh, and the sheriff came to his rescue," she teased.

To her surprise and delight, he leaned in close and dropped his voice low, a smile playing over his lips. "All in a day's work, ma'am."

She gasped. "You made a joke! About your job!"

He laughed, and she could have sworn she felt the low rumble in her belly. "Don't think I'll make a habit of it."

She grinned up at him, and she couldn't resist leaning in until their arms brushed. Even that slight contact stole her breath and left her light-headed.

"I haven't seen you in town the last couple days." His gaze was searching, and her belly did a weird little wobble.

Had he been missing her too? It'd taken every ounce of willpower not to call or text him like some lovesick teen. But she hadn't because…

Well, because this was Levi. The sheriff. The father of three.

They'd shared a fun kiss, that was all.

Her gaze dipped to his mouth, and there was that pull again. Stronger than gravity, it seemed to draw her toward him. And why resist?

He knew she was leaving. She knew she was leaving…

But there was no law saying they couldn't have some fun in the meantime, right?

"What are you thinking about, Miss Daisy?" he teased.

No…he *flirted*.

She swallowed hard against another giddy wave of delight that stole her breath. A serious, stern Levi was too tempting by far, but a flirty, teasing, happy Levi?

Be still my beating heart.

She clamped her lips together to stifle a girly giggle, and when he arched one brow, she shook her head. What was she thinking? Nothing she could say aloud right here and now, that was for sure.

She took a step back, suddenly all too aware that his kids and half the town could be watching them. "Thanks for your help with the chairs, Sheriff."

He opened his mouth to respond but was cut off by someone shouting, "They're here! Let's get ready to celebrate!"

So much for this being a secret engagement party.

Daisy backed away. "I should be there to greet my sister…"

He nodded, and once again he opened his mouth as if to speak and shut it as if rethinking what he'd been about to say. Then, with a sexy, lopsided smile, he murmured, "I'll see you around?"

She nodded, her heart tripping over itself with giddy excitement. "Definitely."

Daisy slipped through the crowd and in the back door to the kitchen, which was already packed with her family. There was a blockade of bodies keeping her back, and she had to muscle her way through.

"Well?" she demanded as soon as she reached her sister's side.

A radiant Dahlia grinned at her as she lifted her hand to show off her engagement ring. "It's official!"

"I'm making an honest woman of her," JJ said from where he stood, leaning against the counter. His arms were crossed, and his grin was smug, and there was nothing but love in his gaze as he watched Dahlia hug Emma, Lizzy, Rose, and then finally Daisy.

"I'm so happy for you, Dee," Daisy whispered.

A wave of emotion hit her hard as Dahlia squeezed her.

"You deserve this." She hoped Dahlia knew what she meant, because she didn't know how to put it into words. "After all you've done for us...all you've given up...you deserve all the happiness in the world."

Dahlia's eyes were swimming with tears when Daisy pulled back. But Dahlia caught her hand and tugged her back in so she could whisper, "You deserve it, too, you know."

Daisy's chest and throat grew so tight she could barely breathe.

"We all do," Dahlia added.

Daisy nodded, forcing a watery smile as she backed away and let the others bombard her with questions about how JJ proposed and their thoughts on the wedding. But Daisy felt too off-kilter to add much.

She'd get all the details out of Dahlia when there weren't so many people around.

"I sure hope you're ready to celebrate," Lizzy warned Dahlia as the group in the kitchen headed out toward the backyard.

"Why?" Dahlia's eyebrows dipped into a frown as she tried to figure out what everyone was up to.

"Welcome home!"

Even from where she trailed behind in the kitchen, Daisy could hear Dahlia's gasp of surprise as the crowd out back cheered and raised their glasses.

"She said yes!" JJ boomed.

The applause and hoots and hollers were deafening, and Daisy laughed so hard that the tears she'd been fighting trailed down her cheeks. She swiped them away. Now was not the time to figure out why Dahlia's words had cut so deep. Now was the time...

She caught sight of Levi stepping inside, shepherding Ronnie toward the hallway leading to the bathroom.

Now was the time to have some fun.

She waited until Ronnie was back outside with his siblings, and then she snagged Levi's hand.

"Daisy." He laughed. "Where are we going?"

She pulled him into the little home office that no one ever used now that Dahlia worked in the ranch's office, and then she turned to Levi with wide, innocent eyes. "Why...fancy meeting you here, Sheriff."

He laughed as he tugged on her hand, sending her tumbling into his arms. She held her breath as he gazed down at her. The soft, warm heat in his eyes made her feel like she was melting. Had anyone ever looked at her like this? Like she was a treasure to be cherished? Like she was something more than fun, pretty Daisy? Something...special.

That look wrapped around her just as surely as his arms tightened their hold at her waist and he leaned his head down.

Her heart slammed against her rib cage when his lips touched hers, softly at first, but then the kiss deepened. His lips were hot and firm as he kissed her more thoroughly, more hungrily, more passionately than anyone had ever kissed her before.

She found herself clinging to his shoulders, pressing closer to his strong chest, trying and failing to keep some sort of control over her wild emotions as he deepened the kiss even further.

But it was no use fighting it. His kiss was magic, making her feel warm and safe, cherished and protected, and a yearning she couldn't quite name. It left her chest feeling just as achy and needy as the rest of her even as his heat filled her senses, making her limbs heavy and her blood flow hot and slow as molten lava.

When he pulled back for air, he chuckled softly into her still-open mouth. "What are we doing?"

He didn't sound upset, just...baffled.

She laughed as well, and he spun her around until he had her pinned against the wall.

"I don't know, but it sure is fun." She grinned.

He laughed again before kissing her hard. "We could be caught..."

She smiled against his lips, wrapping her arms tightly around his neck. "Isn't that half the fun?" She didn't wait for an answer. "Besides, I don't want to see you walking away. Although, you do have a very nice butt." She wiggled her eyebrows.

His growl sent a shiver down her spine. "I couldn't walk away if I wanted to."

Me neither. She swallowed the words because even thinking them gave her a little start. They were just teasing. Flirting. This was all just for fun.

She relaxed into his embrace as his lips found hers once more, and this time the kiss was slow and leisurely as they explored one another, tasting and teasing each other as their hands explored and the heat between them grew.

Once again, Daisy felt like she was drowning in this man, and in the pleasure he made her feel. Her mind was pleasantly blank, that underlying hum of anxiety and fear she was so used to ceasing to exist for a moment. Those ugly emotions didn't stand a chance when this strong, warm, fierce man was holding her like this.

Like he'd never let her go.

She jerked back with a start.

His brows arched. "Daisy?"

But then they both heard it. Someone heading down the hallway. She started to laugh, and then he was laughing too. And she forgot all her cares as his arms held her even tighter and they shook with quiet laughter together.

"We've gotta stop meeting like this," he snickered.

She clamped a hand over her mouth to stifle a loud laugh. When the person passing in the hallway moved along, he took her hand and led her back out. She fixed her hair as he scoped out the hallway.

"All clear?" she teased.

He winked. "All clear."

Together they slipped back into the crowd of well-wishers outside, and Daisy had fun talking and laughing with all the guests and her sisters. But every so often, she'd find Levi watching her from across the yard or from the other side of the table, and every time their gazes connected, her heart went *boom*.

CHAPTER 31

L evi was grateful he was alone in his patrol car when he got Daisy's text.

Daisy: *Where are youuuuuu?*

He let out a huff of laughter, and he couldn't have stopped his foolish grin if he'd tried. He glanced around, smoothing a hand over his beard, but no one in the parking lot of the sheriff's station was looking his way.

He ducked his head and typed back quickly. "Be home soon. Stay for dinner?"

She texted back instantly.

Daisy: *Of course. We already started cooking.*

. . .

She sent back a picture. It was a selfie of her, Mikayla, and the boys pretending to throw food at the camera. Each one of them was sticking out their tongue or making a funny face.

His head fell back with a loud laugh. Man, he couldn't wait to get home. He started to type back "miss you" and stopped himself.

First of all, one of his kids might see. Second, he just saw her the other night when she stayed well after dinner, and long after the kids went to bed. They'd whispered and giggled like teenagers not wanting to get busted by their parents as they watched a movie together.

It'd been three weeks since he first kissed her in the kitchen, and the time had flown by in a whirlwind of fun.

He hesitated with his fingers over the phone screen before slipping it away in his pocket.

He'd talk to her later.

He grinned. He'd also kiss her later. Much later. He'd have to wait until the kids were asleep. He frowned as he pulled out of the parking lot. It really was time they told the kids they were dating. It wasn't just the occasional kiss; it was late-night calls and flirty texts all throughout the day...

He'd even taken a long lunch break last week so he could take Daisy on a picnic.

A picnic! They'd had more fun than he'd had in forever, basking in the sunshine, eating grapes and chicken sandwiches, then making out like teenagers. Surely a picnic meant they were dating and not just a casual fling, right? Which meant they really ought to stop hiding it.

But then again, every time he mentioned their relationship status or where this was heading, Daisy deftly distracted him.

Usually with kisses or wandering fingers that curled into his hair and made his insides turn to cooked spaghetti.

He tapped his thumb against the wheel and ordered himself not to overthink it. They were having fun, that was all. No one had made any promises. No one would get hurt.

He just wasn't used to casual, that was all. It made him antsy.

His thoughts were interrupted by the sight of Cody on the side of the road. He flagged Levi down, but Levi was already pulling over.

"Howdy, Sheriff." Cody waved at him. The ranch hand shared his brother's grin. It was one he'd heard the female deputies call charming and "swoonworthy," whatever that meant.

Cody took off his cowboy hat and ran a hand through his shaggy light brown hair. "I got myself a flat."

"I see that." Levi nodded. "Need a hand?"

Cody smiled again. "I wouldn't say no."

As they worked, they chatted about local gossip and what was going on at the O'Sullivan Ranch.

"You mean the love ranch?" Cody snickered.

Levi chuckled. "Is that what we're calling it?"

Cody shook his head, but he was still smiling that easygoing grin. "I'm happy for all of 'em, I really am. But man, a guy could get nauseous with all the lovey-dovey looks and canoodling going on up there."

"Canoodling, huh?" Levi laughed at the old-fashioned term.

"JJ's so far gone he's getting forgetful on me," Cody continued. "That's why I'm heading into town. He forgot a part yesterday."

Levi winced. "Doesn't sound like him."

"It's not. But I guess falling for a woman has a way of messing with your head."

Levi dipped his head, a smile forming against his will. He couldn't help it. He couldn't think of Daisy without turning into a lovesick fool.

"Well, I know you know what that feels like."

Levi's head snapped up. How did Cody know about him and Daisy?

"You and Beth sure had something special," he continued.

Levi's heart took a plummet, and for a second, he felt like cold water had just been thrown over his head. Cody was talking about Beth.

Of course he was.

Guilt and shame wreaked havoc on his insides, but Cody didn't seem to notice.

The cowboy shook his head with an exasperated sigh. "I'm not one to judge, I guess. I've never been in a real relationship. Heck, I've never even fallen for a woman…" His grin turned impish. "Except for your wife."

Levi straightened with a start, and Cody laughed. "She used to babysit me when I was a kid, you know."

Levi nodded. "Yeah, that sounds familiar."

It made sense. Cody was in his early thirties, and Beth would have been a good eight or nine years older, like Levi was.

He winced. He was pretty sure Daisy was younger than Cody, which meant he was a decade older than her.

Did that matter?

It didn't feel like it when they were together, but maybe he wasn't thinking clearly.

No, there was no maybe about it. When it came to Daisy he definitely wasn't thinking clearly.

"But then she came back from college with some sheriff," Cody teased. "And I was heartbroken."

Levi chuckled at Cody's pout as they finished with the tire.

"That should do it."

"Thanks for the assist, Sheriff." Cody lightly slapped his shoulder.

Levi waved goodbye and ambled back to his squad car. He was so caught up in thoughts of Beth, of Daisy, of how his kids would react if they knew he was making out with Mikayla's music tutor, that he actually jolted when a car zipped past him—way too fast. He jumped behind the wheel and set his siren going, studying the California license plates as he pulled the car over.

He didn't love reckless drivers, but at least it was a distraction from his troubled thoughts.

The man behind the wheel had a tough, city look about him. It set Levi on edge the moment he reached the open window. He'd always had naturally strong gut instincts, and something about this guy just didn't sit right.

"There a problem, Officer?"

"It's Sheriff," he shot back. "Do you know how fast you were going?"

The man looked at the dashboard, then shrugged.

"Twenty miles over the limit, and you're getting mighty close to Main Street. We have a lot of children and families in this place. People around here respect that."

The guy's jaw clenched, and he sniffed, staring out the windshield.

Levi sighed. "License and registration, please."

The man handed it over, and Levi noticed out of the corner of his eye the way the man shuffled in his seat and tapped the steering wheel.

Derek Knox.

Levi read the name, then eyed the guy up again. He had dark shadows under his eyes and scruffy whiskers that needed shaving. Was he growing a beard or just plain lazy?

Derek gave Levi a tight smile that didn't reach his eyes.

Yep, he was definitely not the warm tourist type they usually had passing through here. "You staying in town or just driving through?"

"Hoping to stay." The man nodded, then scratched his chin. "Don't look so worried, Officer. I'm not planning on being here any longer than I have to."

Levi kept a blank expression, not wanting to give away that he was either concerned or offended by the man's derisive tone. If he didn't like Aspire, why the heck was he visiting it?

"What brings you to town, Mr. Knox?"

"Unfinished business." He sniffed and tapped his thumb on the wheel again. "I'm gonna need a place to crash tonight. Know somewhere?"

Levi nodded and gave him directions to the town's most popular motel as he wrote up the ticket.

The man smirked when he snagged the ticket. "Thanks for the welcome, Officer."

"It's Sheriff."

The man snickered. "See you around, *Sheriff.*"

Levi watched as he drove off, making a mental note of the car's make and model, and the license plate.

Those sarcastic quips at the end were just plain rude. They riled him. Anyone who didn't respect the uniform was someone he'd have to keep a very close eye on.

CHAPTER 32

Daisy pointed a finger and ordered all the kids out of the kitchen. "All right, you little hooligans. Get to work!"

They giggled as they filed toward the kitchen door, back to the living room where their homework was waiting. "Hey, Mikayla…"

The girl turned with an expectant look.

"Great work today."

Mikayla beamed. "Thanks, Daisy."

She bounded out after her brothers, and Daisy pulled out her phone for the tenth time in as many minutes, a dopey smile already forming. But alas, no text back…yet.

Levi always replied eventually, though. He was reliable like that. Just like he was reliable with his kids, and in calling her when he said he would, and making sure she got home okay every time she left him.

The sigh that escaped was undeniably sappy. All these years she'd happily dated men who were just as flakey and noncommittal as she was, but these days she was starting to see the merit in dating a man who wasn't all talk.

She headed to the sink to wash her hands before prepping some food for dinner. She'd gotten way more comfortable in this kitchen over the past month. Cooking with Levi, sharing dinners with him and his kids, it was starting to feel almost...normal.

No, better than normal. It felt...right.

She dipped her head with a smile and was about to tuck the phone back in her pocket when it dinged again. It wasn't Levi's face that popped up, so she found herself holding her breath. Something she did often now that the debt collector's text had gotten more threatening. But it wasn't another threat, and she let her breath out with a rush of relief.

And then when she actually read the text, she let out a little whoop of excitement before clapping a hand over her mouth and reading it again. It was from one of her contacts in New York. He had a gig lined up. Hope surged through her. If it paid well enough, maybe she could pay back enough to keep them at bay...

Another text came in right after.

LEO: I have a steady gig coming up soon too. Let me know when you get here and we'll discuss.

She laughed aloud. This was too good to be true! Playing at Leo's bar on a steady basis would bring in a truckload of money. She'd be debt-free in no time, and then she could start rebuilding again.

This was working out perfectly.

She started to text him back and then stopped. Her fingers hovered over the phone.

She knew exactly what she meant to type.

But she couldn't do it.

Something was making her hesitate. Her insides were sinking with disappointment even as she reveled in the win.

Her brows drew together in confusion as she tried to make sense of these mixed emotions. This was what she wanted. So why was she hesitating?

Levi's voice from the doorway had her spinning around. "Just when I think you can't get any more beautiful…"

She grinned, glancing down at the black hoodie she'd borrowed from Mikayla and the scarf turned weapons belt. "Ronnie wanted to play ninjas."

He chuckled as he reached for her, and when Daisy fell into his arms, she felt herself melt against him. Every time, it was like this. The moment he was near, she felt like she could breathe easier, and just…be herself.

He kissed her lightly. "I missed you."

Her heart melted even as her blood heated and her body came alive at the feel of his lips brushing over her cheek and neck. He'd missed her.

"Thank goodness." She sighed as she wrapped her arms around his neck.

He chuckled. "You want me missing you?"

"Well, yeah." Her tone said "duh." "It would be weird if I was the only one."

He growled as he pulled her in closer and nuzzled her neck, making her giggle.

But they broke apart quickly at the sound of Dawson

shouting at Ronnie in the other room. They met each other's amused gazes and burst out laughing.

"Maybe it's time to tell them," he murmured.

She laughed and turned away, avoiding answering just like she did every time he brought it up. Truthfully, she liked keeping it a secret—from the kids and her sisters and everyone else. It meant there were no questions. No expectations. No commitments.

His arms wrapped around her from behind as she started slicing carrots into sticks. "No comment?"

His voice was tinged with laughter, and she smiled. "No comment."

More words filled her mouth and made her fidget with unease.

I got a text today…

There's a gig in New York… possibly something long-term.

What would he say? Would he be happy for her? Would he be sad? Would he tell her to go or ask her to stay? The biggest question was, what did she want him to say?

She didn't know. And so she kept her mouth shut, frowning as she kept chopping the vegetables in silence.

The silence didn't last long, however, because soon enough the kids were coming in to set the table and dinner was being served, and the now-familiar chaos of a Baker family dinner caught her up and kept her pleasantly distracted for the next hour.

After dinner, Dawson begged her to stay because he'd just discovered they could do karaoke on his PlayStation, and he wanted Daisy to sing with them.

"Well, I can't refuse that," she'd said with a grin.

Hours passed with so many laughs, Daisy's face hurt from smiling so much. For the first half hour or so, Levi had sat on the couch and watched with an indulgent grin as she and the kids performed for him—sometimes duets, sometimes solos, and always combined with dance moves that had them all cracking up.

Mikayla nearly brought her dad to tears when she belted out a power ballad and showed off the full extent of her talent.

Heck, Daisy was nearly in tears too. Pride burst through her as if Mikayla was her own daughter.

And then Ronnie and Dawson had them all in stitches as they attempted to rap.

But the best part of all was when Daisy reached for Levi's hand and tugged. She didn't think he'd cave, but after some grumbling and a whole lot of pleading, he finally gave in to Daisy and the kids' persuasion and sang a song.

His voice wasn't perfect, but the sound of his low, rumbly timbre had her heart aching and flipping and twirling and dancing. By the time he was done and he gave her a shy smile, she wasn't sure if she was going to cry, melt, or laugh.

She ended up doing a little of each, throwing her arms around his neck as she whispered, "Nice work, Sheriff."

Eventually the kids' bedtime came around, and Daisy made some excuse about sticking around to clean up while Levi led them through the nighttime routine and got them settled.

He found her finishing up the dishes and silently took her by the hand and led her to the couch. She curled up in his arms, tipping her head back for a long, slow, sweet kiss that made her toes curl.

"I've been waiting to do that all day," he murmured against her lips.

"Mmm, me too."

He shifted her so she was flush against his side.

"You sounded really good tonight." Daisy snuggled up against him. "How come you never told me you could sing?"

He chuckled. "I can't. Not as good as you, at least. Or Beth."

His expression got that sad look it always got when he mentioned his wife. There were probably some women out there who'd find it hard to be dating a man who was still in love with his deceased wife, but it only made Daisy feel more protective of him.

This was a man who didn't guard his heart, and he didn't do anything halfway, least of all love.

And she adored that about him. It was what made him so incredibly special.

"I wish I could have met her," she whispered.

His brows arched in surprise, and she shrugged. "What? It's true. From all I hear about her from you and the kids, Beth sounds amazing."

"She was." His smile was small and sweet. "She would have liked you."

Daisy's chest ached. Would she?

She wasn't sure.

If she could see them now, would Beth be happy that her good, upstanding husband was having a fling with a nomadic vagabond like her? They might both have a nice singing voice, but Daisy suspected that was where the similarities ended. Beth sounded more like Emma than Daisy. She'd been a natural caretaker, and just as responsible and committed as Levi. "I'm sure I would have liked her too."

He gave her another little smile as he squeezed her

shoulders, and then he lightened the tone. "But you were the real star tonight." He nodded toward the PlayStation. "I always knew you were amazing, but tonight…" He shook his head. "You are incredible, Daisy O'Sullivan."

She laughed, but it sounded breathless because that smile and the look in his eyes were doing funny things to her chest. "I'm not."

"But your voice and your ear for music and—"

"But that's all I have. It's literally all I can do," she admitted, her tone rueful. "It's the only thing I'm good at. I mean—" She threw her arm up. "—look at me. I'm homeless and jobless and—" *In debt up to my eyeballs.*

She swallowed the thick choking sensation. Keeping secrets from Levi was getting harder and harder. Every time he held her like this, she had this crazy urge to spill her guts. To tell him all her problems and wait for him to murmur that everything would be okay. His soft, grumbly voice would wrap around her bringing comfort and relief.

She pulled back in his arms a little, her heart suddenly giving a kick of alarm. Let a man solve all her problems? That was the sort of toxic relationship her mother had. That was exactly what she didn't want. Daisy had never relied on a man and she wasn't about to start now.

"Hey…" Levi's grip was gentle but firm as he caught her chin and turned her face toward his. "You okay?"

She nodded and tried for a smile. "Yeah. Of course."

His gaze was troubled. "It's your band, isn't it?"

"What?" She blinked in surprise.

His lips quirked up on one side. "You miss your band, right?"

Her breath escaped in a sharp exhale, and she couldn't quite bring herself to say yes. In all honesty, she hadn't given much thought to her band these past few weeks. And right now, it felt like another lifetime.

Did she miss music? Yes.

But did she miss the drama with her bandmates? No.

She'd been hurt beyond belief when they'd bailed on her before the album was even over, but if she was being honest…a little part of her was relieved to see them go.

"It's over, Daisy," Brian had said that last day in the studio.

And maybe it had been. Maybe it had been over long before they'd parted but no one had wanted to admit it.

Maybe their little band had run its course.

And maybe her bandmates were right to start fresh with new musicians who wanted the same things they did. Because they hadn't wanted what Daisy wanted, and right now…

Right now Daisy couldn't say *what* she wanted. She wanted music in her life, but did she want to return to the lifestyle she'd left behind? Did she want to go on another tour or play the same songs over and over in a tiny studio?

She wasn't sure. Right now, trying to imagine it just left her feeling exhausted.

Her phone vibrated in her pocket, and that only made her tension ratchet up. It could be the debt collector again. Or it could be her contact in New York…

And for some reason, that felt just as scary.

"Hey, hey…" Levi pulled her into his arms. His broad, muscular chest was so familiar, the strong arms around her so comforting, that for a second, she let herself relax and willed her mind to go blank.

His arms tightened around her, and one of his hands stroked her hair. He started playing with the locks and dropping kisses on the top of her head. "How'd you get into music, anyway?"

She shrugged automatically, the trite answer she always gave on the tip of her tongue, but then she shut her mouth and sat upright. "You Are My Sunshine," she blurted.

He stared at her, looking just as shocked as she'd felt. She never told people the truth. Ever. Not even Dahlia and Rose, though neither of them had ever outright asked. But she couldn't bring herself to lie to Levi about this.

So she cleared her throat and met his gaping stare.

"Why are you staring at me like that?" she asked.

"That song, it's what Beth—" He clamped his mouth shut and shook his head. "Never mind. Go on."

"My dad sang it to me as a kid...I guess." She shrugged. "Honestly, I don't really remember much of him at all. But I remembered that song. And I—" She cleared her throat. Dang, being all honest and serious was harder than it looked. "I guess when I was little, I had this stupid idea that it was a connection or something..." She trailed off with yet another shrug. "It was silly. But I made my grandmother teach me how to pick out the notes on the piano, and then I started playing around with my mom's old guitar. She never used it anymore, so it wasn't like she cared."

Bitterness was creeping into her voice, so she cleared her throat again and aimed for a breezy tone. "Anyway, one day, probably when I was around Mikayla's age, I grew up. Or I thought I was a grown-up, at least."

He gave her a knowing, rueful smile.

"And that was when I realized he wasn't coming back. Obviously. And that there was no magical connection. But by then I'd also figured out that I loved music. It was my escape."

He toyed with her hair again, sifting his fingers through the strands, and it was oddly soothing, helping her tense shoulders to relax. "Escape from what?"

"From our home life," she said simply. "I don't know how much you've heard, but our mother was...not much of a mother." She didn't want to elaborate, and he didn't push.

"I'm sorry."

She shrugged. "Me too." She forced a smile. "But the good news is I got some mad music skills out of it."

He chuckled at her attempt to lighten the mood. "Yes you do. And I'm grateful you're sharing that knowledge with Mikayla."

"Me too. I've loved teaching her." Her smile was no longer forced as she thought of all the progress Mikayla had made in such a short period of time.

The sound of one of the kids moving about upstairs had both of them clamming up as they watched and waited.

Then they heard a flush and the footsteps receded, and they both let out a sigh of relief before sharing a little grin.

She could see it in his eyes, the guilt over not having told his kids yet. And she got it. She did. But with the news about a potential gig still in the back of her mind, she couldn't handle a talk about what to tell the kids.

She didn't even know if there would be anything to tell them. She could be long gone in the very near future.

The thought made her heart ache and her stomach plummet.

"Daisy, are you sure everything's okay? You know you can talk to me if something's bothering you."

She nodded. She did know that. Levi was nothing if not a good listener. He was just as attentive and selfless in conversation as he was with everything else. But this was something she couldn't talk about.

He was the root of her confusion. Because her response to her New York contact should be a no-brainer.

She stood up quickly, feeling the loss of his heat instantly and wrapping her arms around her waist. "I should get going."

He nodded, coming to stand and walk her to the door. Once there, she turned back. She had to go. She knew that, but...she didn't want to.

He pulled her into his arms and gave her a crushing kiss that left her breathless.

"I don't want you to go," he murmured.

She smiled even though her throat grew tight. "I don't want to go either."

But what did that mean? How had it come to this? When had she started falling so hard for Levi that she forgot her priorities?

A shiver raced through her. This was what she'd always avoided. She'd never, ever wanted to compromise her dreams for some man. But right now...

She leaned into him, resting her forehead against his chest and soaking up his warmth and his smell. Right now, he didn't feel like just "some man." He was Levi. Her Levi.

And she didn't want to leave him.

Her breath caught at the thought, her mind reeling.

"I really wish I could ask you to stay." His hands were stroking her arms, and his voice was filled with emotion as he murmured. "Daisy, I—"

He stopped short, and when he didn't continue, she

241

pulled back to meet his gaze, sure he would see all her confusion.

But his brows were furrowed slightly, and his gaze was a little distant…a little lost. His throat worked as he swallowed.

"Yes?" she prompted.

He shook his head and let out a sharp exhale. "Nothing." Forcing a smile, he squeezed her arms before stepping back. "Be safe driving home. And text me when you get there."

She winked. "Yes, Sheriff."

CHAPTER 33

D*aisy, I love you.*
A full day had passed, and Levi was still reeling from what he'd almost done. The words he'd very nearly said.

They'd been on the tip of his tongue, ready to slip right out like it was the most natural thing in the world. He gave his head a shake and then walked into the bar on Main Street where most locals went to watch big games.

Levi was much less interested in seeing tonight's game than he was in seeing his friends, but it was a good excuse to meet up, and with Helen's kids in town and offering to watch Mikayla and the boys, he could slip away to meet Ethan and Dex guilt-free.

They cheered when they saw him walking toward their booth, a plate of fries and a couple beers on the table between them.

"Finally," Dex said when he joined them.

"We haven't seen you in ages." Ethan slapped his shoulder with a grin.

It was nice to know no apologies or explanations were necessary.

"It's been too long," he agreed.

"But you're here now." Dex leaned his elbows on the table. "What are you having? It's on me."

"Oh no, I couldn't—"

"Let him," Ethan interjected. "Our lovesick friend here is going to be out of commission soon enough taking care of a newborn."

"Exactly." Dex's grin said he couldn't wait for sleepless nights and a wailing infant.

And Levi couldn't blame him.

When Dex returned, Ethan leaned forward. "So, aside from work and kids, what's been keeping you so busy, Levi?"

Ethan and Dex exchanged a quick look that Levi didn't miss. He set down his drink with a sigh. "What do you think you know?"

"Nothing." Ethan's eyebrows shot up. "Just..."

Dex shifted in his seat. "Rose might have mentioned that Daisy's been spending quite a bit of time at your house..."

Levi didn't know where to look or how to act. He'd yet to tell a single soul that he was so much as dating Daisy, and now...

"I think I may have fallen in love." The words came pouring out, and his friends stared back at him wide-eyed. But their shock didn't last long.

"That's amazing, man." Ethan leaned over to clap a hand on his shoulder.

Dex's head fell back. "What great news," he cheered.

They went on so much with their enthusiastic congratulations that they started to cause a scene.

244

"All right, all right," Levi muttered, but he was chuckling as he said it. Relief flooded him. Their positive responses had been just what he needed. "You don't think it's...?" He scratched at his jaw.

"Too soon?" Ethan offered. He winced. "Man, it's been three years, and moving on doesn't mean that you're forgetting Beth."

Dex nodded. "Neither of us can say we understand what you must be going through, but Ethan's right. It's no crime to move on with life."

"I never had the pleasure of meeting Beth," Ethan murmured, "but from all you've told us, she'd want you and the kids to be happy. And if Daisy makes you happy..."

"She does." His throat felt choked as he admitted it, but the words came easily. "She makes me happier than I've ever been, and..." Guilt hit him hard. "No, I didn't mean that, I just meant..."

Dex grew serious. "Maybe you *did* mean it." He held up a hand when Levi started to protest. "Hear me out. The man who met Beth in college, who fell in love so easily and had three children...you're not that man anymore."

Some of the pressure in Levi's chest started to lift as he nodded, understanding what Dex was trying to say.

"Since I met Rose, I've been thinking a lot about this, about how people come into our lives when we need them most."

"To everything there's a season," Ethan said and then chuckled. "That was the sermon last weekend, remember?"

Levi nodded. "Maybe you're right. Beth's death changed me. And for the longest time, I thought it would never be for the better, that it was only darkness ahead of me. But Daisy makes me feel like…like maybe there's hope. She makes me laugh, and she makes me be a better father, and try new things, and…" He cleared his throat, looking at his hand gripping his drink. "She makes me like the new man I've become."

"That right there sounds like love to me," Ethan said. With a grin, he added, "Not that I know anything about it."

Dex nodded, his smile sincere. "Sounds like you've found something special. Not the same as what you had with Beth, but something wonderful all the same."

Levi's chest throbbed with bittersweet emotions. For weeks he'd been trying to name this sensation, but right now he felt like he got it.

This was letting go. This was loving Beth and the life they'd had together but putting it in the past. This was wanting to move forward…with Daisy.

"You Are My Sunshine" whistled through his head. The moment Daisy had mentioned that song, he'd thought of Beth singing it to their children.

It was a coincidence, he'd told himself at the time. But more and more over the past twenty-four hours he kept thinking of that day in church when he'd asked Beth for a sign. A blessing.

Was this it?

Something as simple as a song?

"Do you…?" He shifted, unable to look directly at his friends. "Do you guys believe in…signs? Or fate or what-ever?" They were silent, but he could sense their minds ticking over. "You know what? Forget it." He brushed his hand through the air. "It's not important—"

"I think," Ethan interrupted. "I think we're always surrounded by signs."

"I asked Beth for a sign," he admitted. "And it was probably just coincidence, but…" He shrugged. "I don't know. It feels kind of real, you know?"

Dex nodded, somber as he considered this. "I don't think that's the sort of thing you can reason or think through. Even as a doctor I've learned there's more to this world than meets the eye, and sometimes you just have to use your intuition or your heart to make sense of it."

Levi nodded. His heart felt pretty darn certain that Beth would be happy for him, and what was more, she'd love to see the way Daisy made her kids light up with joy. "She's good for me," he said softly. "She's good for the whole family. I want her to stay, but I don't know if I can ask that of her. Neither of us made any promises."

"Have you told Daisy how you feel?" Dex asked.

Levi's expression must have given him away because his friends nodded in understanding.

"I honestly don't know how she'll respond," he said slowly. His brows lowered into a frown as he recalled the way she'd drawn away from him the night before.

She was keeping a part of herself from him, and he couldn't say he blamed her. He hadn't exactly been forthcoming with a commitment, and they hadn't talked at all about what they were feeling.

"I don't know if she wants to hear it."

"There's only one way to find out," Ethan said.

Levi nodded and picked up his drink with a sigh. "Point taken. I'll talk to her."

The conversation shifted to Ethan's new coworkers at the fire station and Dex's plans for the baby's arrival. When it came time for another round, Levi walked up to the bar.

He found himself standing next to the man he'd pulled over the day before. "Still in town, I see."

The man nodded, gave a cursory smile, and then turned his attention back to the TV.

"So, haven't managed to wrap up your business yet, huh?" He tried to keep his tone friendly, but there really was something about the guy that had his cop instincts on high alert.

The man cast him a sidelong look. "Don't worry, Sheriff. I won't be in your cute little town much longer."

Levi debated asking more questions, but it wasn't his place. The man hadn't done anything wrong...yet.

The bartender came over, distracting him, and Levi placed his order, then glanced over his shoulder to see Dex and Ethan laughing over something. By the time he turned back to grab the drinks, the man beside him was gone.

But that didn't stop the unsettled churning in his stomach.

CHAPTER 34

D aisy thought she was home alone when she padded into the kitchen in her pajamas to make some tea. She gave a start when she saw Dahlia there, making some popcorn.

Dahlia flashed her a smile. "There you are. I thought maybe you went to bed early. You looked exhausted at dinner tonight."

Daisy slid into a seat at the table. "I thought maybe a cup of tea would help me get sleepy."

She rubbed at her temples. She wished she was asleep. She'd been trying. But falling asleep meant turning her brain off for more than three seconds at a time, and no amount of deep breathing or meditating had managed to do that.

Dahlia gave her a sympathetic wince. "I'll get some hot water going for you."

"Thanks." Daisy rested her elbows on the table and settled her head on her palms. "What are you up to? I figured you and JJ would be doing something fun on a Friday night like Emma and Nash."

The two of them had skipped family dinner for a nice night out at a local steakhouse. Emma had been positively giddy over a date night with her husband.

Dahlia grinned. "I told him to go hang with his guy friends. He hasn't spent any time with Cody or Kit in ages. I think Boone was tagging along as well." She snickered. "He's like their little puppy mascot."

"He is pretty cute," Daisy conceded, thinking of the young ranch hand and how he found excuses to show up at the ranch all the time. He worked for the Donahues next door, but his heart seemed to hang out on O'Sullivan land.

"Yeah, so I told JJ he had to go. He couldn't ignore his buddies."

"Gee, I wonder what's made him so preoccupied lately?" Daisy teased.

Dahlia's giggle was adorable. "I don't want to be the reason he doesn't see his friends anymore."

"That's considerate of you," Daisy murmured. But her thoughts were elsewhere. Namely…where was Levi tonight? What was he doing right now?

And why did she care so much?

She shifted in her seat. He hadn't texted or called today, and that wasn't like him. But then again, she hadn't reached out to him either. And that wasn't like her.

Or it was like her. It used to be her MO.

Any time she'd felt like a guy was getting too clingy, or she was getting too attached, she'd shut it down. But she hadn't done that with Levi…

And look where that left her.

She didn't even realize she'd sighed until Dahlia sank into the seat across from her with a worried frown. "That bad, huh?"

Daisy blinked. "What is?"

"Whatever it is you're stewing over that's had you sighing and distracted all day long." Dahlia's smile was rueful.

Daisy chuckled, even though her heart felt like it was sinking. "Have I been that bad?"

"No," Dahlia said quickly. "It's just not like you to mope, that's all."

Daisy straightened. "I am not moping, I'm just...thinking."

And pining, and stewing, and fretting, and—

Ugh. Dahlia was right. This wasn't like her at all. She covered her face with her hands and moaned.

"Do you want to talk about it?"

"No. Yes." She dropped her hands. "Oh, I don't know. And that's the problem, you know?"

Dahlia nodded as if that comment made sense.

"I don't know anything right now." Daisy told herself to stop talking, but it was like all the whirling, spinning, reeling emotions and thoughts from the last twenty-four hours, ever since she'd realized she was falling in love with Levi...they were too much to keep inside.

Her gaze met Dahlia's, and the sympathy and kindness there sent her over the edge. The tears she'd been battling all day finally welled up and spilled over as her lower lip trembled. "I don't want to feel this way."

"What way, sweetie?"

Daisy sniffled. This was rare. She and Dahlia had been on better terms than ever this past month, but they'd never had this sort of relationship. Not even when they were kids. Rose used to go to Dahlia with her problems, whereas Daisy had resented it whenever Dahlia tried to step in and fix her messes.

But Dahlia had softened...or Daisy had grown up. Or

maybe it was a little of both, and right now she felt a swell of gratitude that she had a sister who cared enough to put up with her sniffling tears. "I don't even deserve him." The words tumbled out, with no thought to whether or not any of it made sense.

Dahlia's brows rose. "Don't deserve who?"

"Levi." She choked out his name on a sob.

"Ahhh." Dahlia nodded, her look of understanding actually quite comforting. "I thought you two were getting close…"

Daisy sniffed. "We've been dating. Sort of. In secret because he doesn't want to tell his kids." Her belly twisted into a knot. "And that probably says something, right? I mean, I didn't want to tell them either. But that's because I knew I was leaving. But he doesn't want to tell them at all, so what does that mean?"

Dahlia stared at her with wide eyes.

"I sound crazy, don't I?"

"No." Dahlia gave her head a quick shake before reaching for a stack of napkins and handing one to Daisy as a tissue. "You don't sound crazy at all. You sound confused and overwhelmed and…" She winced. "Like a woman in love."

"Exactly!" Daisy wailed. "I didn't want to fall in love. I never fall in love."

"Why not?" Dahlia's tone was too gentle. It was the voice of a teacher patiently leading a student to the right answer.

"I don't know," she muttered and then shrugged. "Because it will only get in the way of my music. Of my career."

"Is that the only reason?"

Daisy sniffled, frowning at her sister. "Just say whatever it is you want to say, Dee."

Dahlia gave her a small smile. "It's just... JJ's helped me to see that our childhood wasn't normal, you know? Our father abandoned us, and our mother wasn't there for us, and..." She sighed as she walked over to get the popcorn and bring it back to the table. "I'm only just starting to realize how much that's formed us. How much it affected our relationships. I mean, just look at my dating life before JJ. And don't even get me started on Rose..."

Daisy let out a huff of laughter, and Dahlia grinned.

"We're a mess," Daisy said. "Is that what you're trying to say?"

Dahlia's smile turned sweet and motherly as she reached for Daisy's hand. "Maybe. But I'm working on my issues, and I know Rose is sorting through her baggage, and...I think maybe this thing with Levi is your chance."

"My chance to what?"

"To face what's really going on in there." She pointed to Daisy's head, and then at her chest. "And there."

Daisy sniffed. "I don't know what's going in there. I'm so confused." She pulled her phone out of her pocket and called up the text from Leo, then handed it over. "I got this yesterday."

Dahlia read it, her face brightening. "That's fantastic! It's exactly what you were hoping for!"

"I know," Daisy wailed, tipping her head back. "That's the problem!"

"Oh." Dahlia drew out the word as understanding clearly dawned. "I think I see..."

Daisy nodded, jabbing a finger at her phone. "Gigs in New York, playing at a busy bar—this is what I want. Or... what I thought I wanted." She frowned. "And I always said I'd never let a guy stand between me and my dreams. I'd never let my happiness rest on the whims of a man."

"Like Mom," Dahlia murmured, her voice filled with understanding. "But you know, our mom, she had serious mental health issues. I know she and our grandmother blamed it all on dad's leaving, but...I'm not sure that was it. Or that wasn't all of it. She had her episodes before he left, too, and she would have still had her issues even if Frank had stuck around."

"Maybe," Daisy mumbled. "But his leaving ruined her. She said so all the time."

"But you're not her." Dahlia shook her head. "And Levi is definitely not Frank."

Daisy felt a surge of emotion so strong she couldn't speak for a full minute. Images and memories of Levi bombarded her. Levi with his kids, Levi holding her in his arms, Levi saying he didn't want her to go.

"No, he's definitely not Frank. But I don't know that I could ever be the kind of woman he deserves either." She nibbled on her lip as she tore the napkin into shreds. "You know what I'm like."

"I know what you *were* like," Dahlia agreed. "In your teens and early twenties. But you're growing up just like the rest of us. You don't have to be the flaky sister who can't settle down anymore if that's not what you want. You have a choice in who you want to be going forward."

Dahlia slid the phone back in her direction, and Daisy stared at the message. "What if I don't know who I want to be?"

Dahlia sighed. "Aw, sweetie. I think you do. Deep down I think you know."

"How do I know who I want to be if I don't even know what I want?" She held up the phone. "This is what I've wanted for years. But when I'm with Levi, and with his family, that's what I want. So what do I do?"

Dahlia met her gaze with a soft smile. "You know I can't answer that for you. And we both know you'd hate it if I tried."

Daisy choked on a watery laugh. "I do hate it when you get bossy."

"You'll figure it out, Dais. I know you will." Dahlia squeezed her hand.

"How?" She felt pathetic, like a child.

Dahlia considered her for a long moment. "You know something you've always been good at? Listening to your heart. Letting it be your guide. You, more than any of us, always let your heart make the big decisions. You just need to take a breath and listen to what it's trying to tell you."

Daisy nodded, and after a moment, Dahlia gave her some privacy as she went about fixing a mug of tea for Daisy. When she set it down beside her, Daisy looked up with a tired smile. "Thanks, Dahlia. For everything."

"I didn't do anything—"

"No, I mean for *everything*." She met her sister's gaze. "I've never said thank you for all you did for us growing up. But I'm saying it now."

Dahlia leaned over and kissed the top of her head. When she straightened, her voice was suspiciously wobbly. "Do you want to watch a movie to get your mind off things? I'll even watch that musical about LA that you like so much."

Daisy laughed. She meant *La La Land*, but considering it starred Ryan Gosling and Daisy's first impression of Levi was that he looked just like the actor, the thought held little appeal.

Besides, between the tears and venting about her problems, exhaustion was setting in. "Thanks, but I think I'm gonna head to bed."

Daisy woke up the next morning feeling lighter than she'd felt in days.

Dahlia was right. The answers would come, and it would all turn out for the best. She just had to do what she'd always done—go with the flow.

She got dressed that morning with a smile, humming a new melody she'd been toying with. The sun was shining when she walked out of the house, and she waved to JJ and Cody, who were heading to the stables, as she made her way to her car.

She couldn't spend another day hanging at the ranch. There was way too much peace and quiet here, which gave her too much time to think. And thinking was the problem.

So she cranked up the radio and drove her Beetle into town. First she headed to Rose's house, where she had a nice visit with sister and future niece. She felt the baby kick, her eyes bugging out when she watched Rose's stomach move like she was housing her own personal alien.

"That's simultaneously gross and awe-inspiring," she rasped.

Rose giggled and cradled her belly, looking loved-up like never before. Her little sister was getting everything she needed, and Daisy was happy for her.

After one too many homemade cookies, she drove into town to see if Lizzy was working at the boutique.

She parked a couple blocks away, and when she turned

a corner heading toward Main Street, she spotted Levi walking her way. Her heart soared at the sight of him, and when he spotted her and his face split with a grin, she lost the ability to breathe.

For a second, she was all but useless as relief flooded her. It felt like she hadn't seen him in years rather than just a day. She picked up her pace, her smile growing with each step as he jogged to meet her halfway.

They stopped short when they reached each other, as if they both realized at once that they were in public.

"Hi." Her voice came out breathless and high.

"Morning, Daisy." His words were casual, but the look in his eyes made her knees weak.

Would she ever tire of that look? The way he made her feel like she was the only woman in existence and that she hung the moon with her smile.

"I'm glad I ran into you." He shifted closer and then glanced around as if catching himself all over again. "I, uh…I've been wanting to talk to you."

"Oh yeah?" Why was her heart racing so quickly? And why were there butterflies in her belly as if this was her first time flirting with a handsome man? She gave her head a shake. "What about?"

He tucked his hands in his pockets. "Helen's offered to take the kids for the night."

Daisy's heart took a giant leap in her chest. "Yeah?"

"Her kids are home from college, so they want to have a big cousins' sleepover."

"That's nice."

"Yeah, well, I was wondering…" He rocked back on his heels as he took a deep breath.

Daisy felt like her heart might explode from anticipation, like she might burst with excitement…

"I thought maybe, if you'd like... Would you want to come over for a proper date—"

"Yes!" She burst out laughing at her own overeager response, and Levi's face brightened with a happiness that made her heart swell. How had she ever thought this man was cold and unfeeling?

It was hard to remember a time when his smiles weren't making her head spin.

"Yeah?" He glanced around at the pedestrians passing by.

Her head bobbed like an excited puppy's. "Definitely."

She ought to play it cool. She shouldn't be so very eager. But Dahlia had said to follow her heart, right?

And right now her heart was trying to beat its way out of her chest to get closer to this man.

"Well, okay then." His smile turned to a satisfied smirk.

"Okay then," she agreed, backing up a step.

"I should probably, uh..." He glanced around them meaningfully. "I should get back to work."

"Mmm. And I should go see Lizzy like I'd planned."

"Right." He backed away, too, but neither of them seemed able to turn around. He raised his voice a bit as one of his deputies passed, tipping his hat in acknowledgment. "I'll see you around, Miss O'Sullivan."

Her smile felt just as cocky as she finally forced herself to turn, tossing over her shoulder, "You definitely will, Sheriff."

She heard his chuckle as she sashayed away, her heart soaring with excitement at the night to come. Finally, a true date night without having to worry about the kids finding out.

Her mind was so caught up in fantasizing about the

evening to come, she didn't even see the large man blocking her path until it was too late.

"He told you we'd find you, Daisy," a man growled.

Her head snapped up, and when she saw who stood there, her soaring heart plummeted, and her veins turned to ice.

CHAPTER 35

L evi couldn't stop grinning as he headed toward his patrol car.

Between the talk with his friends the night before and the rush of joy he felt at seeing Daisy this morning, he'd never been more certain about his feelings for her.

He wanted her in his life. The only question was did she want to be there? For right now, sure, but for the long haul? That was another question entirely.

And then there were his kids to consider. They loved Daisy as a friend and teacher, but would they be all right with him moving on?

He reached his squad car and drew the keys out of his pocket.

And then he paused.

His eyes caught on a car across the street, and he recognized it immediately. California plates. But where was the driver?

Derek Knox.

He remembered the name clearly and searched the street for him. His eyes narrowed in on the window of

Mama's Kitchen, but he couldn't see the man inside. Dashing across the road, he walked past the parked vehicle and casually looked in the windows, then ambled along the street, seeing if he could spot him.

"Hey, Sheriff."

He nodded at the friendly greeting but didn't stop to chat.

With each step he took, an agitation grew within him.

He didn't like not knowing where the man was. Probably a little ridiculous. Tourists were entitled to visit Aspire, but something just didn't sit right.

Derek Knox wasn't some innocuous tourist. Levi had felt it in his gut the moment he met the man.

And that wary feeling was only growing stronger, from an underlying caution to a pinching fear. His internal radar was starting to blare, and he picked up his pace, determined to find the man and figure out what his unfinished business was.

Darting back across the road, he glanced in shop windows and searched each corner until he found himself retracing his steps.

And that's when he heard it.

Daisy's voice was high-pitched with fear. "I told you I'll get it!"

Levi ran, his heart racing as he turned the corner to find Daisy...and the man he'd been looking for.

Derek towered over her, his upper lip curled into a feral snarl while Daisy's pale face pinched with fear. He had her pinned against the brick wall, his large hands squeezing Daisy's arms so tight she was wincing in pain.

Blood roared past Levi's ears. It was taking everything in him not to roar like a bear and rush the man. He needed to save his woman! But years of training kept him from

262

charging on impulse, and instead, he unclipped his weapon holster, resting his hand lightly on his gun and reminding himself to remain calm. He had no idea if the man had any kind of weapon on him, and he couldn't risk Daisy's safety. He wasn't about to point a gun anywhere near the woman he was falling in love with unless he absolutely had to.

Pulling in a breath, he quietly approached, praying he could end this peacefully.

"I don't have it yet, but I'll get it. I swear!" Daisy's voice was still shrill and pitching with terror.

It hurt Levi to see her this way, but it also had him curious. How did she know Derek? What did she have to get him?

The man growled and squeezed her arm even harder. "You're out of time. Benny warned you this would happen. Did you think he was just gonna forget about it?"

He yanked her forward, then slammed her back against the wall. She whimpered in pain, her expression tearing at Levi's guts.

Rage fired through him sharp and fierce, but he licked his lips and managed to call out, "Afternoon." His voice was shaking a little. Everything in him wanted to go full-blown warrior, but he was sheriff, and he would remain in control. "Everything okay here?"

The large man stilled, and Daisy's wide, panicked gaze flew to his. He caught her eye briefly, then stared back at the man, moving slowly but steadily toward them.

He wished he could reassure her. Wished more than anything that he could steal her away and hold her close, but there was no telling what this thug would do if he felt threatened.

"We're just having a chat, *Sheriff*." Derek cast a narrow-eyed look his way as Levi moved closer.

It was painfully slow to approach at such a snail's pace, but he was playing it cautiously, reading the scene with each step forward.

"Nothing to concern yourself with." The man smirked, and Levi wanted to punch him.

He had to suffice with imagining it as he swallowed and forced out a casual tone.

"I'd say there is, considering you've got your hands on this nice lady here, and she doesn't seem too happy about it."

Protective rage pulsed through him. The ways he'd like to hurt this man for touching sweet Daisy and scaring her so badly were vast, but he pushed the images from his mind.

He had a job to do.

He had to be calm. He needed to be smart.

"I'd like you to let her go, please." His gaze dropped to the man's hands on Daisy's arms.

Derek's smirk grew, and he squeezed so hard, Daisy's mouth opened with a little whimper.

"Let her go, sir! Unless you want to be arrested for assault."

After a rebellious grunt, Derek released her. But he didn't move back, so Daisy was still trapped between him and the wall behind her.

"This really isn't any of your business, Sheriff." The man tipped his head toward Daisy. "We've got a little something to settle, and then I'll be on my way." He half turned to face Levi.

Good. That was good. He needed to get the man's attention off his woman and onto him. He tried to stay cool and focused, nearly impossible to do when he realized that Daisy was trembling so hard she looked like she was stuck in a snowstorm.

"I'm here to help." Levi took a few steps closer.

"Is that why your hand's resting on your gun?" Derek crossed his arms, looking smug and unaffected by the fact that he was speaking to an officer of the law.

Levi slowly took his hand away, raising both like two white flags as he inched closer and tried for a casual tone. "I'm awfully good at settling disagreements in these parts, and I don't see why we can't all just walk peacefully away from this. If you tell me the problem, I'll help you fix it."

He'd spoken in a slow drawl, trying to calm the man, but all he got was a mocking sneer.

"We don't need your help." The man snickered, the sound harsh and irritating. "I've got a job to do, and I won't be letting my boss down. He doesn't like being let down, lied to, or stolen from." He threw a narrow-eyed glare over his shoulder.

Daisy shrank away from it, curling against the wall and looking to the ground with another soft whimper.

Levi clenched his jaw, his fingers curling into tight fists as he fought instinct over training.

"Care to tell me why you're terrifying a defenseless woman in my town? Or should we talk about it at the station?"

The man shifted, and Levi saw the bulge where his gun was concealed.

Ice replaced the red-hot fury, and some part of his mind raced with images of worst-case scenarios...endings to this situation where Daisy got hurt. Or worse.

A muscle ticked in his jaw, but he kept his voice steady as he lied. "I've already called for backup, so if you'd like to walk away with no trouble, I recommend you let me in on your disagreement, and we'll see if we can settle this here and now."

Derek let out a humorless laugh. "Yeah, sure. Why not? You got twenty grand to clear her debts? That'd settle it."

Twenty grand?

Levi's gaze shot to Daisy, and when she ducked her head as if trying to hide in plain sight, his gut sank. It was true. No wonder she was so terrified. This man was a debt collector and no doubt worked for some loan shark or mafia man.

The idea sent a cold chill sweeping through him, and it was a struggle to ask, "Who does she owe the money to?"

Derek smirked again. "Someone you don't want calling in your debts, you know?"

Levi swallowed hard. Yeah. He knew. And his gut twisted with revulsion at the thought of his sweet, vibrant Daisy in this guy's crosshairs. He'd heard enough stories to know what people suffered when they didn't pay up.

"So, we've got two options here, *Sheriff.* I either get the money, or I'm taking Blondie here back to LA. Benny's got plenty of ways she can pay off her debts, you know what I'm saying?"

Bile surged in Levi's stomach while Daisy shot a horrified look at Derek's back and then started to cry. Her chin bunched and trembled as tears splashed onto her cheeks. Her body was quaking, and Levi wasn't sure how much longer her legs could hold her.

"I don't think that's going to be necessary," Levi rasped, then cleared his throat, trying to sound way more in control than he felt. "If this woman says she'll get you the money, I'm sure she's good for it."

She wasn't, though. Obviously. Her only job right now

was music lessons. She was making a measly forty dollars a week, and he knew it better than anyone.

"No offense, but your word isn't worth much to my boss."

Levi smiled calmly. "Maybe not, but it's worth a whole lot around here. I can't imagine your boss would be happy to know his employee has been locked up in a county jail for harassment, would he?"

The man studied him for a long moment before bursting out in a laugh. "You really want to play that game? All right, fine. I'll let you take this round. But rest assured that I'm not going anywhere until I get what I want. Benny's not someone you cross, and I'm returning with the goods." He spun around to jab a finger in Daisy's direction. "It's the money or your body. You got me?"

Daisy shuddered and leaned into the wall like she wanted it to absorb her.

"The nice lawman here has bought you a couple days' grace. Don't screw me over, Daisy. You don't want to make me mad. You understand?"

Her head bobbed erratically, but she kept her eyes on the ground.

"You pay up what you owe," the man growled before stalking away.

The second he was gone, Levi bounded toward Daisy, pulling her shaking body into his arms. She clung to him so fiercely, his heart clenched in his chest.

"I'm sorry, Levi," she blubbered against his chest. "I'm so sorry."

He held her protectively, pretty sure he'd take on an army of debt-collecting thugs if it meant keeping her safe.

The idea of that man taking her, the way he insinuated how Daisy could pay off her debts made his skin crawl.

Over his dead body he'd let something abhorrent happen to her.

He didn't know how he'd help her solve this, but right now they had a couple days, and he would use every second of that time to make sure Daisy felt secure in his arms.

"I'm gonna take you back to my place, okay? I need to get you safe, and then you can tell me everything."

She nodded with a little sob, pressing her body even closer as she clung to him.

"I'm gonna go pull the car around so we don't face a million questions, okay?"

She nodded. But when he went to step away, she curled her fingers into his shirt. "Don't leave me here."

"I'll be right back, sweetheart." He kissed the top of her head. "I will be right back, and I won't let anything bad happen to you. I promise."

It was a promise he meant to keep, and as he ran to his car and hurriedly put it into Drive, his mind was already racing with ways he could see it through.

He drove around the corner and saw her slump with relief at the sight of him.

He'd keep her safe…but first he had to know what exactly she'd gotten herself into.

CHAPTER 36

Daisy shook so badly, she felt like she might be coming apart at the seams.

Levi didn't say a word on the short drive to his home, and she was shaking harder than ever when he helped her out of the car. Her knees buckled on the sidewalk, and he scooped her into his arms, cradling her like a child as he walked up the front steps and into the house.

It was so quiet without the kids around, but the sofa was familiar and comforting when he got her settled and wrapped her up in a blanket. He shushed her tears and grabbed her a box of tissues, smoothing down her hair like she was his wounded child.

But she wasn't a child. She was a grown woman who'd made such a mess of her life that she didn't know how to even begin to fix it.

"I'll make some tea," he murmured against her hair as he hugged her tight. "I'll be right back, okay?"

She nodded, his sweet tenderness making her eyes well with tears all over again.

She didn't deserve it.

She looked around the living room with its piano and Mikayla's guitar, with the PlayStation and microphones, and Ronnie's ninja weapons.

She'd never deserve any of this. This was a good home with good people, and they needed better than someone who'd never been responsible for anything in her life.

She'd been doing such a good job of ignoring all her problems these past few weeks that when that man had confronted her, when her problems were suddenly there, in her face and looming large…

A violent shiver racked her from head to toe.

It was like something had cracked open inside her. The blinders were torn off, and she was thrown straight out of the sweet daydream she'd been living in. All she'd been avoiding hit with the force of a tidal wave.

She shut her eyes, but that didn't stop the barrage of torturous regret.

What had she done? How had she let it get to this?

He'd found her. He'd said he would, but she'd thought she was safe in Aspire.

But all she'd done was lead a nasty thug into the one place where her family lived.

She covered her face with her hands, unable to control the trembling.

"Here." The sofa sank as Levi sat beside her and pushed a hot mug into her hands. Then he wrapped an arm around her shoulders and held her tight. "You're safe now, sweetheart. You're all right."

"I'm not, though," she rasped, her voice so small and shaky she hardly recognized it. "I'm not all right, Levi. I'm a mess. And I'm sorry. I'm sorry I didn't tell you sooner, and I'm sorry I let us get so close when I had trouble following me, and—"

"Hey, hey…" He pulled her against him until her weight was resting on his chest. "Just drink your tea and calm down."

She did as he said, focusing on the feel of his hands smoothing over her hair and back. It felt nice. Better than nice. She couldn't remember the last time anyone had taken care of her this way. Dahlia and Rose used to try, but she'd pushed everyone away for so long. She'd spent so many years making sure no one got too close.

She sniffled into her teacup. Probably because she'd always known it would end like this if she did. She wasn't cut out for this sort of life. She should have taken off weeks ago. She could have kept running and—

"You want more?" Levi's voice interrupted her thoughts as he took her now-empty mug from her hands and set it on the coffee table.

She shook her head. No amount of hot tea was going to fix this. And when she looked up into his kind, gentle brown eyes, she felt a wave of sadness so intense it made her chest feel like she was being sliced open with a switchblade.

This was it. This was where the fairy tale ended. And of course he was being wonderful about it. Any other person would be yelling at her and telling her what a fool she was, and he was comforting her instead. Waiting patiently for her to tell him the truth.

She sighed as she pulled out of his arms to sink back against the sofa. "I messed up." She shook her head. "I'm such an idiot."

"You're not—"

"I am." She shot him a wry, humorless smile. "My grandmother used to say I was hell-bound. That trouble was my middle name. I used to think she was wrong. But

271

sometimes…" She let out a humorless laugh. "Well, I guess today just proved she was right all along."

"Daisy." Levi reached for her hands, but she moved them away before he could touch her.

She gave him an apologetic wince and sniffed, slashing a hand across her cheek. "You deserve to know everything, and it's time I told someone."

His brows arched. "No one knows?"

"That I owe money to a loan shark? No. I didn't exactly make that announcement when I showed up at the ranch." She sighed again, focusing on her hands clutching the blanket. "We'd always made just enough to get by. The band, I mean. But when we went on tour, we didn't even break even. There were just so many costs that none of us had anticipated, you know?" She didn't wait for a response. Of course he wouldn't know. "Our manager said he had a budget and that we'd come out with enough money to cover the studio space, but the tour…it was just awful." Her eyes darted to his face, but he was just looking at her calmly. It made her edgy, so she focused on the colors in the blanket, staring at the different shades of purple and blue. "I mean, the music part was great. Performing for new audiences and trying out new songs. That was fun. But my bandmates were a couple, and the strain of being on the road together, and the friction within the band about what sort of music we wanted to make next…it was too much."

Levi moved a little closer. She didn't shift away from him, just sat still and closed her eyes when his gentle fingers skimmed the edge of her cheek, then nestled around her neck. His hand was warm and comforting, his thumb stroking soft circles just below her ear.

He didn't say a word, just silently told her he was there. Listening.

She pulled in a shaky breath and forced herself to continue. "So I just…did what I do best. I smoothed things over. I pretended it was all going according to plan. I lied to my sisters and said we were on our way up, when really…" She scrubbed a hand over her eyes. "Really, I was just being optimistic." She sniffed. "No. I was being an idiot. I was seeing what I wanted to see and ignoring everything else." She plucked at the blanket. "That's sort of what I do. Dahlia took care of everyone, and I…I just turned a blind eye. And when I couldn't do that anymore, I left."

Guilt and regret had her curling in on herself. "I left them there. I ran away without even finishing high school. All because I was so sure I could be a star."

Her laugh sounded jaded, and it made her even sadder.

"What happened next?" Levi asked.

She shrugged. "We got to LA without the money we needed for the studio space. And I thought we'd all work to make the money, but my bandmates were already one foot out the door. They were ready to admit defeat and go back home, but we'd already reserved the space, and I was so sure that this was our big chance." She squeezed her eyes shut. "Of course no legitimate places would lend me money, so I…I went to Benny. I got his name from our manager…before he ghosted us."

Levi hissed, and she stole a glance at his wincing face.

"Yeah. You'd think by that point I'd have seen that the end was near, right? But no. I was so freakin' sure I could salvage everything. The band. The money. Our careers." She shook her head. "What an idiot, right?"

He squeezed the back of her neck. "You were fighting for what you loved. That's called passion."

"But that's the thing, you know?" Her voice was getting high and wobbly as she swiped away tears. "I've been thinking lately about what I was fighting for, and I don't know…"

"What don't you know?"

"I was miserable in that studio, desperately trying to make everything work. It's like I forgot all about the music and how it filled my soul. It became this huge drag, and…" She shook her head, feeling that sudden fear of losing something she was so sure she'd been born to do. "I love playing music. I love the way it makes people happy. But I didn't feel any of that when I was struggling to become a star. I mean, what if…?" She sighed. "What if I was fighting for the wrong thing?"

He squeezed her again, and of course he couldn't answer that. And at the same time, the answer was obvious. She hadn't been happy; she'd just been desperate and hadn't wanted to let go of a dream she'd formed when she was no older than Mikayla.

She'd been compelled but not passionate.

It'd been pride, plain and simple, that had kept her from admitting her failure to her sisters…or to Levi.

But it was all out there now, and she couldn't bring herself to look him in the eyes as she finished her pathetic tale about making a terrible loan deal when she didn't know the first thing about interest rates or how quickly the debt would grow. And then the ending, when her bandmates finally ditched her, leaving her with a bunch of unfinished songs, a few unedited tracks, and a mountain of debt.

"And so…you ran." He finished the story for her, filling in the miserable, pathetic pieces.

She nodded. "I didn't have contacts in LA, not like I do in New York, so I couldn't find any paying jobs, and I wasn't qualified for any real work, and…yeah. I ran away. Like I always do."

"Oh, Daisy," he whispered, resting his head against her cheek before pulling her close.

"I know. I was crazy and irresponsible."

"I didn't say that."

"You didn't have to. But the thing that kills me right now is how stupid I was to come here. I thought for sure no one would find me in the middle of nowhere." She clung to his shoulders, murmuring against his shirt, "No offense."

"None taken."

"But now look what I've done." Fear had her voice getting high again. "What if that guy came after me when I was with Rose? Or any of my sisters? Levi, what if he tracked me down while I was watching your kids?"

"Shhh." He leaned back, holding her face and drinking her in like she was precious.

She didn't understand this.

She wasn't precious. She was a trainwreck!

"No more what-ifs. They'll only drive you crazy. What matters is you're here now. And I'm not going to let anyone hurt you or anyone you love."

She sobbed quietly until he caught her chin and lifted her head so she was meeting his gaze. The affection she saw there nearly drowned her.

"Thank you," she whispered. "I know I'm nothing but trouble, but you and your family, and what we've had… it's meant everything to me."

His expression shifted, concern replaced by passion and heat as he claimed her lips in a kiss that was achingly sweet and filled with more emotions than she could handle.

"I'm sorry for the reasons that led you here, Daisy. But I am so glad you came." He ran his hands through her hair and then cupped the back of her head to hold her close for another kiss.

By the time he pulled back she felt like she was drowning in emotions. "I'm falling for you, Levi. I'm falling so hard it scares me."

"It scares me, too, sweetheart." He kissed her forehead, her nose, her cheeks. "But right now you have nothing to fear." He wrapped her in his arms, so tight it helped her tense muscles finally relax. "You're safe here with me. Always."

She snuggled in closer, her eyelids swollen and heavy from crying.

She lay like that for ages until the feel of his hands soothing her and her own soft breathing lulled her to sleep.

CHAPTER 37

L evi watched Daisy sleep for nearly an hour. All the while his head was spinning, but his heart...

His heart had never been more certain.

He stroked the hair back from her cheek, swiping away the tearstains. Had he ever doubted how he felt about this woman? If so, tonight had made it all too real. Seeing her in danger and witnessing her heartache, nothing had ever been more certain.

He'd do whatever it took to protect her. He couldn't stand the thought of her in danger, and he hated the idea of her leaving. She belonged here with him and his family, and right now he couldn't imagine how he hadn't seen it all along.

She'd been sent to him, a gift from heaven. And maybe she had been irresponsible in taking on a debt she couldn't afford...

He winced. Yeah, that had been really irresponsible. But it had been all too easy to see her desperation and to understand it. She'd been trying to make her dreams come true. And while the way she'd gone about it had been reckless, her passion and her enthusiasm were all a part of what made her who she was.

It was her love of music that had brought her into their lives. His temples started to throb as he began to wonder if music would take her out of their lives again.

He couldn't offer her fame and fortune. All he had was love to give. And he wished he could be certain that was enough.

But after a long while sitting there thinking and praying, he realized that no matter what happened in the future, that didn't change where things stood right now.

The woman he loved was in danger. Legally, Derek wasn't allowed to harass Daisy, and he would need a court order to take money from her paychecks. That scum could *not* force her to work off her debts with her body, but that wouldn't stop him from trying. Derek, and no doubt this Benny character, didn't seem the type to worry about breaking the law.

Levi shuddered. The man hadn't even quaked when he'd said, "the money or your body." And he'd said it in front of a sheriff!

The idea of Daisy being stolen away and taken who knew where had rage and fear tearing through Levi in equal measure.

He could fix this. He could keep her safe.

It didn't take much to track down Derek's room number. The receptionist at the motel didn't think twice about letting the town sheriff know which room Mr. Knox was staying in.

Levi stared at the brass numbers on the door—12—and drew in a deep breath before knocking on the wood.

Derek took his sweet time answering, and Levi had to knock again before the door was jerked open. Derek eyed

278

him up with a snicker. "You here to run me out of town, Sheriff?" He looked left and right as if to check for the other deputies. "Or is this a *High Noon* thing and you're here for a shootout."

The man made himself laugh with that one, and his chuckle turned to a smoker's cough.

"Funny," Levi muttered. "I'm here on Miss O'Sullivan's account."

"Is that right?" The man rocked back on his heels. "I hate to tell you this, but you don't have any cause to get involved." He nodded toward his room. "I've got the contract she signed. It's all legit."

"Forcing her to physically work off a debt is anything but legit."

"It says right there in the fine print that if she's unable to pay, she will work off her debt by any means necessary."

Levi growled and clenched his jaw. It was with a sinking sensation that he figured Daisy didn't even read all the fine print. She wasn't the detail-oriented person he was. He could picture her scrawling her signature along the bottom of the contract, desperate for the money…for a way out of the mess she was in.

The idea made his eyes smart for a second, but he sniffed away the burning sensation and managed to calmly say, "I'm not here to talk fine print. I just want to help a friend."

"Ahhh." The man's eyes lit with mocking amusement. "So it's like that, huh? The pretty girl gets herself a hero."

He didn't answer. "You said twenty grand. Is that all she owes? What are the terms?"

The man eyed him for a long moment before turning back to his room and returning with the document.

279

It was signed by Daisy, all right, and one quick scan was enough for Levi to see that while it was a binding contract, it was a terrible deal. "Those interest rates are ridiculous," he bit out. "It's highway robbery."

Derek laughed. "Yeah, well, she still signed on the dotted line, didn't she?"

She did. His temple throbbed once more. Twenty thousand dollars. It would make a massive dent in his savings. But there was no alternative.

There was no way he would let Daisy come to any harm.

"I'll get you the money," he muttered.

The man's eyes widened. "She must be some friend."

He ignored the man's taunting tone. "Just get me the details of where to send it."

The man grew serious. "You got 'til Monday morning. Otherwise, the price goes up again." His smile was cold. "Or we'll have to make another visit to your girlfriend."

Levi fought against a wave of fury. Everything in him wanted to take Derek Knox down, and he had every intention of delving into his boss's business. If there was any hint of illegal activity—and there would be—he'd make sure they paid. But for now…

"You'll get your money." He met the other man's eyes. "And then you'll get out of town."

The man grinned. "That's the plan, Sheriff."

With a weary sigh, Levi turned and left, shooting off an email to the bank manager in the car to get this over with. When he returned home, Daisy was still asleep on the couch, and his heart ached as he watched over her.

So beautiful, and so sweet, and hopefully once this business was over and done with…she'd be his forever.

He kissed her forehead and lifted her into his arms. She

woke only briefly as he carried her to Mikayla's room and set her on the bed so she could sleep more comfortably.

"Good night, love," he whispered as he kissed her cheek. "I promise you, everything will look brighter in the morning."

CHAPTER 38

Daisy woke with a wince as her eyes were speared by bright sunlight.

For a moment, she was confused. Where was she? But it all came back to her in a horrifying rush of memories, and she fell back in the bed with a groan.

Covering her face with her hands, she gave herself a few minutes to wallow before sitting up and forcing herself out of bed to face the inevitable. She tiptoed out of Mikayla's bedroom, although she couldn't hear Levi moving about.

She ran a hand through her messy hair and cringed at the bad taste in her mouth. How had she slept straight through the night after all that had happened yesterday? She wished she could say she felt better, but as she padded through the upstairs hallway and then down toward the empty kitchen, her stomach felt like it was filled with rocks.

It was a sinking sensation that wouldn't quit.

It only grew worse when she saw the note Levi had left for her on the kitchen table.

. . .

Daisy,

Went to pick up the kids from Helen's and take them to church. We'll catch up later.

A cold chill raced down her spine while her belly twisted into a tight, unrelenting knot. The tone wasn't exactly warm, but could she blame him? The most responsible man she'd ever met now fully saw her for the mess-up she was.

And he must hate her for it. She bit her lip, but it was no use. Tears welled in her eyes. She'd lost his good opinion, and it was shocking how much that hurt. She'd gone her whole life not worrying about what people thought, doing whatever it took to not feel beholden or obligated.

She'd made a career out of not living up to anyone's expectations so no one would depend on her and vice versa.

She sank into a chair, which scraped loudly against the floor. It sounded too loud. The house was too silent.

It wasn't the home she was used to without the kids bickering and laughing or Levi's low, rumbly laugh.

It wasn't *her* home. Period.

She dropped her head into her hands.

When had she started to think of this place as home?

She'd known better than to get attached, and yet here she was, her worst fears realized. She'd come to depend on someone to be happy, and now she'd have to leave this town with a broken heart.

She glanced at the clock and stood with a weary sigh. She didn't want to be here when he returned. She didn't

284

want to have to say goodbye. Not to him and not to the kids.

Gathering her purse from the other room, she made sure she had her car keys, and then she fled, walking quickly toward the street where she'd left her Beetle. Fear made her breathing grow shallow, and she kept glancing over her shoulder as she approached the street where the debt collector had threatened her.

She shut her eyes with relief when she unlocked her car and slid inside, hastily locking it behind her. Her heart still slammed against her rib cage, and bile rose up her throat as her mind raced with what-ifs.

It wasn't so much fear for herself as it was the trouble she could bring upon her friends and family. Her stomach churned dangerously as she imagined that same man accosting her when she was with one of Levi's kids.

She couldn't blame Levi at all for being angry with her. She wouldn't be surprised if he wanted nothing more to do with her after the trouble she'd caused.

How had she never considered that they might find her here? How had she been so selfish as to come here in the first place?

She bit her lip to stifle a cry as she put the car in gear and headed home. Not that the ranch was any more her real home than Levi's had been. If that run-in had shown her anything, it was that coming here in the first place was a mistake.

It seemed everyone was at church when Daisy walked into the ranch house, and she was grateful. The faster she packed and got out of here, the better. She was nearly to her bedroom when she ran into Dahlia and JJ, just coming in.

"Hey, Daisy!" Dahlia chirped, a big smile on her face.

JJ nodded, but he was grinning too. They were both glowing and rosy-cheeked, and by the looks of it, they'd just come back from exercising. She was proven right. "I was hoping you'd be up earlier to join us for a morning hike."

"Oh, I, uh…slept in, I guess." *At Levi's house.* She looked down at her feet, a cloak of sadness wrapping around her. It felt heavy and made her knees want to buckle.

Would she ever have a chance to go back there? To see Levi again? Or the kids?

She swallowed hard. No, it would be better for everyone if she just left and took her problems with her.

"Want some breakfast, Daisy?" JJ asked as he moved around the kitchen, pulling out a pan and spinning it. "I make a mean bacon and eggs."

She tried to smile. "No. Thank you. I, uh…" She touched her temple, which really was pounding. "I'm gonna go to bed, I think."

"But you just got up." Dahlia frowned. "You okay?"

"Mmm. Just a headache."

"It's not a migraine, is it? You used to get those all the time as a kid."

"I remember." She tried for another smile. "It's just a headache."

But as if her headache heard her, it chose that moment to grow about ten times worse. With a wince, she waved. "I'll see you guys later."

"Daisy…" Dahlia's voice was filled with worry. "Is something else the matter? You seem…well, you don't seem like yourself."

She couldn't even pretend to smile. She didn't feel like herself. She'd always prided herself on being able to find the silver linings. But right now, she felt like she'd hit a dead end, and there was no way out.

No way but to run again and hope she could scrounge up enough money at these New York gigs to appease the loan sharks who were after her.

She nodded toward her bedroom, which brought on another sharp pain in her skull. "I just need to…" *Pack. Plan. Run.* "Rest."

"Okay, if you're sure." Dahlia nodded, still looking like a worried mother hen. "I'll come check on you in a little bit."

Daisy was already out of the kitchen and halfway to her room. She shut the door behind her with a click and tried her best to block all thoughts screaming through her mind as she found her ratty old suitcase and pulled it from under the bed.

"Someone sure made herself comfortable," Daisy muttered as she went about the task of collecting all her scattered belongings and clothes. She dumped it all unceremoniously in the suitcase. But the headache grew worse with every passing minute, and finally she caved, heading to the bathroom for some painkillers and then crawling into bed.

That was where Dahlia found her a little while later. "Oh, Daisy," she murmured as she came in and sat beside her. She felt her forehead. "I'll go get a cold compress."

Daisy groaned, too miserable to form a "Thank you."

Dahlia paused on her way out, and Daisy saw her take in the open suitcase. She opened her mouth, but when her gaze fell back on Daisy, she closed it again. The sad look in her eyes said she knew exactly what Daisy was up to.

Guilt nipped at her. She and Dahlia had been getting on so well lately, and she'd been having so much fun helping Rose hash out all her plans for the big wedding and the baby's nursery. Not to mention getting to know her new sisters and brothers-in-law.

But they'd all known she wouldn't stick around.

She never did.

This was her MO. She flaked. She bailed.

Daisy sniffled, the onset of tears only adding to her merciless headache.

She ran away.

And it was best that she ran now before she fell any more for the sheriff or his family. Before she hurt anymore people.

When Dahlia returned and murmured to her soothingly as she pressed the cold pack to her temples, Daisy was certain of only one thing.

She'd already lost her heart to Levi…and his kids.

And this time when she ran, she'd be hurting herself more than anyone, because she'd be leaving her heart behind.

CHAPTER 39

Levi didn't realize just how distracted he was on the short drive to drop Ronnie and Dawson at their school the next morning until Ronnie piped up. "You okay, Dad?"

He glanced in his rearview mirror to see his boys exchanging worried glances.

"Yeah. Fine. I'm just fine, buddy."

He wouldn't have fooled any detective worth his salt with that terrible lie. But his boys were easy enough to convince. He flashed them a grin, and they got back to arguing over who was better at the latest video game they'd downloaded.

Levi tuned out and tried his best to focus on the street before him rather than Daisy. But he couldn't stop worrying ever since he'd gotten home from church with the kids to find her gone. No note and no text.

He'd called and texted at least twenty times throughout the day and, in the end, got in touch with Dahlia, who informed him Daisy was suffering from a migraine. It was an awkward conversation as Levi tried to fudge his way through why he was checking up on her sister. He nearly confessed all but instead ended the call in a rush.

Daisy was safe. That was all he'd really needed to know.

He hated the idea of her in pain, but at least she hadn't been stolen away.

At first light, he'd gone to see the loan shark and make the payment.

Derek took the money and said he'd be out of town within the hour. Levi sat in his squad car, watching the motel until Derek pulled out of the parking lot. He then followed those California plates to the edge of town before rushing home to make sure his kids weren't late for school.

The relief at knowing Daisy was safe was hindered only by the fact that she hadn't returned any of his messages. How long did migraines last?

He pulled up in front of the school, and as the boys got out, he spotted Emma talking to one of the other parents.

"Sheriff, hi!" she called when he headed her way.

"Morning, Emma. You seen Daisy this morning?"

Emma's eyes narrowed with curiosity, but she hid her reaction quickly enough. "I saw her briefly before I left for work. She looked a little rough, like she'd been crying." She winced and bit her lips together, like maybe she shouldn't have said that. "Is, uh...everything okay? Did you need to talk to her about something?"

Levi nodded, smoothing a hand over his beard, which did nothing to calm his racing heart. So she'd been up and about this morning. And she'd been crying.

It only made him feel worse. What was with the radio

silence? He wanted to be there for her, but she wasn't going to let him.

He had more questions he wished he could ask, but Emma's brows were drawn together in confusion because, of course, she didn't know they were dating.

All she knew was the sheriff was trying to hunt down her sister.

He tried to force a more relaxed expression. "I, uh… I've been trying to get in touch with her…about Mikayla's piano lessons," he lied. "I was hoping she'd feel better today. Dahlia told me she had a migraine." He mumbled out the last few words and looked to the ground.

"Ahh, I see. Well, I'm sure she'll get back to you today."

His insides clenched as doubts raced through him.

"Dahlia says she used to get migraines a lot when there was stress in their house, but she'd bounce back pretty quickly."

Levi nodded. With the kind of stress she'd been under, he wouldn't be surprised if that migraine lingered for longer than it should.

"Maybe I'll go check on her later." He backed away. "See if she needs anything."

"That would be wonderful. Thanks, Levi."

He waved to Emma before driving away. He had to check in at the station first, but he'd slip off to the ranch the first chance he could. Maybe finding out her debts were cleared would lighten her tension.

Or…

He gripped the steering wheel tighter. Or she'd think he'd overstepped.

Maybe she'd tell him to butt out of her life. Doubt and fear crept in as he pulled to a stop at the station. Was it just the migraine that had her so quiet...or was she pulling away from him?

Did she wake up and realize that what she'd always wanted was in LA and New York, not in some small town with a man who came with a whole lot of baggage? Not to mention a complete family.

He breathed out sharply, trying to regain his composure before he got to work.

Daisy cared for him; she'd told him as much herself. But that reminder didn't do much to squelch this rising tide of fear with every minute that passed without a peep from her.

By the time he drove out of town to the O'Sullivan ranch, his chest was tight with apprehension.

No one answered the front door, but he knew Emma and the others had an open-door policy at this house, so he let himself in, calling out, "Daisy? Are you here?"

He headed toward her bedroom quietly, afraid he'd wake her if she'd been sleeping. But when he nudged the door open to check on her, he froze. "Daisy? What are you doing?"

She glanced over her shoulder with wide eyes before tightening her lips into a look of determination as she went back to stuffing items into an overnight bag. "What does it look like?"

"You're just...leaving?" He hated how dumbfounded he sounded.

How hurt.

She didn't turn around. She didn't respond at all. So he moved farther into the room until he was facing her. Her head was tipped down as she crammed something into the sack, but this close he could see her pain.

Her skin was whiter than white, and there were dark

shadows under her eyes. The lines around her eyes and mouth were tight, and her whole body looked rigid, like she was fighting pain right this second.

"Daisy, if you have a migraine, you have to rest—"

"I don't need you to look after me, Levi." Her voice wasn't mean, but the sharpness of her words and the blank look in her eyes when they finally met his had his heart cracking in two.

She was standing right here, but he felt like the Daisy he knew was long gone.

"Daisy, you're scared and hurt, but that means you need the people who love you and—"

"I don't need anyone. I know it probably seems like I do. I know I've gotten myself into a mess, but..." She threw her hands up. "I never should have come here in the first place."

"Don't say that," he muttered.

She shook her head and reached for some earphones on the nightstand. "It's the truth. I was an idiot when I made that deal. But it was even more foolish for me to bring my problems here."

He went to reach for her, but she pulled away. "You're not alone in this. You're—"

"Well, I should be!" Her voice cracked, and his heart split in two a little more.

"Daisy..." He tried to keep his voice calm and reasonable, but that fear he'd been battling was morphing into anger. She wasn't listening. She wasn't even in her right mind. Her eyes were glassy with pain, and her whole body shook when she tried to lift the bag off the bed. "I know you're scared of the men who've been chasing you, but I—"

"Don't get involved with this," she snapped. "I'm not

your problem to solve." There was a bitterness in her voice that had him jerking back. She didn't sound anything like his sweet, kind, joyful Daisy.

"What does that mean?"

She shook her head, her features pinched. "It means you're so very responsible and mature, and I'm some helpless charity case you have to take care of."

"I never said that."

"Well, I don't need anyone taking care of me. And you certainly don't need another burden in your life."

Anger had his jaw clenching tight as he fought to hold his temper. "I don't see you as a burden."

"Yeah, well, you're not seeing straight, then." She lifted her head and tossed her hair back, her normally sparkling blue eyes dull with pain and regret. "I should have known better than to start something with you. I don't stay in one place for long, and I don't do...complicated."

"Complicated?" he shot back.

"Look at us!" She threw her arms wide. "We're standing here yelling at each other right now!"

"It's one argument," he bit back. "People argue, Daisy. People get angry and sad and hurt, but it doesn't mean there's not real love there."

She turned away, hiding her face from his.

"Couples fight." He sighed. "It's part of the deal."

Her back was ramrod straight, her profile a hard mask. "Yeah, well...I never signed on to be part of a couple. You and me...this...it was only ever a bit of fun, right? That's why we never told anybody."

Ice filled his veins at the softly spoken words. It was worse than any fight he'd had with Beth or any anger he'd had toward Daisy last night.

Her cold, apathetic response spelled a death knell for

whatever it was they'd had between them. Oddly enough, his thoughts turned immediately to his kids. To how they were going to feel when he told them Daisy was gone.

The thought only made his chest ache. "So you're just going to leave?"

She didn't answer, so he shifted again, forcing her to face him. "You were going to go without so much as a goodbye to me? Or for the kids?"

He caught her flinch, but it was there and gone faster than he could read into it.

"It's better this way, Levi." She lifted her gaze, tilting her chin up in determination. "Believe me. I don't belong here."

He wanted to argue, but…

But she didn't want him.

Should he really be that surprised?

He knew all along that what she wanted wasn't here.

It wasn't him, and it wasn't his family.

"So this is it, huh? This is the life you're choosing for yourself? To run away and flit around from one guy to the next, one town to the next—"

"And there it is." Daisy's tone dropped to an ice-cold murmur. "The sheriff who knows it all. Mr. Judge and Jury himself."

His nostrils flared, angry words jamming in his throat.

She stared him down, her eyes fiery with pain and sadness and fury and…

And he couldn't help her. He couldn't force her to stay. And he couldn't stop hearing those bitter comments. Was that really what she thought of him?

Judge and jury?

The words were stinging nettles, wrapping around his heart and making it throb in agony.

"Good luck to you, Daisy O'Sullivan," he muttered before storming out her bedroom door. He drove back to town under a storm cloud of despair and anger.

It wasn't until he pulled up to his house on autopilot that he realized he was supposed to go back to the station to check in.

He slammed his head back against the seat, reliving his argument with Daisy and remembering that he never got a chance to tell her she was debt-free. Those words died in his mouth the second she told him to stay out of it. That she wasn't his problem to solve.

But she still should know she was safe.

Reluctantly pulling the phone from his pocket, he went to text her. He'd keep it brief. Simple. *Your debt's paid. You're safe. Enjoy your life.*

Bitterness curled through him, and he clenched his jaw. Could he honestly send something so cold?

The sound of his own front door slamming caught his attention, and he whipped his head around in time to see Mikayla running down the front steps carrying Beth's guitar. She was dressed in denim shorts that were tight and tiny, cowboy boots, and a tank top that showed enough skin to make Levi's eyes bulge.

He shouldered open the door and jumped out of the car with a growl. "What do you think you're doing?"

She froze, her eyes wide with fear.

"You're supposed to be at school."

"And you're supposed to be at work," she fired back, her chin jutting up just the way Daisy's had.

His stomach clenched, anger rising in him like a volcanic eruption.

"I'm just missing one day. It's not a big deal."

"Skipping school on any day is *always* a big deal. And

where do you think you're going with that?" He pointed to the guitar. "And dressed like that?" He glared at her bare thighs and exposed stomach.

She huffed, planting a hand on her hip. "I'm catching a bus to Bozeman. I'm gonna make some money busking so I—"

"Get in that house right now!" he shouted. He never shouted, but his life was coming apart at the seams all over again. His thirteen-year-old daughter was heading to Bozeman dressed like a…

He shook his head.

And the one woman who'd made him feel like he had a family again…like he had a heart…was leaving without so much as a goodbye.

"Oh, of course, shove Mikayla back into her jail cell, right, Dad?"

"What are you talking about?" he barked. "You're the one in the wrong here. You should be in school right now, not taking off to Bozeman. You're thirteen years old, for crying out loud!"

"Would you just chill? It's *one* day. And it's not like you're letting me do anything else to earn money. You don't even pay me to look after the boys," she huffed.

Levi clenched his jaw, struggling to count to ten in his head. He didn't need this right now. "Get in the house, Mikayla." He gritted out the words.

"No!" She frowned. "I'm going to Bozeman! Busking is a great way to earn some cash and improve my skills. I want a place that's bigger than Aspire, and there'll be more foot traffic there. Daisy says—"

"I don't care what Daisy said!" he thundered. "You shouldn't be taking such awful advice from someone so unreliable!"

"What does that mean?"

"It means she's gone."

Mikayla went pale. "What?"

"She's leaving," he repeated, more for himself than her. "And she's not coming back."

CHAPTER 40

I t was the early hours of the morning when Daisy left a
note on the kitchen table.

She'd wanted to leave sooner, but the house had been
too full, and she couldn't handle the goodbyes. Every time
she went to sneak out the door, someone would show up,
and she knew the second they saw her shoving a suitcase
into her car, they'd send out some kind of O'Sullivan APB.

Her only choice was to quietly slip out in the night.

She hesitated with her hand on the letter. Dahlia and
Rose would forgive her for leaving. They wouldn't even be
surprised that she'd said goodbye in a note. And if Emma,
Lizzy, and the others were hurt, then it only meant they
didn't know her well enough yet.

She lifted her hand from the note and turned toward
the front door, hauling her bag over her shoulder and
rolling a small suitcase behind her. Amazing to think that
the past month could all be packed back up again in two
small bags.

It felt like a lifetime had occurred since she'd arrived
back in April. Her lips twitched with a bittersweet smile as

she climbed into her blue Beetle. She could still remember that day as if it was yesterday. The way Levi had given her that intimidating cop stare when she'd tried to charm him…

A blubbery sob escaped, and for a second, she sat in her car, shrouded in darkness, and let her heart bleed. But then she sniffed and turned the key in the ignition. It was better this way. She cast one last look at the still-sleeping ranch house. Nash would no doubt be up soon. The other cowboys too. But her sisters would sleep until the sun came up. Her heart gave a little pang as she whispered, "Goodbye for now."

They'd forgive her, she reminded herself as she drove down the long dirt driveway toward the main road. They always did. And if they knew the full story of her debts and the trouble she'd brought to their doorstep, they'd likely thank her for leaving.

Would Levi ever forgive her?

She pressed her lips together to stop another sob. No, probably not. He'd expected more from her.

And she'd disappointed him.

She gave her head a shake as she turned onto the main road. If she drove straight through with only a few breaks, she'd be back in New York and working gigs to pay off her debt by the end of the week.

Good.

She tightened her grip on the wheel as her phone dinged with a text. She frowned and glanced at it on the passenger seat. It was almost out of battery, because of course she'd forgotten to charge it last night. She should have just turned it off.

It dinged again, and she let out a huff of frustration. Who would be texting her this early? Had someone heard her leaving? She winced. Was it the debt collector, trying to track her down again?

The thought made her blood run cold. What if he went to the ranch if she didn't respond?

With that thought, she gave in and pulled over so she could read the text.

Her breath caught. It wasn't her sisters or that brute trying to shake her down. It was Mikayla.

Mikayla: *Is it true you're leaving?*

Mikayla: *I get it if you are. I can't stand it here either. My dad hates me. He doesn't get it at all. He just wants to lock me up, ground me for life, and use me as his personal babysitter!!!!! But I want to be like you, Daisy. You get it, right?*

Daisy's heart ached for the girl. Oh yeah, she definitely got it. She picked up the phone and hit Call, but Mikayla's phone went straight to voice mail. Daisy frowned down at the screen, concern and guilt making her heart heavy.

She couldn't leave when Mikayla needed her. She tried calling her again, but it went straight to voice mail. But then she got another text.

Mikayla: *I don't want to talk right now. Just text like a normal person!*

Daisy snickered. So Micky May. Sharp and sassy. With a shake of her head, she went to text back a reply, but another message came through before she could.

. . .

Mikayla: *If you could leave home in high school and make it, then so can I.*

Daisy's heart leapt into her throat. *No. No, no, no.* Fear had her blood turning to ice as she imagined Mikayla out in the big, cruel world on her own.

Her heart slammed furiously as she imagined Levi's reaction if he found Mikayla gone.

With flying thumbs, she quickly texted back a reply.

Daisy: *Running away isn't the answer, Mikayla.*

Mikayla: *Says the woman who's running away.*

Daisy's lips parted on a gasp as the barb dug into her like a poisonous thorn. She swallowed hard and started to respond, but Mikayla beat her to it.

Mikayla: *Dad told me you're leaving. You weren't even going to say goodbye.*

Daisy's heart felt like it was shattering. She hadn't thought she could feel worse than she had after sending Levi away so coldly. It had been the only way to get him to walk out that door. She didn't deserve his love and protection. She cared too much about him to stick around and ruin his life. The minute his car had torn away from the ranch house, her knees had buckled, and she'd knelt on the hardwood floor, sobbing her heart out.

But she couldn't do that again. Not to Mikayla. She couldn't be cold and pretend to not care. The girl was already so fragile and needed a friend.

With a little sigh, she replied, her thumbs trembling.

Daisy: *Trust me, Micky, you don't want to be like me. I'm a screwup. But you... you're strong. And you have your whole life ahead of you. Don't make my mistakes.*

Her lips trembled as she hit Send.

"Don't be like me," she whispered, wishing she could somehow make the girl understand.

When Mikayla didn't respond and didn't pick up again the next time Daisy called, her pulse raced with panic.

What was Mikayla going to do? Was she serious about leaving home?

Daisy had a gut feeling these weren't idle threats. If she was reaching out, then that was a cry for help, right? She didn't *have* to text Daisy and tell her what she was thinking.

She wanted someone to listen.

The thought helped to calm her, but she still wasn't sure what to do. Her fingers hovered over the phone. Should she call Levi?

She winced. She could only imagine his reaction. If Mikayla was still at home, her dad would go ballistic and lock her in her room for life if he thought she was even considering running away.

That wasn't what Mikayla needed right now. What she needed was…

"A friend," Daisy said aloud, her heart aching because she knew what she had to do. With a heavy sigh, she turned her car around and headed toward town.

"Right. New plan," she said as she sped toward downtown Aspire. "Let Levi know the situation and then talk to Mikayla."

She picked up her phone and braced herself to call Levi, but then her phone went black as it died.

She groaned as she threw it down. Of course. *Way to mess up once again, Daisy.*

Trying not to think of how Levi would greet her when she showed up on his doorstep at four o'clock in the morning, she headed toward his house. But before she reached his street, she spotted Rose walking down the sidewalk and pulled over.

She rolled down the window. "Rose?"

Rose grinned. "Daisy! What are you doing out here so early?"

"What are *you* doing?"

Rose gave a soft laugh and shook her head. "I can't sleep. No matter how hard I try, I just can't get comfy. My back, my hips…" She rubbed her belly with an affectionate smile. "This little one is determined to keep me awake. She must be training me for the real deal. Bring on the sleepless nights, right?"

Daisy tried to join in with her laughter but couldn't. "I can't believe Dex is okay with you wandering the streets in the dark. That doesn't sound like him at all."

Rose pointed to the streetlamp she was standing under.

"It's not completely dark, and this time of the morning is so peaceful, don't you think?"

"Ro-se." Daisy narrowed her eyes. "Does Dex know you're out here?"

Her sister's cheeks flushed, and she shook her head. "He got a call about twenty minutes ago. There was a car accident outside of town, and Levi needed a doctor."

"Oh no!"

"Minor injuries," Rose said quickly. "But I couldn't sleep after that, so I thought I'd go for a walk."

Daisy frowned at her sister's look of discomfort. "Are you okay?"

"Yeah, totally fine. I just want this little lady out already, and I've heard that walking can help. All these constant aches and pains, and the swollen feet..." She sighed with a smile. "I'm just so over feeling like a whale."

"Any day now, right?" Daisy said.

"My due date's in about eight days, which feels like a century away." Rose groaned, but then her bright grin was back in place. "I can't wait to meet her."

"Me too." Daisy smiled. And she meant it. Which only made the surge of guilt and regret that much worse because she wouldn't be here when the baby was born. And she had no idea how long it would be before she was back.

"Daisy, are you okay?" Rose asked. "Why are you up and about so early?"

Daisy's eyes welled with tears before she could stop them, not just over leaving Rose but all of it. Levi wasn't home. If Mikayla wanted to run, she'd have done it now while he was out and preoccupied. She needed to tell Levi. "Rose, do you have your phone?

"No, sorry. This dress doesn't have pockets, so I left it

at home." Rose leaned in through the window, alarm in her eyes as she realized Daisy was outright crying. "Daisy, what's the matter?"

"I think Mikayla's run away."

Rose gasped, and Daisy filled her in with the rundown of what Mikayla had texted her. Daisy reached for the door handle. "Get in. I'll give you a lift home to get your phone."

Rose slid into the passenger seat, her brows drawn together in concern. "What you told her about leaving home must have really stuck with her."

Daisy groaned as she pulled away from the curb. "I know. This is all my fault."

"That's not what I meant," Rose murmured.

But Daisy barely heard her. She was turning over what Rose had said. Her story…

She'd told Mikayla about how she'd taken a bus out of town. "Rose, where's the bus station? For buses heading out of town?"

"That way." She pointed in the opposite direction of her house. "But it won't open yet."

"So, what's the next best thing?" Daisy murmured to herself. "If I was desperate to get away and I couldn't catch the bus, I'd probably…" A breath caught in her throat, her eyes bulging when she glanced at Rose.

"Hitch a ride." Rose winced and started blinking like she wanted to cry. "She wouldn't, would she?"

"She's an angry, desperate thirteen-year-old. Of course she would!" Daisy's voice pitched high with panic. "Where's the nearest truck stop?"

"It's miles away."

"Which direction, Rose?"

"Head south." Rose pointed over her shoulder, and Daisy didn't hesitate.

Spinning her Beetle around, she gunned it back down Main Street, the engine straining as fear clutched her insides.

What if Mikayla scored a ride with some creep? She'd no doubt fight to protect herself, but she wouldn't be strong enough to fend off some guy. The thought had bile surging in Daisy's stomach.

Sweet, lost Mikayla. She didn't even know what she was doing!

"It's gonna be okay," Rose kept whispering under her breath, but neither of them seemed to believe it.

She pushed her old car to the limit, tearing down the road out of town and scanning for signs of Mikayla. The sun wasn't due up for at least another hour or so, and the thought of Mikayla stomping along in the dark, chewed up by anger and hurt and betrayal…it was killing Daisy.

She needed Levi to help. She wanted the whole dang town to get out of bed and start searching.

Why hadn't she charged her phone?

Why was she always so irresponsible?

Why hadn't she taken a minute to grab Rose's phone? A little detour would have been worth it, but no, she had to impulsively scream out of town, because that was all Daisy was good for—thoughtless impulses.

She growled in her throat, gripping the wheel and staring out the windshield, desperate to spot Mikayla.

She started praying, something she hadn't done much in her life, but desperation was forcing wild prayers to spin through her mind.

God, please keep her safe!
Help me find her.

Don't let her get picked up by someone with evil intentions.

Help me bring her home. Please! I'll do anything you want me to if you just let me find her!

The prayers continued to whirl through her mind, repeated mantras that grew faster with each passing minute. They were disrupted by doubts—*am I driving in the right direction? Is my truck stop hunch correct?*

But that just made her stomach burn with nausea, so she'd fall back into praying. Begging God to help her solve this in spite of the fact that it was all her fault.

She'd been the worst influence for Mikayla, and guilt wrapped around her like a straitjacket, locking her up and making it hard to think straight.

Levi would never forgive her if she didn't find his daughter.

She'd never forgive herself if she didn't get Mikayla home to her family.

CHAPTER 41

L evi was slumped over as he rested his weight against the trunk of his patrol car.

"You gonna tell me why you look like you haven't slept in a week?" Dex asked mildly as he handed over a steaming cup of coffee.

The passengers in the accident had been picked up by family, and while Levi had dealt with the red tape of wrapping up the report, Dex had gone and fetched them both some coffees from a twenty-four-hour gas station down the road.

He'd taken one look at Levi and insisted that the sheriff was no use to anyone without some caffeine. "Doctor's orders," he'd joked.

Levi took a sip of the coffee and groaned.

"Better?"

Levi scrubbed at his scratchy eyes. "A little."

He hadn't slept a wink last night. His racing mind wouldn't let him even though his heart had been begging for the reprieve of sleep. But he just kept replaying every awful moment of his final run-in with Daisy. And when it wasn't replaying that terrible moment when he'd turned his back on her, he was reliving the awful way he'd had to manhandle Mikayla back into the house. She'd kicked and screamed, cursing him as he carried her up to her room and dumped her on the bed.

"You are *not* leaving this house!" He stomped back downstairs and called the school, then called the station, telling them he wouldn't be back in.

The rest of the day had been a nightmare. Mikayla had wept on her bed, and listening to those sobs tore fresh wounds through his battered heart. He'd tried to bring her lunch as a peace offering, but she'd refused to take it, accusing him once again of being a prison warden and screaming that she hated her life.

He'd quietly shut the door and paced the living room downstairs until he had to collect the boys from school. He'd made Mikayla come with him, and she'd slumped in the back seat of the car, glaring at him the entire way. The afternoon and evening had been much of the same thing, and dinner was a morose affair that had Ronnie and Dawson picking at each other as they tried to navigate the dark, angry vibes pulsing out of their older sister. The picking turned to bickering, which then escalated into a yelling match.

Levi had roared them all into silence. They'd sat around the table staring at him with wide, fearful eyes. It had killed him just a little bit, so he'd sent them all to bed early, then sat in the darkness, staring at a blank TV screen. Hugging a pillow to his chest, he'd lamented the fact that Beth was probably watching from above with sad tears in her eyes. He was failing her and his children, and he didn't know how to fix it. And he couldn't stop missing Daisy and wishing she was with him, curled up against his side with her sweet smell and soft laugh. She was his balm, his sunshine…and she was gone.

Which left him right back where he'd been before she drove into Aspire, except maybe a little more heartbroken.

The future looked bleak, and that didn't help one bit when thinking about returning home to get his kids up and ready for school. The idea weighed a million pounds. Mikayla probably still hated him, and he didn't know how he was going to talk to her. What would he even say after the worst day they'd ever had?

Guilt spiraled through him, shame right behind it.

"I'm a horrible father," he muttered.

"You're not," Dex said automatically. "You know you're not."

"What I know is that I love those kids more than life itself," he said. "But that doesn't make me a good father."

There was a pause as Dex thought that over. "If unconditional love doesn't make you a good parent, then I don't know what does."

Levi's head tipped forward. "I messed up everything. With Daisy and with Mikayla. I have no idea how to make things right."

"You want to tell me what happened?" Dex rested against the car beside him. "It might help to talk it out."

Levi was silent for a long time as he weighed his options. He felt terrible talking about Daisy's debt issue without her consent, but at the same time, he was so confused right now he couldn't tell if he was coming or going. Finally he turned to Dex. "This is just between us…"

Dex nodded, his expression serious. "Let's just say you're my patient at the moment." He winced. "Frankly, you look like you need a doctor."

Levi gave a huff of weary amusement. "Well then, Doc, maybe you can tell me where I went so wrong." He spilled it all. He found himself telling Dex about how he'd tried to fight his attraction to Daisy, and then how good she'd been for his kids...and for him. How she'd brought joy and laughter and love and music back into a home that had never recovered from Beth's death.

And then he told him about how it had all gone wrong. About the debt collector and Daisy's mistakes. About how she'd run from her problems, and now she was set to run all over again.

"She's leaving me, Dex. That's the part that I really can't stand. I don't care about the money. I know she's learned her lesson about being irresponsible, and she's grown and matured so much in the short time she's been in Aspire. I've seen it. I know her sisters have seen it. But Daisy doesn't seem to realize."

Dex nodded. "That's the sort of thing you can't force a person to see. You can help people all you want, but ultimately, they have to make the changes in their lives. It's Daisy's decision."

"I know." His voice sounded way too gruff. "I know, and that kills me."

"Trust me, I understand," Dex said. "It's hard to stand back and watch someone repeat their mistakes. But you can't fight someone else's battles for them."

"Yeah," Levi grudgingly agreed. "I know you're right." His mind turned to Mikayla and the horrible way they'd left things.

He hadn't even apologized for his angry reaction. He didn't know where to begin or how to make things right. He'd been too caught up in his own hurt to really listen to Mikayla. Rather than carrying her into the house, he

312

should have heard her out. No wonder she called him a prison warden.

He cringed and shook his head.

Now he was afraid the rift between them would never be healed. With Daisy around, he'd been hopeful. But without her there…

"I might not be able to help Daisy, but what about Mikayla? She's still young."

"She is, but she's growing up too." Dex sipped his coffee. "You can't fight her battles either. All you can do is love her. And that's what you do."

Levi scrubbed a hand over his eyes. "I know you're right." His mind called up a memory. Something Daisy had said about how children were still people. It sounded so simple, but he suddenly knew what she'd been trying to say.

Mikayla didn't just need his love, she needed what all people need. Trust. Understanding. The freedom to make some mistakes and learn from them…

Skipping school to busk in Bozeman would have been a pretty big mistake!

But you could have gone with her. You could have let her have one day and turned it into a fun adventure. That's what Daisy would have done.

He shut his eyes with a sigh. "I need to apologize to my daughter. What she tried to do was wrong, but the way I handled it was so much worse."

"And Daisy?" Dex asked.

Levi shook his head, his heart hurting so badly he thought it might give out on him. "I need to let her make her own decisions. She was right that I can't take care of her…not if she doesn't want me to."

"I know it's tough, but hang in there, buddy." Dex

clapped a hand on his shoulder. "Now you go home and take a dose of decent sleep." He grinned. "And call me anytime you need me."

Levi nodded, and soon they were both climbing into their cars and heading back into town. He felt a little better for having vented it all to Dex. But he couldn't stop thinking about what he'd said about Daisy.

She didn't want him taking care of her. That hurt, but what really killed him was she wouldn't let *anyone* take care of her, just like she wouldn't let anyone too close to love her. He'd known it from her stories about her past. She ran before anyone could hurt her.

She ran before she could let anyone down.

She ran to avoid all the bad feelings that came with deep, meaningful relationships. But that was no way to live. There were no real ups without the downs. There were no rainbows without rain.

But he couldn't make her see that the pros outweighed the cons. He couldn't force her to have faith.

He was so lost in his own thoughts that he nearly missed the fact that Ethan's pickup was parked in front of his home. He stopped behind it, his insides jolting when he saw Ethan dashing out of the vehicle.

"Ethan?" he barked. "What's wrong?"

Ethan was heading to the front door, a frown creasing his face. "The boys called me. They woke up and found Mikayla was gone."

"What?" Levi checked his watch, his insides trembling. She must have left in the dark. But how long ago? He'd been gone for over two hours.

They both entered the house and saw the boys waiting with wide eyes and stricken features. "Why didn't you call me?"

Neither boy answered, but it was so obvious it was like a punch in the gut. They'd been too afraid to call their own father. They likely didn't want to get Mikayla in trouble or put up with his yelling over the phone. Guilt swamped him as he moved forward, then knelt in front of them. Spreading his arms wide, he beckoned them in a choked-up whisper. "Come here, boys."

They launched themselves into his arms.

"It's going to be okay," he promised. "We're going to be okay."

"Where's she gone, Dad?" Dawson blubbered.

"I don't know. But we're gonna find her, okay?"

Ronnie clung to his shoulders, whimpering against his shirt.

"Hey, boys, let's get you something to eat," Ethan murmured. "Everything's more manageable on a full stomach, right?"

Levi flashed Ethan a grateful smile.

The tall fireman winked and murmured, "Let me know what you need me to do."

Levi nodded as he pulled out his phone to call Helen. She hadn't heard from Mikayla. Then he tried Daisy, but her phone went straight to voice mail. He thought about calling Mikayla's friends or their moms, but with a pang of regret he realized he didn't even know where to start. Her friends seemed to change daily, and she never talked to him about any of it.

It was still too soon to say she was missing and too early for most people to be awake. The thought gave him pause. The coffee crew would be awake. Maybe one of the old men who camped out at Cal's Coffee Shop saw her on Main Street. He rang Norman, who asked around.

No one had seen Mikayla.

He was about to hang up when Norman added, "But Cal saw Daisy and Rose speeding off like their tails were on fire. He was only just getting to work, which means it must have been around four in the morning. What were those O'Sullivan sisters up to? You have any idea? Chicken Joe reckons Rose might be in labor, but I said it's still too soon. Her bump wasn't sitting low enough when I saw her the other day, and—"

"Yeah, thanks, Norman." He knew it was rude, but he hung up before he could get trapped in some long-winded call with the town gossip.

"Any news?" Ethan walked in, drying his hands on a dish towel.

"Why would Daisy be awake and in town?" He shook his head. "Why would Rose be with her?"

Ethan stayed silent, and Levi dialed Daisy again. Another voice mail.

So he called Dex, putting it on speakerphone so Ethan could be part of the conversation as well.

"I got home to an empty house," Dex said, confusion clear in his voice. "Rose left her phone behind, so I have no idea where she went."

Levi filled him in on what Norman had said.

"If Rose was in labor, she would have called me. I can guarantee it." Dex sounded so calm and sure.

"But she doesn't have her phone with her."

"She wouldn't have left the house to go walking around the streets in the dark. Daisy must have come to collect her, and they left in a rush."

"It has to have something to do with Mikayla being missing." Levi's stomach was rapidly filling with cold, hard dread. "Maybe Mikayla texted Daisy to warn her she was running away or something."

"Would she do that?" Dex sounded skeptical.

"I don't know." Levi sighed, starting to doubt his theory. "I just have to find my daughter. I'm going to drive around town and see if I can spot her."

"I'm coming with you," Dex said.

"Why don't you take your own car? We can cover more ground that way."

"Good idea. I'll head north."

"I'll work my way south."

"And I'll stay with the boys and make calls to her friends," Ethan added.

"Thanks, guys." He headed for the door, trying his best to be the cool, calm cop. But it was impossible.

God, please, help me!
My little girl is missing…
And it's all my fault.

CHAPTER 42

The sun was creeping over the mountains, and Daisy was starting to worry they'd gone the wrong direction or worse... Mikayla had already been picked up by someone.

"This is all my fault," she muttered. "Why did I tell her those stories? Why did I make my life sound so freaking awesome when it hasn't always been! I needed to get away from Mom—we all did—but I left you guys! And although it felt like freedom for a little while, it was also kind of lonely, and all the people I fought so hard for, and gave all my loyalty to, have totally abandoned me, and the ones who loved me all along are—" Daisy's voice caught as she fought a succession of quick sobs. They made her belly jerk and heave.

"Daisy, calm down. I need you to concentrate on driving. We're going to find her, okay?"

"How? When?" Daisy practically screeched. "What if we're too late?"

"There!" Rose jerked in her seat, pointing ahead of them down the road.

Daisy squinted, gasping when she spotted the young girl with her thumb in the air as she walked along the country road.

"Thank you, God," Daisy blubbered, pulling her Beetle to the side and jumping out. "Mikayla!"

The girl jerked and spun around, her eyes bulging wide. "What are you doing here?"

"I came to find you."

"Yeah, right! And then you'll drop me back at Baker Prison before being on your way!"

"No, that's not…" Daisy walked toward her. "Micky May, come on."

"Don't call me that!" she snapped, her eyes wild.

She'd been crying. Daisy could tell from the way her makeup was smudged. The mascara and dark eyeliner had smeared beneath her eyes, and she looked like a Halloween ghoul in the pale morning light.

Daisy's chest tightened with empathy. She knew exactly what Mikayla was going through, that desperate need to get away, to start over in the hopes it would make all the bad stuff disappear. But it didn't work like that.

Mikayla was so much younger than Daisy had been when she left home. She didn't understand how cold and unfeeling the world could be.

Her thoughts jumped to Levi. He loved his daughter so very much. He'd be devastated if he knew she was out here all alone.

She's not alone. You're here. So make it right. No matter what, make sure Levi doesn't lose his little girl.

"You need to come home with me."

"I'm not going back!" Mikayla spun on her heel and stormed away, yelling over her shoulder, "You can't make me."

Desperation flared, and Daisy glanced back to see that Rose was hovering behind her. She gave Daisy a little nod as if to say "You've got this."

Did she? She wasn't so sure.

Licking her lips, she ran after Mikayla, snatching the girl's arm and pulling her to a stop.

"Let me go!" she screeched, yanking her arm free.

Daisy raised her hands but moved in front of Mikayla to block her way. "Look, I know I can't drag you back home, but if you think I'm just gonna stand here and watch you make a huge mistake, you'd better think again. Not only is hitchhiking to who knows where insanely dangerous, but you are going to break your father's heart, and I won't let that happen."

Mikayla's chin jerked back, her eyes wide with surprise.

Daisy supposed she wasn't used to hearing her talk like this...like a stern grown-up. But right now, that was what she was. She was the responsible one here.

The thought almost made her laugh. Her, responsible? Who would believe that?

She swallowed hard. Mikayla had better believe it, because everything was riding on this. Daisy couldn't fail Levi...not on this.

She bent her knees, chasing Mikayla's wandering gaze until she caught it. "Running is not the answer."

"That's rich coming from you." Mikayla scoffed.

Daisy's jaw tightened, but she didn't pretend not to know what the girl meant. "Look, I know—"

"You ran away when you weren't much older than me," Mikayla interrupted. "If you could do it, why can't I?"

"I was seventeen, okay? There's a big difference

between thirteen and seventeen. But that's not even the point. You don't want to be like me." Her voice was so emphatic, but not quite enough to stop a sharp huff coming out of Mikayla.

"What do you even care? You're leaving town anyway." The girl tried to keep a stoic expression, but Daisy caught the way her mouth worked and her breathing grew shallow.

She was trying not to cry.

Over her.

Daisy's chest ached, and the wave of shame was nearly too great to bear. "I'm sorry," she whispered. "I'm just trying to do the right thing."

Mikayla turned to face her, and in her eyes, Daisy saw the battle between anger and hurt. "Leaving without saying goodbye is not the right thing."

Daisy reached a hand out, but Mikayla jerked back before Daisy could touch her. She let her hand drop. "Mikayla, I—"

"Everyone I care about leaves." Mikayla's voice had a bitter edge to it.

Daisy's breath caught at that. "That's not true. Your father—"

"Hates me," Mikayla finished for her. Her eyes swam with tears as she frowned. "I can't do anything good enough for him."

"You know he loves you," Daisy said, her voice firmer than she intended. "You have to know he'd do anything for you."

"No, he loves *you*." Mikayla jabbed a finger at her, and when she caught Daisy's wide-eyed look of surprise, she sneered. "Did you honestly think I didn't know that you and my dad were hooking up?"

322

"I...what...how...?" She caught Rose gaping at her over Mikayla's shoulder and winced.

Great. Someone else she'd managed to disappoint and hurt.

Rubbing her forehead, she cringed and muttered, "We should have told you."

"You think?" the girl spat. "I'm not a kid, you know. I could have handled it."

"I know, and it wasn't that. It was..." She trailed off and struggled for a way to explain. "We didn't tell you because we weren't sure ourselves what was going on, if... if there was a future."

"And it didn't work out, right?" Mikayla sniffed as she scuffed her boot on the ground. "My dad was a jerk and drove you away, didn't he?"

"Mikayla, no!" Daisy shifted forward, wishing she could shake some sense into the girl. "Your dad was good to me. He was..." Her mind called up an image of Levi cuddling her and reassuring her after she'd made such a mess of everything. "He's better than I deserve."

Mikayla's brows drew down. "What do you mean?"

"I..." Daisy scrambled for a decent reply. She wasn't about to open up about Benny and her terrible decision to borrow money off him.

"Forget it." Mikayla shook her head. "I'm not going back there no matter what you say."

"Well, I'm not letting you go anywhere alone," Daisy shot back. "So if you go, I go."

Rose made a little sound, and Daisy looked over to see her clapping a hand over her mouth, tears welling in her eyes as she shook her head. She was looking at Daisy like...like she was proud.

The thought made Daisy feel choked up, too, but it

gave her the confidence to turn back to Mikayla and tell it to her straight. "Look, I know I told you all those stories about skipping school and then leaving home, but you know what I left out? That it wasn't perfect. There were so many dark times, and I just didn't want to acknowledge any of them. I put up this happy, sunshine-y shield so I didn't have to deal with the bad stuff, but that didn't mean it wasn't there."

Mikayla arched one brow in a dubious frown.

"It's true. For as long as I can remember, I've tried to run away from pain. I thought…" She threw her hands out wide as if she could summon the words to make Mikayla understand. "You were lucky, Micky May. You had a good mom."

Mikayla's lower lip quivered at the mention of Beth.

Daisy's eyes filled with tears, but she kept going. "I'm so sorry that she was taken from you when you were so young, but your mom loved you more than anything in the world."

Mikayla nodded. "I know."

"And your father doesn't show it in the same way your mom did, but he loves you just as much."

"You don't know that."

"I do, though. I know it with every fiber of my being. It was the first thing that drew me to your dad. I saw the way he loved you and your brothers with all his heart. I saw the way he stuck around even when you were being a brat."

"Hey!"

Daisy arched a brow of her own. "He never stopped trying, and he never will. You could push him away every day for the rest of your life, and he will still be there waiting for you, trying to get through to you. Tell me you don't know that."

Mikayla frowned and then shrugged.

"Oh, come on. He'd walk through fire for you. And that's what I love about him!" Her voice rose. "You don't want to be like me, Mikayla, because I am a coward. I always have been."

Mikayla started to shake her head.

"It's true." Daisy glanced over at Rose, who was giving her a look of love so sweet it made her choke on a sob. "I wasn't there for my family the way I should have been when I was a kid. I ran away instead of toughing it out. And it was tough, living in a home where our father abandoned us and our mother wanted nothing to do with us most of the time." She swallowed hard. "And when I left home, I decided I would never get hurt again. I'd never care enough to put myself in that position. I wanted everything to be light and fun. I wanted to be free and independent. I wouldn't rely on anyone, because then I couldn't get hurt." She shook her head.

Mikayla eyed her for a long moment, and Daisy saw it. The realization that she was doing the same thing Daisy had done all her life. She was pushing away the people who loved her most before they could leave her like her mother did.

"Did it work?" Mikayla finally whispered.

Daisy's chest deflated with a sigh. "No. Pain follows you no matter where you go. I was a coward when I ran. I thought I could keep myself safe. But pushing people away didn't keep me safe, it just kept me alone…and empty."

Mikayla's eyes softened, her lips trembling. "Really?"

Daisy nodded. "I'd been so alone for so long, and then suddenly your dad was in my life, and you and your brothers, and…" She swiped at tears. "I didn't mean to fall in love with your father any more than I meant to fall in love with his kids. But I was just so happy that I couldn't stop myself."

"You fell in love with us?" Mikayla let out a shaky laugh.

Daisy stepped forward and wrapped her arms around her. "Of course I did. How could I not?"

Mikayla stiffened for just a moment, then relaxed on a shuddering sob, wrapping her arms around Daisy and clinging to her shirt. "Then why do you want to leave us?"

"I don't." Daisy buried her face in the other girl's hair. "But I've made so many mistakes. And I have to make things right. I don't deserve your dad right now, and the thought of his disappointment kills me. I couldn't bear seeing that in his eyes, you know?"

Mikayla nodded. "I'm afraid of the same thing."

Daisy leaned back so she could look at Mikayla's face. Tears ran down her cheeks, and Daisy brushed them away with her thumbs. "You push and you push just to see if he'll walk away, don't you?"

Mikayla's answer was a sob.

"I get it. I really do." Daisy sniffed. "But he's never going to leave you. He's never going to let you go."

"I've screwed up so many times," Mikayla admitted in a low voice.

"Me, too, sweetie." She pulled her back into a hug, rubbing her back. "Me too."

They were quiet for a long time as they cried in each other's arms, and then Daisy found herself thinking of something Dahlia had said to her the other day.

"You're growing up just like the rest of us, Daisy. You don't

have to be the flaky sister who can't settle down anymore if that's not what you want. You have a choice in who you want to be going forward."

She pulled back to meet the other girl's gaze. "Mikayla, I've made so many decisions based on fear. But every second of every day is another chance to choose who you're going to be. Nothing is set in stone. Just because I was a coward before doesn't mean I have to be for the rest of my life, and the same goes for you."

Mikayla sniffled and swiped her nose on the back of her sleeve. "I don't know how to be the kind of daughter he wants."

"Then tell him that," Daisy whispered, her eyes filling with tears all over again. "He loves you so much, and it would mean the world to him if you opened up. Talk to him about your fears and your pain. He wants to hear it." She pushed the girl's hair off her face where it clung to her wet cheeks. "All he wants is to love you. Let him love you."

Mikayla nodded, and Rose walked over, placing a gentle hand on the girl's back. "What do you say we get you home before your dad realizes you're gone and goes into a panic, hmm?"

Mikayla nodded, slowly turning to face the car.

Rose wrapped an arm around her shoulders as the three of them headed back toward Daisy's Beetle.

"You ready to do this?" Daisy asked.

Mikayla nodded but stopped to glance up at her. "Will you be there with me?"

Daisy's heart gave a frantic whir of panic at the thought of facing Levi again, but she forced a small smile. "Of course I'll be there."

CHAPTER 43

The car was filled with the sound of sniffling by the time Daisy stuck the key in the ignition and turned it on. Daisy glanced in the back seat, where Mikayla was swiping at the tears on her cheeks and looking out the window at the sky.

The sun had risen, and Daisy felt a surge of urgency to get back to Levi's home before he came back to find Mikayla missing.

She heard Rose sniffle as she buckled her seat belt.

"Are you okay, Rosie?"

Rose nodded and waved a dismissive hand. "Don't mind me. I'm a sympathetic crier these days."

She and Daisy shared a little smile. "Sweetie, you've always been a sympathetic crier."

"I know, but it's worse than ever now." She wiggled in the seat to get comfortable. "And, Daisy, what you said back there...about you leaving. About our family..." She reached a hand out and squeezed hers. "You know you have nothing to feel guilty about, right?"

Daisy swallowed hard and looked at Rose's hand on hers. "You're sweet, Rose, but—"

"But nothing," Rose interrupted. "Dahlia feels guilty for being too hard on us, and I feel guilty for being a burden, and..." She sighed. "I think it's time all three of us forgive ourselves, that's all."

"Yeah?" Daisy blinked and fought another wave of tears.

Rose nodded. "We were kids." She glanced meaningfully back toward Mikayla. "We shouldn't have had to deal with a lot of the things we did, and we can't blame ourselves for the way we handled them."

Daisy nodded, her throat tight. "I think you're right."

She squeezed Daisy's hand with a sweet smile. "Have I mentioned how happy I am you're here with us?" She patted her belly. "With all of us. We really don't want you to leave." Rose's voice hitched.

Daisy smiled, but regret nagged at her. In all the chaos, she hadn't told Rose that she'd been on her way out of town when she'd gotten Mikayla's text. She cleared her throat. First she had to get Mikayla home to Levi. Then she could deal with saying a proper goodbye to her sisters.

And the kids.

She winced as she pulled away from the curb. She couldn't even begin to imagine saying goodbye to the kids...or Levi.

She clamped her lips together and focused on the road in front of her.

How was she supposed to say goodbye to Levi? It had been impossible to watch him walk away the first time. She couldn't push him away again. But what if—

Her thoughts were cut short as a deer stepped foot in the road right in front of her. Her heart leapt as she swerved to miss it, but that had them angled straight for the ditch.

Slamming on the brakes, the car screeched, and Mikayla screamed as the Beetle dove into the trench on the side of the road before coming to a jarring halt.

The engine sputtered and hissed before clunking off. For a second, all Daisy could do was sit there and stare at her white knuckles still gripping the steering wheel.

"Mikayla? Rose?" she asked in a shaky whisper. "Are you hurt?"

"I'm okay," Mikayla said from the back, but her voice was small and trembling.

Daisy turned to Rose, who was paler than she'd ever seen. "Rose?"

Rose lifted a hand. "I'm fine. Just a scare, that's all."

Daisy sank back in her seat. Well, at least no one was injured. But the car...

She groaned as she unbuckled. The car was going to have to pay another visit to Fred.

"Mikayla, you have your phone on you, right? Can you call for help?"

She got out to inspect the damage and scowled at the deer, who was leisurely crossing the road as if it hadn't just given Daisy the scare of her life.

When she climbed back in, she saw Mikayla holding her phone up over her head and glaring at the screen.

Daisy sighed. "Please don't tell me..."

"No reception," Mikayla murmured.

Of course not. They were in the middle of freaking nowhere.

"Rose, how far do you think—" She stopped short when she caught sight of her sister's expression. Fear shot through her at Rose's pained grimace. "Rose? Rose, sweetie, what's wrong?"

"I think my water just broke," she panted.

Daisy's gaze shot down to the seat, and sure enough, liquid was dripping down Rose's legs. "Oh my gosh. Is the baby coming?"

Rose groaned. "I think so."

Daisy's jaw dropped in horror as her gaze dipped down to Rose's swollen belly. "Now? But you said eight days. You said—"

"Due dates aren't exactly hard and fast, you know?" Rose's voice was tight with pain. "Babies tend to have a say in the matter, and…" She trailed off with a whimper that made Daisy's heart rate skyrocket. She turned to find Mikayla watching from the back seat with wide, terrified eyes.

"Maybe the accident triggered something. I'm not sure, but…" She panted. "These contractions feel really strong." She whimpered again, holding her belly and wincing. "Daisy, I need help."

Right. Okay.

Help. You can do this, Dais.

Her mind felt like it was scattering with the wind as she tried to come up with a plan. But in the end, with no working phones and no working car, there wasn't much for it but for someone to start running into town.

"Mikayla, out of the car," Daisy quietly ordered. Then she came around to Rose's side and tipped the seat back as far as it would go. "Is that better?"

"Yeah, maybe," Rose murmured. Her skin was still so pale, but she wasn't wincing anymore. "I need to time how long it takes between contractions."

"Okay." Daisy nodded. "Mikayla, use your phone. You sit there." She pointed to the driver's seat.

The girl slipped behind the wheel. "What are you gonna do?"

"Go for help." She looked down the road, trying to remember how far they'd come. Mikayla had gotten a long way before they'd spotted her. "Keep her as comfortable as you can, okay? I'll be back with help as soon as possible."

Mikayla nodded. They shared a slightly panicked look before Daisy mumbled goodbye and started running.

At this early hour of the morning on this isolated road, she didn't think she'd have much luck waving down a car, but as soon as she saw a mailbox, she would be racing down that driveway and banging on a farmhouse door.

Please let me find a mailbox!

It wasn't much of a plan, but it was the best she could do.

Her lungs were aching, and her sandals were giving her blisters, but she kept running. All the while regret chased her. Why hadn't she reacted quicker when she'd seen the deer?

This whole morning had been one big mess, and most of it was her fault.

Mikayla's running away. Rose being stranded on the side of the road when she went into labor. Her stupid phone dying when she needed it most.

Regrets hammered at her, just as surely as her heart hammered in her chest. Her cheek was starting to ache, and she realized belatedly that she must have gotten banged up and not even realized it.

Fear turned her blood to ice. What if Rose had internal injuries? What if Mikayla was hurt and didn't even know?

Please, God, just help me get Rose to the hospital and Mikayla home safe and sound. And then...

And then what?

Then she'd stop wreaking havoc. She'd stop causing trouble. She'd leave this town like she should have weeks ago. She'd pay off her debts and stop putting the people she loved in danger.

It was time to face the fact that wherever she went, trouble followed. And Levi and his family deserved better.

Her sisters deserved better.

For once she wasn't running away for selfish reasons. She'd leave because it was the right thing to do.

CHAPTER 44

L evi squinted when a familiar figure came into view. He'd been driving around for what seemed like forever, begging God to make Mikayla appear on the roadside.

Well, he wasn't seeing Mikayla right now, but...

"Daisy!" he shouted as if she could hear him. His heart clenched painfully with relief as he sped toward her. But his relief quickly turned to terror as he grew closer.

Her cheek was red like someone had hit her, and her face was a mask of pain and panic.

Where was her car? Where was Mikayla?

What the heck was going on?

He pulled over and jumped out. "Daisy!"

She sobbed at the sight of him, throwing her arms around his neck. "I'm so sorry, Levi."

His heart stopped. "Where's Mikayla?"

"She's okay," she quickly reassured him, then winced. "I think she's okay."

"Where is she?"

She pointed back the way she'd come. "She's with my

car and Rose, and…" She gripped his arms, her eyes flaring with panic. "Rose is in labor. We were heading back to your place, and a deer came out of nowhere. I swerved, and…" Her eyes welled with tears. "I'm so sorry, Levi."

He pulled her shaking body close as he wrenched the phone out of his pocket and called Dex.

"You found her?" Dex asked by way of greeting.

In clipped tones, Levi updated his friend on what was happening, and Daisy spoke over him, giving Dex the location of her car as Levi nudged her toward the passenger side.

They barely spoke as he gunned it, sirens wailing while he raced to get to his little girl.

"Rose needs an ambulance," Daisy was saying.

Levi nodded, putting in a quick call. His training was taking over, shutting off his emotions and keeping him calm and efficient.

"I'm sorry, Levi," she murmured as soon as he hung up.

She'd said it so many times now, and he cast her a quick sidelong look. "What for?"

She shook her head, her gaze on the road as she craned her neck to spot them. She never did answer, and while he had a million questions about how Mikayla had come to be in her car, and why Rose was with her, he let them go for now.

There'd be time for questions later when Rose was at the hospital and Mikayla was home safe. Daisy let out a little cry of impatience when they spotted the car on the side of the road. He'd no sooner parked than they both jumped out.

"Dad!" Mikayla shouted.

She'd shot out of the car as soon as she saw him pull

up. He raced to her, pulling her into his arms and holding her tight. "Mikayla." His voice was gruff with emotion as he crushed her to him. "I thought I'd lost you."

"I'm okay." Her voice was small as she burrowed into him. "I'm okay."

He didn't even realize he'd started to cry until he had to sniff and wipe his nose. He heard Daisy's voice coming from the car, assuring Rose that Dex was on his way, that she'd be at the hospital soon, and everything was going to be okay.

She sounded perfect—confident and calm. He suspected he was the only one who knew how panicked she'd been just a second ago, and how much she was blaming herself.

Dex pulled up and was out in a heartbeat. "Rose?"

"I'm okay." Her soft voice said otherwise.

Levi pulled Mikayla out of the way, and Daisy moved so Dex could lean into the car. "Hey there, my love." His voice was calm and his smile sweet, as if he found women in labor on the side of the road every day of the week.

Rose smiled back at him. "Hi, honey."

"She just couldn't wait, huh?" He kept up the easy chatter to keep Rose calm...and no doubt Daisy and Mikayla too.

"An ambulance is coming." Dex shifted to give her a brief exam, asking questions about pain levels and contractions.

"They're about four to five minutes apart but getting closer all the time." Mikayla held up her phone.

"Good job." Dex gave her an impressed smile, and Levi squeezed her shoulder, pride illuminating his chest.

"The last one was four minutes and—"

Rose tensed, hissing and gritting her teeth as another contraction tore through her.

"It's okay, honey. Just breathe. Remember your breathing." Dex gripped her hand, talking her through it until she flopped back on her seat with an exhausted sigh.

He shot Levi a worried frown over his shoulder. "This has come on really fast. I don't think we have time to wait for the ambulance."

"What?" Daisy looked horrified.

But Levi understood at once. "Take the squad car. You can have the sirens going and get there that much faster."

"Are we allowed to do that?" Daisy gaped.

"You are today." Levi nodded, throwing Dex his keys.

He caught them and then looked at Daisy. "I need you to come with me. You can sit in the back and help Rose through each contraction while I drive us to the hospital."

Daisy blinked wide eyes, clearly taken aback. "Wouldn't I be better to drive?"

Dex eyed the Beetle, haphazardly resting in the ditch, with a dubious frown, and Daisy tutted.

"Good point." She huffed and took Rose's other side, walking her to the car. "You ready to be a mom, sis?"

"I am so ready," Rose breathed. "I feel like I've been waiting forever."

Dex kissed her. "Well, there's not long to wait now, my love."

Levi helped them get Rose into his car and then turned to Daisy, who looked wide-eyed and frightened as she waited to get in behind Rose. "You're doing great."

"I got her into this mess," Daisy whispered. Then she glanced at Mikayla, who was waiting behind him. "I got everyone into this mess. And I'm so sorry."

He gently squeezed her arm. "Just take care of Rose.

We'll be fine here. I'll stay with the car until the tow truck comes, and then I'll take Mikayla home."

She nodded and spoke in a soft whisper, "Okay." And then, with that feigned confidence, she climbed into the car and happily chirped, "Okay, lil' sis, let's go meet your baby."

It was all for show, everyone knew it, but that was Daisy. No matter how scared she felt, she just threw a little more sunshine on it until everyone around her felt better.

CHAPTER 45

The drive felt interminable. Dex was so very calm, talking Rose through her breathing techniques though he sped as fast as Levi's car could go, blasting the sirens the entire way. Rose was anxious, holding Daisy's hand with a vise grip that only grew stronger when each contraction hit.

She tried to breathe through the pain but at one point screamed at Dex to stop telling her what to do before bursting into tears. He just smiled into the rearview with one of those compassionate, forgiving looks that told the world how much he loved his wife and how he'd bear her pain in a heartbeat if he could.

Daisy sat beside her sister, silently freaking out. She was trying her best to hide it as she smoothed Rose's hair back and gave her sips of water between her contractions.

They seemed to be rolling around faster by the second.

What if something was wrong with the baby?

Over and over she replayed the moment when the deer had appeared, trying to figure out if she could have done something differently.

She wasn't sure, and in the end, it didn't make a difference. She couldn't turn back time.

Just take care of Rose. Daisy repeated the words over and over until they became a beat in the back of her brain.

She heard Levi's strong, steady voice in her head every time she started to panic. *"Rose. Just focus on Rose."*

So that was what she did...or what she tried to do. And finally they pulled up in front of the hospital. Dex was in his element, issuing orders and filling in the ob-gyn on how far along his wife was. A wheelchair was brought to the car, and Daisy helped her sister in and then took a step back, ready to pace the waiting room.

But Rose gripped her hand tight. "Stay with me," she pleaded.

Daisy's eyes widened with alarm. She'd never seen Rose look so scared. There was no way she could say no. And so Daisy found herself joining Dex and Rose and the doctors and nurses.

The delivery was fast. Everyone marveled at how quickly it went considering Rose was a first-time mom. It was pretty hard going for Rose, who sank back, exhausted, while Dex kissed her forehead and told her how amazing she was.

Daisy stood in awe, gaping at the sound of the baby's wail. It was a feeble, beautiful cry that tore Daisy's heart wide open. Little arms and legs flailed while the nurse cooed and wiped her down before passing the squirming infant to her mother.

Dex had tears in his eyes as he curled the blanket back from the baby's face, then kissed Rose's sweaty brow again.

Daisy blinked at her own tears, pressing her fingers

against her quivering mouth as she drank in the most life-affirming, precious moment of her life.

Rose kissed her daughter's little nose. "Welcome, baby. I'm your mom, and this…" She glanced up at Dex, mirroring his loving gaze before whispering, "This is your daddy."

Dex's chin bunched as a fresh wave of tears filled his eyes.

Daisy sniffed, realizing how much this must mean to him. He wasn't the biological father, but he was being treated as such.

"I love you," he murmured, kissing Rose's lips before turning to their daughter and smiling. "And I love you too. Always and forever."

Daisy had never been more grateful to witness something so precious. Her heart swelled with love—for her sister, and for the baby girl who was now family. She was Rose's to look after…and Daisy's too.

Daisy knew with utter certainty that her new life mission was to be a better sister and a worthy aunt.

She started to back away quietly. She wasn't that person yet, but she would be. She had to be.

"Daisy, wait." Rose's call stopped her just as she reached the door. "Don't you want to hold her before you go?"

Daisy's heart stuttered. "Really?"

Rose and Dex both grinned.

"Of course," Dex said. "You helped us get here."

"If it weren't for you running for help…" Rose gave a little shiver at the thought.

Daisy's smile faltered. If it weren't for Daisy, she would have been home safe and sound when she'd gone into labor, not on the side of the road.

But when Rose lifted the baby in her direction, Daisy couldn't resist. She took the soft, warm little bundle and smiled down at the wrinkly cutie in her arms. "Well, aren't you something," she whispered, her heart so full of emotion she could hardly breathe. "You are perfect and sweet, just like your mama, aren't you? And I bet you'll be just as smart and noble as your daddy too." She caught Dex's gaze and winked at him before looking back down at her niece. "I cannot wait to see you grow up, sweetheart."

When she handed the baby back, her heart was aching with it all. The regret, the shame, the fear…and the realization of how much she'd failed everyone. In the past and today.

But she would do better. For their sakes, she'd start over, and she'd grow up.

"I'm gonna go call Dahlia and let her know," Daisy said before slipping out to give the new family some privacy.

But it turned out she didn't have to call Dahlia because she and JJ were already in the waiting room.

How did they know?

Levi, Daisy guessed. He must have called them. And Daisy had never been more grateful to see her twin sister.

"Congratulations, Aunt Daisy." Dahlia laughed and hugged her tight.

"Congratulations to you, Aunt Dahlia," she shot back.

Dahlia squeezed her shoulders. "Levi told us how you chased down help. You did good, sis."

Daisy's throat was too choked to respond, so she just nodded and then pulled away. "Go on. I'm sure Rose can't wait to see you."

Dahlia glanced at JJ, who gave her a smile. "I'll stay out here with Daisy to give you guys some privacy."

They shared a gooey look that made Daisy want to cry all over again. She was so happy for Dahlia and for Rose and all they had. No one deserved love and happiness more than her sisters.

But right now she was so achingly aware of all she was walking away from that she couldn't even bring herself to respond when Dahlia said, "I'll be out soon."

Daisy walked over to a row of chairs and plunked into one. Now that the adrenaline was fading and reality was settling in, she felt like a weight was resting on her shoulders.

JJ slid into the seat beside her. "How you holding up?"

She shrugged. *Okay. Fine.* She couldn't quite get the words out.

"You've had quite a day, considering it's only midmorning."

She nodded.

He shifted until his shoulder brushed hers. "Saw your note on the table."

She stiffened. She'd forgotten about that. "Oh. Um…" She glanced over. "Did Dahlia see?"

His gaze was kind as he nodded. "Gotta say, I do not enjoy watching my woman cry."

"I'm sorry." She winced and slid down in her seat, hunching her shoulders.

"Nah." His voice was quiet. "I wasn't trying to make you feel bad. Just thought you should know is all."

"That I was a jerk for not saying goodbye?"

"That you'll be missed." He turned to face her. "A lot."

She pressed her lips together and nodded. "Thanks."

"Dahlia and Rose are so happy to have you here, Daisy.

Emma and Lizzy too. Just wanted to make sure you knew that. And today, with all this going on...well, I hope you know how proud of you they are."

Daisy stiffened. Was he being sarcastic?

No. He sounded and looked totally sincere.

She gave him a confused frown, but he just sat back in his seat with that quiet smile of his.

Silence settled over them, and Daisy told herself not to fill it. She didn't want to talk anyway. But Dahlia had mentioned more than once what a good listener JJ was, and suddenly Daisy understood why. It was the fact that he wasn't prying, wasn't judging, wasn't giving her a hard time at all...

It had words bubbling up and spilling out before she could stop herself. "There's nothing to be proud of. I made a mess of things, just like I always do. Dahlia was constantly cleaning up after me as a kid, did you know that? Not like I was a messy kid kind of way, but in the sense that I was always getting into trouble. And it was Dahlia who cleaned it up."

He pursed his lips and nodded. "That sounds like my Lia."

"And now...now she shouldn't have to do that anymore." She bit her lip as she thought of the debt collector who could be at the ranch right now looking for her. "I'm done letting her take care of me. And I'm done resenting her for it too."

After a beat, he replied in that slow drawl of his, "Well, I'm sure she'll be real glad to hear that. But Dahlia takes care of the people she loves. It's who she is. And everyone needs help now and again, but that doesn't mean they're too much trouble."

"But I am," Daisy said, her voice shaking. Her mind

346

was with Levi and his kids. It was her fault that Mikayla ran away. She'd thought she'd been bonding with the girl, but really she was just a bad influence.

"It's my fault this happened." She gestured toward the delivery room.

"You got your sister knocked up?" JJ's voice held a tinge of laughter, and Daisy rolled her eyes.

"She was with me because Mikayla ran away, and it was my fault. And it's my fault Levi hates me, and now Ronnie and Dawson will, too, because they'll think I'm abandoning them, and I should never have come here because bad people are looking for me, and if I'd just remembered to charge my phone, then none of this would have happened!" Her tirade came to an end so she could take a breath, and when she let it out, tears slipped down her cheeks.

She swiped at them in annoyance. She was tired of crying. Tired of feeling sorry for herself.

No, she was tired of herself. Period.

"I want to change." She sniffed. "I *need* to change if I'm going to be the sister they deserve."

Her lips trembled. She wasn't sure she'd ever deserve Levi and his family. And she didn't have the right to ask him to wait while she tried to…

What? Grow up?

She dropped her head into her hands. "That's why I have to go, JJ." She lifted her head to look at him. "Make sure Dahlia knows that, okay? I'm trying to do something right for once."

JJ arched a brow. "From where I'm standing, there's a whole lot you do right. Dahlia, Rose, Emma, Lizzy, not to mention the sheriff and his family…I've seen them all light up like Christmas trees these past couple months. You did that, Daisy. You brought joy and life to this town in a way I've never seen."

She sniffled, swiping a finger under her nose. "Thanks, JJ. That's really sweet." She shook her head with a rueful grin. "I'm glad Dahlia found you. You two are so perfect."

"I found *her*, thank you very much," he teased. "And we love each other because of our imperfections. Not because we're perfect. That's how love works."

She drew in a shaky breath. She knew where he was going with this, but it wasn't the same. Dahlia might have her issues, but she was responsible. "Dahlia would have never been a bad influence on Mikayla or gotten Rose into an accident," she muttered.

"You're being too hard on yourself." JJ nudged her with a teasing smile. "I forget to charge my phone all the time."

"Yeah, but you're not a flake."

He gave her a lopsided grin as he slung an arm around her shoulders. "Nope. That's one name I haven't been called. But seeing as I'm almost your brother, I'll clobber anyone who calls you a flake from here on out. Deal?"

Daisy choked on a laugh, but then the laugh turned into a sob.

JJ curled his hand around her shoulder, tugging her close and murmuring kind words of comfort as she wept against his chest.

CHAPTER 46

I t took a little while for Fred and his tow truck to arrive, and while they waited, Levi called Ethan to tell him Mikayla had been found and to spread the word to anyone who might have been worried. Then he checked the car out, making sure to grab anything Daisy might need.

He found himself staring at her luggage in the trunk with a heavy heart.

"She really is leaving," Mikayla murmured.

He hadn't heard her approach, and now he didn't have words to comfort her, so he wrapped an arm around her shoulders instead. Truthfully, his own heart ached with rejection at the sight of her luggage. They might not have ended things well the day before, but he'd thought he'd see her one more time. He thought he'd have a chance to fix things.

But clearly she didn't want to fix this. With a heavy heart, he kissed the top of Mikayla's head. "I'll always be here," he rasped. "You know that, right? No matter what you do or say, no matter how far you run...I will always be your father, and I will never, ever stop loving you."

She stared up at him, her chin starting to quiver as tears filled her eyes. And then she burst into tears, pressing her face to his chest as he held her tight, rocking her gently from side to side.

He rubbed her back and shushed her as best he could, but she obviously had a lot to get out. Her escape into the darkness was catching up with her. Relief that she'd been found was overwhelming, and he fought his own tears as he battled nightmare scenarios of what could have been.

Thankfully, the tow truck showed up, and Levi was able to pull himself together quick-smart.

Fred's eyes lit with recognition when he saw the car. "Is Daisy all right?"

"She's fine," Levi answered.

"That's good." Fred moved to the back of his truck to get started. "That girl is a real angel."

He nodded. He'd thought so too. Heck, he still believed it. For all her faults, he'd never seen so much love or joy in a single person. He'd never met someone who gave her affection so freely, asking nothing in return.

And maybe you couldn't hold someone like that down. Maybe with someone like Daisy, you were only meant to take what they were willing to give and then let them go.

The thought made his chest constrict, and it was an effort to sound calm and bright the way Mikayla needed him to be.

"Come on, kiddo." He led her to Dex's car. "Let's go home."

They rode in silence for a little while, and then Levi cleared his throat. "So, uh...what were you doing out so early?"

He'd already guessed the scenario. Daisy and Rose flying through town, chasing after his daughter. They found her out in the middle of a country road in the early morning darkness. His kid had been trying to run away.

The idea wounded him deeply, but he didn't want to let it show.

And so he waited.

Mikayla didn't answer right away. Instead, she perfected her swallowing, lip-biting routine.

"What were you doing with Daisy and Rose?"

The silence stretched so long he thought maybe she'd never answer. But when he parked in front of the house, she finally spoke up. "I ran away."

His heart lurched painfully, but he kept his lips clamped shut. Some part of him had hoped there was another explanation. "Why?" The one word felt like glass.

Was he such a horrible father? He scrubbed a hand over his eyes.

"I just felt like… I thought…" She sniffed. "I thought you wouldn't care."

"What?" He spun to face her. "How could you think that?"

"I know, I'm sorry. I…" She met his gaze warily. "I always make you angry. And I hate school. And—"

"You don't make me angry. I worry about you, that's all." He kept his tone soft and sincere. "I'm afraid for you and your brothers all the time." He took her hand and squeezed. "I thought losing your mother was going to kill me. It hurt so much."

Her lips parted, and her eyes widened. "Really?"

He nodded. "And the thought of losing you…" He squeezed his eyes shut. "I know I'm not the best father, but I will try to be better."

"You're not a bad father," she whispered. "I just feel like I can't do anything right."

He winced and then swallowed. "I'm sorry I make you feel that way."

"I thought…" She looked out the window, her face bunching. "I don't know. You never talk about Mom. And you always seem so miserable at home with us. Or…you did before Daisy. And when I found out she was leaving, I knew you'd go back to being all sad and grumpy again. I don't want to feel like we're the reason you're miserable, you know? I don't want to go back to feeling like…like… like you wish you'd never had us."

Her soft admission was spearing his chest with a broadsword. "Is that what you thought? Mikayla…" He waited until she looked at him. "You and your brothers are the best thing that ever happened to me."

"But when Mom died—"

"After your mom died, I was grieving, and I was scared because I don't know how to be everything for you guys. Your mom was the one who cuddled you and sang songs and tended to your boo-boos."

Her lips twitched at the "boo-boos" comment.

"All I know how to do is keep you safe. So that's what I did." He eyed the cut Mikayla had gotten during the fender bender. "That's what I try to do, at least."

She nodded slowly. "Yeah. I get that."

He wasn't sure what else to say but wasn't ready to give up on this "breakthrough" conversation. "Why do you hate school?"

She shot him a sidelong look. "Do you really want to know?"

"Of course."

She took a deep breath and launched into a story about

her friends that he could barely follow. Every time he felt like maybe he should add his two cents, she said, "But Daisy told me I should just…" or "Daisy says girls do that when…"

So he kept his mouth shut, because apparently Daisy had it covered. He scratched the back of his head. Good thing, too, because he had no idea how to deal with teen girl social issues.

"Well, I'm, uh…I'm glad Daisy helped you out," he finally murmured once Mikayla was done.

"Yeah." She nodded. "She said I could call her too." She shot him a quick look. "Even if she's not hanging around at our house anymore."

She was prying, but he refused to acknowledge it. "Did she?"

"Yeah. She said…she said no matter where she is or what she's doing, she'll pick up when I call. That's pretty cool, right?"

"Yeah," he agreed, his heart heavy.

No matter where she is…

She wouldn't be here, that was what that meant.

"I hate that you were going to run away from me, from us…" He gestured to the front door, where the boys were waiting and watching anxiously in the doorway.

Mikayla turned to him with wide, teary eyes. "I am sorry, Dad. I wasn't thinking. Daisy made me realize that running isn't the answer, and I promise I'll never do it again."

She said it so solemnly and with such conviction…

He drew in a breath and gave her a watery smile.

She turned to open the door, but he stopped her. "Mikayla, wait."

She spun back, and he pulled her into his arms. "For

my part, I promise I'll never go back to being so closed off, okay?"

She nodded against his shoulder.

"I know I sort of…shut down after your mom died. I was living in fear and only focusing on your physical safety and health. I wasn't there for you three the way I should have been. I forgot that it's not just about keeping you safe, it's about making sure you know you're loved. Unconditionally and forever." He pulled back to meet her gaze. "And you are, Mikayla. I love you always and with all my heart."

"I love you, too, Dad."

She hugged him so tight he was choking, but he refused to be the first to pull away.

"So, no more Warden Baker?" she whispered against his shoulder.

He heard the playful tone and sat back with a soft chuckle. "I'll do my best. Just do me a favor and don't act like a delinquent."

"No promises." She laughed. "But I will try my very best."

She winked and jumped out of the car, making him think of Beth.

She looked so like her mother it took his breath away.

Racing up the walkway, she greeted the boys, who threw themselves at her.

"Thanks, Beth. They're good kids."

His mind jumped to Daisy, and he couldn't help thanking her, too, even though she wasn't there to hear him. She'd reminded him of all the joys he'd been over-looking.

And even though he had a feeling that very soon she'd

be long gone, he had to be grateful for what she'd given him in the time she'd been here.

It was a gift, and all he could do now was cherish what they'd had and let her go.

CHAPTER 47

Daisy adjusted the little beanie on baby Kiara's head. The pale pink fabric was covered with yellow hearts. "Look at you, all fashion savvy."

The baby cooed, and Rose laughed. "That was from Lizzy. She and the twins went a little overboard with onesies and accessories."

Daisy grinned as the baby latched on to her finger, her tiny digits so soft and delicate. "Thanks to your Aunt Lizzy, you're going to be the most fashionable little girl in town, aren't you?"

Rose laughed again when the baby answered with a gurgle. "I think that's a yes." Her gaze lifted to meet Daisy's. "Are you sure we can't convince you to stick around a little longer?"

Daisy shook her head, her heart heavy despite her smile. "I'm afraid this is something I have to do."

Rose's brows drew together, but she didn't argue.

"Thanks again for pitching in to get my car fixed. I owe you and Dee big-time. And I promise to pay you back... eventually." She cringed.

"Is your situation really that bad?" Rose mirrored her expression.

Daisy hesitated. In the few days that had passed since Mikayla ran away, Daisy had been doing a lot of thinking about who she wanted to be going forward. And honesty was one of the traits she'd been trying to work on.

She'd come clean with Dahlia about her debts and the loan shark on the drive back to the ranch that very night. And while Dahlia had been trying to convince her to stay —she was so sure that she could help Daisy sort out her mess—Daisy was equally sure that she needed to fix her own problems.

No more running when things got tough.

She watched the newborn yawn, and her heart pulsed with adoration. She was besotted with Kiara, and if she was going to be a good aunt, she had to make sure the next time she came to visit, there was no one following her.

If she was going to be a good sister, she had to find a way to sort out her mess once and for all.

And she would. She'd responded to her contact in New York and had lined up some gigs in the weeks after her return. And if her heart was heavy as she kissed her niece goodbye and told Rose she'd see her when she got back, then that was all just part of her penance.

"We'll be waiting for you." Rose gave her a sad smile, opened her mouth, hesitated, then sighed and said, "You do know there's a difference between shirking responsibilities and letting people help you, right? It's not a crime to count on your family. And letting someone help you is just as much a gift to them as it is to you."

Her gaze moved to Dex, who was in the kitchen with his grandfather. The old man had been doting over his great-granddaughter with more affection than Daisy thought possible. He'd been near giddy from the moment he first held her. Daisy had been in awe of the display, wondering how different her life would have been if she'd had a male role model like that. All three of them would have grown up feeling secure, loved, wanted.

But that had not been their path. She cringed, thinking about how far all of them had strayed before love found them new homes.

Home. Levi. The kids.

Daisy fidgeted while her heart pulsed and yearned for the things she couldn't have.

It was impossible to stay. The Baker family deserved joy and security, not threatening debt collectors.

Levi had helped her for now. She had no idea what he'd done—maybe flashed his badge around and made a few legal threats of his own—but Derek Knox had been scared away for a little while.

It was a short reprieve. Her debt was still unpaid, and he'd be back soon enough.

Daisy was determined to be as far as possible from the people she loved when that happened.

After she'd worked her butt off and saved up that money, she could head west again, maybe even settle down in little ol' Aspire. Her family would welcome her with open arms.

But would Levi?

He hadn't called.

And she had to assume he got it now...that she was more trouble than she was worth.

She couldn't blame him. Not after it was her influence that led Mikayla to run in the first place.

"Daisy," Rose prompted. "You do know it's okay to let

people help you, right?"

Daisy smiled. Dahlia had said something similar when she'd said her goodbyes to everyone at the ranch this morning. She suspected both her sisters had grappled with this to some extent or another. One didn't grow up the way they had without some monster trust issues, especially when it came to men.

Rose looked expectant, so Daisy said what she'd said to Dahlia. "I'm working on that."

Rose's eyes were filled with sadness on Daisy's behalf. "I just don't want to see you walk away from love because…well, because of our mother's experience."

Daisy nodded, but she turned away before she could get choked up about the topic. For the first time in her life, she had let a man get close. Levi had stolen her heart right out from under her nose. He'd slipped past her defenses before she'd even realized what was happening.

And his kids…

She swallowed hard at the thought of those kids. They'd gotten to her in a way she hadn't seen coming. She'd never in her life imagined being a mom. She'd never daydreamed about being a part of a family.

But lately she'd started dreaming of it, finding solace in the prospect of settling down.

She needed it. And maybe with a little luck and a whole lot of hard work, she'd get it.

Sucking in a determined breath, she forced a smile and gave Rose and the baby one last kiss goodbye.

"I'll see ya, sis."

"Hopefully soon." Rose's sweet smile was disrupted when Kiara started to fuss.

"Aw, does baby girl need a hug from Pop Pop?" Dex's grandfather walked into the room, looking young and vibrant as he reached for his great-granddaughter with a tender smile.

"She'll be due a feed soon."

"All right." He bounced the baby in his arms. "Just a quick cuddle, then back to Mama."

Daisy walked away from the heartwarming scene and stepped into the kitchen.

Dex was busy making Rose a cup of herbal tea. It smelled delicious.

"You're a good man," she murmured.

Dex spun around with a grin. "It's easy when you've got a good woman to look after." He caught Daisy's expression, and his smile fled. "You leaving already?"

With a nod, she opened her arms for a hug, and he drew her close.

"We're all going to miss you, you know," he murmured.

She nodded again. She'd been hearing that a lot. Before she came here, she'd said her goodbyes at the ranch and swung by Lizzy's house. She'd debated long and hard about going to the sheriff's place to say goodbye to the kids.

And to Levi.

But maybe she hadn't shed all of her cowardly tendencies yet. The thought of having them all within hugging distance and turning her back on them…she couldn't do it.

So she'd written them each a card instead. Mikayla was right, leaving without a goodbye was wrong, so she'd worked late into the night perfecting a message to each of them. A stack of discarded notes lay in a wastepaper basket at the ranch, and four sealed envelopes were in her bag.

She drew them out and passed them to Dex.

"Would you…?" She shifted from one foot to the other. "Could you please give these to Levi and the kids the next time you see them?"

Dex's brows lowered with concern as he took the labeled envelopes. "Daisy…" He sighed. "Are you sure you don't want to pass these on yourself?"

She swallowed, indecision warring inside her.

The truth was she wanted nothing more than to see Levi one more time. To touch his beard and be held in his arms. Just the thought of that comfort—of his scent and his arms wrapping around her—it was enough to make her lungs hitch.

She'd give just about anything to feel his lips against hers one more time, to hear his laugh, which had been so rare when she'd first met him but had become the sound-track to her life for a few weeks there.

But to then walk away from that?

Impossible.

She sniffed and shook her head. "Please, Dex. I can't."

"Okay." He laid them on the counter, then winced and shook his head. "I just really think you should see him on your way out of town."

Her throat felt raw when she swallowed. "I'm not, uh…I'm not sure he'd want to see me right now."

"I don't know about that."

She shook her head. "I've caused him enough trouble, but if you could please pass these on, I—" Her breath caught, and she had to clear her throat before she could speak again. "It's just explaining why I'm going and that I'm not out to hurt anyone. I'm trying to do right by him and his beautiful kids." She sniffed. "I have some debts I have to clear first, and maybe…maybe if God's merciful, He'll help Levi to forgive me." She blinked, but it was pointless. The tears broke free anyway.

She scrambled for a tissue and mopped up her face while Dex stood there frowning at her. "Debts? Did you borrow from more than one guy in LA?"

She blanched and shook her head, about to ask him how he knew, but of course Rose would have told him.

Ashamed, she looked to the floor and muttered, "No, just Benny. But the interest rates are a killer, and I need to get on with paying it back, you know?"

"But…" Dex's brows furrowed further with confusion. "They've been paid."

A rueful laugh escaped. "No they haven't. Benny is one determined guy, and—"

"Levi told me about him. And that jerk Derek who threatened you."

She blinked, her belly twisting with humiliation. "He did, huh? Well then, I guess you understand why I have to go back to New York and earn the money to clear my debt."

"Daisy." Dex lightly squeezed her shoulders. "Levi paid him off."

Her lips parted, and for a second, she was sure she'd heard him incorrectly. "Excuse me?"

"I thought he told you." Dex looked as surprised as she felt. "You're cleared. Levi promised to keep you safe, and he did. He's a man of his word."

Her mouth opened and closed, and her belly swooped and soared as she tried to make sense of it. He'd paid her debt?

"But I owed…so much money."

"Yeah." Dex looked grim.

"How did Levi...?"

"He had to dip into some savings, but if it meant you'd be safe..." Dex's lips curled into a soft grin. "He didn't hesitate."

Breathing was becoming hugely difficult.

She rested a hand on her chest and had to lean against the kitchen counter.

Twenty thousand dollars. He'd paid twenty *thousand* dollars. For her.

Why hadn't he told her? Why had he done it at all?

She had the urge to laugh and cry all at once because... of course he'd paid the guy.

Of course he'd do that.

She shook her head, clapping a hand over her mouth.

The man was too honorable for his own good.

And while she loved that about him—while everything in her wanted to fly off to him right now and hug him until he laughed—she didn't have the right to.

Twenty thousand dollars.

No doubt Mikayla's college fund.

Daisy closed her eyes, guilt ripping through her.

The man was too noble for his own good. He felt obligated toward her, and he shouldn't. She wasn't his to worry about. He shouldn't have to put up with that kind of nonsense. He deserved a good, kind woman who would take care of him and the kids, not someone who chewed into his savings and denied sweet Mikayla the education she deserved.

She really was an unworthy screwup.

"I'm gonna pay him back. Every last penny," she said, her voice a fierce whisper. "You make sure you tell him that."

Standing tall, she pulled Dex into a quick hug before walking out the kitchen door. She'd never felt more determined to get to New York and start making money. She wanted to prove to Levi that she wasn't some flake.

Mikayla was going to college. Daisy wouldn't stop until she'd made certain of it.

CHAPTER 48

It was a peaceful Saturday morning for the Baker household. Levi soaked in the quiet as he finished up the dishes. After a little while, though, the quiet became worrisome.

Levi looked over at the kitchen table to see Ronnie still picking at the last of his pancake, Dawson absorbed in a graphic novel, and Mikayla on her phone.

He felt a tug of pride as he looked at them. It had been a tough week all around. Lots of family talks had taken place, and while things were far from perfect, he liked to think maybe they were settling into a new normal. One where they talked about their problems. One where everyone had a voice.

There was only one thing missing. There was an empty chair next to Ronnie that felt like a gaping hole.

Daisy should be here. This current silence was nice, but he missed her laughter. This house and his kids—none of it was the same without her enthusiasm and light, her laughter, and her music. She'd brought this place back to life after Beth's death left them in a sort of trance, and he couldn't stand the idea of going back to the way things had been before she'd come along.

He couldn't bear the thought of her not being in his life. It was nearly as painful as grieving. But rather than mourning a life lived, it was like mourning a life that he'd never truly had.

He threw down the wet rag with a sigh. Maybe he should call her. He needed to. For one, he'd never had a chance to tell her that she didn't need to worry about her debts anymore. He'd been putting it off, worried that she might tell him off for muscling in on her business. She was an independent woman, all right.

But he'd also been putting it off because he wanted to talk to his kids about it first.

The next time he invited Daisy into his home, he didn't want it to be a secret. And he didn't want her there as a music teacher. He wanted her there as the love of his life.

He wanted her as his wife.

It was a big step, and they obviously wouldn't rush into things. For all he knew, Daisy could be leaving town as soon as Rose and the baby were settled.

Or maybe she'd stay a little longer.

Please stay, his heart begged.

He glanced over at his kids.

Did he really want to upset this new delicate balance he'd found with them?

Yes. You do. Because her light and energy are needed in this house.

A spark of energy shot through him, and he cleared his throat.

None of them looked up.

With a small frown, he stepped up to the table and lightly tapped his knuckle on the end of it.

"So I was thinking…" He trailed off because they were each too absorbed in what they were doing that they clearly weren't listening. He let out a sharp exhale and mentally rehearsed.

I was thinking about asking Daisy to be my girlfriend. How do you feel about that?

He winced and smoothed a hand over his beard. Too abrupt?

I asked your mom for a sign, you see, and…

He shook his head. Too weird.

No, all four of them had agreed to be more straightforward with each other, so he'd just say it like it was.

I fell in love with Daisy, and I want her to be a part of our lives.

He took a deep breath, ready to try again. But his phone rang before he could speak. Dex's name lit up his screen.

"Hey, Dex." He forced a cheerful tone. "How's the baby?"

"We're all happy and healthy here. Rose and Kiara got home yesterday and are settling in just fine. But I'm actually calling to…" He sighed.

"What is it, buddy? Everything okay?"

"Maybe it's none of my business."

Levi heard Rose call something out in the background, and Dex chuckled. "Rose says if it's not my business, it's hers."

Levi frowned in confusion. "What are you talking about?"

He heard Rose's voice in the background again. Something about sisters looking out for each other. He straightened, fear stabbing him in the gut. "Is it Daisy? Is she all right?"

That got his kids' attention. Suddenly all three of them were staring at him wide-eyed.

"She's fine," Dex said slowly.

Too slowly. There was a "but" coming, and Levi braced for it.

"But she's heading out of town."

"What?" Levi barked. "I thought she was staying a little longer. Her car's not even fixed yet."

"She got it back this morning."

"And she's left already?"

"Just now," Dex admitted. "She gave me goodbye letters to give you and the kids. She just couldn't bring herself to say goodbye face-to-face. She was a wreck, and aw, Levi." He hissed. "I think she's trying to do the right thing by you and your family. And maybe Rose and I shouldn't intervene, but…we thought you should know."

Levi's heart galloped. His rib cage felt too tight as panic hit him straight in the chest. He was losing her before he'd even had a chance to win her back.

He'd been too slow. He should have gone to her right away. Why had he hesitated?

You fool!

"I'm sorry if this news is upsetting you. I just… We wanted to give you a heads-up."

"Yeah, thanks, Dex." He hung up and started to pace.

"Dad, what is it?" Dawson asked.

"Has Daisy gone?" Ronnie's little face puckered with worry. "I thought we'd get to see her soon."

Mikayla stayed silent, but her big eyes were too dark and knowing. Levi suspected she'd guessed straight away that Daisy had never planned on seeing them again.

"I, uh…" He met his kids' curious stares as his mind raced.

370

He couldn't let her leave. He needed her.

Rubbing a hand over his aching chest, he faced his children. This wasn't how he'd planned to tell them, but there was no time left to dally. "Dex told me Daisy's just left."

"No!" Dawson bolted out of his seat.

"Dad, you can't let her go." Ronnie was right behind him.

Mikayla stayed quiet, but her lips were pressed together tight. She was watching him expectantly, almost…encouragingly.

"Here's the thing, guys." Levi stepped toward them, his hands out wide. "I've fallen in love with her."

Ronnie gasped. "Like you want to kiss her and stuff?"

Levi felt the heat rising up his neck and nodded with a soft chuckle. "Something like that."

His kids gaped at him, Dawson blinking in wonder while Mikayla narrowed her eyes to really study him.

"This doesn't mean I love your mother any less." He spoke directly to her. "I'll never stop loving her."

There was a brief silence before Mikayla finally nodded. "We know that."

Ronnie nodded, too, and Dawson added, "Of course you love Mom. We all do. But we love Daisy too."

Levi's brows arched. "Yeah?"

"Of course!" Ronnie looked offended. "Daisy's the best."

Mikayla's lips quirked up in a small grin. "We've known about you two for a while."

"You…you…" He stopped. "You did?"

Dawson grinned. "You're not very good at being sneaky."

He choked on a laugh. "No, I guess not. We wanted to

tell you. We just weren't sure…" He winced. "I'm still not sure."

"You're not?" Mikayla's wide eyes said she didn't believe that for a second.

"No, I mean, I am. I just…" He sighed in exasperation. He couldn't believe he was trying to explain his feelings to his kids. "I'm sure about how I feel. I'm just not sure if this is what she wants."

His kids stared at him for so long he thought maybe he'd said something profound. But then Ronnie scratched his head, his nose wrinkling as he asked, "So why are you still standing here?"

Mikayla snorted out a laugh, and Dawson grinned. "Yeah, Dad. You're not gonna find out if she feels the same unless you tell her."

She lifted a fist. "Time to be brave."

His heart picked up its pace as he nodded. "Yeah?"

He met each of their gazes in turn and found them all so certain and so happy, he couldn't believe he'd waited this long to talk to them about it.

"Come on!" Ronnie was already running for the door, Dawson right behind him.

Even Mikayla was moving with some urgency as they headed outside.

"You guys don't have to—"

"Daisy stopped me from making a mistake." Mikayla spun to talk to him, suddenly looking like a grown-up as she met his gaze. "I'm not gonna let her do the same thing."

He opened his mouth, but she looked so determined that he couldn't bring himself to argue. Besides, he wanted to believe her that Daisy was making a mistake.

Because the alternative, that Daisy had decided he and

his family weren't worth it...that she didn't want to give up her life on the road to be with them...

His chest roared with pain. *Please don't let that be it!*

He grabbed the car keys and followed his kids out the door.

Ronnie was right. There was only one way to find out if she felt the same.

And there was no time to waste.

CHAPTER 49

D aisy did not leave town the way she came in. For one, her taillight was fixed, and in better shape than ever thanks to Fred's recent handiwork. For another, she wasn't speeding.

Far from it.

Her car inched down Main Street as she let her gaze linger one last time over the spot where she'd tried busking that first week in town before getting busted by Levi for not having a permit. And then the coffee shop where they'd had their first date. Sort of.

She waved to Norman and Chicken Joe, who were the last of the coffee crew still lingering this late on a bright, sunny Saturday morning. She slowed to a crawl as she passed a crowded Mama's Kitchen, glancing in the front windows in the hopes of spotting someone she knew.

Oh, okay, fine. Who was she kidding? She was hoping that maybe Levi and his kids were in there and she might get one parting glance.

She was pathetic.

She gripped the steering wheel tighter and turned her

attention back to the road. She'd made her decision. Pressing a little harder on the accelerator she made her way southeast, heading for the main road that would take her to New York.

She braked at a stop sign and lingered far longer than necessary as her mind raced. Was she right to leave without a goodbye?

Were those cards enough? Would the kids understand? Would Levi forgive her?

She closed her eyes for a second as if that might make everything clear. A car honked behind her, and she opened her eyes with a jerk. "Sorry!" she called out her open window. She cut through the intersection and turned onto the road that led to the highway.

He'd cleared her debt.

No matter how many times she thought about it, she still couldn't quite believe it. Why had he done that? Was it just duty? Some feeling of obligation because they'd been secretly dating?

She shook her head. Of course it was. And she'd find a way to pay him back if it killed her. Her focus turned to the upcoming gigs she'd lined up, which at one point might have made her excited, but these days just made her weary.

What does it mean if the thought of doing something you love exhausts you?

She tapped her fingers on the wheel as she stewed that over. She supposed it meant she didn't love it anymore. She frowned as she passed the church. Its doors were open, and the choir was rehearsing. The gorgeous sound spoke directly to her soul.

She *did* love music. She'd never stop.

But the closer she drew to the outskirts of town, the

more she found herself dreading what was to come. The late nights, the endless schmoozing, the auditions for people who didn't care about the music, just the show, and the compromises when it came to what she played and sang.

It was the business of music she was tired of. For a second, she tried to remember what had kept her going for so long. The mental image of fame and fortune as she played for sold-out amphitheaters used to drive her on a daily basis.

But right now, it didn't feel like a goal or even a dream. It felt like she was imagining something from a movie. Someone else's goal. Someone else's dream.

She'd been clinging to that teenage fantasy for so long, but at some point...

At some point, she'd changed, and she hadn't allowed her dreams for her future to change with it.

But if she let herself fantasize now...

If she let her mind wander to the perfect life and the way she truly wished to live...

Well, it definitely wasn't flitting from one city to the next, and it didn't involve hustling to make someone else's music. Her mind's eye filled easily with an image of what her dream future looked like, and it was right here in Aspire.

She took her foot off the gas as the town limits approached.

Her dreams were all set here, in this town with one particular man and his three adorable kids. Her breath caught, and her heart stumbled.

This was a mistake. She shouldn't be walking away from happiness. Not without explaining to them why she was going.

Wasn't there a way she could earn money here?

Or at least promise that she'd be back as soon as possible?

If Levi even wanted her to return.

Her heart sank.

That was a big if. But maybe—

Whoop! The sound of a siren cut through her thoughts so suddenly she gasped. And then her heart soared when she looked in her rearview mirror and spotted Levi's patrol car behind her.

A huff of disbelief escaped as she warned her heart not to get its hopes up. She might have a busted taillight again or…or…

Her eyes swam with tears when she saw him in her side mirror. He looked more handsome than she remembered with his trimmed beard and those crinkles around his eyes. He wasn't in uniform, but those snug jeans and white T-shirt were still sending her insides into a frenzy.

His gaze was fixed on her, and for a second, she couldn't bring herself to breathe, let alone move.

What was he doing? Was this goodbye or…something else?

He was nearly at her door, and she pushed it open, swiveling to watch him. She drank in the sight of him as he approached, all too aware that this might be the last time she saw him…at least for a while.

She nibbled on her lip and fidgeted with her bracelets. What was she supposed to say? He couldn't have gotten her letter yet, and suddenly she couldn't remember a word of what she'd written.

And then he was there. Right in front of her. And his heat, his scent, the look in his eyes was all-consuming. She could barely breathe as she managed a teasing "Something wrong, Officer?"

His lips twitched, but his dark gaze was unreadable. "It's Sheriff."

Her heart faltered. He was teasing her back. He remembered their first meeting, and he was…teasing.

Her mouth went dry as she tried to swallow. "Hi, Levi."

He moved closer, gently taking her hand and helping her out of the car. She leaned back against her door and gazed up at him.

"Don't go." His voice was so low and gruff that she nearly didn't hear him over the breeze.

She blinked, sure she'd heard him wrong. "W-What?"

He reached out and snagged her around the waist, tugging her so close they were pressed together. He rested his forehead on hers, his breath hot against her lips. "Please. Don't go. I can't let you go."

He sounded so pained, so heartbroken. Her chest cracked, and all the emotions she'd been trying to keep in check spilled out in a blubbery sob. "I don't deserve to stay."

"Yes you do." He leaned back, catching her eye with a desperate look that made her heart beat a wild new rhythm she'd never heard before. "You're safe now. You don't have to run away."

A breath caught in her throat, and she let out another little sob. "Dex told me what you did and…" She lurched forward, kissing him soundly. "Thank you. Thank you."

"Shhh." He pulled her in tighter, holding her close. "I don't need your thanks. I don't want it. I did what I had to do to protect you, and I'd do it again in a heartbeat."

"But you shouldn't have to… I didn't want you to…"

"I know, but, sweetheart…" He pulled back until his gaze met hers again. "I love you."

Her breath left her in a whoosh. "What?"

"I love you." He said it so evenly, so steadily, making a mockery of her frantic, whirring heart.

"But…but I'm a mess."

His lips quirked up on one side. "So am I. Or…I was." He glanced back toward the car. "We were. Until you came along and helped us."

Her eyes widened in surprise as Mikayla, Ronnie, and Dawson poured out of the back seat. "What are you all doing here?"

Levi's deep drawl brought her attention back to him. "We're here to stop you from leaving us, Daisy O'Sullivan. I know…" He cleared his throat. "I know I can't offer you the fame and glamor you deserve. And I don't want to come between you and your dreams, but there's got to be a way for you to have it all, and I'll make that happen. I swear to you—"

"That's not my dream," she blurted before he could continue.

He stared down at her. "What?"

"I thought it was." She wet her lips as she tried to explain what she was only just starting to understand. "I thought being a famous musician would satisfy me, you know? I thought…" She searched for the words with frustration, her fingers curling in his shirt as he held her. "I thought if a whole lot of strangers adored me, that would be enough. It would make me feel loved without actually having to…" She swallowed hard as his gaze searched hers. "Without having to risk my heart. Or rely on a man who could…who could hurt me…"

"Oh my darlin' Daisy," he growled before kissing her thoroughly. "I would never hurt you."

"You wouldn't mean to," she said quickly. "But love makes us weak."

He shook his head. "No, it makes us vulnerable. Not weak." He reached a hand up and cupped her cheek, trailing a thumb over her tears. "You helped me realize that. I thought after losing Beth that I could never leave myself open to that sort of hurt again. I didn't want to love another woman, because then I could potentially lose her, and..." His throat worked. "I didn't think I could survive it. So I shut down and protected my family and my heart." His smile was gentle. "But then you came along. And suddenly there was sunshine in our dark days. There was music and laughter and...hope. And what I realized, Daisy..." He leaned down until his nose grazed hers, and his whispered words hit home. "What I realized is that a life without an open heart, without someone to share all the ups and the downs with...a life without love, it's no life at all."

She went up on her toes to kiss him, her heart pounding harder as he kissed her back with so much heat and passion that Ronnie called out, "Gross, Dad."

Levi lifted his head, his eyes dancing with amusement as he kissed her nose and cheeks. "I forgot we had an audience."

Daisy laughed, the sudden burst of happiness making her feel lighter than air.

Then Ronnie added, "Does this mean she's staying?"

Levi's eyes were rich with affection as he gazed down at her. "That's the question, isn't it? Daisy O'Sullivan, will you stay and be my girlfriend?"

Her smile was instant, and her answer required no

thought. "Yes!" She leapt into his arms, and he crushed her to him, lifting her off her feet with a triumphant growl.

The kids came running, circling them and hugging Daisy, until they were one big mass of arms and legs, laughing and dancing and hugging in the middle of the road.

Levi included.

CHAPTER 50

L evi held Daisy's hand as she sniffled and squeezed his fingers when Dahlia said, "I do."

Aside from maybe Cody, Kit, and JJ's father, there wasn't a dry eye among the small group gathered by the lake on the ranch's property.

Apparently this was the sight of Dahlia and JJ's first date when he'd taken her ice fishing, and it was the perfect location for this intimate sunset wedding. With just their immediate families and close friends nearby, the happy couple only had eyes for each other as they exchanged their vows.

JJ's parents and sisters had arrived the day before and were only staying a few nights. To say they brought a certain tension to the ranch was the understatement of the year. Daisy had never seen JJ quite so ruffled, but in this moment right here, his eyes were focused solely on Dahlia, and the way he was gazing at her made Daisy's heart flutter out of control.

Dahlia deserved this, and Daisy was so excited for the future they were going to have together.

Her heart swelled as JJ slid the ring on her sister's finger, and little baby Kiara chose that moment to gurgle with happiness, making Rose, Dex, and everyone around them smile.

When the minister declared them married, the crowd burst out in cheers, and Levi stole the moment to lean over and whisper gruffly in her ear, "You ready to start talking marriage, sweetheart?"

She shot him a feigned look of exasperation. "No!" But then she went up on tiptoe to kiss his cheek and add, "Not *yet*."

He gave her a wink that made her heart flutter. It seemed to do that a lot lately. And every time he mentioned the M-word, her heart grew ever more frantic. One of these days, she was going to say yes, but it had only been a month since she'd decided to stay, and they'd promised to take things slow for everyone's sake.

Granted, two days into "taking it slow," Ronnie had asked when she was moving in, and Dawson had declared her his stepmom, so the kids weren't really on board with the whole slow-going thing. And shortly after that, Levi had started dropping hints about how he couldn't wait to call her his wife.

Daisy was now the only one taking things slow. Which was kind of hilarious considering she was supposed to be the impulsive one. But that was exactly why she was trying to keep a level head. This was the dawn of a new Daisy, and she'd spent the past month not just enjoying the heck out of her new boyfriend and his loveable kids but working on getting her act together.

She'd taken Dahlia up on her offer to help her budget and plan. No matter how much Levi protested, she was determined to pay him back. Not because she doubted his intentions but because it felt right. It felt responsible, and that was the kind of person she wanted to be.

They'd spent one evening arguing back and forth, but it was Mikayla's college fund that was the clincher. He'd given her the sweetest smile and finally caved.

"All right. I'll let you contribute to my children's college fund, then."

"Thank you." She raised her chin, feeling most triumphant, then dissolved into peals of laughter when Levi had grabbed her with a growl and ended their argument with a series of very heated kisses.

Emma had been helping her, too, and now Daisy's days were filled with private music lessons along with some part-time classes at the high school. Summer school was in full swing, and much to her surprise, there were students who were keen to keep their lessons going throughout the long summer days. She was happy to oblige, plus it made her look good for the coming school year. She was hoping to get a permanent part-time gig that would bring in a steady income.

Slowly but surely, she was figuring out new dreams and goals...ones that matched who she was today.

She sidled closer to Levi as the gathered crowd started to head back to the side-by-sides and trucks that would take them back to the ranch for a simple lunch.

Dahlia and JJ had been intent on keeping it simple, saving their pennies for an extended honeymoon. They were leaving the very next day.

Levi slipped an arm around her shoulders as they joined Dex and Rose. Rose handed the baby over to Daisy, who doted on her as always. "What did you think of your aunt Dahlia's dress, hmm?"

"Well, I for one think she looks amazing," Lizzy answered as she joined them, Kit at her side.

Levi's kids had offered to look after the twins during the ceremony, and Daisy spotted all five of them playing in a nearby creek.

"Their good wedding outfits are going to be ruined," Emma said with a laugh when she saw where Daisy was looking. Nash followed close behind her.

Lizzy waved a hand. "That's what the laundry is for."

Emma took the baby from Daisy for a snuggle of her own and then looked to Kit with a shake of her head. "Seriously, what have you done with my high-maintenance little sister?"

He grinned and kissed the side of Lizzy's head. "Oh don't worry, she's still in there." He adopted a stage whisper. "Ask me how many wardrobe changes she's done already today."

Lizzy playfully slapped his arm as the others all laughed.

Levi slid his arms around Daisy's waist. "What do you say, beautiful? You ready to party like a rock star?"

Daisy laughed. "I'm only playing a few acoustic songs. Hardly a rock star event."

"You're always a star in my eyes, darlin'." He nuzzled her ear, making her giggle.

She turned to give him a light kiss. "And that's why you're the best boyfriend ever."

His grin turned wicked. "And that's why I'll make the best husb—"

She clamped a hand over his mouth with a laugh. "One wedding is enough for one day, don't you think?"

His eyes glittered with amusement. He knew her so well, better than anyone ever had. Even though they'd

386

only been dating a short while, she felt more secure with him than anybody. He no doubt knew exactly why she was shutting him up, and he probably also knew exactly how much her heart leapt every time he mentioned wedding bells of their own.

She removed her hand and replaced it with a kiss.

"All right, lovebirds," Nash said, clapping a hand on Levi's shoulder. "Let's head back to get lunch started."

By that upcoming Monday, the new bride and groom were off on their honeymoon, and JJ's family was on their way back home.

The ranch house was back to normal, if a little quieter without JJ and Dahlia around. Daisy made her way to the kitchen that morning with a yawn and a stretch. She found Cody leaning against the counter with a coffee cup in hand. "Morning, Cody."

"Mornin'."

She poured herself a mug and added some creamer and sugar.

"You gettin' excited for your camping trip?" Cody asked.

Daisy winced, thinking about her pending trip to Colorado. "I think so. Although, I've never been camping before. I just hope I don't embarrass myself in front of Levi's family."

Cody laughed. "You won't. Levi will take care of you."

She felt her cheeks heat with color and enjoyed the warm feeling that sizzled through her every time she thought about her boyfriend. Drinking her coffee with a grin, she did a little dance over to the window so she could gaze out at the sunshine.

"It's a beautiful day," she murmured. "Is it going to be a busy one for you?"

Cody snickered. "You know it. With JJ gone, it puts the pressure on, but we'll be just fine. Boone will pick up a little of the slack. Nash's father has agreed to share him between the two ranches."

"Well, that's good. He seems like a nice kid."

Cody grinned. "You know he's twenty-two, right?"

"That's still younger than me, so I'm happy to keep saying 'kid.'" Daisy laughed, then paused with the mug halfway to her mouth. "I think April's in her early twenties as well."

"Yep." Cody nodded. "I'm pretty sure she and Boone went to high school together."

Daisy whipped around to face him. "Does he know where she is?"

Cody shook his head with a glum smile. "They lost touch when she left town. Her mother was real sick, and… I don't think she was coping very well."

"That's so sad." Daisy slumped against the counter, sipping her coffee as she imagined what poor April must have gone through. "I wish she'd respond and come here. We'd take care of her."

"I know you would. You'd take care of both of them. What's the other woman's name again?"

"Sierra." Daisy wiggled her eyebrows, putting on an ominous voice. "The eldest O'Sullivan."

Cody laughed. "If she even exists, right?"

"True." Daisy bulged her eyes and tipped out the rest of her coffee, rinsing the mug before stacking it in the dishwasher.

He passed his over with a mumbled "Thanks."

"So, with JJ gone, you must have the bunkhouse all to yourself."

"Not for long. All the summer workers are due here any day now, and the place will be packed."

Daisy turned to study Cody's expression and softly murmured, "You're still gonna miss him, though."

He sighed, dipping his chin and finally nodding. "Yeah, I am. But he's a happily married man now, and I wasn't about to stand in the way of that."

Daisy wrinkled her nose, wincing in sympathy. "All these men falling in love left, right, and center. Must be making you a little crazy."

Cody snickered. "I've had my moments."

"Do you think you want to fall in love one day?"

He shrugged, but Daisy noticed a soft pink tinging his cheeks.

Her eyes lit with amusement, and she was about to start peppering him with questions.

Have you met someone already?

Who is she?

I want details, man!

But the sound of a motorcycle rumbling up the drive made her pause. Cody's eyebrows dipped together, and he walked past her, heading to the front door to investigate.

"Who could that be?" Daisy asked.

He shrugged. "No idea." He was already leading the way out the door, and she hurried alongside him. They stepped onto the porch to find a leggy redhead climbing off her motorcycle. Her hair was bottle red, not natural, and she had big shades on, so it was hard to really see who this woman was. Unzipping her leather jacket, she looked up at the ranch house with a scowl.

"Who is this?" Daisy murmured, glancing at Cody.

But he didn't say anything. He was just staring at her with his lips pressed together, like somehow he knew but he didn't want to say.

Was she part of some old town secret Daisy didn't know about?

Gossip had a way of lingering in Aspire; surely there was a story attached to this woman.

"Hi." Daisy trotted down the porch steps with a smile, raising her hand in greeting.

The woman paused, yanking off her shades to give Daisy a narrow-eyed glare.

Daisy dropped her hand back to her side and swallowed, kind of wishing Dahlia hadn't taken off already. She'd know how to handle Miss Unpleasant.

"I'm, uh, Daisy. And you are?"

The woman ignored her, her gaze roaming the house like she was assessing the property for purchase.

"This is the O'Sullivan ranch," Daisy offered.

"I know," the woman murmured, her nose wrinkling as her eyes traveled across the house, then landed on the porch.

She stilled, her lips parting in obvious surprise.

Daisy whipped a look over her shoulder and spotted Cody's pale expression. He'd stepped forward into the sunlight and was staring at the woman, his hands shoved into his pockets.

"What are you doing here?" the woman snapped.

"This is…where I work," Cody mumbled, scratching the back of his head.

Daisy pointed between them. "You guys know each other?"

They both said nothing, and Daisy let out a huff. "Can

someone please tell me what is going on?" She threw her hands up before pointing at the woman. "Who are you?"

Yet again, the woman ignored her, shaking her head at Cody and muttering, "You didn't think to mention that."

"I didn't think it was important at the time."

"Oh, it's important." She pointed to the ground. "This is my land."

"Excuse me?" Daisy balked. "I don't think so. This place belongs to the O'Sullivan sisters."

The woman stepped forward, towering over Daisy with a look that had her shuffling back.

"I'm Sierra, Frank's eldest."

"Sierra," Daisy breathed, happy surprise rocketing through her until her brain caught up to remind her that this woman was being kind of rude and… Oh man! Were they seriously related?

Be nice, Daisy.

Forcing a bright smile, she stuck out her hand. "Well, welcome. We've been looking for you. I'm so glad you finally came."

The woman scoffed, ignoring Daisy's outstretched hand. "Enough with the small-town plastic-coated pleasantries."

Daisy frowned. "I was just trying to be ni—"

"This land belongs to me. It's my right. I'm the oldest. I should get first claim."

"It's not…" Daisy shook her head, irritation sizzling through her. "It doesn't work like that. I can show you the will. Frank left the land to all of us. He—"

"Frank gave me nothing!" Sierra snapped. "My whole life, he forgot about me, treated me like I didn't even exist. Now he's dead, and finally it's my chance to take a little something back. He owes me this place." Her fierce green eyes flashed with emotion, and Daisy struggled to figure out if this woman was mad, wounded, or just plain heartless.

"Sierra." She softened her voice, hoping to appease her. "This land is yours, but it's also mine and Emma's and Lizzy's and Rose's and Dahlia's... and April's." She winced. "If she'll ever choose to acknowledge it. We've been trying to find you both for so long now. We want to—"

"Enough." Sierra frowned, rubbing her forehead. "I don't want a list of names I've never heard before. I just want what's mine." Her voice broke, then started to tremble. "Frank owes me this."

Her eyes turned glassy, but when Daisy reached forward to offer a small hand of comfort, she flinched back.

Her gaze darted up to Cody, and she pointed an accusing finger at him. "You should have told me."

"I didn't know who you were," he mumbled, walking down the stairs to stand next to Daisy.

Sierra's face was etched with sadness as she gazed at Cody for a long beat, then shook her head and walked back to her bike.

Swinging her leg over the seat, she gunned the engine, then gave them both a hard look. "This isn't over," she shouted. "I'm going to be contacting my lawyer about this. I want what's mine." And with that, she spun the bike around and took off down the driveway.

Daisy watched the cloud dust bloom for a moment before spinning to look up at Cody. "You know that woman?"

He shook his head. "Not really."

Turning for the house, he started up the stairs, and

Daisy chased after him. "You better tell me something, Cody Swanson!"

He paused with his hand on the screen door and let out a sigh. "I'm sorry, Daisy, but...I don't want to."

With an apologetic smile, he walked through the house and disappeared out the back, grabbing his hat along the way.

She frowned after him, crossing her arms and then spinning back to glare out the front window.

Well, isn't this just grand?

She huffed and shook her head before snatching the phone and texting her sisters. Shocking news like this needed to be shared. She didn't care that Lizzy and Emma were having a girly day at some spa in Bozeman, and she didn't care that Rose was knee deep in dirty diapers and baby toys. Dahlia was offline, but the rest of them could step up and at least tell her that this was all going to be okay. That the place they'd all come to love and cherish was not going to be snatched away from them by Sierra O'Sullivan.

EPILOGUE

Crickets chirped from the surrounding trees, and the river beside them was a pleasant roar. Moonlight illuminated the log Daisy was sitting on, while the light from her phone illuminated the frown on her face.

Levi leaned over with a soft chuckle and plucked the phone from Daisy's hands.

"Hey!" she protested.

He brought a finger to her lips and then shot a meaningful gaze toward the tents where the kids were fast asleep. He kept his voice low. "You do know that no matter how you hold this thing, you're not getting reception, right?"

Daisy sighed and then snatched her phone back, tucking it in her back pocket. "I know. I just hate being out of contact with all the drama going on back home."

He pulled her into his arms and rubbed her back. "You're really worried about what Sierra might do, huh?"

She pursed her lips and nodded. She'd told Levi all about that weird incident the week before.

"Emma checked with the lawyer, though, right? Sierra doesn't have a leg to stand on."

"Maybe not, but she seems set on causing trouble. The ranch is finally going to be making a profit, but we don't have endless money at our disposal for a lawsuit if it comes to that."

Levi nodded. "Then hopefully you and your sisters can make sure it won't come to that."

"Yeah, I hope so. I just hate being away when Emma, Lizzy, and Rose might need me."

He smiled and kissed the tip of her nose. "You're a good sister."

She laughed. "I'm trying. But honestly, it's Dahlia we need right now. She's the one who understands legal jargon. Not to mention she knows how to intimidate." She huffed and mumbled, "I bet she could have gotten the truth out of Cody. I don't know why he's being so dang stubborn about this. Couldn't he just tell us how he knows Sierra? It might help stave off some hideous lawsuit."

Levi squeezed the back of her neck. "It's going to be okay, sweetheart."

She leaned into him. "I just wish Dee was here," she lamented yet again. "I can't believe she'll be gone for so long. Twelve weeks!"

"Only eleven now. The time will fly by quick enough." He kissed her forehead. "You'll be just fine without her." He leaned back so he could see her face in the milky moonlight. "You know you have me on your side. Not to mention the entire town. They love you and your sisters."

Her smile grew as she nodded, wrapping her arms around his neck and climbing onto his lap. "You're right. And I'm so glad I have you. That means everything to me."

His eyes darkened as he ran his hands up her thighs, then pulled her close. He brushed his lips over hers before he whispered, "Thank you for being so wonderful these past few days."

She giggled. "Why are you thanking *me*? Your family is seriously the best. I love them so much, and it's been easy to hang out with them. I can't believe I was ever nervous about coming here and meeting them."

They'd only been here two days, and already she was in love. They'd canoed, swum, hiked, roasted marshmallows over the fire. Card games had been played with raucous laughter, along with a very energetic game of charades. The kids and their cousins had fished, climbed trees, and played a lengthy game of Go Home Stay Home. Hearing their laughter and squeals had filled Daisy with so much joy, she'd run in to be part of the game too.

Levi grinned, tucking her hair behind her ear. "They've loved every second with you too."

The Baker family camping trip was an annual tradition, practically sacrosanct. It was booked twelve months in advance every year, and everybody always made it. Even the year Beth passed away, they still got together to support Levi and the kids as they mourned the aching loss.

So this year had been particularly special as Levi brought his new girlfriend to meet the Baker clan. Levi's parents, brothers, and sisters-in-law had embraced her warmly from the start. His mom and dad had each taken her aside to tell her how relieved they were that he'd found her.

"Yeah, well, having you here, and with the kids..." He kissed her soundly. "You've made me so happy, Daisy."

She smiled at him, running her fingers through his hair

and cherishing this moment together. Having this time with his family had been wonderful, but these snippets of alone time were precious. She leaned into him, pressing her lips to his and letting his warmth wrap around her, savoring the feel of his heart beating in time with hers.

This man. She'd had no idea what real love was until he'd shown her. And he kept showing her every day. Sharing his kids with her, welcoming her into their home and their lives...

"You make me feel like the luckiest woman alive, you know that?" she murmured.

"Always," he said, his voice a low rumble in her ear.

Always. She liked that. No, she loved it.

This moment. This feeling. It was all so right.

Here and now, she was exactly where she needed to be, and she saw exactly where her future lay.

Leaning back, she held his face in her hands and smiled at him. "Marry me, Levi."

He blinked in surprise and then pulled back a little more, like he was trying to get a better view of her face. "Seriously?" Excitement laced his voice. "Are you serious right now?"

She beamed as she nodded. "I love you. I love your kids. You and your family..." She took his hand and pressed it to her heart as if he could feel all the love she had there. "You are everything to me. I want you to be my future. And I want to be there for you and your kids whenever you need me. Whenever you want me—"

He cut her off with a crushing kiss that made her giggle, then melt against him. His sweet lips and warm tongue sent her senses on a quick orbit around the planet before he pulled back just long enough to say, "I will always want you. I will always need you." He wrapped his arms around her tight. "And nothing would make me happier than to be your family. To have you as my kids' stepmother."

She squeezed his shoulders, pressing her lips into the crook of his neck with a soft laugh. "So is that a yes?"

He chuckled, low and rumbly, and just as perfect as always. "That is most definitely a yes."

He cupped her face, guiding her off his shoulder so he could kiss her again, but she held him back. "Wait, I should talk to the kids about this first. Ask their permission."

He arched a brow, his lips twitching into a smile. "Ask their permission?"

"Well, get their blessing."

He rolled his eyes. "Daisy, they adore you. They already call you their stepmom."

"I know, but I want to do this right."

He opened his mouth but then closed it again with a little nod. "Okay. Before we make it official, you can get their blessing."

"Excellent." She moved to get off his lap, but he caught her hips, tugging her back down again.

"Tomorrow," he murmured. "Tomorrow you can wake the kids to ask them. But tonight..." He caught her lips in a warm, sweet kiss that sizzled right through her. "Tonight I want to enjoy my bride-to-be in private."

She laughed as she pressed her body against his, wrapping her arms around his neck and murmuring against his lips, "That sounds like an excellent plan, Sheriff."

Thank you so much for reading Daisy and Levi's romance.

I love how sunny and bright Daisy is compared to Levi's sensible demeanor. It was so fun to play with that dynamic.

I'm also looking forward to having some fun with Sierra and Cody's dynamic. She may come across as a fiery redhead at the end of this book, but there's a lot more to this amazing woman than meets the eye. She's going to sweep into town and change this ranch hand's life...

HOME IS WHERE THE COWBOY IS

Can a feisty loner teach this cowboy what it means to find home?

Sierra O'Sullivan never got anything from her father when he was alive, and considering she wasn't even told he was dead, she doesn't have any expectations there either. So imagine her surprise when it turns out her deadbeat dad left her a ranch in Montana. Well, he left it to her . . . and the six sisters she never even knew she had. But her father's attempt to make peace with his firstborn is too little too late. She has a life, and a future, and there's no room left for a family that never wanted her.

The only saving grace in this blink-and-you'd-miss-it town of Aspire is the hottie ranch hand with the killer smile. His easy humor and laidback charm make it hard to remember that this is just a pit stop. And his kisses . . . they could make even a jaded drifter dream of happily ever afters.

The eldest O'Sullivan sister is shrouded in mystery to everyone in Aspire . . . except Cody Swanson—everyone's favorite, dependable cowboy. He met the feisty redhead before anyone knew she was the long, lost daughter they'd been searching for, and that meeting wasn't one he'll forget anytime soon. Like a burst of fireworks, Sierra comes into his life with passion and intensity. But more than that, she brings questions. Like, does he really want to be tied to a ranch for the rest of his life? For a guy who's spent every day as a devoted brother, son and uncle, the question isn't so simple. But every time he holds the outcast O'Sullivan sister in his arms, he can't help but feel like he's found the answer.

As tensions rise on the O'Sullivan ranch, Cody finds himself caught between two worlds—the one he's always known and the one that sets his heart on fire…

AVAILABLE IN FEBRUARY 2023

ACKNOWLEDGMENTS

Dear reader,

Daisy is such a breath of fresh air and I love the sunshine she brings into Levi's life. This book has been so delightful to work on. Daisy makes me laugh and that scene with her baking cookies with the kids is my favorite. What a treat it's been to see these two find their happily ever after.

If you enjoyed the book, I'd like to encourage you to leave a review on Amazon and/or Goodreads. Reviews and ratings help to validate the book. They also assist other readers in making a choice over whether to purchase or not. Your honest review is a huge help to everyone.

And speaking of help, no book is complete without a team of people, so I'd like to thank Deborah for this gorgeous cover - you found the perfect Daisy! Thank you Kristin for being such a wonderful copy-editor, and to my proof-readers who caught those last few mistakes and then helped me promote the book.

Thank you, my reader, for visiting Aspire. It's a very special place, filled with loving people and the ability to heal. I'm excited to see it work its magic on Sierra O'Sullivan too.

And just before I go, I'd like to thank God for his creation. He's given us so many reasons to smile and filled this world with His constant beauty. How blessed we are.

xo,
Sophia

ABOUT THE AUTHOR

Sophia Quinn is the pen-name of writing buddies Maggie Dallen and Melissa Pearl Guyan (Forever Love Publishing Ltd). Between them, they have been writing romance for 10 years and have published over 200 novels. They are having so much fun writing sweet small-town romance together and have a large collection of stories they are looking forward to producing. Get ready for idyllic small towns, characters you can fall in love with and romance that will capture your heart.

www.foreverlovepublishing/sophiaquinn

Made in the USA
Monee, IL
31 March 2023

30960634R00239